THE BOOK
of
WONDERS

Permissions requests may be addressed to:

SixOneSeven Books
21 Wormwood Street
Ste. 325
Boston, MA 02210
www.sixonesevenbooks.com

Publisher's Note: This is a work of fiction. Names, characters, places, and incidents are a product of the author's imagination. Locales and public names are sometimes used for atmospheric purposes. Any resemblance to actual people, living or dead, or to businesses, companies, events, institutions, or locales is completely coincidental.

"The Librarian" first published in the Michigan Quarterly Review (2010). "Sonnet 126" first published in the Michigan Quarterly Review (2013). "The Novelist and the Short Story Writer" first published in the Minnesota Review (2014). "The Program in Profound Thought" first published in the Notre Dame Review (2014). "Faucets" first published in Midwestern Gothic (2015). "Endymion" first published in The Iowa Review (2015). "The Detroit Frankfurt School Discussion Group" first published in Ploughshares Solos (2016).

Cover design by Whitney Scharer.
Interior by Eliyanna Kaiser. Author photo by Emilio Azevedo.

Boston / Douglas Trevor — First Edition
ISBN 978-0-9848245-5-7

Printed in the United States of America

The Book of Wonders

A collection of short stories by
Douglas Trevor

(sixoneseven)BOOKS

Boston, Massachusetts
2017

Contents

And now I will unclasp a secret book,
And to your quick-conceiving discontents
I'll read you matter deep and dangerous . . .

William Shakespeare, *1 Henry IV*

In the blest kingdoms meek of joy and love . . .

John Milton, "Lycidas"

Endymion

CYNTHIA NEVER WENT TO HAPPY HOUR. She preferred to head straight home, light one of her aromatherapy candles, and take a bath. After her bath, she might make something simple for dinner or order from the Thai place she loved. But she had heard earlier that day from a friend on Don Corsyth's team that the numbers for the Majestic account weren't adding up, so Cynthia felt a fact-finding mission at O'Doul's, the Irish pub up the street from her firm, was in order.

Cynthia was a senior corporate accountant for a small firm in Porter Square. The firm was arranged by teams, each of which handled different accounts. Cynthia was her own team. She was in charge of all internal audits. Basically she cleaned up everyone else's mistakes.

The CPAs had slid several tables together and were gabbing when Cynthia walked in, gave a perfunctory wave, and headed to the bar in the adjoining room to get an Amstel Light. Cynthia didn't like light beer; she preferred stouts, but she had ruled out the latter, at least until she started going to the gym she had joined several months before. Cynthia was keenly aware of, and exasperated by, the ease with which her squat frame accumulated weight: first beneath her armpits and then again, like a bad joke told twice in too-quick succession, in her already round, full hips. Granted it was the height of tax season, but still: she hadn't worked out once since paying the initiation fee.

Standing at the bar, she felt a man step up behind her, then his hand graze her hip as he raised his arm to motion at the bartender. He was practically on top of her, and the bar wasn't even that crowded. Cynthia turned around to glare and found herself staring at a black T-shirt. She looked up. The man had thick black hair that hung halfway down his neck and olive-colored skin, overlaid with a thin sheet of stubble. He had to be at least six five. She had no idea how old he was. Twenty-five? Thirty? Thirty-five? All were possibilities.

The bartender had walked over to them by now. "Go ahead," the man behind her said. His voice was gravelly but also—somehow—meek.

But Cynthia Lyly just stared, her back to the bar. She was fairly certain she had never before stood so close to a man this good-looking.

"No, no, you go ahead," she finally muttered.

He shook his head. "Please. What are you drinking?"

"An Amstel Light. Not by choice. I mean, that's what I'm drinking, but it's not my preference."

He tilted his head at her but didn't say anything in response. Instead he nodded at the bartender. "Just your well whiskey, straight up, and an Amstel Light," he said.

They waited for their drinks in silence, the tall man looming over her, although in an oddly timid sort of way. She liked how he had said *please* to her. And that now he wasn't talking. Or at least she liked that he wasn't chatting her up in some forced, insincere way. Then again, Cynthia wasn't sure if she had *ever been* chatted up. She had been approached countless times by people asking if she could break a dollar or if she knew the bus schedule. And yes, sadly, in these instances she nearly always *could* break a dollar and invariably *did* know a full range of public transportation options regardless of where she was in Boston.

Now she racked her brain, trying to think of something clever and flirty to say. Nothing came to mind.

When the drinks arrived, the man placed a ten-dollar bill on the bar, lifted his glass, and—in one gulp—finished his whiskey.

"Thank you," she said.

"No worries. You going to join the nerdapalooza in the other room?"

"That's the plan."

Before she could trudge off, he reached down to the floor and looped the strap of a tiny, crumpled knapsack over his shoulder.

"Well, this isn't really my scene; I just wanted a drink. Have fun with your co-workers."

"Oh, I'm anticipating a real barn burner."

He turned to leave, but then he stopped. "Why don't you come with me instead?"

"Excuse me?"

"Let's just leave. We can walk around, or at least head down Mass Ave. together. That's where I'm headed—down Mass Ave."

Two women, standing at a high table off to Cynthia's left, were looking this man up and down. Really, he could have had a role on a Spanish-language soap opera. He could have been an underwear model.

"I'm sorry, but as you suspected, it's kind of a work thing." She pivoted her upper body as if she were about to walk off, but her feet remained planted firmly beneath her. "Thanks again for the drink."

"I just wish it was something you liked." He cupped her shoulder with his hand. His black eyes had a sleepy quality to them. "Have a nice night."

Under the touch of his fingers and the gaze of his eyes, Cynthia's body tottered. God am I lonely, she thought. Not just lonely emotionally; in recent years, she had felt *physically* alone, *spatially* set apart from others, as if a force field of some kind had been silently conjured around her. She hadn't had sex in four years, and that was with the only truly serious boyfriend she had ever had: Duke Lester, a financial consultant who had dumped her for his secretary. The two of them were married now with a kid out in Dedham. In the years that had followed, Cynthia had mostly declined opportunities to meet men, unwilling to risk heartbreak. Obviously, walking out with this man would be more than just impulsive and irrational. For all she knew he might have a van idling outside, with accomplices ready to tie her up and take her out into the woods somewhere. But his languid pose certainly didn't hint at a planned abduction. Anyway, her loneliness changed the way she calculated risks.

The man had begun to walk away when Cynthia called out after him. "Wait a second!" She left her beer untouched on the corner of the bar and caught up with him.

He pointed at a door on the far side of the bar—one that would enable her to avoid her work associates in the other room. A moment later they were outside, in the chilly spring air.

He remained silent as they moved along, occasionally clearing his throat as if he were about to speak but then catching himself. Cynthia told herself that he was a shy person, imprisoned within his body like the Elephant Man, only burdened by horrific physical perfection rather than imperfection. But of course that was absurd.

They traversed one block, then another. At the corner of Everett Street, she stopped. "You walked me home," she said, pointing across the street.

"Did I?"

There was an awkward pause. Lit by passing cars and streetlights, the man's skin gave off a luminous, otherworldly glow. And Cynthia, much to her surprise, touched him on the elbow. "You can come up, if you want," she said.

His half-drawn eyelids lifted for a moment. "Okay," he said, with neither enthusiasm nor reluctance. They walked over and took the elevator to the third floor.

Cynthia's one-bedroom apartment was filled with potted plants and even some small, flowering trees. Wickerware baskets—philodendron and bougainvillea—hung above her tiny balcony, which overlooked the Cambridge Common.

"I have a green thumb," she said apologetically, setting her keys on the small table in the foyer as they stepped inside.

"I love Italian food," he replied. She hooted with nervous laughter at his non sequitur, but he just looked at her distractedly. Okay, so maybe he didn't possess what the wiser sort in Cambridge would have termed blinding brilliance, or a rapier wit, but she liked him all the more for that.

Suddenly, he dropped to a knee and began to rummage through his knapsack. Cynthia, startled by the rapid movement of his hands, stepped back. But then, once more, his languidness reasserted itself. He carefully withdrew a folded black T-shirt— identical to the one he had on—and a toothbrush and a tube of toothpaste. Who carried toothpaste and a change of clothes with him? Was he living out of his knapsack? How could someone who looked like him live out of a knapsack? He asked where the bathroom was and, rather than direct him to the half bath just behind him, she led him around the corner, through the small dining room, into her bedroom. She pointed at the door on the other side of her queen-sized bed.

"There you go," she said.

He walked through her bedroom and shut the door behind him. Cynthia sat down on the corner of her bed. She couldn't believe how forward she was being; it was so unlike her, but she was just so attracted to him. She wanted to re-apply her make-up, but all of it was in the bathroom. Instead she grabbed the soft brush off her bedside table and began to comb the tangles out of her not-quite-shoulder-length brown hair, the bangs of which rested just above her eyes.

As she combed her hair, Cynthia had no choice but to listen to the racket made by the enormous man in her bathroom. For at least a minute she could hear him, scrubbing away at his teeth. She listened to him expectorate loudly, then gargle with what she presumed was water from the sink. Next, she heard the toilet seat crash against the tank. His stream seemed unusually loud to her. In the wake of this waterfall, the toilet flushed meekly. She set down her brush.

He opened the door, crossed her room in two strides, and sat down next to her.

The two of them were still for a moment. Cynthia could feel her palms sweating. She was aware of herself swallowing, again and again. He put one hand on her knee. She shut her eyes. Nothing happened. She peeked. He was sitting there, just staring ahead. Nervously, she leaned over and kissed him.

They kissed for several minutes, very slowly and quietly. Then he stood up and, leaning over her, picked her up in his arms as if she weighed absolutely nothing and gently set her in the middle of the bed. They kissed some more. He tasted of nicotine, lightly sprinkled with peppermint. Time passed. Cynthia finally directed his enormous hands toward the bottom of her sweater, which he lifted off, and next toward the back of her underwire bra, which he unclasped. She squirmed out of her pleated corduroy skirt and black nylons. In contrast, like some enormous bird lifting off a lake with water trailing behind, he gave a tug here and there, and his clothes seemed just to fall away effortlessly from his body.

Now naked, the two of them slipped under the comforter and sheets. His hands pressed against her breasts, then squeezed the excess flesh on her hips and the backs of her thighs. Painfully aware of the tautness of his frame compared to her own pudginess, Cynthia could bring herself only to touch his body with the point of her index finger, which she used to trace the muscles of his torso.

When he entered her, she heard him sigh. She knew she couldn't get pregnant because of her IUD, which she had never bothered to have removed after her relationship with Duke had ended, but of course there was still the risk of STDs. Nonetheless, she didn't ask him to go fish around in that knapsack of his for a condom. At that moment she just wanted to feel as close to him as was physically possible.

He moved very slowly, very timidly, in and out, and together they fell into a rabbit hole where there was darkness and rocking and breathing and nothing else. Then he gasped and convulsed slightly in the shoulders. She pinned him tightly to her waist with her legs.

And Cynthia Lyly felt whatever you might call it, her soul, the kernel of her being, what she preferred to imagine as a seedling, for so long crimped and crippled inside of her, sprout to life.

They lay next to each other, sharing the silence. Then he stood up on her mattress, fully naked, and carefully extracted the battery from the smoke alarm on the ceiling. He lit a cigarette from his knapsack and smoked it next to her, in bed. Cynthia had always believed that smoking should be outlawed. It was a disgusting habit that supported a disgusting industry. But she liked the smell of his cigarette. As she drifted off to sleep, she pulled herself closer to him. She took in his sweat, mixed with burning tobacco and the slightest hint of some other odor, ever so faintly discernible: the barest whiff of dog.

THE NEXT MORNING, when Cynthia woke up, he was not in the bed, but his knapsack remained on the floor. She showered and dressed, the whole time waiting to feel the onset of acute shame and embarrassment, but she never did. When she walked out of her bedroom, she saw him sitting on the floor in the far corner of the living room, ashing a cigarette into the pot of her jade bonsai.

"Cynthia," she said.

"I know." He pointed at the neat pile of bills on her trundle desk. "Damian."

"What do you do, Damian?"

He looked at her with confusion. "I breathe, I eat, I sleep . . ."

"I mean, what's your occupation?"

"Animal control."

"Oh."

He tilted his head at her. "Do you have an extra key? I could use one, to get in and out."

"I don't think so." Cynthia looked down at her shoes. Was he kidding? He stared at her inscrutably. "It's tax season," she added, since that was the excuse she routinely used to get out of things during the first four months of the year, but of course she hadn't told him that she was an accountant, so the sentence must have confused him. Nonetheless, he didn't ask for clarification. As they left her apartment together, Cynthia noticed that Damian didn't have his knapsack. She didn't remind him of it.

He said goodbye to her at the Porter Square T stop. Cynthia worked in the brick building across the street. The first thing she did, when she sat down at her desk that morning, was type a quick e-mail to her sister, Telly. "I think I picked up a homeless guy last night," she wrote. But she didn't send it. Sitting in her cubicle, she wondered if perhaps he had come home with her simply because he needed a place to sleep. The explanation made so much sense, she spent the rest of the day slumped in front of her desk, spiritlessly doing her calculations.

That evening, when Cynthia returned from work, Damian walked up just as she was about to enter the building. He must have been waiting for her on the other side of the street. She felt a surge of euphoria when he joined her at the door. They walked inside and stepped into the elevator.

"How was your day?" she asked him.

"Lots of mutts, a few terriers," he replied. "You?"

"Lots of accumulated depreciations, a few exemptions."

She was tempted to ask him about his motives, but she didn't. She was just so happy to see him again.

Once they were inside her apartment, Cynthia led Damian into her bedroom. They undressed. The bed was unmade from the night before, and they crawled back into it: reentering the hollow shell of their bodies' coupled smells. After they were done, Damian smoked another cigarette. Then he suggested they order a pizza with everything on it for dinner, along with spaghetti and meatballs. "Of course it's on me," he added.

"I hope you're hungry," Cynthia said. "That's a lot of food."

Waiting for their meal, she told herself not to think about

what the two of them were doing together. She told herself to resist the urge to ask him a million questions. He was a person of few words, after all; she didn't want to scare him off.

When the delivery guy arrived, Damian put a bath towel around his waist, withdrew several bills from his knapsack, and then went off to retrieve their food. He brought the containers back to her bed and they began to devour pieces of pizza, one after the other, while the grease dripped from their fingers onto the comforter and pillows.

Cynthia reconsidered her prior hesitancy to ask him a few questions about himself. There was, after all, an undeniable strangeness to the situation they found themselves in—this bizarre nesting they had apparently undertaken. If he intended to stay at her place, she surely had a right to know more about him.

"So how long have you been . . ." She dabbed at a string of cheese on her chin. She was ravenous. "I don't know the right word . . ."

"Wandering?"

"Yes."

"Awhile."

"And the whole time, you've been alone?"

"Yeah." Damian didn't chew his pizza so much as engulf pieces, one after the other, the way a woodchipper might consume logs.

"You aren't using me, are you?"

"Using you? For what?"

"I don't know, a place to sleep?"

He leaned forward, peering at her as if she were a display in a museum. "Are you serious?"

"I don't know," she stammered.

He stood up, the towel still tied around his waist, and walked into the bathroom. Along the base of his neck, she noticed, were green tattoos of numbers, overlapping and faded. Once more, she listened to his powerful stream.

"Where did you live, before you started wandering?"

He said nothing.

"Did you have the same job as the one you have now? Were you in a relationship?" Cynthia wasn't sure if she had ever heard anyone pee so loudly and for so long before. "Tell me, Damian. I'm curious."

"I'd rather not talk about my past," he said, over the sound of the toilet flushing. He walked back into the room and plopped onto the bed. "Can we just go to sleep?"

"No, no." She playfully slapped him on the arm, but he just stared at the ceiling. "What's wrong?"

He squinted at her. "Nothing, I'm just trying to sleep." He stared some more. "Do you really think I'm using you for your bed?"

"No, I don't. I swear I don't."

"Have you ever slept beneath the moon, on a still night? There's nothing more beautiful. Why would I give that up for an off-white ceiling?"

"Of course you wouldn't. Please, forget it. I'm just . . . I have doubts. They're more about myself than anything. You are so, so good looking and I am . . . Well, you know the way we see ourselves isn't always flattering."

A silence fell between them.

"Can I be honest about something?" he finally asked her.

"Of course." She sat up on her knees, relieved that he had spoken.

"I think you're very beautiful. I love your frame. Your legs and buttocks and shoulders. I just wish you were bigger. Would you ever get bigger for me?"

"Bigger?"

"Yeah. Heavier. Rounder. Like the moon. Would you do that for me? Would you get big like the moon?"

She peered at him. "Like the moon? Don't you mean like a pig before the slaughter?"

"What? Come on, don't act like you've slaughtered an animal."

"I wasn't. It was . . . a figure of speech."

"It's nothing to joke about."

20

"I didn't mean to." She was so confused. "You want me to gain weight?"

"Yes." He looked at her blankly, then turned away. "There's nothing more beautiful in the world," he said softly, as if to himself, "than a full moon, shining in the night, and a woman beneath the moon, but—like her—full and radiant."

She smiled at him in wonder. Could he really be as innocent, as pure, as he sounded? Or maybe he had fried his brain somehow, on acid, or meth. Did she really care? When he spoke, with his husky, oddly solemn voice, it was as if they were the only two people on the planet. Everything beyond them seemed to fade away.

She put her hand on his cheek and redirected his gaze back toward her. Their eyes locked. She reached into the box, withdrew another slice of pizza, and took an enormous bite.

IN THE MORNING, when her alarm buzzed, Cynthia looked over at Damian. He was lying perfectly still, his eyes open, his hands beneath his head. Cynthia gasped. She thought he was dead. She waved her hand above him and he suddenly started.

"You woke me up," he said.

"You sleep with your eyes open. Has anyone ever told you that?"

"Yes."

She wished that he hadn't answered that last question. "Well, time to get up."

"I don't work on Wednesdays," he mumbled.

"Really?" She had started to comb her hair, some of which fell out in the teeth of her brush, loosened by Damian's hands the night before. "So what do you do when you don't work?"

"I sleep," he said.

"With your eyes open?"

"I wouldn't know."

"All day?"

"Yeah."

"That sounds depressing. Are you depressed?"

"No." He pushed his black hair from his eyelids. "I just love to sleep. Are you depressed?"

"I used to be," she said.

"But no longer?"

"Nope. Not anymore."

He put his hand on her knee, which was covered with black nylon. It pained her not to be able to feel the rough texture of his palm. They sat still for several minutes.

"I know you don't like questions," she began, "but could you tell me your last name? It feels funny, not knowing it."

He paused. Then again, he always seemed to pause before speaking. "Endymion," he said. "Damian Endymion is my full name. Go ahead, if you want to run a background check."

"I'm not going to run a background check." Cynthia smiled, then bit at her thumbnail. She was thinking again. "What kind of name is Endymion?"

"Greek."

"It doesn't sound Greek."

He stared at the ceiling. Or he had fallen asleep. She wasn't sure which.

"Damian?"

"Yes."

"I said it doesn't sound Greek."

He didn't say anything. She decided to let it go.

Right when Cynthia arrived at work, she Googled *Damian Endymion*. Nothing about her Damian came up, but there were lots of references to the Greek myth of Endymion, and she began to read them. In the myth, Endymion was a beautiful young shepherd who slept with his eyes open and never aged. Selene, the moon, fell in love with him. But in another version, Endymion fell in love with Selene. How peculiar. And nothing Cynthia found online seemed to explain what happened between the shepherd boy and the moon, just that one loved the other, or vice versa. It was a weird, amorphous myth—one without even an ending. Still, the similarities between her Damian Endymion

22

and this mythic figure were too obvious to be a coincidence. She wondered how in the world she would broach the subject with Damian.

When lunchtime arrived, rather than dart across the street, as she normally did, for a cup of soup and salad from Au Bon Pain, Cynthia remained at her desk. She worked right up until six o'clock without taking any breaks, except to go to the restroom a few times. Once more, when she arrived at her apartment building, he was waiting for her outside. In the elevator, just as the doors shut, she snapped at him.

"Do you think I'm so insecure, Damian, that you can get me to do whatever you want? Follow along with whatever twisted script you've come up with?"

His mouth opened slightly in shock. "What in the world do you mean?"

"I'm not going to get bigger for you. No way. If anything I want to lose weight." As she spoke, Cynthia realized how famished and irritable she was.

His sleepy eyes bore into her. "Okay. I'm so sorry." He put his enormous hand on her cheek. "Of course, it's your body, and I treasure it in whatever form it takes. Forgive me, please."

And she did. Before the elevator doors opened on her floor, she told herself that sure, what she had read online had an uncanny bearing on their situation, but it was just a crazy coincidence, nothing more. It was easy to think in such a manner standing next to Damian. He had a way of making logic and rationality disappear.

A short time later, when they were making love, Cynthia felt their two bodies fold into and around one another, so that where one form stopped and the other began was no longer discernible. Afterward, she apologized profusely for acting the way she had in the elevator, but Damian told her she had done nothing wrong. He ordered lasagna and—once it arrived—it took them about fifteen minutes to finish the entire tray.

The next day, at work, Cynthia canceled her gym membership. For lunch, she had a cheeseburger and large fries delivered to her desk.

THAT SATURDAY, Cynthia proposed to Damian that they go for a drive somewhere, in the car she owned but never used. She explained that they needed to get out more—experience the world together, that sort of thing.

"I don't have a license," he said.

"That's okay. I can drive. Where should we go? How about one of your old haunts?"

"I'd rather not."

"Come on! It'll be fun."

He was silent in a brooding rather than a blank sort of way. "I think it's a bad idea," he said finally.

"Well, we can't just sit inside all day."

"Why not?"

"Because it's boring."

"I don't think it's boring."

Cynthia didn't either, but she felt that she couldn't back down now. "Doing things together, Damian, things outside, that's important."

"Okay," he said, shrugging. "If that's what you think."

She led him out the back door of her building, into the parking lot, and over to her black Camry. For someone without a license, Damian seemed to know the web of Boston's highway system exceptionally well. He directed her out to Lowell. They parked and walked around the downtown. Damian seemed particularly quiet. She asked where he had lived, where he had worked, where he had hung out. She tried her best to sound upbeat and laid back. He answered her with shrugs and vague hand gestures. "Over there," he mumbled more than once. Before heading back to Boston, Cynthia suggested that they get something to drink. Damian said he wasn't thirsty, but she led him to the coffee shop across the street from where they had parked.

While they waited in line, Cynthia noticed that the young girl behind the counter was staring at Damian differently from the manner in which most women stared at Damian: less like she

24

wanted to undress him and more like she was unsettled by his appearance. When it was their turn to order, the girl slipped away into the back room. A heavyset, older woman, perhaps the manager, came out and prepared their espresso drinks. The whole time, she never once looked at Damian.

"Did you know that girl in the coffee shop?" Cynthia asked him during their drive home. Damian just shrugged and Cynthia felt this incredible frustration, bordering on anger. Why couldn't he just answer her questions?

That night, rather than abandon herself to his caresses, Cynthia claimed to be tired. The entire next day, she tried but failed to put the coffee-shop encounter out of her mind. She told herself she was imagining things. Still, she couldn't stop thinking about what might have transpired in Lowell. The following morning, when it was time to leave for work, she offered Damian a ride. "I have to drive in," she lied. "I have a meeting to go to." Damian said he preferred to take the T. Cynthia phoned work and told them she'd be in a little late that morning. Then she drove out to Lowell and returned to the coffee shop. The young girl was behind the counter. She was a wisp of a thing, bony and pale. If Damian really liked big women, what could he have possibly seen in her?

When it was her turn to order, Cynthia asked for a triple-sized caramel latte with whipped cream and chocolate sprinkles. While fumbling with her billfold, she tried to formulate the impossible question she wished to ask this girl, but the girl made it unnecessary.

"Do you know what he does for a living?" she asked Cynthia.

"Who?"

"Damian." She pulled the sleeves of her long-sleeved T-shirt up to her elbows. "He kills dogs. For the city of Boston. Strays." Purple scars traced her forearms, some bulging, others very faint, like rivers and streams. "He did this to me," she whispered.

Without picking up her drink from the counter, Cynthia rushed out of the coffee shop. Back in her car, she sobbed with her head on the steering wheel. *I am so stupid*, she said to herself. *So, so stupid.*

THAT SAME NIGHT, when Damian tried to kiss her, Cynthia pulled away from him. When he asked her what they should have for dinner, she snapped at him, "Anything but Italian." So he ordered tacos and burritos. But when the food arrived, Cynthia refused to eat any of it. Finally, he asked her what was wrong, and she confessed that she had lied to him and driven back to Lowell to interrogate the girl in the coffee shop. She didn't even ask if he had cut her arms. She just said, "How could you?" And Damian replied, "I didn't touch her, not like that. She did it to herself, after I left her, to try to get me to come back."

"She carved up her arms?"

"Yeah. It was really disturbing." He said this without sounding very disturbed. But then again, his intonation, his gravelly voice, always sounded the same, regardless of what he was saying.

"She said you kill dogs? For the city?"

"I euthanize strays, yes. Someone has to. There are too many to keep in the cages."

"So you kill them! You? You do that?"

His eyelids shut for a moment. Cynthia wasn't sure if he was just blinking or internally weighing her shock.

"It's humanely done."

"But how can you do that? Day after day . . ."

"It's very hard."

"No, I mean *how* do you do it. I need to know. Is it violent?"

"Of course not." He looked into her eyes. "Okay, I'll tell you. First," he whispered, "I move very slowly, so as not to alarm them. I pet them like this." He put his fingers on her cheek and let them drift toward her chin. "I pet them for as long as it takes for them to calm down." Once more he ran his fingers down the side of her face. "Then I administer an injection right here." And he put his other hand just below her rib cage on the left side, beneath her heart.

Cynthia couldn't help it. Under the touch of his fingers and hand, she closed her eyes and felt herself float away.

THE NEXT DAY, Cynthia couldn't concentrate at work. She thought of Damian, out there in the city, euthanizing dogs. She thought of the girl working in the coffee shop in Lowell with the scars on her arms. Desperate for someone to talk to, she phoned Telly.

"What's going on?" Telly asked her before her sister even had a chance to ask her how she was doing. Cynthia proceeded to give her a very censored version of her situation with Damian, in which she excluded—for example—the girl from Lowell, any direct references to the myth of Endymion, and Damian's job. All those details that were troubling her the most. When she finished, Cynthia could hear Telly clicking her tongue in her mouth, a sound she had always hated.

"You can't date a guy," Telly began, "who sleeps all the time and wants you to get fat. I'm sorry, sis. Regardless of how . . . hard it's been for you the last few years, you just can't be with a guy like that. That's just the way it is."

Cynthia had expected her to say as much. She thanked her for listening and hung up the phone. In her cubicle, over a large pastrami sandwich, she choked back tears and wondered why she hadn't kicked him out of her apartment the minute she had read about the myth. Was it just because of his beauty? He certainly wasn't a fascinating conversationalist.

When she was finished at work, she scurried down Mass Ave., let herself into her apartment, and marched into her bedroom. Damian was asleep with his eyes open, his shirt off, the sheet just barely covering his midsection. She caught her breath, then kicked at the mattress.

"Get up!" she screamed. "Get out of here!"

He lifted his head with confusion. "Cynthia?"

"Get out!"

27

"What's wrong?"

"Don't treat me like an idiot. You know what's wrong. You're . . . you're trying to turn me into the moon."

"What?"

"The moon. You're . . . I'm gaining all of this weight—"

"What are you talking about?"

"Don't try to make me crazy."

"I'm not trying to make you crazy." He wiped the sleep from his eyes. "I'm in love with you."

"Stop it, Damian. Or whatever your real name is."

"I don't understand what you're saying."

"Just shut up."

"Why are you screaming at me?"

"SHUT UP!"

He was silent for a moment.

"If you just believed what I'm saying we wouldn't be fighting."

She wiped the tears from her eyes and caught her reflection in the standing mirror in the corner of the room. It was true; with her round shoulders and her head leaning down and forward, her body seemed almost spherical.

"What are you saying, Damian?"

"I think you're beautiful."

A FEW NIGHTS LATER, in the throes of intercourse, Cynthia felt as if she were sliding down the bed, toward the floor. She opened her eyes just as Damian—his own eyes open, although Cynthia didn't know if they were open such that he could see around him or open such that he saw nothing—tumbled off her. In fact, they were both sliding onto the floor. The bed frame had broken. Behind them, the headboard had been stripped from the frame and was slumped—as if exhausted—against the wall.

The two of them crawled out from beneath a mass of blankets and pillows. Then Damian dragged the mattress off the box spring and dropped it onto the floor. He took the sheets and resituated them atop the mattress. Together they reclined on the improvised bed. With his hands, he began once more to roam about her body, but Cynthia pushed him away. He leaned back.

"What is it now?" he asked.

She crossed her arms over her breasts. She felt exposed and fat and unattractive. "I just don't see how you can be with someone like that girl and then someone like me. How old is she? How old are you?"

He shrugged. He seemed, now that she had started to keep track, to shrug an awful lot.

"Answer me!" she cried out. She couldn't help it. She was consumed by the opacity of Damian's story. His vague past, his unknowable future. She found herself awash these days with morbid thoughts. Damian had dealt drugs. He had stolen cars. He had run some kind of sex ring. He had been a pimp, a thief, a rapist, a murderer. He had committed crimes against the elderly and infirm. He had never paid his taxes. He was going to be murdered by someone he had wronged. He was going to be arrested. She was going to be arrested for harboring him.

He turned away. Through the doorway, the dining room light shone faintly on his profile, and he looked horribly, excruciatingly beautiful.

"Can I ask you a question?"

She was caught off guard. He never asked questions. "Of course."

He cleared his throat. "Why do you think it's so hard for people not to dwell on what they don't know, what they can never really know? Why is that so hard for people?"

She shifted her weight, propping herself up on an elbow. She couldn't focus on what he was asking; she was distracted. She felt as if she could glimpse her own dark sadness, cast on the same wall at which Damian stared, waiting to envelop her once he was out of her life. And yet, even as she loathed this darkness, she felt herself moving toward it, inexorably.

"I have no idea," she said. "Why do you think it's so hard?"

He stroked her hair with his hand. "I think because, deep down, most people are afraid of being happy."

THE FOLLOWING WEDNESDAY, she awoke to the now familiar sound of his stream in the toilet, then the toilet flushing, then water running in the sink. Cynthia felt cheerful, even giddy; she had no idea why. Perhaps it was just that she had slept well the night before, her head nestled in Damian's armpit, his hand resting in her hair. She knocked softly on the bathroom door. Damian let her in. Together they brushed their teeth. Cynthia opted to get dressed and then apply her make-up after he was done shaving. She put on one of her no-nonsense work outfits, then found herself standing in the doorway, watching as he dragged the razor slowly down his cheek before reversing direction and going from the base of his neck to the bottom of his jaw. Her eyes lingered on the base of his neck.

"Where do you get tattoos like that?" she asked him.

"What?"

She paused. She told herself that she should not repeat her question. Then she told herself that she should. "Those green numbers, all around the base of your neck. Where do you get tattoos like that?"

He took his razor and threw it into the sink. The blade detached, flipping into the air and landing on the floor. "Where do you think!" he said, his fists clenching. And then he suddenly screamed, his voice garbled with rage, "WHERE THE FUCK DO YOU THINK!"

Cynthia backed away from the doorway. Turning to scurry out of the bedroom, she tripped over the mattress on the floor. She hopped to her feet and rushed out of the room, past the dining room table and into the narrow kitchen of her apartment. There she stood, waiting. What did she want to happen next? Did she want him to follow her here, into this space? To trap her? Maybe grab her by the shoulders and push her down onto the floor? Oh God, she realized, pressing her hands against her mouth and inhaling sharply. That was exactly what she wanted.

But he didn't come after her. The minutes passed. Although

there was no sound of running water, no sound of the toilet seat crashing against the tank, no sound of anything except the traffic outside, Damian remained in the bathroom. Finally, after calling out to him and hearing nothing in response, Cynthia left for work with her hair uncombed, her make-up unapplied.

She decided that she was going to end their relationship before the close of the workday. She was going to call and tell Damian to be out of her place by five. He would be sleeping, since he didn't work on Wednesdays. So she was going to wake him up. Then, after he had left, she'd call a locksmith and get new keys made, just to be safe. But all her planning was for naught; she couldn't bring herself to pick up the phone.

When Cynthia arrived back at her apartment, rather than rouse him and subject herself to his statuesque form, splayed across her mattress, she called to Damian from the dining room. Once he had stumbled out of the bedroom, she asked him to sit across the table from her.

"You know, Damian," she began, but he interrupted her.

"I'm sorry I screamed this morning," he said. "There is pain in my past. There is confusion and pain." His eyes lingered over her. "Please forgive me, Cynthia."

She leaned back in her chair. "Does this feel . . . sustainable to you, Damian?"

"What?"

"This. What we have. Our relationship. Does it feel like it's working?"

His milky eyes lingered over her. "We seem to talk a lot more than is probably necessary," he observed. "But you are what I've always wanted. When I'm awake, when I'm not sleeping, you're all I want."

He leaned toward her, across the table, and beckoned her to lean toward him. And she did. Perched like this, Cynthia could see the individual, tiny hairs that made up Damian's scruff. She could see the edges of the pores out of which the hairs grew.

She looked into his sleepy eyes. All the plants in the apartment were dead from his cigarette ash. He slept all the time.

31

He killed dogs for a living. It was not a viable relationship.

"You need to leave," she said with finality, her nose starting to run. She was determined not to let herself fall into the black holes of his eyes. Even though she wanted to, she told herself she couldn't permit it to happen. "Before the sun rises. Before the morning comes. You need to be gone."

Afterward, they lay in bed for a long time without saying anything. Cynthia was convinced she would never fall asleep, but she did. When she awoke in the middle of the night, she looked across the room, toward the far wall, for the dark outline of Damian's knapsack, but it wasn't there. She looked back, over her shoulder. Damian was gone.

She sat down at her desk, in the moonlight. Had he done anything wrong to her, other than stare at her and encourage her to eat like a horse and raise his voice that one time? She wasn't sure if he had. Had the whole affair been some kind of ruse, intentional or otherwise? She had no idea. Was she afraid of being happy, as he had implied? But why would she be? Because she didn't think she was worthy of being loved, or couldn't bring herself to trust in what others told her wasn't normal? As if normalcy had ever brought her anything beautiful in her life, anything joyous.

Cynthia didn't move. She sat perfectly still under the cold moon. She was alone once more. There was just the real around her, nothing else. In her solid flesh and heft, she could hear— beyond the rumble of the traffic outside, and the heater clicking on—her soul, squirreling away once more, deep into the shadows.

The Book of Wonders

1. *Before*

Annabel Crouch's most treasured item sat on the top shelf of a nineteenth-century walnut deux corps dresser in the den of her colonial home in Amherst, Massachusetts. *The Book of Wonders*, as it proclaimed itself to be, was actually a leather ledger book that had been sold at the 1893 Chicago World's Fair. The folio-size cover of the book featured an embossing that depicted the famous Ferris wheel—the first of its kind—from that six-month celebration. When Annabel stumbled upon *The Book of Wonders*—at the first estate auction she ever attended—she decided to make a bid, even though she knew nothing about rare books. There actually ended up being a fair amount of interest in the piece, but the other bidders were all timid amateurs. Annabel had never bid on anything in her entire life, but there was nothing timid about her. Looming as she did in the front of the room, nearly six feet tall, her large hands unfurled at her side, her even larger feet encased in leather espadrilles she had to special order, Annabel paused dramatically each time she raised her offer. Her performance and demeanor managed to scare off the competition in less than a minute.

In a home that soon became filled with antiques and collectibles, *The Book of Wonders* nonetheless held a privileged place. During the day, Annabel kept the volume safely locked behind the inlaid glass doors of the walnut deux corps dresser. But at night, typically after dinner, she would unlock the dresser doors, take the book down, and write in its pages. When she was finished, usually after fifteen minutes or so, Annabel would return the book to its small wooden display stand on the top shelf of the dresser and carefully lock the doors.

Annabel's only child, her daughter Simone, became aware of *The Book of Wonders* as a little girl, largely because her rules of engagement with the object were painfully clear. She was neither to touch the tome—not that the opportunity ever presented itself—nor bother her mother when she was seated on the couch in the den, pen in hand, with the bulky book open on her lap. Perhaps because of these prohibitions, Simone always regarded *The Book of Wonders* with fascination. Why, she would ask herself as a young girl, did her mother only handle and use *this* item from her considerable collection of precious goods? All the other ones were so ignored as to disappear entirely into the background of the Crouch home. *The Book of Wonders* alone stood out.

The singular status of *The Book of Wonders* only increased in Simone's mind until—still a young girl—she finally summoned the courage to ask her mother how much the object was worth. She knew Annabel Crouch would frown at such a question. What a crass way of thinking. How gauche. Still, Simone couldn't help herself.

Surprisingly, though, Annabel didn't frown. Instead, she replied with a chuckle, her head poking out over her sternum as she did. *Oh, it's not valuable per se,* she had replied. *It's of value to me, that's all.* In the years that followed, Annabel only elaborated a handful of times on why she was so attached to her book. *If you must know,* she observed one night over dessert when Simone—now a teenager—dared to ask her yet again what the deal was with the whole book thing, *I trace my decision to become an antique dealer to that fateful day in 1978 when I bid on* The Book of Wonders. *The thrill of the auction experience convinced me that I might find at least a measure of contentment buying and selling antiques. I never dreamt of being a homemaker. Changing diapers and figuring out, night after night, what to prepare for dinner.* She lifted her nose with disgust while Simone and her father, Ralph, traded uneasy—but also sympathetic— glances. *Indeed,* Annabel went on, The Book of Wonders *serves as a reminder to me of breaking free from such domestic shackles. That's why I've always used the book to record the purchases and sales of my antiques. Which is not to say,* and here she reached out and tapped her husband's wrist, a little like a game show contestant might strike a buzzer, *that I could have gone into business without your generosity, Ralph.*

Ralph Crouch had gladly funded Annabel's career as an antique dealer, and paid for the string of babysitters and nannies that had taken care of Simone in her mother's absence. He was a highly successful estate attorney—often one of the first people to know of auctions in their area. As a result of his earnings, Annabel could bid on antiques aggressively. In addition, if she fell in love with a particular item, there was nothing to stop her from buying it for herself. Although he was from an old New England family, Ralph was hardly stingy with money. In fact, he didn't care very much about possessions in the first place. Perhaps that explained his utter lack of interest in not only *The Book of Wonders*, but every artifact Annabel acquired. Rather than sit in the midst of these prized treasures, Ralph preferred being outside; he enjoyed fly fishing, hiking, and—perhaps most of all—splitting wood. Usually he undertook these activities with Simone in tow, although Annabel objected to having their daughter nearby whenever he was swinging his ax.

Then, in the early 1990s, in spite of never having smoked a cigarette or chewed tobacco, in absolutely splendid shape all around—particularly for a man in his late fifties—Ralph came down with cancer of the esophagus. He was dead within a year. On the heels of his passing, Simone, now a sophomore at Tufts, had the courage to ask—granted, over the phone—if her mother might consider downsizing. *What on earth for?* Annabel had replied. The house, onto which a not-disastrous addition had been made in the late 1800s, was of course completely paid for. Moreover, what would she have done with her antiques if she moved? Put them in storage? Sell them? How absurd. No, Annabel wasn't interested in *downsizing*.

The problem, Annabel ended up discovering, with maintaining a large home as a widow, was that it gave the impression one had room for visitors. This was precisely the issue with which she was struggling today, as it was Thanksgiving, and Simone and Bart—her son-in-law—had come up from Boston with their twins. Annabel had a hard time masking the annoyance she felt around these boys. They were—it seemed to her indisputable—rather awful children. Hyperactive, smelly, and loud. Like bumbling puppies without the charm. They screamed and hooted. They smeared food on one another. And now they were in her house for the day and night, because of course there was plenty of *room* for them all.

As she basted the turkey, Annabel felt a tide of irritability rising inside of her. She could hear the boys in the living room, banging into her antiques, making the dishes in the pantry tremble against one another whenever they stampeded by. It was hard not to stare as her daughter struggled to cut up a carrot for the salad. Apparently Bart did most of the cooking in their home, even though Simone had given up a promising career to spend her days with the twin terrors. So it would have made more sense, from a practical point of view, to enlist her son-in-law for assistance in preparing the dinner. But, in Annabel's judgment, Bart was more mindful of the boys, at least in her house. That left her in the kitchen with Simone, who seemed to be mulling over something—what, exactly, her mother wasn't sure.

"My head is starting to ring from all of this racket," Annabel blurted out, just as a herd of footsteps clamored through the front hallway. She had tried her best, but she just couldn't restrain herself from saying something.

"Mom, they're children. They're going to run around some."

"They shouldn't. Not in my house. They should observe *my*

rules, and I say no running."

"And I say you're being a little unrealistic. They're boys, and they're feeling cooped up."

Annabel told herself her daughter had a point. Bart couldn't very well take them outside, not with the sub-zero temperatures, howling winds, and a winter advisory warning. She smiled mischievously to herself as she imagined having matching treadmills installed in the basement downstairs, where Ralph's old medicine ball sat gathering dust.

"What is it, Mom?"

"Nothing, I'm merely looking forward to dinner." Her daughter, Annabel couldn't help but notice now, had finally finished with the carrot and—perhaps as a reward—was pouring herself yet another glass of chardonnay.

"That's the other thing with the boys," Simone added. "They're hungry."

"Well, let's sit down then, like civilized people, and have some cheese and crackers. The turkey won't be ready for another hour. Would you get the chèvre out of the fridge for me, please." Annabel reached down beneath the counter at which she stood and pulled a tray out of the top drawer.

"How are you doing in there, Bart?" Simone called out to her husband.

"Just living the dream," Bart called back, above the swell of the boys' cries.

"Come in and get yourself a beer. We're going to have some cheese and crackers."

"We can bring him something," Annabel observed. "The boys blasting into the kitchen might not be safe, with the oven door so hot."

"Annabel?" Bart's voice approached, and now the door to the dining room swung open. He appeared in his wrinkled blue oxford and brown corduroy pants. Bart was a frumpy man, but also affable and smart—very easy to be around. Sometimes he struck Annabel as perhaps a tad too sarcastic for her tastes, but that was true of most men his age. They all wanted to be like

David Letterman—witty and irreverent and showy. Annabel preferred humor of the British sort that was dry and devastating and didn't draw attention to itself.

Bart cleared his throat, a touch dramatically—or so it seemed to her. She looked away, in search of the cheese knife in the cutlery drawer, only to discover she had already placed it on the counter.

"Hey, Annabel," Bart began. "Can I ask you a question?"

"You *may*, yes."

"The boys noticed that Ferris wheel book in your hutch and I was wondering—"

"ABSOLUTELY NOT!"

"Mom—"

"That is a valuable book, Simone. Very valuable. Not materially, as you know. Not like the Chinese jade water bowls on the Victorian corner shelf in the living room, with which your boys cannot under any circumstances play. But the book means a lot to me and the boys may not touch it."

"I wasn't thinking *touching*," Bart added. "I thought maybe I'd show it to them."

"Out of the question." She felt herself swoon slightly and leaned against the counter for support.

"Mom . . ."

"That's fine, that's fine." Bart rubbed the scruff on his face.

Simone knew there was nothing in the house that meant more to her mother than *The Book of Wonders*. Bart should have known this by now, as well. And yet the two of them had suggested deploying the item as if it were being displayed at a hands-on museum. Now, from a different perspective, she reappraised her son-in-law. Perhaps *frumpy* was putting it too generously. Ralph Crouch would have been more circumspect toward an elderly woman making him Thanksgiving dinner. Not to mention, he would have shaved. Not that he had been a saint, certainly, but he would have looked the part.

Annabel pointed toward her son-in-law's legs, around which one of the children was poking his head. "Let's keep them out of the kitchen, shall we?"

"You heard your grandmother." Bart scooped up the boy—a string of snot now extending from his nostril—and disappeared from view. Annabel wondered where the brother might be. Probably breaking something, although she had done her best to put away everything she could, from the Tiffany figurines and vintage matryoshka dolls the boys were simply obsessed with to the antique Japanese fans she usually displayed on the mahogany perimeter table in the entryway. The water bowls to which she had just referred were high up on the corner shelf and should have been out of harm's way, provided Bart kept a close eye on his offspring. Maybe she had overestimated his capacities in that regard.

As she babbled on like this to herself, Annabel was actually thinking about something else entirely. That comparison she had just made between Bart and Ralph had caught her attention. She couldn't recall the last time she had thought of her husband. She regularly mulled over the things he had left behind—the medicine ball in the basement, the bookcase filled with P. G. Wodehouse novels upstairs—but rarely Ralph himself. True, their relationship hadn't been a very intimate one, and he had been gone now for some time. But they had been married for more than twenty years. Should she feel guilty because she had a hard time visualizing this man, and an even harder time summoning his voice? How could she help what faces came to her mind, and what voices? How was that all supposed to be within her control?

"You're talking to yourself, Mom. At least your lips are moving."

"Well, that's what happens when you get old and accustomed to being alone. You learn to amuse yourself."

Simone helped her mother arrange some rice crackers on the tray, along with the cheese and a sprig of grapes. "There's no reason to snap at Bart over a book, Mother."

"It's not just a book, Simone. You know that."

"You nearly tore his head off."

"And now you're exaggerating."

Simone withdrew from the refrigerator one of the beers Annabel had purchased for Bart. That was hardly tearing the man's head off, stocking her house with the whatever-it-was-called—a porter something. Last Thanksgiving, he drank the whole six-pack in one evening. That explained the jiggle in his belly and haunches. Annabel's own weight had been going down over the last few years. A doctor on the *Today* show (the only television Annabel ever watched) had suggested just the other morning that loss of appetite was a key sign of depression, even among the elderly. Annabel wondered, though, if *elderly* and *depression* weren't redundant terms.

The tray of crackers and cheese appeared ready to go, but Simone was leaning against the counter now, apparently ready to have it out with her. She had always wanted Simone to stick up for herself, but Annabel found the way her daughter now spoke of her feelings and needs to be a little tedious. She blamed the shadowy therapist to whom Simone occasionally referred for mobilizing this whiny version of self-empowerment—one that seemed entirely dependent on pointing out her faults. Of course, Annabel knew she was hardly a perfect mother. Couldn't they just agree on this, without lingering so much on her specific failings, and move on?

"What is it?" Annabel asked her.

"I'm feeling frustrated, Mom."

"With me, I assume?"

"Well, yes, with you."

About to be attacked, Annabel instinctively straightened her posture. Even with her frame settling, she still towered over Simone. "Is this about the birthday party?" Two weeks before, the twins had turned three. Annabel had decided to skip the party down in Boston. The boys were having a dozen or so friends over, and Annabel feared she might ruin the whole affair by losing her cool around the children.

"Yes, it is."

"I'm sorry, Simone. I wish I were better suited for such events."

"Well, why aren't you? Or why can't you try to be? Bart's parents were there, Mom. They attend *everything*—from the craft shows at the art center to the movement classes at the Y. And they live in Brooklyn. You're twice as close, but you don't ever come down."

"They travel together. On the train, isn't that right? I would, of course, be coming by myself, probably via the bus—"

"You get on the bus in Amherst, you get off in Boston. How hard is that?"

"That isn't the hard part." Why couldn't Simone understand that it was the situation *after* getting off the bus in Boston that she dreaded? Not just the children, but Bart's parents. They were perfectly pleasant people, but they were also *so* attentive to the twins, and so enamored with one another. Always holding hands and saying *love. Oh, yes, love, I would like some more tea. Thank you for asking, love. No, thank you for sitting with me, love.* Annabel knew, by some standards, she might be termed a crabby person, and perhaps she was even a little jealous of the companionship those two clearly had, but that hardly invalidated her desire not to be around them. If anything, she felt her own circumstances—materially comfortable, yes, but my goodness, she spent a lot of time alone—justified her unwillingness to be exposed to all of these vivid examples of the joy that was out there, to be gorged upon by everyone but her. What a shame. Loneliness seemed to beget only more loneliness.

"You're not an easy person," Simone muttered under her breath. Annabel didn't bother to contradict her claim. She watched as her daughter began to glance around the kitchen, surveying it as if she had never been in the room before.

"Why don't you have any family photos in the kitchen?"

"Excuse me?"

"These photographs . . ." Simone pointed around them, at the framed images hanging on the wall above the counter, atop the refrigerator, even on the narrow wall that divided the doorway from the stovetop. "Why do you have all of these photos here?"

41

"What do you mean by *these photos?*"

"I mean the photos of you with your Radcliffe classmates."

"Simone, there are plenty of photos of you, Bart, and the twins throughout this house."

"But you've chosen to put the photos of these women in the two places where you spend the most time. The kitchen and the den."

Annabel didn't know if she could handle this latest assault. "Simone, I am not going to defend the placement of photographs in my own home—"

"I'm not asking you to defend yourself. I'm asking you to explain why you've made the choices you have. That way, I can better appreciate where you're coming from."

If she had just started to weep, would that have made her daughter relent? When had she last cried? Annabel couldn't recall. Not at Ralph's funeral. She had been quite composed then, as the situation had dictated, but even in the privacy of her home, her husband's death had not brought her to tears. Simone, she had thought at the time, had cried enough for both of them.

In an effort to remain calm and collected, Annabel looked down at her hands, which rested on the counter. Wrinkles and liver spots covered her fingers, the nails of which were yellow and brittle. There was no denying her advanced age, not when she regarded her body with an objective air. She was seventy-eight, after all.

"What did you guys call yourselves?"

"To whom do you refer?"

"The people in all of these photos." Simone motioned around her as if she were erasing her mother's past from a chalkboard. "What did you guys call yourselves?"

She was after something, posing these questions, the answers to which she knew perfectly well. "We weren't *guys*; we were young women. The Cambridge Women's Club."

Simone turned from the counter now and began to peruse the various photographs on the walls. Nearly all of them had been taken at the annual Cambridge Women's Club reunion, a reunion that had carried on for almost thirty years. "These are all Radcliffe girls, right?"

"Young women, yes. You had to be a student at Radcliffe to be in the Cambridge Women's Club."

"Isn't that a little elitist?"

Annabel decided just to let that question go. Simone lifted one of the photos off its hook. What was her daughter up to? She felt under attack, under scrutiny, from all sides. The children were blasting around in her living room (she could hear one of them making some kind of hideous siren noise), while their mother poked and prodded at their grandmother as if she were some laboratory animal. Nonetheless, Annabel managed to stand still, breathing slowly through her mouth until—after what seemed like an eternity—Simone returned the framed photograph to the wall.

"Tell me about these friendships, Mom. Clearly they've meant a lot to you, but you've never really discussed them. Every August growing up, when you disappeared to that home on the Cape for your reunion—"

"*That home* was the vacation residence of Margaret Worthen, one of the first female CEOs of a major American corporation. A very accomplished woman."

Simone didn't appear to take in that bit of information. "I just remember," she continued, "how you'd sit me down right after school ended and remind me that the third week of August you were going to be on the Cape and that the trip could not be canceled for any reason. *Even if you break your leg,* you'd say, *I'm going to the Cape.*"

"I find it hard to believe I put it like that. This is absurd, Simone. You had a group of close friends at Tufts and I've hardly interrogated you about them."

"Again, I'm not interrogating you. I just want to know why they meant so much to you. You're right, I do have a group of friends from college, but I don't have pictures of them all over my house."

"Well, you might one day, you never know. After they begin to pass away, you might put their pictures everywhere." She looked over at the nearest group photograph, framed and set at the end of the counter. And now she felt indeed like she might actually cry. For the first time in forever. This was the last group photo taken at their last reunion. Melinda Cranley, there in the back row on the far left, had died of cancer just the year before. She had been perhaps the spriest of the bunch when they were young. Once, on one of their walks along the Charles, she dashed ahead and then called down to them from atop one of the syc-amores—had just scampered right up its trunk before anyone could so much as blink. Anymore now, when she thought of the past, Annabel returned to these moments—back to the time when she was twenty, twenty-one. And she would conjure new scenes from these days, too. New memories that she would then stitch to older ones. This past was there, waiting for her—fertile and inviting. The rest of her life, what had followed, seemed to have disappeared. She wondered why she felt on the cusp of tears now, when her evenings were mostly spent gazing at these photos. Perhaps it had something to do with her daughter's pres-ence, her daughter's questions.

"It's not easy for me to turn my feelings and memories into words," she said, pulling her eyes off the photograph and settling them back on her daughter. The weight Simone had first put on with the twins had shifted from her stomach to her hips and thighs. Her shoulders were rounded, as well. A shame, as Simone had once had a nice little figure. "I am not a cassette recorder," Annabel added. "I don't have a *play* button. You wouldn't under-stand, of course, as your generation has been taught to external-ize everything."

"You have a point there," Simone said. "Although your met-aphor is a little outdated."

Well, that was somewhat conciliatory. Once more Annabel's eyes were pulled off her daughter, lured by one of the oldest photos she had of the Cambridge Women's Club. It hung just to the left of the refrigerator, between the hinges of the door Bart had burst through a few minutes before. "It was such a love-

44

ly time, the mid-sixties in Cambridge." She stepped around the counter to get a better look at the photo. My, how they all smiled beneath their graduation caps—their crooked teeth unstraightened by braces. Her nose just inches from the print, Annabel noticed that the colors had faded substantially and the frame sorely needed dusting. "I nearly missed it all," she said softly. "My father—very much a company man (worked for IBM, as you know)—he didn't understand why a young woman might need a serious education. My mother convinced him to foot the tuition bill only by insisting that Boston would be an ideal place for me to find a husband."

"Did you date anyone in college before you met Dad?"

"I didn't cross paths with your father until after I graduated, when I was working as a teller at the Bank of Boston on Boylston Street." Annabel sensed that her response had failed to satisfy her daughter's unprecedented curiosity, so she added: "I didn't go to Radcliffe to date. No, I went to college to learn, as did my friends. We were very serious about our studies."

"Well, you must have done *some* socializing."

"Of course. We had dance parties. I remember the Four Tops on the turntable, and The Supremes. Always The Supremes."

"You danced to The Supremes?"

"I was young then, remember. We'd go to the beach together, too. We'd sit under these enormous umbrellas, drink Coca-Cola out of glass bottles, smoke cigarettes."

"Were there ever any boys at these beach parties?"

"What are you getting at, Simone?"

Her daughter looked at her then, almost pleadingly. Annabel struggled to remain inexpressive. What did Simone want from her? Some victory at the expense of her last shred of dignity? How could she lack such basic compassion? Didn't she realize that her mother spent night after night alone, preparing her dinner only to eat it by herself at the dining room table? And then, for Simone to arrive on the scene and torment her like this. How could she?

"I just want to know, Mom."

"*What* do you want to know, Simone?" She stared back at her daughter. Why not make her just say it? That's what Simone wanted from her—an unambiguous declaration. Like a child at a magic show demanding that all the sleights of hand be revealed. She blamed the tawdry nature of American culture in general for stripping her daughter of much of her intellectual subtlety. She knew that Simone read those horrible gossip magazines, for example. On the one hand, that was her choice, but on the other hand, she was hardly alone in making it.

"Have you two forgotten about me?" Bart hollered from the living room, making them both start. "I'm outnumbered in here."

"We're coming!" Simone hollered. She seemed quite relieved by the interruption, as was Annabel, who picked up the tray while her daughter grabbed her glass of wine and Bart's beer. Apparently she was herself not deserving of a beverage. Although she imagined stepping into a scene of utter chaos and destruction, the living room didn't look so bad at all. Bart had set up some toys on a large Red Sox blanket, and the boys were banging their trucks on the floor, which she preferred to them banging them against her furniture. Oh, now one was off and running. Was it absolutely terrible that she couldn't tell them apart? They were identical, after all—must have been a by-product of the fertility drugs Simone had decided to take after trying through much of her thirties to get pregnant. Although Annabel had sympathized with Simone's struggles, and had tried her best to be supportive during them, she nonetheless felt some disappointment in her daughter for letting the importance of reproduction loom so large in her mind. There was really so much else, beyond having children, in which one might invest one's energies. So much in life that merited attention. Annabel, of course, had chosen antiques. She had thought buying many of them and selling some would fill the void in her life that had first opened after college. What a difficult time that had been. She sometimes wondered what might have happened in her life if she had refused to take that job at Bank of Boston, suspecting as she had that there would be little chance of promotion. Would she have accepted Ralph's proposal if she had, for example, been employed by Sotheby's? Well, she wouldn't have met Ralph then. But the Eastern Seaboard was filled with Ralphs in the 1970s. Would she have been able to evade them all?

"I said"—Bart did a half cough, presumably to draw her attention—"what have you two been up to?"

The other boy had made it over to the Morbier grandfather clock in the corner; Bart managed to lure him back by saying his name, Jason, over and over again. So that meant the one on the blanket was Michael.

"Just catching up," Simone said.

"Anything interesting to report?"

Was she being paranoid, or was Annabel right to detect a tone on Bart's part that implied some measure of complicity in the barrage of questioning to which she had just been exposed?

"Nothing at all," Simone replied. She handed Bart his beer, and he lifted the glass without getting up from the floor. "Happy Thanksgiving, Annabel," he said.

Annabel indented her cheeks in the semblance of a smile, then bent over to set down the cheese and crackers.

That was when the artery in her brain exploded. It was as if a thin, tight line of wire had been snapped in the middle of her head. In a millisecond, Annabel Crouch felt a tension to which she had previously been unaware grow slack. Life had been this tension, it turned out, not something vegetative and languid but something hard and taut. *Remarkable*, she observed to herself, *the swiftness of the end, and its heaviness.*

She saw Revere Beach then. The summer of 1965. One of her beloveds, a fellow member of the Cambridge Women's Club, stood to shake the sand off her towel. Looking back at Annabel, she smiled at her in a fantastic pair of oversized sunglasses, the sun blazing over her shoulder. There was not even enough time to recall her name. Just her beautiful smile and sunglasses, and then the crash of darkness.

2. *After*

When she made an appointment to see a therapist the year before, Simone did so because she thought she wanted to discuss the challenges she was facing in trying to raise twins, the regrets she sometimes felt about stepping back from her own career in advertising in order to be a stay-at-home mom, and the difficulties she was having with—among other things—motivating herself to do anything other than chat on the phone with her friends, watch TV, and inattentively thumb through *US Weekly* in the checkout line at the store.

Once her sessions started, however, Simone found herself incapable of talking about anything other than her mother. She began to express, in tonal registers she sometimes didn't even recognize as her own, the enormous anger she felt toward Annabel Crouch. For the cold way she had always treated her father. For her emphasis on tidiness, which had ruled out the possibility—when Simone was growing up—of having a cat or dog. And for all the pressures her mother had always placed on her, particularly when she was young, to look and carry herself a certain way, to care about the quality of everything, from furnishings to food, and in general, to be judgmental and discerning about all things, great and small.

Beyond the anger, Simone also discovered a need to process her unified theory about why her mother had been the way she was. This theory led inevitably back to *The Book of Wonders* and her conviction that in its pages her mother had expressed herself more candidly than she had in person. Simone had long thought that her mother had been gay—that she had repressed these tendencies after college and resented both her husband and her daughter as a result of this repression. *When I started liking boys she so clearly disapproved*, she observed in one of her sessions. *That's when I could really feel my mom losing respect for me. Before she had lost her patience with me—when my clothes looked shoddy or my hair wasn't done right. After my first boyfriend, she lost her respect.*

As her therapy continued, Simone found herself repeatedly voicing a fantasy she had. She wanted to get her mother to discuss her sexuality by forcing her to talk about her time at Radcliffe. Her therapist cautioned her against expecting that such a conversation would help her understand any better her relationship with her mom. *What you're feeling is in you,* she pointed out. *What your mom might say won't necessarily change that. Our desire for our loved ones to confess their true natures is often a desire for clarity about our relationships with them. But such clarity is elusive.*

Bart had been more sympathetic about Simone's desire for a direct confrontation with her mother than had Simone's therapist. Halfway up to Amherst during that fateful Thanksgiving break, he proposed a plan. What if he asked to show *The Book of Wonders* to the boys, and Simone used her mother's response as a way to approach the subject of her college years? Simone had quickly agreed to give it a try, never thinking for a moment that her mother would die minutes after her attempt.

Now, six weeks later, having buried her mother and barely survived the holidays—or so it seemed—Simone returned to Amherst with Bart in order to organize the estate. The boys were staying with Bart's parents for the remainder of their winter break, by the end of which Simone hoped to have her mother's affairs settled and the house on the market. But first, all of Annabel's many collectibles and antiques, along with her carefully stored linens and her meticulously arranged dinnerware and stemware, would need to be inventoried and organized.

"How does an estate auction even work?" Bart asked. "Explain to me again why can't we just do it ourselves?"

The two of them were sitting on the floor in the den as the sun set. Simone felt that her mother could have rounded the corner at any instant. The only thing that seemed out of the ordinary was the space in front of the couch in the living room, where the nineteenth-century rosewood coffee table had once sat. Her mother had shattered it beyond repair when she had fallen from her aneurysm.

"Mom always said I had to use Sotheby's. They'd know the value of what she owned. If we sold the stuff ourselves, everyone would underbid."

Bart took a sip of his beer. On the way up, he had tried to joke about the two of them doing something a little silly to break up the solemnity of the occasion, like smoke a joint in the backyard. *As if we know where to buy pot in Amherst,* he had added, chuckling. Simone knew his intention was to cheer her up, but she had started to weep in the passenger seat. She couldn't help it; the guilt was really overwhelming. And it was hard, too, knowing that both of Bart's parents were still alive and thriving, and that he had two siblings to boot. Simone was alone now in the world, except for Bart and the boys.

He rubbed her shoulder with his hand. "You know what I've been thinking? Your mom was kind of a badass. A no-nonsense gal, definitely, and tricky to have as a mom—I get that—but she named you after Simone de Beauvoir; how cool is that?"

Simone shook her head. "I feel like I killed her. Like we killed her. With that prank of ours. And my failed cross-examination."

"Well, she didn't have a heart attack; she had an aneurysm. You can't upset someone enough to cause an aneurysm, can you?"

"I don't know. Regardless, it was an act of violence, the way I questioned her."

"I wouldn't go that far. The way she raised you, *that* was an act of violence. Always making you feel inadequate. Walking around in her Armani pantsuits at seven in the morning. But I don't feel too good about Thanksgiving either, as you know."

Simone cupped her hand over her eyes. She felt so fragile since her mother's death, so weakened. "I don't think she really loved me," she said, looking down at the Persian rug beneath them.

"I disagree. She just had a hard time showing it."

"She didn't love the twins."

"That, I'm afraid, might be true."

They laughed.

"So are you sure you want to do this?" Bart stretched his short legs and twisted slightly at the waist, his back cracking loudly in response. "You don't have to. Certainly not tonight,

50

but not ever, not if you don't want to."

"No, I do. The boys aren't here, and I think it might bring me a little closure, whatever I find in its pages."

Bart tapped the worn corduroy pleats that covered his knee. "You really think she was gay?"

"I don't know."

"But you think there are answers in her book?"

"I think there might be. You don't?"

Bart shrugged. "What do I know? Your mom always said she used the book to keep track of her antiques, right? Sometimes the most straightforward explanation ends up making the most sense." He leaned back on the floor, cradling his head in his hands.

"I think all of her scribbling, her uptightness in general, might have been compensatory for the dissatisfaction she felt about the direction her life took after college." Simone had said all of this before. Still, it eased her mind, to voice these thoughts yet again. "I mean, she was *so* upset when Radcliffe merged with Harvard. She wept in that chaise longue over there." She pointed toward the far wall. "I know I've told you this, but she was desperate for me to go to Smith or Mount Holyoke. She *begged* me to apply to those places. She wanted to raise a strong, take-no-prisoners kind of woman. I let her down when I chose Tufts."

"And met me." Bart grinned. He took his hand and gently wrapped it around Simone's ankle. "Isn't that something? Her generation got to be feminists, but they didn't get to be gay, really, at least not without a lot of fuss. I wonder what your generation of women is losing out on, besides equal pay . . ."

Simone wasn't really listening. She was occupied by what awaited her that evening. Surprising even herself, she abruptly rose to her feet. "I think it's time," she said. She lifted the Ziploc bag filled with keys, extracted weeks before by a locksmith from the safe in her parents' bedroom, and walked over to the deux corps dresser. With Bart standing next to her, she began to insert one key after the other into the lock on its doors. Each time a key either jammed in the lock or didn't fit into it in the first place, she handed it to her husband. She was on the fifth key when the bolt turned with ease and the doors sprung open. Simone lifted her hands and took the surprisingly heavy book down from the top shelf. Then she walked into the living room and sat on the couch.

Bart followed her, but he didn't sit next to her. Simone assumed he was trying to give her some space, and smiled as she watched him wiggle into one of the really uncomfortable Louis XIV armchairs that faced the couch.

"I'm afraid to open it," she said.

"Then don't."

"No, I've wanted to peer into this book pretty much my entire life. Is that crazy?"

"No, of course not."

"And now I've got it right here." She was starting to tear. It had been an emotional few weeks, and yet she had hardly scraped the surface of all the challenges with which she would now need to contend. In a matter of months at most, her childhood home would belong to another family, and nearly all of her mother's prized possessions—Simone was planning on keeping just a few items—would be owned by strangers. What would it feel like to no longer be tethered indirectly to all of this stuff? To no longer know her mother as constituted, to a large degree, by what she owned?

With a deep inhalation of breath, she placed her index finger beneath the top right corner of the volume's cover and opened *The Book of Wonders*. Her mother's cursive handwriting was painfully neat—perfect, really. She read the first page of Annabel Crouch's entries, then the second, and then began to skim. In line after line, antiques were listed and curtly described, usually with a price that followed. *Chippendale end tables, one leg worn, $1,400 . . . Tiffany lamp, impeccable, $38,000 . . . English Regency round rent table, poorly restored, $7,000 . . . Federal Secretary with drop-front desk, utterly pedestrian, $9,500.* Simone began to turn the pages rhythmically, her eyes glazing over at all the entries—decades worth, hundreds and hundreds of items, duly recorded.

"Any revelations?" Bart asked her.

She shook her head. "Just lists of antiques, like she said. She certainly couldn't have bought and sold all of these. Maybe they were her recollections of all the pieces she saw at auctions and estate sales? My God, it's just endless."

"Well, you always said she was detail-oriented."

Simone nodded in agreement. She flipped the pages, one after the other. The minutes ticked by. She felt her attention wane. Absentmindedly glancing down, she suddenly noticed a break in the pattern. Halfway down, this particular page was blank, as was the next. Turning another page, Simone saw not an item but a quotation, attributed to Virginia Woolf, written in the same immaculate hand as the list she had just traversed, but with the ink less faded than on the previous pages.

I is only a convenient term for someone who has no real being.

That sounded like something her mother might have said, although Simone wasn't sure what it meant. Was her mother rejecting the notion of an individual self? Her own self, perhaps?

Simone turned the page. Here, the list was different. Not antiques but women's names, neatly arranged in a vertical row beneath the heading *"The Cambridge Women's Club." Melinda, Beatrice, Margaret* . . . Simone leaned in, looking for asterisks or some other denotation, but there weren't any. She focused on the ink itself, to see if it had pooled in certain letters, where the pen might have paused affectionately, but she detected nothing. Slowly she turned the page.

The next opening was blank, as was the one after that, and the one after that. Simone had only a few pages left to go. On the cusp of setting down the folio, she glanced at the book's final opening. To her surprise, one last line was written—attributed to the poet James Wright.

I have wasted my life.

Her mouth fell open slightly and Bart, who was sitting there, watching her every move, rose to his feet.

"What is it?"

Simone set the book down on the couch cushion next to her. She felt the air empty from her lungs. Bart walked over and put his arm around her.

"Tell me, Simone. What did you find?"

She sat still for what seemed like a very long time to her. Bart twisted with curiosity. "Simone?" He teetered next to her, waiting for a response. Then he added, hurriedly—"I'm sorry; I'll shut up."

Simone felt herself spin for a moment, as if she were rising off the couch. Then she settled back into her body, back onto the cushion beneath her. What *had* she found? Wasn't it more or less what she had suspected? Evidence that her mother had regretted the path she had taken in her life. And yet there was something so terribly sad in having her assumptions confirmed. Simone felt, for the first time in her life, a bewildering surge of love for her mom, mixed with a sudden desire to protect her in death as Annabel Crouch had so rigorously—so ruthlessly— protected herself in life.

"What is it? You can tell me." Bart squinted at her affectionately. "Come on, Simone. Please."

She took his hand and squeezed it. He really needed to shave; his attempt at growing a beard that winter had produced facial hair that was splotchy, mostly gray, and thick only around his chin. She placed the back of her hand softly against his cheek. "There was nothing in there, honey," she said. "It was just a ledger book, after all."

The Novelist and the
Short Story Writer

SHE HAD WRITTEN TWO NOVELS by the age of twenty-seven and was known, by the time she went to the Upstart Conference in the Hills to teach, as an author of peculiar power and enviable sales numbers. Her first novel, *Hand Job*, was about a teenage girl in a small town who used her considerable finger dexterity as a pianist to satisfy the various adolescent boys who courted her relentlessly, until a carnival came to town and she discovered the love of her life: a diabetic, deaf, asexual pony wrangler with whom she ran off at the book's conclusion. Yes, there were some contrived elements in play here, as reviewers noted, but they also praised the way the author balanced her treatment of sexual frustration with a meticulous account of carpal tunnel syndrome. In addition, the book's depictions of what the effects of a steady intake of high-fructose corn syrup can be on an unnamed but clearly red-state community were universally praised. "Junk food has never looked so junky," one critic noted.

Ellen's second book, *The Sodomite*, detailed a fourteenth-century young nun's affair with an abusive Dominican who offered the girl comprehensive knowledge of Scholastic philosophy in exchange for a kind of love that pretty much dared not speak its name. On the heels of this work, one reviewer enthusiastically described Ellen as "the illegitimate daughter of a carnal union between Umberto Eco and the Marquis de Sade." Just a week before the conference was scheduled to begin, the novelist's agent optioned the book to an Italian movie producer.

The short story writer was older than Ellen: thirty-three. He smoked continuously—cigarettes he rolled himself to save money, and also because he was particular about the kind of tobacco he liked. Thom wore a long beard. His hair rested on his shoulders. He was very tall and gaunt and looked and carried himself more than a little like Jesus Christ. Unlike Christ, however, Thom coughed a lot and professed to suffer from both claustrophobia and acrophobia, although in both cases he was lying.

More than anything, Thom identified himself as an experimental writer. He identified himself in this manner a lot; he had to, since no one had ever heard of him before. Faculty positions at the Upstart Conference in the Hills were all endowed and came with differing—although unpublicized—compensation. Ellen, for example, was the Dow Corning and Norwesco Septic Tank Distinguished Author. She received an honorarium of $15,000 for her ten days of work. Thom, on the other hand, was the Arthur McKendrick Author of Experimental Fiction. Harry McKendrick, Arthur's father, lived a few miles from the conference and had occasionally attended the public readings, although not so much anymore. He had used some of his considerable inheritance to build a bomb shelter on his property and fill it with *Star Trek* memorabilia. His son, Arthur, had taken after his father. Midway through high school, however, Arthur's attempt at launching an assortment of kitchen flatware into space via a homemade rocket resulted in a serious conflagration that killed him and torched about three acres of the McKendrick property. (True to form, the bomb shelter remained unharmed.) In memory of his son, Harry had offered to cover the airfare for a writer of experimental fiction to come and teach at the conference annually. Each year, when it came time to select the Arthur

McKendrick Author of Experimental Fiction, the director of the conference wrote the names of all the applicants on tiny slips of paper and then drew one from the pile randomly. In this manner, Thom was selected as an instructor.

The Director of the Upstart Conference in the Hills was not a fan of experimental fiction. Notwithstanding his general dislike of the genre, if he had bothered to read Thom's work, he might very well not have tossed his name into the pile in the first place. Thom had published nearly all of his stories in journals run by his friends. The journals had names that couldn't be pronounced, like *Sthc__Kal8*. "That doesn't sound like a magazine," his father would say, when he stumbled upon one of them in his son's tiny home in the Midwest. "That sounds like a staph infection." In spite of their author's avant-garde claims, however, Thom's stories were incredibly formulaic. There was, for example, a very discernible, but nonetheless curious, presence of the Russian literary tradition in Thom's writing. That is, every one of his stories began with an opening line from one of Anton Chekhov's stories. These lines were always appropriated verbatim, if in translation. The odd thing was, Thom never returned to any element of this opening sentence. So if one of his stories commenced, for example—as one did—with the sentence, "A medical student called Mayer, and a pupil of the Moscow School of Painting, Sculpture, and Architecture called Rybnikov, went one evening to see their friend Vassilyev, a law student, and suggested that he should go with them to S. Street," Thom immediately—in the next sentence—absconded with every element he had evoked through Chekhov. There was no further reference to Mayer in the story, or to the Moscow School of Painting, or to Rybnikov, Vassilyev, or S. Street. Moreover, if one of Thom's stories started—via Chekhov—in the third person, Thom would immediately shift to first or second. Often there would be a long string of numbers with which the first paragraph would conclude. These numbers were *always* repeated, without variation, throughout the given story. Furthermore, American city names like Cleveland and Houston were only used in Thom's work to designate animals, and these animals *always* spoke. If asked to comment on these features of his work, which he was never asked to do but sometimes did anyway, Thom always said, "I aim to disorient the reader. I am a disoriental."

One last thing: Thom had an obsession with Nazi bombing runs. In every story, in spite of the customary nineteenth-century feel of his borrowed opening lines, at some point, usually quite quickly, the Luftwaffe appeared.

Ellen met Thom at the faculty get-together held the night before the students arrived in the big barn that also served as the central gathering place during the conference. The director began the proceedings by introducing himself and asking each faculty member to do the same. Everyone immediately looked at Ellen, who was standing next to the director on his left. "I'm Ellen Dubrow," she said softly. She had a beige cashmere pashmina thrown over her shoulder, and her long brown hair was pinned and barretted, with curls evenly descending on either side of her long, elegant face. As she looked around the barn, her cheeks turned red. "I've written a couple of novels and . . . I'm thrilled to be among you." And with that she gave an effusive, but nonetheless humble, wave to the rest of the faculty, none of whom had garnered nearly as much public attention over the preceding two years as she had. It was an endearing self-presentation.

The other writers introduced themselves one after the other, following Ellen's lead by also insisting upon how thrilled they were to be there. Thom, who lurked back behind the others, in the shadows cast by the enormous barn doors, stepped forward last. "My identity is of no consequence," he said. "I write so as to take the idea of character and shatter it into broken pieces, so that *what* we see does not cohere, and *how* we see becomes fractured, rocking, and spastic. I write, as Chekhov might say, to wipe away the stain of man's false memory." For those, like Ellen, who had actually read more than the opening sentences of Chekhov's stories, the approximated quotation was a confusing one. "My stories are meant to assault the mind," Thom continued. "To disassemble it. And then, deliberately, *refuse* to put it back together. I see myself working against the corrosive, debilitating effects of poetry and poets: all the fake beauty they have spewed over the millennia. I say death to all that."

There was a collective gasp among the other writers, except Ellen. She had noticed, while Thom spoke, the way the index finger of his right hand picked at the thumbnail. She had detected droplets of perspiration trickling down his brow. She didn't know if he had meant what he said, but she suspected that he was on the verge of having a panic attack, so she felt sorry for him. Besides, it was never an altogether bad thing to have someone at a conference such as this one stir up things a little. Otherwise the days could get pretty boring pretty fast.

Following Thom's comments, the Director of the Upstart Conference in the Hills, himself a highly acclaimed poet, took a moment to gather his composure. "Well, before we begin executing the poets, let's all have a drink and chat," he said finally. And with that, everyone began to mingle.

Thom immediately made a beeline for Ellen, cutting off several other writers in the process. "I find you to be very interesting," he said as he stepped in front of her and positioned his nose just inches from hers. "You sell so many books. And you radiate such warmth. You are a radiator."

"Thank you." Ellen smiled. She had a read on him now: kooky, socially awkward, probably with a little chip on his shoulder. He was a short story writer, after all.

"I love the circle jerk in *Hand Job*," he said. "The first one."

Ellen continued to smile and nod her head ever so slightly. Ever since the publication of *Hand Job*, she had grown accustomed to receiving praise from complete strangers for her literary depictions of group masturbation scenes.

"The second circle jerk, however," Thom continued, "the one toward the end, after the carny folks hijack the Hostess Snack Cakes truck, I hated that one. To me it was like some Nazi youth rally, celebrating a false ideology."

Ellen's eyebrows wrinkled just as three of the other writers approached. "Is he bothering you?" one of them asked Ellen.

"No, no," she said, shaking her head. She was rattled, not because Thom had aligned her somehow with Joseph Goebbels, but because the second circle jerk scene in *Hand Job* hadn't been her idea. Her editor had pushed it on her and Ellen had given in. The whole thing had seemed forced to her as well, even more forced than your average circle jerk.

"What are you working on?" she asked him.

"My latest story is called *Fireside Missile Potato*. It's narrated by John the Evangelist and Saint Louis, a Doberman who survives the incessant Nazi bombing of an unnamed Russian town on the Volga by dressing like a UN peacekeeper."

He really was kooky. Ellen wondered what kind of journal would publish a story like that one. A student literary review, maybe?

Thom continued to speak in a droning monotone for several minutes before stopping abruptly and disappearing for the rest of the evening. In his absence, the three other writers—who had been shielded from Ellen by Thom's tall, looming frame—stepped forward.

"*That* was interesting," one of them said, his voice dripping with sarcasm.

"I don't know what *he* was talking about, but I loved that circle jerk scene in *Hand Job*," the second one added. "When the guys are eating their Twinkies with their pants down around their ankles! You didn't pull any punches there."

"And what an indictment of Middle America," the third writer observed. "Twinkies are a powerful metaphor for self-abuse."

Ellen didn't say anything. She had already tuned them out. Ever since her first book had become a bestseller, people so rarely said anything frank to her about her work. So she gave Thom credit, even though his public manner was a little jarring.

By the official start of the conference the next morning, all the writing instructors other than Ellen had decided that they couldn't stand Thom. The nonfiction writers thought he was inauthentic. The novelists thought he was pretentious, disclaiming personal identity the way he had. The poets thought he was a poser. And the other short story writers thought he was a really terrible writer. Like the other faculty members, Thom had brought along some of his publications. These journals were on display in the bookshop set up in the corner of the barn, where they could—at least hypothetically—be purchased. Early that morning, before workshops commenced, several of the short story writers combed through these publications so that they could arrive at a collective understanding of Thom's oeuvre. They found his limitations in terms of craft to be absolutely infuriating. It wasn't just the verbal, numerical, and stylistic repetitions that were so annoying. In addition, and there was no delicate way of putting this, but *a lot* of Thom's characters, not simply central characters but even the people in the background, waiting for the bus or working in a supermarket or going through the rubble after yet another Nazi bombing run over yet another unnamed Russian town on the Volga, nearly all of these characters were crippled, physically or emotionally or both: missing hands, confined to wheelchairs, blind, burn victims, incapable of whispering, incapable of shouting, possessing extra limbs, possessing no limbs at all, lacking an understanding of verbs, suffering from untreatable restless legs syndrome, rendered mute by an overwhelming fear of giraffes, and so on. Not just shit, all of it, but every sentence in every story seemed to show off just how shit-filled it was. The other short story writers really took exception to this. For them, good writing really mattered. For another short story writer to flaunt his bad prose like Thom did made them all look worse, especially in the eyes—they imagined—of the more commercially successful writers. If they couldn't at least claim higher literary standards for their own work than the novelists, what could short story writers claim?

The Arthur McKendrick Author of Experimental Fiction got into his first bit of serious trouble in the first hour of his first workshop that first day, when he led his class outside, into a field, and assumed a toadlike position on top of a large rock, around which he asked his students to gather. While they sat uncomfortably in the tall grass around him, Thom remained squatted down on his calves, in shorts that were strikingly short, and—disturbingly—void of any underwear beneath them. For the better part of an hour, Thom spoke about what it meant to be a short story writer. "You have to forget about fame," he insisted. "Even your close family members will never read a word of what you write, and what they will read they will misunderstand so fantastically that you will end up daydreaming about how best to murder them in their sleep."

At this moment he stood up, rolled himself a cigarette, lit it, and then squatted back down on his haunches. "Stories shouldn't have beginnings and middles and ends," Thom observed languidly. "Rather, they should imitate the mind of Saint Augustine's God, only on LSD. Everything—past, present, future—should be jumbled together." And suddenly, without any warning, Thom farted loudly. "The music of a short story," he opined, closing his eyes and lifting his head up toward the sky, "is made up of cymbals and screams and the metal of a DC-10, twisting and crashing into the cold, dead earth. No survivors, friends. No one makes it out alive."

A few of the workshop students seated some distance from the rock were still listening, but everyone up close was not. They had been distracted now for some time by Thom's extended peep show, courtesy of his short shorts. Immediately after the workshop ended, with Thom leading the group in what he described as a Tantric chanting ritual but what sounded suspiciously to some like the lyrics to the Los del Río "Macarena" song, only slowed down and delivered in even more of a monotone than the rest of Thom's performance, one of the older students wasted no time in seeking out the director to complain about what she had been forced to confront in workshop. The nature of the complaint necessitated a meeting with Thom, which the director called for immediately after lunch in his office.

"We can't have you hanging out of your shorts during your workshop, Thom," he said, after Thom had settled into the chair in front of his desk: a desk large enough, thankfully, to obscure any view of the region immediately below Thom's waist.

The short story writer had begun to shake his head and laugh even before the director had made it through the sentence. "Your hatred of the male phallus, and your animosity toward creativity, is not surprising in a Herr Director, Director. Still, it's disappointing."

The director, who as an openly homosexual man was not accustomed to being accused of hating the male phallus, simply smiled, his lips pursed. "I don't have any animosity toward anything," he replied, "except our students complaining about your potato salad. Just wear some underwear under your shorts when you teach and everything will be fine."

Thom acknowledged the directive by shutting his eyes for a couple of minutes. The director wondered if perhaps he had fallen asleep. Then, abruptly, Thom hopped out of his chair and rushed from the room.

The morning of the second day of the conference was uneventful. Thom taught his workshop while wearing a pair of pants, shorts, and some pajama bottoms. That afternoon, during lunch, Ellen offered to meet on the manicured lawn just beside the barn with any of her students interested in discussing strategies for revising one's work. Every one of her workshop participants showed up. Thom glimpsed the group, and Ellen, as he exited the dining hall, where he had eaten a quick lunch at a long table at which no one else had sat down after he did. He watched from afar as she spoke and gestured toward the students, watched them laugh and sigh and move in, closer and closer toward her, so that they wouldn't miss a word of what she said. She was wearing a white linen dress that hung from her shoulders, cascading onto the grass around her. And suddenly Thom had an idea. Checking to make sure he had his wallet, he walked off the grounds and headed into town, about two miles away, in order to pick up some supplies.

The next day, when Ellen once again offered supplementary instruction during lunchtime, Thom was ready. While her students gathered around her in the grass, he climbed the ladder inside the barn up to the loft, and from there popped open the window that led out onto the narrow, flat border—about three feet in width—that wrapped around the bottom edge of the steep roof. He tied the piece of rope he had purchased the day before around the window jamb and his ankle. Then he dipped his hand in the large jar of petroleum jelly he had also bought and lacquered his face and body with the substance. Finally, he pulled his newly acquired lighter wand from his pocket, stepped onto the roof, and walked around to the side that faced Ellen's class.

"ELLEN!" he called down to her. She had to turn around and crane her neck in order to see him. Her students, who were already facing the barn, had an easier time. "ELLEN, I'M STANDING UP HERE, TERRIBLY AFRAID OF HEIGHTS, SO THAT I MIGHT IMPRESS UPON YOU WHAT I THINK IT MEANS TO BE A WRITER."

Ellen seemed entirely unfazed by this pronouncement. She simply set her hands in her lap and stared up at him. Inside, though, she was confused. Why was Thom trying to impress anything upon her? Why was he trying to win her over? She just assumed that any experimental writer wouldn't care what she thought about his view of writing, and yet here he was, making this scene. It was puzzling, almost as if he wanted something from her.

"FOR ME," Thom continued, "BEING A WRITER MEANS BEING ABLE TO DO WHATEVER YOU HAVE TO DO IN ORDER TO WRITE WHATEVER YOU HAVE TO WRITE. SO IF I NEEDED, FOR EXAMPLE, TO LIGHT MYSELF ON FIRE AND JUMP OFF THIS BARN IN OR-DER TO WRITE THE STORY I NEEDED TO WRITE, I WOULD DO THAT. AND I TRUST YOU WOULD AS WELL, ELLEN. JUST AS I TRUST THERE IS A REASON WHY YOU ARE DOING ALL OF THIS EXTRA TEACH-ING."

He paused. Was he waiting for her to respond? That wasn't going to happen. For starters, Ellen was a very thoughtful per-

The Novelist and the Short Story Writer

son; she wasn't fond of spontaneous, public banter. What's more, when viewed from below, with the sun behind him, Thom's similarities to Jesus Christ were more than a little unsettling. Ellen didn't consider herself to be a religious person, but the research she had done for *The Sodomite* had made her sensitive to the power of Christian iconography, a twisted version of which Thom was presenting to them now.

"What's going on with his skin?" one of the students asked the rest of the class.

"It looks like he smeared Vaseline all over it," another one responded.

"I HAVE SMEARED VASELINE ALL OVER MY SKIN," Thom announced, "TO MATERIALLY EMBODY HOW WE ARE, EACH OF US, MELTING INTO NONBEING. WE ARE ALL FRACTURED. THE *I* IS A LIE!"

Thom began to wave the lit wand above his head and rock his hips from side to side. Ellen and the class watched him for several more minutes, until Ellen noted the time and suggested they get back to work so that they would be done before the afternoon reading. So Thom was left, eventually, to make his way back into the barn, where he untied the rope around his ankle and used the T-shirt he was wearing to wipe as much of the Vaseline as he could off his body.

After this stunt, the director requested a meeting with Ellen, not Thom. "Is this guy bothering you?" he asked her. "Because if he is, I'll have him out of here within the hour."

"No, he's fine. Really." Ellen nodded for emphasis. "Absolutely fine. The thing today, I think it was great for the students to see someone with as much passion as Thom has."

"You're being very generous," the director added. "And I'm sorry to ask you here, but I know how inundated you are with attention from so many . . ." And with that he produced hardcover, first editions of both *Hand Job* and *The Sodomite*, which Ellen quickly—and thoughtfully—inscribed to him.

What Ellen didn't say, either to the director or to any of the other writers, was that after his performance, Ellen had thought

65

a little more about the question Thom had posed to her from the top of the barn. Not about the extra teaching, but the question having to do with whether she was willing to do whatever needed to be done in order to write the story she needed to write. Her response, she decided after some deliberation, was that—as a novelist—she had learned very early in her career to pace herself. Maybe, as a short story writer, you could throw yourself into a piece intensely and even a little recklessly for a time, the way a Hollywood actor might inhabit a role for six weeks or so, but as a novelist, you needed to remain balanced and measured. Otherwise you wouldn't make it to the end of your book. So, if asked to employ Thom's set of terms, Ellen would have said that no, she wouldn't light herself on fire and jump off a barn in order to write the story she needed to write, because she didn't quite see how being in traction or otherwise laid out, not to mention maybe dead, would help her finish a novel.

By the next morning, Ellen had endeared herself to everyone at the conference, in part due to her accessibility, but also in part due to how gracefully she had handled Thom's barn-top performance. That same morning, while Ellen taught and chatted and taught some more, Thom slept until 12:30, missing breakfast, his workshop, and lunch. Later that day, a small delegation of his students visited the director to ask if they could switch into another class, preferably Ellen's, about which they had all heard so many great things. The director asked the students for their continued patience for one more day. Then he called Thom in for a meeting.

"I'm not sure," he began by saying, "if your presence at our little conference is working out."

"Maybe I should apologize," Thom retorted, "for not helping you affix your white hood as you light a cross on the front yard of American literary endeavor."

The director of the conference, who was not only homosexual but also African American, asked Thom to leave his office and told him that there wouldn't be another meeting between the two of them. Any more issues or outbursts whatsoever and

Thom would have to leave.

"Good luck with your pogrom," Thom replied. And with that he stormed toward the barn, where two of the poets were on a small stage, about to begin a reading of the dramatic monologue they had written and published together. Thom made his way through the crowd, hopped on stage, and yanked one of the two microphones out of its stand. "POETRY IS DEAD!" he cried out, over a terrible screeching sound. "POETS ARE FASCISTS! POETS WORK FOR MICROSOFT! POETS PLAY GOLF! POETS DON'T RECYCLE!"

The guys who ran the AV equipment pulled Thom off the stage just as the director, who had heard Thom's amplified, demonic-sounding voice as he made his way up the hill from his office, burst into the barn. He put his hand on Thom's shoulder. The short story writer offered no resistance as the director marched him outside. Once they were a comfortable distance away, the director asked Thom to please go collect his belongings so that he could drive him to the airport.

"I don't need my stuff," Thom replied. "I'd just like to leave."

"Fine, then. I assume you know your way to town?"

"I do. One problem, though: I'll need a few bucks, once I make it there, to get a taxi out to the airport."

The director gave Thom all the cash he had, about thirty dollars, and watched him trudge off. He waited until the short story writer had rounded the bend and was completely out of view before returning to the barn.

Ellen, who had been teaching a craft seminar on how to write a good paragraph down at the lake so that she and her students could take a swim when they were done, heard the details of Thom's final eruption that night at dinner. Several faculty members joked about throwing a party to celebrate his departure, but Ellen didn't feel like partying. She was genuinely curious about Thom; she felt that the party line on him being just an untalented asshole was itself too simplistic a reading. That night, as she left the dining hall after dinner, her iPhone suddenly chimed.

"Ellen!"

"Yes?"

"This is Thom."

She hadn't placed his voice immediately, in part because he wasn't screaming.

"How did you get my cell phone number?"

"Immaterial. Listen, I need you to do a favor for me. When I was escorted off the grounds earlier today, I left all my stuff behind. Now, I don't care about my clothes, or my toothbrush, but there are two notebooks I need you to get to me. All my work is in those notebooks. One is called *The Originator*. The other is called *The Destabilizer*. Could you grab them for me, before the director—you know—torches them or whatever?"

"Of course. I assume the front office has your address?"

"Oh, you can't send them to me."

"What do you mean?"

"I mean, I don't want them in some brown envelope, in a plane over western Pennsylvania. No, that wouldn't be a *favor*, dropping my life's work in the mail. The *favor* I'm asking you to do is to drive the notebooks out to me, here in Akron. If you leave the last day of the conference, you can be here in six hours. It's just straight west on I-80 from the Poconos, at least until around Youngstown, where you merge onto 76."

Ellen paused. How did he know that she had a car out here? And what in the world was he thinking? She had an event back in New York shortly after things wrapped up here. Not to mention, she didn't really feel like driving to Ohio.

"When you get here," Thom went on, "you can meet Amelia and Jeremy, which is crucial."

"Amelia is . . ."

"My wife."

"And Jeremy?"

"My seven-year-old son."

"Okay. . . ."

"Thank you, Ellen. Thank you so much." And with that he hung up the phone.

But she hadn't consented to the road trip. Her *okay* had been intended to communicate the shock she felt at hearing about his family in this manner. Of course, she had assumed that Thom's outlandish behavior toward her had been in part a form of flirtation. Ellen was used to men throwing themselves at her, but not so used to having these men suddenly ask her to drive to Ohio to meet their wife and child. She checked the time. It was still early. Standing around a bonfire, drinking—the usual, post-dinner activity at the conference—held no appeal, particularly after this phone call. So she turned in her tracks and headed over to the cottage where Thom had once had a room, along with several of the other short story writers.

The two, blue-bound, chemistry lab notebooks were the only items on Thom's bedside table. On one, in scribbly, slightly deranged-looking handwriting that could only be Thom's, **THE ORIGINATOR** had been written with a thick black pen. On the other, **THE DESTABILIZER**. Ellen opened to the first page of the former and read the following:

1. The boy cannot distinguish between his voice and the voice of others. He has no I. So to establish any distinction for the reader is to disavow the experience of the boy in this world. The boy doesn't attribute any special significance to his status as a human being. The boy likes listening to stories, but he cannot follow them, so he often asks for the first sentence to be read over and over. Since he cannot connect this sentence to what ensues, the first sentence of every story about the boy must be disconnected from the rest of the story.

   When the dog barks, the boy thinks that the dog is talking to him. Noises unnerve the boy so much, it is as if he lives in the rubble of a city under siege. But in other ways he is utterly unflappable. A ten, a twenty, a thirty-digit number recited to the boy will be repeated perfectly, without a transposed digit, upon request.

Next Ellen opened *The Destabilizer*. On the identical page as in *The Originator*, she found the following passage, also numbered.

1 . The deputy examining magistrate and the district doctor
were going to an inquest in the village of Syrnya. *My name
is Milwaukee. I like hot dogs and sprinklers.* Snow, grass, into the
truck with you. The Junkers come in low from the Cau-
casus oilfields. Who is she? The woman who lives in the
ditch! The one allergic to water who lost her ankles playing
in the sand. Who is she? Just a screen door. Spinning and
spinning, looking for the red and blue spider. Why does the
house hide him? The rooms change on their own, when the
bombs hit. 71857463899382658473.

And so the two notebooks went, with passages numbered
and paired: the one listing attributes of the boy or describing
scenes, the other transforming these attributes and descriptions
into something else, something at once more immediate and
more opaque.

Ellen took the two notebooks back to her room and spent
the rest of the conference, when she wasn't teaching and being
smiled at bashfully, reading them. It didn't take her very long to
decide that it wasn't really appropriate to term Thom a bad writer. That is, while *The Originator* wasn't by any means technically
dazzling, the writing was crystal clear. It was only when one read
The Destabilizer that one wondered what the hell was going on,
but one wondered this a lot less with *The Originator* nearby.

Six days later, the conference came to an end. Ellen spent
some time consoling a few of her more distraught students.
Then she climbed into her car—she drove a beautiful green Mini
Cooper—and headed west, toward Ohio. An hour into her trip,
she pulled over for gas and phoned Thom to get directions to
his home. It was closer to an eight-hour drive than a six-hour
one, but eventually she turned off the highway at the exit he
had specified and took a left down one street and two rights
down two others before pulling up in front of a very modest,
aluminum-sided, one-story home. In front of the home, on the
stoop, a woman with long red hair, in sweatpants and a T-shirt,
sat with a magazine pinched under her arm. A boy was sitting
up on his knees before her, rocking, his arms furling and unfurl-
ing, his head rolling back and forth unrhythmically. A golden

retriever rolled around in the grass next to him. Thom stood in the driveway that ran up the left side of the house, in front of a lawnmower that was partially disassembled and a pile of tools. Behind him, in the beat-up truck that sat in the open garage, Ellen spied two more lawnmowers in its bed.

The woman—it had to be Amelia—stood as Ellen made her way up the driveway, Thom's notebooks in her hand. She waved at her and Amelia waved back, her face forming the semblance of a smile, only void of warmth and good cheer. Then she opened the screen door behind her and called out, "Jeremy! Detroit!" The dog bounded immediately inside. Jeremy acted as if he hadn't heard his mother's voice or seen the dog disappear. Amelia called to him again. He still seemed not to hear her. "Jeremy," Amelia said softly. "Jeremy." He ducked his head beneath the elbow of his left arm. Then he rose to his feet and stepped forward gingerly on the grass, as if he were walking on ice. Amelia, Thom, even Ellen stood there, waiting. Suddenly, the boy turned and—in a gallop—rushed into the house. Amelia followed him inside, the screen door slamming behind her.

"How are you?" Thom asked.

"Fine. A little tired." Ellen handed him his notebooks.

"Thank you. Hold on a second, I want to run these inside. Do you want anything to drink?"

She shook her head and stood there. A moment later he reappeared.

"So . . ." he began, but his voice trailed off. Clearly he wasn't going to invite her in. This was even more awkward than she had imagined. Why in the world had she made this drive? Curiosity? Or was it because she just assumed Thom wanted her opinion of his work and she felt that was the least she could offer a writer like him: one without a multibook contract, movie options, or any social media following?

He pointed toward their feet. "I repair lawnmowers. Not year-round. Just in the summer. In the winter I clear driveways and repair snowblowers." He bent down and plucked a wrench off the driveway, which he then twirled loosely in his hand. "So that was my family: Amelia, Jeremy, and our dog, Detroit."

Thom's voice sounded oddly subdued. At least there were none of the grand gestures on display that she had come to associate with him at the Upstart Conference in the Hills.

"I take care of Jeremy during the day," he said. "Amelia works at a bank. In case you didn't notice, she wasn't crazy about you swinging by."

"Actually, I picked up on that."

He shrugged with his palms open to the sky. "In the summers, I mostly work in the evenings, when she gets home. And on the weekends."

She found it odd, the manner in which he was giving her all of this incidental information, as if she were interviewing him.

"I write at night," he added. "At the kitchen table. When everyone else is asleep."

She heard a loud scream from inside the house, then some barking. Thom turned around and cupped his hands around his mouth. "Need a hand?"

"He's lost his Spider-Man cup again," Amelia called back. "It's in his room, I think."

There was more screaming, some more barking, then relative silence. Thom turned back toward her, almost as if he wanted her to issue a report of some sort.

"So your son is autistic?" she asked tentatively.

"That's not a word we use."

"Oh, okay. I'm sorry." She leaned back on her heels slightly. Something about his demeanor suggested to her that he was on the cusp of some dark mood: the way his eyes were squinted, maybe, or the slight contortion of his mouth. "You change your stories all around for him: to try to approximate how he sees the world. Is that right? Then, at the conference, when you were antagonizing the poets, when you screamed those incongruous things, it was you . . . acting like him, in a way?"

"I call it *acclimating*. Like being a town crier. There are a lot of kids like my son. Every day, there are more and more like him. Someday, they're all going to grow up, and the world is going to meet them. So in anticipation of that, I'm an acclimator." With his hair tied back in a ponytail, Thom looked less like a figure from the New Testament and more like the lead singer of an alternative country band.

"Of course I read your notebooks. That was what you intended, I assume."

He didn't say anything. He flipped the wrench in his hand and nudged his foot up against the side of the lawnmower.

"Do you want to know what I think about your writing? I think what you're trying to do is really fascinating, I just wish you could give your reader some more help. I feel like you might be able to broaden your audience if you did. Maybe you could include the material from *The Originator* at the beginning of each—"

He waved her silent. "Please. Stop. Stop. I don't believe in sustained narrative. I'm not a novelist. If I made what I'm trying to do easier to read, then it would be a different project. My project is about reality: about not understanding your situation, about being confused and lost." He pinched the wrench underneath his arm, pulled his tobacco pouch out of his jeans pocket, and began to roll a cigarette. "I don't want to mislead you, about my behavior at the conference. I mean, some of what I did was inspired by Jeremy, but some was because I was just acting out, why I don't know. Maybe I didn't feel like I deserved to teach there, so a part of me wanted to sabotage the whole thing. Maybe I was just trying to put myself at ease, somehow." He put his pouch back in his jeans, lit his cigarette, held the smoke, then exhaled over her head. "It was really overwhelming, being around so many other writers. And I'm definitely not good with structure and authority. On the roof of the barn that day, I guess I was kind of showing off for you. No, that's not right. I was trying to encourage you to think about taking a creative leap or risk—you know, when you start your next book." The wrench slipped through his fingers and clanked against the top of the lawnmower. "For the record, what I said in the barn that first night, about hating poets because they talk about false beauty . . .

well, I meant that, but I haven't really read much poetry: just Keats, in community college, and he really got under my skin."

"Thom!" Amelia called out from the window on the side of the house, the only one that faced the driveway. "When you finish up with that lawnmower, we have to get Jeremy to the picnic."

"All right." He took a drag on his cigarette. "Want to know something odd? Noises, like if you drop a plate in the kitchen when Jeremy is having his lunch, they really upset him. He'll scream, even hit himself sometimes. Motorcycles, if the TV volume is set too loud, a door slamming: all that stuff. But when I run lawnmowers and snowblowers, it doesn't faze him at all. He doesn't even blink."

"Why don't you write about *that!* From your point of view?"

"I'm not going to write something that pimps my son. Why, so I can *maybe* get a story in a semi-respectable literary journal? Besides, that's not where my strengths lie as a writer. I'm not good at setting a scene, or narrating. But you . . ."

Oh, God. She got it now. "You want me to write a novel based on your son!"

"Yeah, that was my idea—"

"But why? If you don't want to pimp his story, why would you ask me to?"

"Because that's . . . no offense, but that's kind of what you do, isn't it? And it wouldn't be pimping if you wrote it. Jeremy isn't your son. Besides, I figured, in the course of writing about him, he'd change and become, you know, a character in one of your books." He took several puffs on his cigarette, then flicked the butt into the driveway. "I'm not much of a town crier when only six people read what I write. But you have the whole literary marketplace in the palm of your hand."

"Just because people read what I write doesn't mean that I don't have any artistic investment in what I do."

"I didn't mean to make it sound like that—"

"And it doesn't mean that my next book will be anything like my first two."

"That's why I thought a story about a boy like Jeremy, set in the Midwest, might appeal to you. It'd be so different."

At some point in the last few minutes she had crossed her arms. Of course he had been insulting her. He didn't think she was a good writer, and that bothered her because she wasn't sure if she was a good writer, either. It was hard to know what to think of her own work anymore, surrounded as it was by all the investments and observations made by others.

"I can't write a book about your son," Ellen said. "I'm sorry. I don't have enough to go on." That wasn't exactly what she was thinking. She was also trying to imagine what the arc of a story about this family would look like. It couldn't just end where it began. Novels had to go somewhere. Where could this story possibly go?

"Why don't you stay here for a few days? Take some notes . . ."

"I can't. I have prior obligations."

"You don't research your books?"

"I do, as a matter of fact." She was beginning to suspect that Thom hadn't read *The Sodomite*. "Do you research your stories?"

"I live my stories."

Ellen let out a sigh. This wasn't the first time she had heard such a pronouncement made by a short story writer. For them, writing a novel was easier than writing a short story. You just turned on your computer and started typing. They didn't know what it was like to go back to the same text, day after day, month after month, year after year. To build and build and build, then clear away, then build again. They were mesmerized by brilliant bursts of fireworks. She was, in contrast, an urban planner.

She decided to be conciliatory. "I feel for you," she said. "As a writer with this material, I'm not sure I'd know what to do, either."

He shook his head. "It's awful, it really is."

She checked her watch. It was a little past four; she needed to get moving if she wanted to get back to New York that night.

"I love writing," Thom said. "Again and again, it saves me.

75

Every day it saves me. But it kills me, too. The sentences, the work, the people who don't think it's work, the rejections."

On that they could agree, except about rejections. Ellen didn't really get those anymore. But that meant she worried about writing shit that people would read, as opposed to writing the gospels and having them languish. She wasn't sure which was worse.

"I'm sorry," she said again.

"I am too," he said. "But I appreciate you driving out here."

"Good luck, with your family, and your writing."

"Good luck to you, too."

She walked back to her car. Standing next to her open door, she watched as Thom reattached the front cover of the lawn-mower. Then he primed the engine, straightened his back, and yanked on the starter cord. It roared to life. With the noise of the lawnmower spread like a cocoon over the house, Ellen stepped into her car and turned the key in the ignition. She pulled away from the curb, turned around, and began to retrace her path back to the interstate.

God, did she miss Brooklyn: her routine of getting coffee in the morning, going to her office for the day, meeting with friends for dinner. It felt as if she had been away for a year. She sped onto the ramp that merged with I-76 East. Traffic was light now. As she settled into the right lane, nestled not too far behind an enormous eighteen-wheeler, she thought more about Thom's claim that he was interested in reality and that she—as a novel-ist—was presumably interested in something else. What if you granted him his premise? What if you just took as a given the idea that the form of the novel was aligned against reality, with its typically sustained narrative and its divine-like control of time and relationships? Did that really make her any less of an artist than a short story writer? Because that's what he was implying, wasn't it? Occasionally, in conversations with other writers, on panels, in the Q&As that followed her own readings, Ellen was asked why, in an era in which attention spans were narrowing noticeably, most readers still avoided short stories. She had never been able to offer much of an answer, but now she thought that maybe Thom had given her one. Readers willing to take on fiction were looking for refuge from reality, and short stories didn't provide much of a refuge. They were . . . well, they were short. And so many of them were so unpleasant: just these morbid snapshots of life, so rarely uplifting. The ones that were funny or silly seemed too trivial to care much about. The ones that were serious were usually deathly so.

Ellen drove east, out of the Midwest, farther and farther away from Thom and his family, into the waiting arms of her fantastic, adopted borough. The sun, orange and hazy, set in her rearview mirror. She had yet to decide what her next book would be about, but it would come to her soon; she could feel the idea stirring within her. Her career, as great as it was at that moment, as sublimely unreal, was really just getting started. Who knew where she would be in another couple of years. She had just begun to blossom.

The Program in Profound Thought

HERBERT SHIFTED UNCOMFORTABLY in the antique wingback chair that sat directly in front of Dean Meriwether's enormous mahogany desk. He had it on good authority that even before Dean Meriwether had arrived on campus that summer, the new head of the Humanities Division at Excellence University had arranged for this awful chair to be shipped ahead, with instructions that he wanted it placed exactly eight feet from the front edge of his desk. Apparently Meriwether derived some kind of sick pleasure, both from grilling the beleaguered professors of Excellence and also from watching them shift and contort while they tried to squeeze their plump, decidedly twenty-first-century bottoms into this rigid, Puritanical chair: this chair that was so uncompromising and inflexible, so creaky and cold to the touch.

Herbert also had it on good authority that Dean Meriwether was always late to meetings. When he called in faculty members, he instructed his administrative assistant, Betty, to show them in and let them sit there for a little bit. *Cool them off*, was the term he used. Betty was Herbert's source for all of this. Before getting bumped up to the dean's office, she had worked for a decade as the chair's secretary in the English Department. During that time, Herbert had served a not-completely-disastrous term as the undergraduate curriculum chair, so the two of them had gotten to know each other pretty well. Betty liked him; at least Herbert thought she did. Right when things had blown up with Priscilla, Herbert had confided in Betty in—of all places—the photocopier room, and he remembered Betty patting him on the back while he fumbled with the paper tray that always jammed, saying to him over and over, the chain from the arms of her glasses swinging as she spoke, *Oh goodness, Herbert, oh goodness me, you poor thing, you poor, poor thing.* . . . Even to this day, in his weaker moments, Herbert would hear her voice, saying, *You poor thing, you poor, poor thing,* and nod his head in agreement.

Herbert Baker had begun to attract Meriwether's attention earlier in the fall when the new dean began an audit of all academic units in the humanities. Two weeks into September, when Herbert received a letter in campus mail instructing him to send along all receipts and documentation related to the Program in Profound Thought, he knew he was in some serious trouble. Herbert had started the speaker series eight years before, and now the program was in the last year of its second, four-year grant, with one-third of the funding coming from the English Department and the rest from the dean's office. Although the e-mail from Betty requesting that he meet with Meriwether the following Wednesday had not disclosed why his presence was desired, Herbert knew it had to be because of the program. What other reason could there be? Failing to publish articles and monographs at the expected rate didn't land you in the dean's office. They had a dreary faculty workshop set up to tackle that issue (Herbert had been "invited" to attend twice and had actually shown up once, but it had still been more than twenty years since his name had appeared in print: "Renaissance Prose Style: The Example of Thomas Nashe," by Herbert Baker, *Rhetorical and Prosody Review*, vol. 53, number 3 [1983], pp. 128–143). If you were tenured and the dean needed to see you, it had to have something to do with either money or sexual misconduct, and the one thing no one could pin on Herbert Baker for several years now was sexual *conduct* of any kind, not to mention of the collegiate, inappropriate variety. So of course this meeting was about the Program in Profound Thought. And Herbert was a nervous wreck, because his little speaker series had actually never brought in a single speaker. The whole program was a sham.

Dean Meriwether sauntered through the doorway with a manila folder in his hand. "Don't get up, don't get up," he said, swinging his thin, athletic frame around his desk and sliding into his chair, which was leather and reeked of ergonomic design. Herbert shifted again in his colonial iron maiden. He had no intention of hopping to his feet and shaking Arthur Meriwether's hand. These were the people ruining higher education: bean counters who read spreadsheets instead of books. It didn't help that Meriwether was only in his mid-forties—ten years younger than Herbert—and that Herbert had seen him just the other Sunday morning at the one decent restaurant in town, having brunch with his wife, a real stunner, and a couple of little boys decked out in seersucker suits like miniature stockbrokers.

Meriwether leafed through the papers, then shut the manila folder out of which they spilled. "So"—he strummed the desk with his fingers—"give me the history, if you will, of this program you run, with the largesse of university funding. What is it, the, uh . . ." He made a show of opening the folder again and rearranging the pages within while he waited for Herbert to finish the sentence for him.

"The Program in Profound Thought?"

"Yes, the Program in Profound Thought. Thank you for reminding me."

Meriwether folded his hands in front of him: some Catholic schoolboy pose of attentiveness. Oh, this guy was trouble. He was on a mission, the likes of which Excellence University had never seen, or at least hadn't seen in Herbert's time, and Herbert's time at the university had been a long one. Meriwether was going to make people accountable. He was going to cut the budget. If he couldn't make the humanities profitable, like the beloved medical quad, at least he was going to make them cost less. When the search for a new dean had begun, none of the faculty had heard of Arthur Meriwether, and once they had, none of them wanted him hired. But the board of trustees certainly did. They loved the idea of having someone keep closer tabs on people like Herbert Baker. And now that Meriwether was here, the man was clearly going to follow through on all of his proposed cost-cutting measures, if only because—at least as Herbert saw it—if he didn't, then he'd never have a chance of getting another job and leaving Excellence behind.

"The history, well . . ." Herbert shifted in his chair, his kidney aching from the pressure of the armrest on his right side. Actually, the history behind the Program in Profound Thought had shaped Herbert's middle age. Not that Meriwether was going to hear a bit of it. The origins of the program were quite literally *in* Herbert Baker's house, or at least in its deficiencies: deficiencies noticed painfully back when Herbert and Priscilla were still married. The two of them hadn't started to fixate on their home until right after Priscilla's last round of in vitro had been completed—unsuccessfully—and they began to talk about adoption. These conversations were conducted in the Baker's tiny living room, one corner of which served as Herbert's study. Although he had been able to summon enthusiasm at first, and eventually longing—as the many years of trying went by—for his own child, adopting someone else's never appealed to Herbert. "These kids that come over from Russia," he had remarked at one point, "some of them have been dropped on their heads a lot, and when they turn five they try to kill their caregivers. A switch just goes off." "That's ridiculous," Priscilla had snickered. "No, it's true," Herbert had added faintly. "I read about it somewhere."

As the months went by and their conversations about adoption grew more and more pointed, Herbert felt their home closing in on them. This wasn't entirely imagined, as the foundation on which their house sat had been sinking gradually in its middle for some time now, the old wooden support beams in the basement bowing a little more every year. After they decided to set aside the subject of adoption once and for all, and had endured night after night of edgy silence, Herbert observed aloud that the two of them should think about creating a new space where they might try to restart their marriage: a space that wouldn't be littered with all the indicators of failed conversations they had had in the recent past—the frayed fabric of their couch; the crooked, framed print advertising the Santa Fe Music Festival which, every time Herbert shifted on its nail, shifted right back. What they needed was to start over. They couldn't sell their house, not without reshoring the foundation. An addition to the home was out of the question—too expensive. But a back deck was within the realm of possibility, and that's what Herbert proposed.

So you could say the Program in Profound Thought began with the thought of a deck: a place to grill and eat dinner, a place to sit in the summer and look out at the grove of oak trees behind their house, beyond which the interstate roared endlessly. The Bakers lived on the far side of the unfashionable part of Excellence: not too far from the landfill, a short walk from the rail yard. The program began with the deck, which was simply Herbert's ill-conceived attempt to save his marriage.

But he didn't save the marriage. Priscilla left Herbert at the end of that summer, just days after the deck was finished: first for Joni, the woman who would dump her a short time later and then leave town, but the woman who nonetheless marked the beginning of Herbert's ex-wife's pilgrimage through the middle earth of bisexual and then gay self-identification until she arrived, really not that long ago, as an active member of Excellence's lesbian community, one whose partner owned the biggest art gallery in town. This was the woman with whom Priscilla had adopted two healthy, beautiful Haitian girls—girls who had just turned five and four, respectively. In spite of all the setbacks, Priscilla had managed to have a family after all, only without Herbert.

But no. In point of fact, the Program in Profound Thought

had begun well before this. It began when Herbert's younger brother, Pete, got out of rehab the second time and swore to his older brother that he had to stay clean this go-around or he'd end up dead. And this time Herbert knew that Pete was being serious, that his little brother's life (Pete was thirty-nine at the time, eight years younger than Herbert but every bit a child), really was dangling there, even if Pete's body exuded not anxiousness so much as proof that a person could indeed be fast asleep in spite of the fact that he was standing there, talking to you about God knows what. Even before he had become a junkie, gotten cleaned up, and then become a junkie again—a darker, more ominous version of his first, junkie self—Pete had never made a bit of sense.

When Herbert first mentioned the idea of a deck to Priscilla, he wasn't thinking only about saving their marriage; he was also thinking about saving his brother's life by giving him a job and keeping him busy, even putting some money in his pocket. Not that the gesture was simply a charitable one. Pete was a genius at building stuff. But to pay him six grand, which was what Pete said the deck would cost—quite a bit more than they had assumed, but a figure that held up when Priscilla actually had a few contractors come out and bid the job—Herbert had to get creative, and the truth was, Herbert wasn't so good at being creative. That's when he was reminded of the idea he had entertained himself with in faculty meetings for some time: the Program in Profound Thought.

Back in the nineties, Excellence University had become obsessed with interdisciplinarity. The idea was to bring together people from different departments, people who otherwise had no interaction with one another, and encourage them to share ideas. Back then, pre-Meriwether, central administration really pushed the whole initiative. To incentivize professors to "think outside their disciplinary boxes," as his e-mails put it, the dean at the time proposed a variety of inducements. Research money was made available for faculty members who partnered with their equivalents from different units, or cross-listed their courses. Very briefly, really for just a single semester, a course release from teaching was offered to professors who "fostered interdisciplinarity," either by organizing conferences or setting up groups of "diverse thinkers to tackle topics or issues in an invigorating, interdisciplinary manner."

From the first moment he heard of it, Herbert had real doubts about the whole interdisciplinary thing. He didn't like how the usual suspects in his department, the ones who always seized on new funding opportunities, effortlessly repackaged themselves as interdisciplinary types and quickly put together proposals with their friends from other departments. He didn't like the premise that academics needed to organize more meetings; if anything, he thought they should organize less. And he didn't even really understand the concept of interdisciplinarity itself. His own field, Renaissance English literature, had never been about simply literature; every discipline was, it seemed to him, interdisciplinary if you looked at it long enough. What's more, Herbert didn't buy the assumption that by throwing a bunch of professors with different doctorates together, an institution like Excellence could produce some kind of intellectual revolution. If the cocktail parties he had suffered through over the years were any indication, sticking academics in a room who were mostly unknown to one another seemed to produce more in the way of complaints about being academics than it did any riveting ideas. *Interdisciplinarity* sounded like another tool of academic self-promotion to him, and since Herbert Baker had never been any good at self-promotion, the whole initiative felt like another, institutionally coordinated effort to remind him that his career had seriously stalled.

But he kept these thoughts to himself, in large part because no one asked him what he thought. No one in his department asked Herbert much of anything. Then, as he heard his (invariably) younger colleagues produce more and more interdisciplinary proposals in faculty meetings—mind-bending proposals to, for example, bring together professors from English, kinesiology, religion, and electrical engineering to explore "the very circuits by which we think, move, and live"—Herbert started to think about a program that would make fun of all these programs. That's when he concocted the Program in Profound Thought: just came up with the idea, nothing more. But then years went by and when he had his other brilliant idea—saving his marriage by employing his drug-addled brother to build a deck on the back of their house—Herbert remembered his program. Because, it occurred to him then, it probably wouldn't sound *that* ridiculous to his colleagues if he asked for funding for such an initiative. The economy had yet to tank; there was still money to be made being interdisciplinary. So Herbert tossed together a proposal and brought it before the department. It flew through. Colleagues sent Herbert warm e-mails, congratulating him for "reinventing himself." A short time later, the old humanities dean signed off on the program and—as so often happened back then—once the initiative was up and running, with Herbert given direct access to the account, everyone more or less forgot about Professor Baker's interdisciplinary contribution to profound thought, at least until the economy fell apart and Meriwether came along.

So that's how the program had begun, but why in the world had he stuck with it, even after filching the money he needed to pay Pete for the deck? Even after Priscilla had fallen in love with Joni and left him, Herbert had continued the sham. Why had he continued to steal money from Excellence University? That was Meriwether's real question. And the truth was, Herbert had kept up the charade because now that he knew he'd never have a child, not to mention an academic career of any distinction, the Program in Profound Thought was—oddly, sadly, because it didn't actually exist—his only pride and joy.

But he said none of this to Meriwether. Instead, he droned on about the program's mission, the need to carve out a space for intellectual exchange in an increasingly complex world, all the while his voice fluttering, his heart pounding, the sweat pouring from his armpits. Herbert wondered if he was having a panic attack, or maybe a heart attack. But didn't a heart attack constitute a panic attack? He wondered what Meriwether would do if he collapsed on the floor of his office. Let him die there? No, he'd call Betty and she'd call the paramedics. He'd be okay.

"So let me get this straight." The dean flipped through the computer-generated expense reports for nearly eight years of profound thought. "You invite these people in and they give talks?"

"Yes, that's right. They are experts in the . . . field of profound thought." Herbert's nose was running. Sweat dripped off his earlobes.

"And what exactly is the field of profound thought?"

"Well," Herbert said and cleared his throat, "*profundis*, as you know, is a Latin word. It was used by Neoplatonists like Pico to describe a state of inner contemplation." Dean Meriwether remained conspicuously silent. Herbert started over. "The Program in Profound Thought has as its aim . . . well, its aim is two-fold. As the initial grant application explained, there is quite a bit of speculative thought on metaphysics and *ontology*"—Herbert dipped his chin as he emphasized a word, the meaning of which he had never been entirely sure of—"that can't be placed *squarely* in a single academic *circle*." He paused in admiration of his own, deliberately mixed metaphors, and then continued. "But this thought is important nonetheless, or important perhaps *because* it is outside of the academic profession. So the program intends to tap these human resources by inviting speakers to Excellence in order to see what more or less unconventional, or at least non-institutional, thinkers are generating regarding . . ." But that was enough; he couldn't go on.

Meriwether twirled his pencil on his thumb with his fingers. He was really good at it, too. The pencil spun like a gyroscope. "So you've brought in independent scholars exclusively in order to give these talks."

"That's right. It's my belief that academics have a lot to learn, in *interdisciplinary* terms, from thinkers who work outside of academia entirely—"

"And these scholars have given talks like"—Meriwether

pulled a sheet out of the folder—"'Red Fruits, Green Vegetables, and the Mind Diet of Post-Structuralism.' That was the title of one of the presentations given last year?"

"Yes, it was. And what a talk that one was—very enlightening."

"'Relativity, Bikram Yoga, and the Automotive Arts?'"

"I believe that one was given the year before."

Meriwether held a blank stare for several seconds, the whole while his pencil spinning round and round. Herbert had to look away. "And these talks have been held where?"

"In our building. Third floor. The conference room."

"And how has attendance been?"

"Oh, good. Very good. Most of our speakers have had to come in on Friday afternoons, since they have *real jobs.*" Herbert painted quotation marks in the air with his fingers. "And, to be honest, not all of my colleagues make it in on Fridays." He rolled his eyes with mock disdain. Herbert himself hadn't been on campus on a Friday since the end of 1988, when he had ransacked the house looking for their title deed so he could try to refinance their mortgage and ended up driving onto campus to thumb through his filing cabinet in search of the scrap of paper. Right now, though, at this juncture of the interrogation, he held the upper hand. Meriwether would never be able to get him by calling in his colleagues; they'd claim to have attended the talks to cover their own asses.

"Any presentations scheduled in the near future?"

Stop here, Herbert said to himself. *Stop right here. Tell Meriwether there aren't any talks scheduled. Tell him the momentum behind the Program in Profound Thought has, in fact, waned. Explain that, surprisingly, a lot of profound thought has appeared to have dried up lately. Agree, if necessary, to refrain from asking for any payouts this semester. But whatever you do, Herbert, don't take the bait.*

"Because I'd like to attend." Meriwether permitted himself a smile. "I'd like to see what all of this . . . profound thought is doing on campus. You might be surprised to learn, Professor Baker, that I seem to have been the first administrator to take a good look at your books, and I have found some very interesting anomalies. For instance, it seems odd that *all* of the reimbursements to your speakers—for airfare, accommodations, et cetera—have always been paid out to *you*, not to them."

"Yes, I can explain that." Herbert pressed his palm against his forehead to try to steady himself. In his field of vision he suddenly made out tiny black dots, floating around. What did they mean? Were his eyeballs about to explode? Would Meriwether stop snooping around the Program in Profound Thought if his eyeballs exploded? Or would he get charged for steam cleaning the carpet? *Keep it together, Herbert,* he said to himself. *Keep it together.* He cleared his throat again. "Excuse me. Yes, these are men, and women, some of whom don't *believe* in having bank accounts, for—you know—ethical reasons."

"Well, that certainly explains a lot." Meriwether leaned toward him, across the enormous expanse of his gigantic desk. "And I suppose the utter absence of receipts for such expenses is because your speakers don't believe in leaving paper trails?"

Herbert shut his eyes for a moment, took a few deep breaths, and straightened his posture, which alleviated some of the pain he felt on his side. "Well, yes, there are some people who take ecological considerations to heart when asked to submit a printed receipt for reimbursement—"

"In which case they could provide an electronic image of their expenditure." Meriwether scooped up the papers that had begun to accumulate in front of him and shoved them unceremoniously back into the manila folder. "Professor Baker, I'm going to need to see a real ledger sheet, and a real paper—or electronic—trail to explain where the funds made available to you by this institution have gone, and I'm going to need to see these materials soon. I should remind you that defrauding the university is grounds for termination of one's contract, irrespective of whether the employee in question has tenure. What I've discovered up to now concerning your Program in Profound Thought is an utter joke. It's a joke that this university, that *any* university, would reimburse speakers in such a manner. I ask people about short codes around here, and they look at me with blank faces. Really, it's unfathomable. It's a complete joke. Well, perhaps you haven't heard, but I got hired to stop the jokes. That's what I'm doing here at Excellence. I'm here to get rid of the laugh track."

Herbert re-crossed his legs. There were thick sweat rings beneath his armpits and a pool of perspiration in the seat of his pants. He was melting, but his heart wasn't racing quite as much as before, and his vision had returned to normal. For some reason, being told flat out that he might lose his job had a calming effect.

"Or perhaps I am mistaken." Meriwether had begun to twirl his stupid pencil again. "Perhaps your program is as robust and interdisciplinary as you describe it, and your strength is simply not in bookkeeping. I would be happy to reconsider my request for past receipts if I could meet one of your profound thinkers and be reassured that this program is, in fact, legitimate. You could consider this meeting today a good-natured warning—a shot across the bow of all your profound thought, so to speak—and attend more scrupulously in the future to documenting your expenses. That is, if you have any scheduled events in the near future. So, are there any on the docket?"

Their eyes locked. Herbert was not a violent man. He had never struck Priscilla. God, the very idea. He had never laid his hands on anyone before. Even when Pete probably could have used a slap to the face, Herbert had never administered one. Nonetheless, he could have taken Meriwether apart right then. Not because he was questioning him about the Program in Profound Thought, but because he was so goddamn condescending. He had sold out years ago. Before Meriwether had bought in, he had sold out. He wasn't any smarter than the people he made squirm in this ridiculous chair. He was just part of this movement of fuckheads that were everywhere on campus, everywhere in academia, as far as Herbert could tell, having conferences on efficiency, putting out articles in *The Chronicle of Higher Education* that made your eyes bleed with boredom. Meriwether was the reason people like Herbert had stopped being productive as scholars. The idea of being assessed by someone like this guy, being pressured to be *active in the field*, made scholarship seem distasteful, even shameful. So if Meriwether was, in Herbert's mind, the living embodiment of everything that was wrong in American higher education, the Program in Profound Thought was, in a way he couldn't quite explain, even to himself, an example of the best that the academy had to offer. Even though it was a sham. Maybe precisely *because* it was a sham.

Herbert cleared his throat. "In fact, we're having Gerhard Hindenburg in from Munich this Friday. He'll be discussing Heidegger and . . . plumbing. He's a plumber, see? He works on plumbing and, uh . . ."

"Let me guess: Phenomenology?"

"Exactly! 'The Phenomenology of Plumbing.' That's the title of the talk. Gerhard Hindenburg. A brilliant thinker. This Friday. Don't miss it."

"Oh, I won't. I'll be sure to be there." Dean Meriwether stood up behind his desk.

Herbert took the cue and hopped to his feet. "See you on Friday," he said.

Meriwether pointed at the door, and Herbert turned and headed out of the oak-paneled office. *Walk slowly*, he whispered to himself. *Walk with nonchalance, as if you don't have a care in the world. Don't think about your job, hanging by a thread.* But in spite of himself, Herbert couldn't saunter, and in less than a minute he had sped past Betty's desk after offering the briefest of waves and retrieved his overcoat from the coatroom on the ground floor where—in the dark ages—an attendant had actually worked. A moment later he was outside, facing the stiff winds that blew through Excellence every fall, scattering leaves and snapping car antennas, after which would come the snow and ice storms, but never, it seemed, never the rebirth of spring.

"WHAT THE FUCK WERE YOU THINKING?" Pete asked him. They were bundled up that night, out on Herbert's frozen patio furniture on the deck in the dark, all because Herbert didn't let Pete smoke inside his house. Not because cigarette smoke even bothered him; the rule had been Priscilla's—no smoking indoors—and even after all these years, Herbert enforced it without exception.

"I don't know. I just couldn't stop myself. That man Meriwether, I swear he's the Antichrist."

"Yeah, but he was just daring you to double down on that bet of yours, and you did. And now he's got your balls in his hand. He's holding your balls, right there in his hand."

"Thank you for that visual, Pete." Nothing like having your younger, mess of a brother weigh in on your own stupidity.

"I'm just saying, you're fucked."

"Yeah, I got that."

Pete took a drag on his cigarette, then ashed carefully onto the deck. "So what the hell are you going to do?"

Herbert tapped his foot. "I'm going to do what I have to do. I'll publicize the talk: flyers, posters, one of those listserv e-mails, the works. I'll try to get a big crowd there. Then I'll phone the office right before the talk is scheduled to begin, disguise my voice, and explain that Gerhard Hindenburg has unfortunately been detained in customs. Or that his flight was canceled. No, Meriwether could check that. Maybe I'll say that he couldn't get a visa. Wait, do you need a visa if you're coming from Germany? I'll just say that the State Department blocked his entry into the country, some post–Nine-Eleven bullshit."

"The department secretary won't be able to figure out that it's you on the phone?"

"Oh hell, she barely knows me. She's brand new. The old one quit after they cut her benefits."

"Betty?"

"No, the one after Betty." Good lord, he couldn't think of her name, not to mention the name of the current secretary. "Then I'll sit there in the conference room with Meriwether and anyone else who has shown up to hear the talk, and when the secretary rushes in with the news that Hindenburg won't be attending, I'll get up and say how outrageous it is that people in our government are making connections between Al-Qaeda and German plumbers."

Pete whistled softly. He was a tremendous whistler, Pete. He could imitate any bird you could think of, and let loose a howler with two of his fingers jammed in his mouth that brought every dog in Excellence to a halt. "I don't know, Herbie. Having Meriwether sit there with you, waiting for this sausage link to drop by, that sounds risky to me. Besides, wouldn't you know the day before if customs had detained him? It's not like he'd fly all the way here from Germany the same day he was giving a talk."

Herbert warmed his hands with his breath. He found himself as unsettled by his brother's occasional lucidity as he was by his flights of deadheaded babbling. Perhaps he could try not to be quite so short-tempered with him. But Pete had exasperated Herbert for so long: doing all those drugs, then laboring so hard not to do them. In a way, the recovering addict's affects were nearly as annoying as the junkie's, they just didn't bring with them squad cars and creepy dudes living out of their vans. The truth was, Herbert had always blamed Pete for his marriage falling apart, and not simply because of all those times his drug problems had interrupted Herbert and Priscilla's domestic life. Whenever he had been asked to imagine adopting a child, Herbert had always ended up wondering what he would do if that child grew up to be like Pete—a question, curiously, he had never considered when he thought of having his own child with Priscilla, a child that would have at least shared some of his younger brother's genetic makeup.

"Could I do it?"

"Do what?"

Pete leaned toward him. Like some 3-D special effect, his tangled eyebrows continued to advance even after his body had stopped moving. He was wearing a plaid shirt and jeans. Pete was *always* wearing a plaid shirt and jeans, and rarely a coat, although he had one on then—not his own, one of Herbert's old down parkas he had dug out of the closet in the front foyer after professing to be a little cold. There were, Herbert noticed now, specks of gray in Pete's unkempt Fu Manchu.

"Could I make the call to the department secretary? I've always loved the German accent— fell in love with it as a kid watching *Hogan's Heroes*."

Herbert shot him a withering glare: the kind he usually reserved for his students. "This is serious stuff, Pete. I could lose my job."

"I know! That's why I'm trying to help."

Herbert bent his head to the side, waiting to see if his brother would crack a grin, but he didn't. He was being utterly sincere; he had no idea how ridiculous he sounded. "That's okay. I mean, I should probably handle it myself."

Pete took out his tobacco pouch and began to roll another cigarette. "You should let people help you more, Herbie. You're too proud. And what has it gotten you, being so proud? Bro, look how empty your life is now."

Herbert stood up. He could sit in the cold and watch Pete smoke—actually, he found that doing so relaxed him—but he couldn't sit in the cold and let his younger brother give him advice, or opine about the barrenness of his life. This was a man he had once retrieved from a dumpster. One night, it must have been at least ten years ago now, the phone rang—not the first time—at just a little past three in the morning. "Is this Pete's older brother?" a woman asked, her voice hoarse and tired. "Yes, it is," Herbert had replied, already fumbling for the pen and pad of paper he kept on his bedside table: once used to jot down notes to himself for articles he envisioned writing, now exclusively a means by which he recorded the addresses where his younger brother was encamped in some altered state, in need of a lift home. "Your brother," the woman continued, yawning, "I think he might have OD'ed. He's in the dumpster behind Logan's Pub. You know the alley there? It's one way off Excellence Drive. That's where he is." And Herbert had driven over there, parked next to the dumpster, and waded in to pull out his brother, whose body was limp, his clothes wet with beer, egg yolk

(Logan's served breakfast 24/7), and general filth. He pulled him out—barely—set him in the backseat of his Subaru, and raced over to the hospital. And now, years later, Pete was telling *him* not to be too proud.

Herbert walked toward the sliding doors that led into the living room. "I've got some grading to do," he announced. Pete said nothing in reply. He was gazing off into the darkness, spaced out for a moment. Technically, Pete didn't live here; he rented out a basement apartment from a retired couple on the other side of town, lodging that Herbert had found for him when he finished his last stint in rehab. But Pete slept on Herbert's living room couch fairly regularly, since Herbert lived just around the corner from Post-Colonial Lanes and Pete bowled there every night, without fail.

Herbert shut the sliding door behind him and walked past the couch, over to his desk in the far corner of the room, on which a pile of student writing more than a foot high sat waiting for his attention. He scooted in his chair so that his soft belly nudged up against the desk and began to flip through the papers: one had two-inch margins, several didn't have the pages numbered. Here was one with its staple mangled and twisted. Did students do this thing with their staples intentionally, in order to draw blood? He plucked the top paper off the pile and leaned back in his chair.

The student's name, printed in the top right corner of the page, didn't ring any bells; then again, Herbert had quit learning his students' names years before. He plunged into the one-sentence opening paragraph. When he was finished, Herbert had learned that *Paradise Lost* was a novel, Milton was still alive, Eve had attention deficit disorder, and Satan was best understood as the head of a motorcycle gang. Actually the last bit wasn't so terrible, in its own, idiotic way. He looked back over his shoulder, through the sliding doors that led out onto the deck. Pete was whistling, low and hypnotically, trying to attract one of the raccoons that had nested in the woodpile out beyond the farthest reach of the deck. Pete was obsessed with raccoons.

Herbert returned to his grading. And while he tried his best to resist the awful temptation, he nonetheless could not stop himself from reflecting on his life. Here he was, reading the drivel of a twenty-something who was probably drunk when he put pen to paper while his own brother was outside being a raccoon whisperer and his ex-wife was probably receiving another award somewhere, maybe for the Haitian adoption support network she had helped to start in the Midwest, or for the pedestrian mall that had just opened in downtown Excellence, thanks to Priscilla's tireless fundraising. And then, the following day, Herbert would find himself in class, standing in front of a blank chalkboard, and one of his students' hands would creep into the air. "Yes," Herbert would say. The low lid of the kid's baseball cap would lift slowly. He'd clear his throat. "I don't know, Professor Baker, but sometimes I kind of, like, wonder if Milton even, you know, like, believed in God." And Herbert would recoil in theatrical horror. "Milton not believe in God! Insane!" He would flap his arms. He might even snap the piece of chalk in his hand, provided it wasn't the last piece left in the room. Since its state funding had been slashed, Excellence had cut way back on supplies. While the student in question sank into his seat, Herbert would drone on for a bit about Milton's *Christian Doctrine*, the entirety of which he had never managed to finish. He would remind the class of the opening lines of *Paradise Lost*. He might even read them aloud. "Does that sound like the musings of an atheist?" he would ask.

But all the while, in the darkest recesses of his heart, the inanity of such a student wouldn't seem that inane, and for a brief moment Herbert would feel the temptation to tuck his dog-eared copy of *Paradise Lost* under his arm and say to his class, "You know, go ahead and write this down: I wonder sometimes myself if maybe all of the people we've been reading, not just Milton, but Shakespeare and Donne as well, I wonder sometimes if they all didn't end up deciding that religion was a pile of shit. Otherwise, why would Shakespeare make so much fun of the Trinity in Sonnet 105? Why would Donne talk about his profane mistresses in Holy Sonnet 13? And why in the world would Milton ever let the Heavenly Father in *Paradise Lost* come across like such a horse's ass?"

But Herbert would say none of this. Instead, he'd simply read a large chunk of Milton's verse until his students were cowed into submission, all because he didn't want to risk any conversation, any exchange in which a logical question might be posed, an interesting response to which he wouldn't be able to articulate. So, out of self-defense, Herbert Baker chose to bore his students to tears, and—two days a week, every week—he succeeded brilliantly.

He set the student's paper back on the pile. Who was he kidding? He couldn't grade tonight, not after learning that he might be fired for embezzlement. But he couldn't just sit there, either; he had to try to distract himself. So he withdrew a legal pad from the top drawer of his desk, on which he had been scribbling a personal ad that, in his weaker moments, he contemplated sending into *The New York Review of Books*. Of course, Pete *was* right; his life was empty. It was barren and windswept, save for the Program in Profound Thought, but Dean Meriwether was about to come down on that with all the delicacy of a sledgehammer. He looked over his ad.

> *DWM, overly educated, burned-out, fifty-something academic seeks a cheerful female nihilist of any age or ethnicity who is unambiguously committed to heterosexuality. Ideally she, too, is tired of the information age, jazz, Marxism, actually all –isms, young people, exercise, and NPR. A passing interest in baseball that peters out in late May wouldn't be bad, along with some sense of what to watch on TV that doesn't immediately inspire a desire for a meteor to wipe out this planet. But in truth, interests themselves are entirely optional. Comfort in shared silence is probably a good idea, as well as patience with eccentric siblings. . . .*

Oh, this would be a real hit. He slid the legal pad to the side, put his elbows on his desk, and rested his head in his hands. For the sake of argument, he imagined some poor woman actually responding to this cry from the wilderness, some woman whose anti-psychotic medication was set at a dosage that did not disrupt her motor skills to the point where she could no longer send an e-mail. He imagined receiving a little electronic note from this woman, along the lines of, "Hi! I've been searching for years for someone just like you, someone filled with a fascinating mixture of bitterness and torpor. What do you say we get together?" At which point Herbert would have to consider how the hell to get this person out to Excellence, in the dead center of the Midwest, in the middle of soybean crops, meth labs, and anti-abortion messages painted on the sides of barns. *Jesus Hates Baby Killers!* was just a few blocks away, followed by—three miles down the county road—*Every Fetus Deserves A Christmas.*

Pete whistled softly right behind him, the perfect imitation of a plane plummeting from the sky. How could Herbert not have heard him come in?

"Bro, that is one depressing piece of writing."

Herbert shoved the pad back into the drawer. "Excuse me, Pete—"

"What *was* that?"

"Can you give me just a little bit of space—"

"Was that a personal ad? I hope it was, bro, because I think that'd be a great move for you. Get a profile out there on the Internet. Why the hell not? But you've got to put your best foot forward. Dig up a picture from a few years ago. Maybe a decade ago. Make up some shit—you know, so you sound a little cool. Say you like to hang glide. Don't say you hate young people!"

"But I don't like to hang glide, Pete."

"You can tell the woman that on your first date. Say you had an accident and now you spend your time mostly reading old poems. Kind of ease her into your world, that's all I'm saying."

Pete slapped him on the back and made his way into the kitchen. If only I did spend my time mostly reading old poems, Herbert thought wistfully, as he listened to his brother rummage through the cupboards. "Sorry there's not much to eat," he called out apologetically. "I have to go to the store."

"Oh, I can make something work here for the little guys."

Herbert picked up a pen. For a moment he contemplated trying to twirl it on his thumb like Meriwether had, but he had never been any good at tricks like that. "What are you talking about?"

"The raccoons. I'm going to make them a little dinner."

"Dinner? Just give them scraps from the garbage."

"If you were a raccoon, would you want scraps from the garbage?"

"Yes, I think I very well might."

"I don't think you would."

Herbert rose to his feet and walked across the living room. He stood in the doorway that led into the kitchen. Pete had placed some tortilla chips on a plate and was sprinkling cheese over them.

"What are you doing?"

"I'm making them nachos. Do you have any salsa?"

"Pete, please do not make nachos for the raccoons who live out in the woodpile."

"Herbie, I don't know if I've told you this, but the last time I was in rehab—"

"Pete, you've told me this every night *since* you got out of rehab—"

"—one of the exercises we did was to choose an animal that we thought embodied who we were. And I chose raccoons. I did so because raccoons are demonized and feared for no reason. Also because they are resourceful, and nocturnal. And they have OCD tendencies. Now, do you think it's a coincidence that virtually the same day I got out of rehab, a family of raccoons moved into your woodpile?"

"Pete, there have been raccoons living in the backyard for no more than three months and you got out of rehab the last time more than eight years—"

"Time is a fiction, Herbie. Think of the Buddha, or at least consider the female orgasm. Sometimes you sound like such a child."

Herbert said nothing. What was the point? Pete was not

someone with whom you could reason. He returned to his desk. Once more he told himself that he really should dive into his grading, instead of putting it off for yet another night, but all he could think about was Meriwether, digging into his little program. Jesus Christ. What if he just came clean about the whole thing? Blamed his divorce, said he had made some bad choices? Like this academic Frankenstein, built in a basement somewhere by vengeful bureaucrats, would care. The only chance he'd have to save his ass in the short term would be if Gerhard Hindenburg's nonappearance somehow altered Meriwether's view of the Program in Profound Thought, not that Herbert saw exactly how it could.

The microwave chimed. Pete shuffled out onto the deck, his plate of nachos carefully held in front of him, like a vase filled with flowers. Herbert watched him cross the deck, then turned back around in his chair. Once more he looked at the pile of grading he had. *I myself am hell*, he muttered. What if he told his students that, as an educational exercise, he wanted them to grade each other's work? There was some term for that: peer-response something. It was a credible form of instruction. Maybe he could make all of his courses peer-response based. Then he'd have no grading. He wondered what percent of his listlessness stemmed from grading, or—more accurately—from not being able to bring himself to grade. Thirty percent? Fifty? What if it was more like eighty? What if he got out from under his grading altogether? Maybe that would really change his life.

Herbert had just reminded himself that his students could peer-respond until the end of time, but that wouldn't change the fact that Meriwether was breathing down his back, when he heard an earsplitting scream, followed by a stream of abuse.

"You little fuckers! I will bury you! I will eat your fucking children! I will douse your home with gasoline and light a fucking match! I will kill you all!"

Herbert rushed outside and over to the far side of the deck. Down at the woodpile, Pete turned toward him, his hands spread in front of his face, blood streaming down his fingers.

"You're going to have to take me to the hospital, bro," he said, his speech now garbled. "One of those fucking raccoons bit me in the fucking face."

THEY PULLED RIGHT INTO THE EMERGENCY ENTRANCE at the Excellence Medical Center. A couple of orderlies helped Pete into a wheelchair and then sped off. At the check-in desk, Herbert filled out his brother's paperwork. For a long time, Pete had been without any health insurance. But then, after his divorce had been finalized and Herbert had a little money left over from blowing up his retirement account in order to give Priscilla half, he took out a health insurance policy for his brother with the understanding that he would make the payments initially, until Pete found steady work. Pete never did, though, and Herbert had continued to pay the bill. At times he wondered why he worried about Pete's health insurance when Pete himself didn't seem the slightest bit concerned. But on nights like this, he understood his own logic.

The waiting room was deserted. When he had finished with the forms, Herbert nodded at the empty chairs to the nurse seated behind the desk. "Slow night, huh?"

"Oh, the moped accidents and alcohol poisonings don't kick in until after midnight," she explained.

Herbert checked his watch. It was just half past seven. What a long day.

He was directed back into the ER: a cluttered area shaped like an octagon, its outer edge comprised of small bays, each of which was cordoned off by a curtain. Herbert approached the large, circular counter in the middle of the room, behind which a single nurse stood, staring down at a computer screen. Off to his right, he heard a loud voice denouncing raccoons and all their wretched progeny. He followed the voice to one of the bays, the curtain of which was only half drawn. Pete was sitting on the edge of a bed while a nurse wiped blood out of his Fu Manchu. The raccoon, it turned out, had bit him right on the fleshy point of his chin.

"I'm having flashbacks," Pete exclaimed. "I can see its little rat face, bearing down on me."

The nurse stepped back just as a man in green scrubs entered the room.

"What have we got here?" the doctor asked as he walked over and peered at the bite marks.

"Fucking raccoon," Pete grumbled.

"No kidding! Bit you on the chin, huh? How about that."

"Give a raccoon a plate of nachos and this is how it repays you."

The doctor turned and looked at the nurse, who looked back at him. They used a local anesthetic to numb Pete's chin. Then, without a word, the doctor sewed up the wound, which required six stitches. When he was done, he told Herbert that Anne—the nurse—would take care of the rest, and Anne followed up by saying she'd be back in a jiffy.

Once they were alone, Pete swung his legs onto the hospital bed and shut his eyes. Herbert looked down at him. There was some dried blood on the collar of his plaid shirt, and his chin was purple and swollen, the stitches gleaming under the fluorescent lights.

"Can we get the hell out of here?" Pete asked. He kept his lips pressed together when he spoke so Herbert had a hard time understanding him.

"The nurse said she'd be right back."

"I don't give a shit what she said. I want to go." For a man keen on escape, Pete had a funny way of showing it. He remained listless on the bed.

"You can walk home then. I'm waiting for the nurse."

Pete sighed. "My face feels like it's made of Silly Putty." His eyes flipped open. He regarded the ceiling blankly. A couple of minutes passed before Herbert heard a rattling coming toward them. Anne pulled back the curtain, revealing a cart, on the metal top of which sat two needles and syringes, two small, sealed jars of medications, and a pair of latex gloves.

Pete turned his head toward the cart, then pushed himself

up in bed. "We need to give you an immunoglobulin shot and a rabies vaccine," Anne said. "Then, three more vaccine shots over the next two weeks, the next one in three days."

She slipped on the gloves, flicked the syringe with her index finger, then inserted the needle into one of the small jars, out of which she drew the immunoglobulin. Pete watched her work with his mouth open, a bead of saliva on the corner of his lip. Then he looked over at his brother. "Ask her if she has to use needles, Herbie. See if she can't give me pills instead."

Herbert turned toward Anne, who wrinkled her brow at him for clarification. "My brother has a thing, a past history . . . with needles."

Pete turned his wrists and held out his arms so that she could see the tracks and scars that marked his pale skin: those puckered, red tributaries of abuse. The nurse studied them with sympathy. "There's no other way," she said. "I'm sorry."

Herbert leaned over the bed. "Here, grab a hold of my hand, Pete. And shut your eyes. You'll get through it just fine. Then I'll bring you back here for the next shot. I'll bring you here for all of them. I'll stand right next to you and you can squeeze my hand each time. So there's nothing to worry about."

Pete wiped the sweat from his forehead. He stared down at his dirty jeans.

"I'll need to . . ." The nurse pointed at Pete's mangled chin. "We need to get this shot as close to the wound as possible."

Pete looked pleadingly at his brother.

"I bet we can leave right after these shots are done," Herbert said. "Is that right?"

The nurse nodded. "Yes, that's right. Dr. Martin signed the release papers. But we have to do them first. It's very important."

The nurse and Herbert stood there, waiting for Pete. After a minute or so he groaned, wiggled over to the edge of the bed, and took hold of Herbert's fingers tightly. Then he shut his eyes. The nurse rubbed a tiny pad of alcohol on his chin, then drew the needle toward Pete's face. Herbert watched his brother's expression, waiting for him to grimace in pain, even cry out, but when the needle plunged into his skin, Pete just smiled, his eyelids fluttering.

A FEW MINUTES AFTER THE SECOND SHOT had been administered, they were back in Herbert's rusted-out Subaru, the front dashboard of which was now stained with flecks of Pete's blood. They turned off the hospital grounds, onto Excellence Drive. Dozens of students were milling at the bus stop on their right, waiting for a lift to the bars that were lined up on Main Street, about four blocks away.

"What time have you got, Herbie?"

"Eight-twenty."

"Okay, you got to hightail it over to Post-Colonial Lanes. My B League starts to roll in ten minutes."

Pete bowled in at least three leagues that Herbert knew about. When he didn't have league play, he hustled games with friends, or he bowled by himself. Almost all of Pete's socializing, at least all of his socializing with which Herbert was familiar, occurred at Post-Colonial Lanes.

"You sure you don't want to skip tonight? You look like hell."

At the stoplight, streams of students passed in front and behind their car, some calling out like coyotes, others holding their hands in the air, like kids on a rollercoaster. The next morning, some of these very students would squint at Herbert while he propounded the worthiness of a few lines of poetry written four hundred years ago, their heads no doubt throbbing, their throats parched, their bowels churning.

"Herbie, if you don't fucking get me to Post-Colonial Lanes right away, I swear to fucking God I'll be under the bypass, shooting up before sunrise. I am not shitting you. I need a bowling ball in my hand, bro. It doesn't even have to be mine. But I got to bowl. Believe me."

Herbert drove quickly past Main Street, over the very bypass Pete had just referenced, back to the unfashionable side of town. Post-Colonial Lanes was lodged in a barely renovated, enormous industrial shed that had—up until the last farm crisis—housed surplus tractors, headers, and windrowers for the John Deere dealership on the other side of the lot. When that dealership closed, one of Herbert's former colleagues, Arun Kumar, decided to leave academia and pursue a dream he had been harboring since his earliest days in the States: opening a bowling alley. Post-Colonial Lanes was coined out of deference to Arun's intellectual interests. Rather than number the lanes, he had named them after prominent Post-Colonial theorists, which meant Herbert had become accustomed to having Pete say things like, "Hey, I rolled a 248 on Spivak the other night," or, "There is no action on Said these days, I mean none!" In lieu of a concession stand, Arun's wife, Gita, ran an Indian buffet and rented out Bollywood films, a number of which Pete had brought home to watch on Herbert's TV. Most importantly, at least from Herbert's point of view, Arun either hadn't been able to secure a liquor license or hadn't cared to; all he and Gita served were soft drinks and various kinds of tea, so Pete wasn't tempted by any alcohol when he bowled.

Even though his brother had been going to Post-Colonial Lanes since its opening night three year before, Herbert had never stepped foot inside the place. All of his information about Post-Colonial Lanes had been culled from Pete, and the rapturous articles about the place that appeared regularly in the *Excellence Gazette*. Neither did any of his colleagues hang out at Post-Colonial Lanes, but for reasons different from Herbert's. In a fairly short period of time, Arun's income from his bowling venture had managed to meet and then surpass the modest salary he had once earned at Excellence as a professor, and this was a source of frustration and envy for his former colleagues in the humanities. So they stayed away. Once it became known around town that Post-Colonial Lanes was the one place where you could hang out without having to worry about encountering any faculty from Excellence, the place only became more crowded and popular. Still, Herbert Baker didn't share his colleagues' jealousy. He steered clear of Post-Colonial Lanes simply because he didn't know how to bowl, and he didn't want to intrude on Pete's world. But he didn't begrudge Arun's success. In fact, he saw the two of them as kindred spirits; Post-Colonial Lanes was simply a more successful, more tangible version of the Program in Profound Thought.

The two of them stepped through the aluminum doorway and made their way—enveloped by clouds of cigarette smoke— to the long counter that ran behind the lanes. A plump Indian woman walked over to them.

"I'll need to borrow some shoes tonight, Gita," Pete said. "Size eleven. I didn't have time to swing by my place."

Gita reached beneath the counter and pulled out a pair of shoes. "What happened to your face, Pete?"

"A little encounter with a raccoon." Pete winked at her. Gita asked Herbert for his shoe size, but Herbert explained that he was just there to watch.

"What lane are we on tonight?" Pete asked.

"You guys are over on Bhabha. Have a good night." Gita waved at them both. They began to walk but progressed slowly through the place, as Pete stopped every few feet to explain his injuries to different groups of people and check the racks for a ball that might work for that evening. Herbert hung back and watched as his brother joked around with his friends and flirted with one woman after another, many of whom wore wrist braces and brightly colored league shirts. Herbert had spent so much time in his life worrying about his brother, thinking him lost, even doomed, that to watch him now in his element filled him with wonderment, even a little envy. Here was a man who had tried, really tried, to throw his life away time and time again, but who had also always managed to surround himself with people who adored him: people who laughed at his jokes and eagerly exchanged awkward, middle-aged high-fives.

With Pete now engulfed by his teammates at the far lane, Herbert found a chair and sat well behind the bowlers. Pete hadn't missed a frame, but he wouldn't be able to warm up. He put on his shoes hurriedly and stretched his arms. Then he stepped onto the upraised wooden floor from which the Homi Bhabha Lane, like all the others, extended. Pete raised the ball up to just beneath his chin, straightened his posture, and stared at the pins. Then, suddenly, he turned around. Setting the ball down in the return, he held up his hand to his teammates, asking for a second. Quickly he skipped over to where Herbert was seated.

"Can I make the call, Herbie? Please."

"What are you talking about?"

"To the department secretary. Can I call her and say the German dude you invented isn't going to show up? It'd mean a lot to me, to be involved in this a little, since—you know—you started the whole *profound thought thing* pretty much to get me straightened out."

Herbert was shocked. He had assumed that Pete didn't remember, or had never really known, that he had first asked for funding for the program in order to pay him to build the deck. He had just figured that this gesture, like so many others he had made to help his brother, had been forgotten, or not even fully fathomed in the first place.

"Hold on, I have an idea." Pete brushed his hair out of his eyes. "How about we have a little wager? If I bowl a strike with my first ball, you'll let me make the call. If I don't, then you can do it."

Herbert grinned. That seemed fair. Besides, his brother was still slurring his words. He liked his odds. "Okay, deal."

Pete rushed back to the match. Picking up his ball, he once more assumed his pose at the top of the lane. Then he took five quick steps forward, extending his arm as he did so. Upon releasing the ball, his fingers curled up toward the ceiling. Even before the pins came crashing down he had spun around, his hips twisting, his fingers shooting invisible bullets at his brother, his face discolored and swollen, his eyes sparkling with pure joy as he cried out, "I am back, baby!! I am so back!!"

AFTER LEADING A PARTICULARLY DISMAL CLASS on *Lycidas* the next morning, in which his students remarked that Milton was "like, so totally into himself," that the poem was "so, like, all over the place," and that the genre of elegy itself was "like, such a total downer," Herbert spent the rest of the day plastering his department with handouts and poorly made posters advertising the brilliance of a German plumber named Gerhard Hindenburg. He tried and failed to send out a mass e-mail, but he did manage to corner a younger colleague and beg him to forward the lecture information to everyone imaginable in the Excellence community. In the afternoon, he sat down and wrote out exactly what he wanted Pete to say when he phoned the department as Hindenburg. Minutes after Pete had bowled his coveted strike, it occurred to Herbert that a single phone call from the latest invitee to the Program in Profound Thought Speaker Series wouldn't do the trick. If the department secretary was informed the day before that Hindenburg wasn't going to be able to make the talk, then she'd simply cancel the presentation right then and there, only raising Meriwether's suspicions that much more. So Herbert decided, much to Pete's delight, to have him phone as Hindenburg *twice*: once on Thursday to announce that he was encountering some difficulties with authorities in the Munich airport and would be taking a later flight that would get him into Excellence with just a little time to spare before the talk, and then—right before the scheduled lecture the following day—another call canceling once and for all. Herbert would be seated in the conference room along with everyone else when the second call came through, so when the department secretary walked in with the news, he wouldn't look any more to blame for the failure of profound thought than anyone else. At least that's what he tried to tell himself.

"I've written out exactly what I want you to say each time," Herbert explained to his brother over the phone. "How about I swing by and we make the first call from your place?"

But Pete took offense. "You don't think I can pick up the goddamn phone myself, Herbie? You think I'm that fried?"

"It's not a simple call. You have to make sure to dial star 67 and then the department number; otherwise, the secretary will see that you're phoning from town."

"Anyone who has ever called a new dealer has used star 67, Professor Shithead. Just read me the script over the phone. You'll make me a nervous wreck anyway, standing over my shoulder. Besides, this is about you letting go. This is about you learning to let people help you."

"No, this is about trying to get out from under years of profound thought."

"Herbie, you are such a stick in the mud—"

"All right, all right. Take this down EXACTLY as I say it. . . ."

Herbert recited the speech slowly before letting Pete go. Fifteen minutes later, the phone on his desk—the phone that never rang—rattled in its cradle. It was Lucy. That was the department secretary's name. She related the travel difficulties being faced by the speaker who was flying in from Germany, although she also confessed that his thick accent had made it difficult for her to follow everything he said—something about an issue with his passport. In any event, he would be arriving on a later flight. Herbert thanked her for the update and asked her to call the airport shuttle and arrange for them to take their customer right to the department. Lucy said she'd be happy to do that, and that the dean's office had instructed her to make all travel arrangements for speakers in the future. Herbert said that would be enormously helpful and hung up. Then he called his brother.

"Okay, you're halfway there."

"That was awesome, bro! I really feel like I get this guy, you know? As an actor, I mean. I feel like I can really inhabit this dude."

"Well just inhabit him once more. You'll need to phone again right at three tomorrow. Where will you be then?"

"Home."

"Fine, I'll call you at two thirty and we'll go over things."

"Super, talk to you at three thirty—"

"Two thirty!"

"I'm shitting you, Herbie. Jesus, take a pill."

"Okay, very funny."

Pete yawned slowly and loudly into the phone. "So what do you think, bro? Me as an actor: can you see it?"

Through his office window, Herbert overlooked the Excellence University Power Plant. He watched the plumes of pollution stream out of the plant's smokestacks. Not exactly postcard worthy, his view. My God, how did things end up unfolding like this? He had shown promise—certainly as an undergraduate, but even in graduate school he had received some notice, only to end up here at Excellence. He should have never encouraged Pete to move out here from Rochester when their mom died, but what was the use second-guessing himself now?

"I can definitely see you as an actor, Pete," he said to his brother. "Crystal clear."

FRIDAY MORNING, Herbert showered, shaved, and dressed in attire he hadn't worn in years: pleated corduroy pants, a worn white Oxford, and a tweed jacket with patches on the elbows. All morning he puttered around the empty hallway of the Excellence Department of English. At noon he ate a bagel in a corner of the student union. After lunch, he dug up a yellow legal pad in his office: his prop to give the appearance that he was prepared to take notes during Hindenburg's talk. At two thirty he phoned Pete and they went over his next call. He would just say that he missed his flight. That was it. No further explanation. Lucy would rush over to the conference room with the news, and Herbert would take it from there. In spite of his generally fatalistic nature, Herbert couldn't help but feel pretty good about how the ruse was playing out. He phoned Pete at ten to three, just to make sure he hadn't fallen asleep, then shut his office door and walked down the hallway.

The chairs that had been arranged to face a podium on the far side of the department's conference room were nearly full, with Dean Meriwether seated prominently in the front row. All of Herbert's colleagues were there. Someone, probably Betty, must have spread the word that the dean would be attending a talk in their department. Herbert nodded and smiled as he made his way across the room. He shook Meriwether's hand, then took the only empty seat he saw, right next to the dean. Only then did he permit himself to glance at his watch. It was two minutes before three. He looked over his shoulder, at the doorway, waiting for Lucy to burst in.

A minute ticked by, then another. Finally Dean Meriwether leaned over to him. "I believe you are missing your speaker, Professor Baker."

"Some travel delays, apparently. He's on his way." Herbert allowed himself a knowing nod. Another minute went by. On the cusp of excusing himself in order to run back to his office and phone his brother, Herbert sighed with relief when he saw Lucy step through the doorway. But rather than rush over to him, she took a spot against the back wall. Apparently she was settling in to hear the talk. Herbert excused himself and zipped around the swelling crowd, until he stood just inside the doorway to the room. He had to motion at Lucy several times before she walked over to him.

"Are we okay?" he asked her.

She grinned. "Yeah, he just called—said he was two minutes away. You aren't going to meet him downstairs and walk him up?"

Before he could even process what she was saying, a figure rushed into the room. The man was wearing an obviously fake, short, crooked moustache and black lederhosen, beneath the suspenders of which a baggy Led Zeppelin T-shirt hung over his waist. In his hand, he swung an enormous lug wrench.

"Greetings, fellow Profounders," Pete began, making his way to the podium. The accent sounded less Bavarian than it did early Muppets. "Howzabout we kick this beer hall into gear, Munich style!"

Herbert watched as his colleagues and Dean Meriwether first took in the human spectacle before them, and next turned in their seats to see what his reaction was. But Herbert had no visible reaction. All he felt was the sensation of being turned to stone.

"Whenever I work on a toilet," Pete continued, fumbling with a napkin he had pulled out of his pocket, on which he had apparently jotted down some talking points, "I am always thinking about the phenomenology of . . . toilets. What does a toilet look like to me? What does a toilet look like to you?"

"Hold on there." Herbert snapped out of his immobilized state and ventured out, in front of the chairs that faced the podium. He couldn't let his brother do this. Holding up his hands, he nodded deferentially toward the dean, the man who—together with all the other people who had never cared about books, about reading, about poems or stories or ideas in the first place—would take apart Excellence, along with every other college and university in the country, until all that would be left would be departments and programs devoted to documenting the ugliness of the world, rather than the achievements of dreamers and misfits. "You win, Dean Meriwether. There is no such thing as the Program in Profound Thought, or Gerhard Hindenburg. This is my brother, Pete. Just to be clear, I've been embezzling money from Excellence University for more than seven years. So go ahead; treat me as you see fit."

"YOU GOT TO RESPECT THE FACT that he told you on the spot he was going to move to have you terminated immediately. I mean, he didn't leave you dangling there. Now you can get on with your life."

The two of them were sitting out on Herbert's deck. Pete was having a cigarette. Herbert had already helped himself to the Scotch in the pantry. They had shared a largely silent dinner: pick-up Thai food devoured at the dining room table, without place mats or plates. Herbert had never felt hungrier in his life. He assumed that he was in a state of shock. He felt oddly calm, but calm in an unnerving way, like someone thrown out of an airplane without a parachute who chooses not to worry about the landing and just takes in the scenery as he falls.

"What's happened to me?" He looked over at Pete for an answer. Really, whom else did he have to consult? "First my marriage falls apart, then I lose my job. No one with tenure loses his job! Good Lord."

Pete shook his head. "Priscilla's not your bad, bro. That's just bad luck; that could happen to anyone."

Herbert regarded his brother with a touch of envy. He did have a worldview of sorts: a kind of personal philosophy, cobbled together from drug rehab, self-help books, and daytime TV programming. But it was a worldview. It helped Pete make sense of his existence, at least some of the time. In spite of all of his reading, at least all the reading he had once done, Herbert had no such interpretive confidence.

"Shit, I'm sorry, Herbie. Showing up like I did . . . I was really trying to help. Your whole plan—no offense—but it looked to me like it was going to crash and burn. How would another speaker *not* showing up for one of your little rodeos get Meriwether off your tail? That's what I didn't get. Not to mention, you were the one who really got me thinking about the whole acting thing in the first place. I kind of got into the research I did online and I thought if I went in there and smacked a home run you'd be off the hook. I really thought I might hit the jackpot."

Herbert let out a long sigh. That was a really impressive string of mixed metaphors there. Surely some advanced life form somewhere in the galaxy would regard his brother as a kind of genius. But such a form had yet to be detected; for the foreseeable future, Pete was stuck with the assessment of mere earthlings.

"I'm not mad at you, Pete. I know you were just trying to help."

Pete took a drag on his cigarette. "I have my clear moments and then I have my fuzzy ones—even now that I'm clean. I think it's kind of always been like that with me."

Herbert agreed. "So I'm assuming that was a fuzzy one?"

"The idea of playing Gerhard Hindenburg? No, that was as clear as can be. I was going to march in there and save your ass: kind of right the ledger sheet a little. The clear moments, those are the ones that always get me into trouble, not the fuzzy ones. Like when I can see the pins crashing, when I *know* I'm going to get a strike, then I never do."

Herbert finished his drink. "The Hitler moustache was a nice touch."

"Yeah, turns out they don't sell those at the Excellence Costume Emporium. You have to buy a Groucho Marx and trim it down."

Herbert looked out over the far end of the deck, at the moon rising on the horizon, just above a band of dark clouds. The raccoons had been rustling around when they first moved outside, but Pete had quieted them down by screaming over and over again that he was going to murder them all and burn their carcasses.

"You're a good brother, Herbie," Pete said, crossing his arms behind his head and looking up at the sky. "What you did in your department today, coming clean like that, that was something else. You've really done some growing here lately. I like what I'm seeing."

"Thanks, Pete."

A minute or two of silence passed.

"I'm sorry about Priscilla, too," his younger brother added. "She let a good guy go. Personally, I think it's better that you're no longer married to a lesbian. But I know that was hard on you."

He couldn't recall if his brother had ever commented on his divorce before in such a manner. And suddenly, Herbert felt a tear form in the corner of his eye. He sneezed twice in rapid succession. "You give yourself to someone; I mean, you just give yourself away." He shook his head as his eyes closed. "Then she decides to give you back, only there isn't anyone to give you back to, so you're all alone, and what you thought you were building ends up being a dream . . . ." His voice broke. Once more he sneezed, like a man with hay fever, only Herbert wasn't allergic to anything.

"No, no. You're forgetting, bro: there's me. She gave you back to me. I'm sitting right here. I'm not going anywhere." Pete reached over and squeezed Herbert's forearm. "You did what you needed to do, and the choices you made, they brought you here and you want to be here. It might not seem like you want to be here, but you do. The present moment is the sum total of your past, see? And you want to live in the present. Like God. You getting me? He's just in the present, not in the future or the past. He's in the eternal present. That's why God doesn't worry any and seems so removed: because he can't be troubled. There is no addiction in the present, just being. God never did smack because he's always in the present. You follow?"

Herbert's head was buried in his hands. He was really sobbing. He couldn't help it. He was just sobbing.

"You saved my life, bro. Don't think I don't know it. I'd be dead if it weren't for you."

Pete rubbed his arm for a bit, until Herbert's crying let up. Then he rose to his feet. "Hey, I got an idea. How about we go over to Post-Colonial Lanes and I show you how to bowl? A free lesson. Just you and me. What do you say?"

Herbert wiped his nose with the back of his hand. He rubbed his eyes for a moment. The very thought of sitting around the house filled him with dread.

"You don't have any league play tonight?"

"Not tonight. Come on."

Herbert followed his brother out to his car and drove the two of them over to the bowling alley. Pete rented him a pair of shoes. He asked Gita if they could use Fanon: the lane on the farthest end. He picked out a ball for him. When they made it over to their lane, he set the ball in the return, had Herbert lace up his shoes, and showed him several stretches for his arm and back. Then he instructed Herbert to pick the ball up out of the return and step onto the upraised floor in front of their lane.

"You want to keep your hips in. You bowl with your hips, not your arm."

"I'm not sure what that means." Herbert cradled the ball in his hands.

"Now line your feet up there behind those little arrows. There you go."

Herbert looked over at the bowlers in the adjoining lane. They were laughing and high-fiving one another. *I need to invent my own Post-Colonial Lanes*, he said to himself. *Something real this time. Something I can take a little pride in. Maybe I could open a bookstore. But no one buys books anymore. I've always wanted to volunteer for Habitat for Humanity. But I'm no good with tools. Oh, crap, what am I going to do?* He felt his throat tighten. How much did this ball weigh, anyway? He stared down at the bowling pins at the end of their lane. *Maybe, instead of worrying about what to do with myself, I should tell myself what I'm not going to be doing anymore. For instance, I'm not going to be boring any poor undergraduates. I'm not going to steal any more money from Excellence. Tomorrow morning, I'm not going to sit in my office and read a bunch of insufferable e-mails. And in the summer, when the guys in the hazmat suits come in to pull more asbestos out from above the ceiling panels, I'm not going to run into them in the hallway of the department and try to engage them in conversation. "Just curious," I won't be saying. "You know, you guys are in here for a few days each summer in those suits, but I work here year-round and I don't even wear a face mask . . . ."*

"Now take five steps forward, swing the ball back, keep your arm straight, and let it fly."

Maybe, for the next few days, or weeks, or months, maybe I can just take it easy. Or, better yet, maybe I can go back to the poems that led me to graduate school in the first place. Maybe I can become a reader again. Doesn't that sound nice? I can sit on the back deck and read Paradise Lost, *beginning to end—just lose myself in it, like I did when I first read it in college.*

"Empty your brain, bro!" Pete intoned. "Tell yourself you're a bowling ball, made of resin and plastic. All you have to do is take a spin down the lane."

Herbert nodded. He reset his feet behind the little arrows. He told himself not to think so much. Then, he took five swift steps toward the pins, shut his eyes, and let the ball go.

The Librarian

HE HAD TO TOUCH THINGS. He couldn't control himself. Before he had been able to, at least for a while, but anymore now he couldn't. Why, he didn't know. Maybe because his dad was still gone? But his dad had been gone for a long time. So he didn't know.

On the subway, on the way to work, he would touch the hands of the people holding onto the same pole that he was. They would pull away. Sometimes, when the train paused at a station, they would move to the other end of the car. That was okay. There were always plenty of hands to touch on the subway.

When he entered a room, he would envelop the doorknob fully with his hand. He would touch the doorframe. He would run his hands against the backs of chairs, along the walls. The curtains he would let ripple in his fingers. Curtains were his favorite things to touch in rooms because they were so fine and thin, and because no one had ever objected to the way he handled them. No one, in fact, ever seemed to care.

In the park, he would pet every dog he could. He would cup their flews in his hand. If they were gentle and their walkers permitted it, he would place his cheek against their panting sides.

Most things he touched with his hands, but his preference was to touch with his cheeks. That was his favorite way to feel.

He was a librarian at the reference desk in the New York Public Library.

He had been beaten for touching people. Just the year before, at McDonald's, he touched the prickly beard of a black man standing in front of him in line. He touched it with the back of his hand. The man had five friends with him. They beat him in the restaurant, then outside on the street corner. No one tried to stop them. First they punched him in the face and stomach. Then, when he fell onto the sidewalk, they kicked him. They did this to him until the cops arrived, at which point they ran away.

He had been called many things. He had been called a "fag." He had been called a "faggot." He had been called a "pervert." (He had been called that one a lot.) He had also been called a "freak show." He didn't like being called names (who does?), but it didn't change anything. The librarian still had to touch things.

He was twenty-eight years old.

As a boy, they had owned a vacation home out on Long Island. The librarian, who was then, of course, not yet a librarian, loved touching the sand. It was his favorite thing to touch. But it was frustrating, too, because on the beach it wasn't easy to feel the sand touch your body, all at once, and that was what the librarian wanted to feel. One day, the librarian had an idea: he would take off his swimming trunks and leap from the top of a gazebo they shared with their neighbors and land in the sand with his arms and legs spread wide, so that each pore of his skin would feel the sand at the precise same moment. But the librarian miscalculated the distance from the roof to the beach and landed in between the two, on a concrete path. He broke his right arm and leg and fractured his chin and two ribs. He spent the next several weeks in the hospital. The librarian who was not yet a librarian did not like having a fractured chin and ribs, but he loved the feeling of his arm and leg sealed in plaster; it made him feel very, very calm.

When he got out of the hospital, his father was gone. His

mother sold the house on Long Island, and the two of them moved from their apartment on the Upper West Side to a two-bedroom in Astoria, where she was from. After he was out of his casts, she started to drop him off for a few hours here and there at the Queens Library on Fourteenth Street—just a few blocks from their place—while she ran errands. She also took him to see a psychiatrist.

The psychiatrist was a very serious man. At their first session, he looked at the librarian for a long time before saying anything. Finally he said that he had heard from the librarian's mother that he had broken his arm and leg the summer before. He asked how this had happened, and the librarian explained that he had jumped off the roof of a gazebo. The psychiatrist asked him why he had done this. The librarian didn't want to tell him that his only intention was to feel the sandy beach encompass his body, all at once. He didn't think the psychiatrist would understand. So he said nothing. Several minutes went by. Then the psychiatrist asked him if he had wanted to hurt himself. The librarian said to the psychiatrist, "Why would I want to hurt myself?" The psychiatrist didn't answer. More time passed. Still staring at him, the psychiatrist asked the librarian if he wanted to fly. The librarian said to the psychiatrist, "Why would I want to fly?" The psychiatrist said nothing. Then the librarian thought about the psychiatrist's question some more and asked, "Doesn't everyone want to fly?" The psychiatrist wrote something down on his legal pad when he said this. The librarian was ten years old at the time.

He saw many other psychiatrists over the next fourteen years, and the conversations he had with them became stranger and stranger as he grew older and older. After he had touched a man's hand at a urinal in a bathroom in Grand Central Station, his psychiatrist at the time asked him what he thought of the male body. He asked him what he thought of the female body. The librarian who by now was a librarian laughed. He had a very soft laugh. "I love men's bodies and women's bodies," he answered. "Isn't it silly, the idea of loving a male body rather than a female body, or vice versa? To your fingers, the differences are so tiny." He had offered this observation again and again, but none of his therapists had ever written it down.

Eventually the librarian began to tell the therapists he saw about how much he loved to touch things. He would touch them on the knee sometimes, or the hand, while he told them that he liked to touch people on the knees and hands. The librarian found that in general, therapists didn't like to be touched. Neither did custodial workers. They would ask him sometimes, not the custodial workers but the therapists, why he liked to touch things. The librarian would answer with a question himself: "Why do we like to do anything?" They never answered his question, and the librarian, in turn, never answered theirs.

The last therapist he saw asked him what he wanted to touch more than anything else. The librarian remembered this session, because just the day before he had been leafing through the enormous books they had in the natural sciences section of the Queens Library on Fourteenth Street. The same library in which he had once passed away the time as a boy was now where he worked as a reference librarian. Book after book in the natural sciences section was filled with pictures of beautiful beings, but none more beautiful than the butterflies the librarian encountered in these pages. The librarian had never thought about butterflies before. Now he realized that, more than anything else he had ever seen, he wanted very badly to touch them. Right away he surmised that it would be very difficult to do so. Then, the more he thought about it, the more he wondered whether or not the intensity of such an interaction might kill him. So he decided instead that it would be best to pursue approximations.

It was at this moment that the librarian began to fantasize about touching people's eyelids. They were, after all, the thinnest sheaths of the human body, and he reasoned that feeling someone's eyelids with his fingers, or better yet, his cheek, would probably be as close as he would ever get to touching his true loves. But he also knew that it wouldn't be easy, figuring out a way to touch someone's eyelids. It wouldn't be like touching a curtain in a room. And not all eyelids, he realized very quickly, were equally thin and appealing. Like everything else, some were particularly mesmerizing, and others less so.

Although the question posed by the last therapist he saw about what he wanted to touch more than anything else was a very easy one to answer, the librarian didn't answer the question. He already knew that his desire didn't map onto the kinds of desires he saw figured all around him in the city. Sometimes, when he passed a billboard on the street or a wallpapered advertisement on a subway platform or a display in a store window, what he loved might be indirectly evoked, or even represented as something incidental, something in the service of another, presumably more noteworthy figure of beauty, but the kernel— or rather the wisp—of what the librarian desired to touch still needed to be imagined most of the time. Butterflies didn't unfurl themselves as did other objects of yearning. They weren't nearly so common.

Then he began to collect pictures of his true loves. He cut some of them out of books at work. Others he found in magazines, but not many. He kept the pictures in his desk drawer at the library so that he could look at them whenever he got a chance. Along with helping patrons find books, this was mostly how the librarian passed the day.

Two years went by. The librarian turned twenty-six. A position opened up at the New York Public Library, and the librarian applied. Much to his surprise, he got the job. The librarian was very happy about this, because there were no more pictures of butterflies left for him to cut out from the books at the Queens Library on Fourteenth Street.

Starting his first day at his new job, the librarian sat at a desk next to one occupied by a woman named Mrs. Higgenbottom. The librarian thought it was ridiculous that anyone in the twenty-first century could really be named Mrs. Higgenbottom, but that was her name. She was one of two people in the world, along with his mother, that the librarian didn't want to touch. The librarian didn't want to touch his mother because she was his mother. He didn't want to touch Mrs. Higgenbottom because he hated her. Her skin was cracked and hard and pink. It bulged around her wedding ring. When she wore shoes without panty-hose in the summer, the flesh around her ankles swelled like summer sausage. Before she shook someone's hand, or exchanged a book, Mrs. Higgenbottom would douse her meaty fingers and doughy palms with antibacterial ointment. The librarian thought this was really gross. He didn't see how you could hope to feel anything with your hands drenched in soap.

For the next two years, the librarian spent his time at work sitting at his desk, nearly always with a book open in front of him. The librarian loved to touch books. That's why he had gotten a degree in library science: you could touch books all day as a librarian, and no one batted an eye or called you a pervert or a fag. He liked to touch old books especially, with their stiff spines and their soft, yellowy pages. And he really loved touching books filled with images, because these images made the texture of the pages shift and change, and the librarian loved to feel these shifts and changes beneath his fingers and cheeks.

For as long as he could remember, the librarian had always loved to touch things, but it was getting worse now. Before, he would place his hand or his cheek against something thin and soft and smooth, and that would be enough to satisfy him for a day or two. But now it was no longer sufficient for him to cup the flews of a dog or feel a curtain curl against his fingers. Each sensory experience just made him want to touch something else, and something else after that. There was no end to it all, and he didn't know what to do.

One day, while he was touching a bound facsimile of the first edition of Audubon's *Birds of America* at his desk, a girl walked up. "I would like to find an atlas?" she said. She had an accent; the librarian thought it was Eastern European. He pointed behind him, toward the back wall of the reference room. "We have atlases over there," he said. He looked over her shoulder, for her trailing parent or care provider or older sibling, but there was no one behind her.

The girl looked at him with confusion. She had very big, brown eyes. They were round and corpulent, like stuffed olives. The librarian didn't like her eyes. But when she blinked, as if in slow motion, he watched her lids close and then open, and the librarian loved her eyelids very much. They were the thinnest he had ever seen, with very fine, long eyelashes, as well. He wanted to touch them so badly that he lost his breath for a moment.

So he told her that he would help her find the atlases. Mrs. Higgenbottom raised her head, which was actually quite small, in spite of the fact that she was otherwise swollen and puckered. It was unusual for the librarian to leave his desk in order to help a patron, unusual for him even to lift his fingers from one of his books, so she was curious. She watched the two of them walk off. The librarian could feel her eyes on him, like some bird of prey with hard, jagged feathers and a sharp, crinkled beak.

He led the girl toward the back of the reference room. There were long wooden tables on either side of them, filled with students and researchers, typing on laptops. There were no other children in the room. In the far corner, there were several shelves, filled with atlases. The librarian stood before the shelves.

"What kind of atlas would you like to see?"

"One of Europe," the girl said.

"Aren't you a little young to be here by yourself?"

"I am not by myself." She spoke very deliberately. She didn't blink as much as the librarian would have liked. "My father is upstairs. He is working on a book."

"What does your father do?"

"He is a scholar. He is writing a book on Czech landscape poetry."

"He must look at a lot of large books."

The girl didn't understand this statement.

"Why do you want an atlas?" the librarian asked her.

"I want to look at my country," she said. "I miss my country."

AFTER WORK, HE WOULD GO HOME and have dinner with his mother. During their meals, the librarian's mother would try to engage her son in conversation.

"How was your day?' she would ask.

The librarian would never say. Instead he would usually criticize the meal. "The pasta is cooked too much," he would say. "The noodles are stiff. They should be airy and light, almost translucent. That's how pasta is supposed to be served."

"I make no claims as a cook," his mother would reply. "You know that."

The librarian liked placing thin pieces of food on his tongue—the thinner the better—but he didn't like swallowing. He preferred, when his mother wasn't looking, to remove whatever food he had placed in his mouth and ball it up in the paper napkin in his lap. As a result, the librarian had a slim build, with pointy shoulder blades and a neck that looked longer than it really was. He kept his black hair short and wore it without a part. In addition, he shaved each morning with a fresh blade to keep his cheeks as smooth as possible. Because he was so slender, and had such an odd hairstyle, and no stubble whatsoever, the librarian looked much younger than he really was.

"Perhaps it's time for you to get your own place," his mother would often opine while clearing his plate. "You could prepare your own meals just the way you like them."

"Get my own place in the most expensive city on the Eastern Seaboard?" The librarian would chortle. He chortled only with his mother. "I don't think so."

After dinner, he always retired to his room immediately. Without a full nine hours of sleep, the librarian found it very hard to stay awake during the day.

Once he shut his bedroom door, the librarian's mother would fret over her son. He had been so odd as a child. Then, in high school, he was even odder, always getting beaten up: coming home with an eye swollen shut, with an arm scraped up, with his lip split. After he graduated and went to Queens College, he wasn't so odd for a while, but then he got *really* odd when he started working on his degree in library science. He had never been on a single date, not one. He never went out. He didn't care about movies or sports. He didn't look at the weather report in the morning, or read the paper. She had sent him to one therapist after another, but eventually, with no signs that her son was making any progress, their insurance provider refused to authorize any more sessions. When he had been younger, the librarian's mother had wanted him to have a girlfriend. She had even daydreamed about him getting married someday and having a family. Now she had much more modest wishes. She wanted her son to have a friend or two. She wanted him to go out occasionally at night. She thought he was disturbed, in part because of how much time he spent indoors. She thought he might feel better if he wasn't penned in so much.

Every once in a while, in moments of weakness, when her son had already left for work, the librarian's mother would snoop around his room. She never found anything. The librarian led an utterly uncluttered life. On his bedside table he kept a few old issues of *National Geographic*. On the top of his dresser, a mirror leaned against the wall. In his closet, on the floor, were three pairs of shoes and a pair of slippers. He never brought any books home from the library; the librarian's mother had always thought that was very strange, that even though he had chosen to spend his professional life surrounded by books, he had never seemed to take any interest in reading.

Their bedrooms adjoined, and after the librarian had said goodnight, his mother would go into her room, change into her nightgown, and sometimes put her ear against the wall in the hope, and fear, of hearing something: some noise that would help her understand her son. But she never heard anything.

After she had assumed he had fallen asleep, the librarian's mother would do the dishes in her blue bathrobe. On Thursdays she played canasta at the Y.

HE SAW THE GIRL THE NEXT DAY. She didn't come by

the desk. She went straight back to the atlases. He noticed her after lunch. She was wearing jeans that only made it down to her mid-calf, white sneakers, and a T-shirt that didn't make it to her narrow hips. He didn't think she should dress like she did, not in New York. He didn't think it was a good idea for her to show so much of her iridescent skin.

He walked over to watch her blink. She was tracing the border of the Czech Republic with her index finger. She had nice fingers, nice hands—very light looking. The librarian himself had beautiful hands. His fingers were exceptionally long, and he kept his nails and cuticles neatly trimmed.

"While your father is working, why aren't you with your mother?" he asked her.

The girl bit at her lip. She looked back down at the map. The librarian stood there, touching the table.

"While your father is working, why aren't you with your mother?" he asked again.

"My mother left my father," the girl said. "She was unhappy. I can't be with her now. She is in the Czech Republic. When she comes back, I will be with her."

The librarian looked at her. When she began to cry, her eyelids shut completely. There were very fine, purple veins on both eyelids. The librarian wanted so badly to touch the veins on her thin eyelids that he felt as if he might topple over.

"My father left us," the librarian said. "Afterward, my mother would drop me off at the library near our apartment in Queens."

The girl sniffled loudly. A rope of snot coiled up her nose. The librarian didn't like snot, but he loved it when the skin of her nostril flattened against the bridge of her nose.

"She was mad at my father," the girl said, "because he fell in love with a student."

"My father was mad at me," the librarian said, "because I fell in love with sand."

AFTER HE LEFT FOR WORK, the librarian's mother would

shower and dress. Then she would do the crossword puzzle in *The New York Times*. The librarian's mother worked behind the register at the corner store across the street from where they lived. Sometimes a man in his twenties or thereabouts would come in and ask her for a copy of *Hustler* or *Penthouse* or one of the other pornographic magazines they kept behind the counter. They had one for a while called *Asian Fetish*. They didn't carry *Asian Fetish* anymore. When the men would ask her for these items, they always looked right at her, unashamed. And it was terrible because, staring back at them, the librarian's mother never saw their faces. For some reason, she always saw her son's.

"SOMEONE IS CUTTING PICTURES OUT from some of our best holdings in natural sciences," Mrs. Higgenbottom said the next day.

The librarian didn't bother responding.

"I found a book yesterday that had been utterly ruined. It had also been misshelved. Since it was in the closed stacks, it must have been someone who works here."

The librarian said nothing. The book had not been misshelved. Mrs. Higgenbottom was always taking books that were properly shelved and reshelving them incorrectly with her fat, antibacterial coated paws. Mrs. Higgenbottom was a beast. She was an animal with needles for hair, like a porcupine, or one with chafed, leathery skin, like a rhinoceros.

"It's revolting, what this person is doing," she said. "It's appalling." She lowered her eyes so that they glared at the top drawer of the librarian's desk. "Why do you always keep your desk drawer locked?"

"Why do *you* always keep *your* desk drawer locked?" The librarian got up and walked over to the girl, who was looking at a different atlas from the one he had pointed out to her three days before. She was no longer looking at the Czech Republic. Instead she was looking at the Western United States.

"How is your father's book going?" he asked her.

126

"Very well. He is just checking the notes." She sat with her hands folded in front of the book. "When he is done with it, we are going on a vacation."

"Where are you going?"

"To Colorado. To see the mountains."

"That sounds very nice." He peered down at the atlas that was open on the table. Then he had an idea. He placed his index finger softly on the girl's wrist. "These aren't the best books, you know: the ones on the shelves in this room. They're all so worn. You can't feel the ink, raised slightly off the pages, and the spines are cracked and rough from being opened and closed so many times. The best books are in the closed stacks. Would you like to see some of them?"

The girl just stared at him. She didn't even blink. She said nothing.

The librarian tried a different approach. "I would like to meet your father," he said.

She nodded at him, as if she were in trouble. "He is coming to get me at four."

"Please have him stop by my desk."

"Okay."

"My name is Daniel," he added, running his hand along the wooden table.

"My name is Sasha." She turned in her seat and extended her hand. Daniel held his palm and fingers out so that they were barely touching hers, like magnets resisting one another. That was how he liked to shake hands.

"How old are you, Sasha?"

"I am thirteen."

Daniel giggled. "That is so, so old," he said. He was used to measuring age in terms of days, not years. "That is very, very old."

SASHA AND HER FATHER approached Daniel's desk that day promptly at four. Sasha's father had a beard that engulfed the bottom of his face, but just beneath his cheekbones it was shaved neatly along a line. The librarian very much wanted to touch his cheek where the hair stopped and the smooth skin re-emerged.

"Thank you for looking after my daughter," Sasha's father said.

"My pleasure," Daniel said.

"It is not an easy time. My proofs are due next week. The book has already been very delayed. We are up in the air at home a little. We have just arrived in New York. We know no sitters."

"New York is filled with many untrustworthy people, even in places where you'd least expect it." Daniel glanced over at Mrs. Higgenbottom, who snickered at him while he ran his fingers across a page of the Braille edition of Charles Darwin's *The Various Contrivances By Which Orchids Are Fertilized By Insects* that sat open on his desk. Daniel loved Braille books because of the contrast between the tiny, upraised bumps that spelled words tactilely and the smoother parts of the paper that spelled nothing.

Sasha's father smiled with uncertainty, dipping his head slightly at the same time.

Daniel lifted his fingers from the book as he stood up. "Perhaps I could give your daughter a tour of the stacks tomorrow? The closed stacks, where we keep the best books."

The father looked down at his daughter. "Would you like that, Sasha?"

Sasha shrugged.

"Thank you very much." Sasha's father shook Daniel's hand vigorously. "Thank you so much." His eyes beamed. Daniel stepped around the desk and embraced the man. He wore a wool overcoat that Daniel did not love touching. When he stepped back, Daniel's hand grazed the man beneath his eye. The man recoiled slightly.

"You had something, on your cheek," Daniel whispered.

The man smiled. Sasha smiled. Mrs. Higgenbottom watched them walk away. "We don't do individual tours of the stacks," she said to Daniel after they had disappeared from view. "At least not for patrons. Not to mention children."

"Her parents are splitting up," Daniel said. "Have some sympathy, you elephant."

It was the coarsest animal he could come up with on the spot.

THE NEXT DAY, Daniel began to prepare for the tour the moment he woke up. He told himself that he should approach the rendezvous not as someone who wanted desperately to touch a girl's eyelids but rather as a thing himself, a beautiful thing—say, a flower—with which another beautiful thing—say, a butterfly— would be thrilled to come into contact. So he dressed in a brightly colored purple shirt and green slacks. He rummaged through his mother's old perfume bottles and put a touch of what he determined to be the sweetest of her scents on his neck and wrists so that he smelled like a coneflower. At work, he went into the stacks on the north side and placed some of his favorite books from the library's collection on a small table at the end of one of the aisles. He pulled another chair over to the table. Then he opened the books so that the images of flowers faced the chairs: their blossoms red and orange and deep blue and pink.

He met Sasha back at his desk in the reference room. She was wearing a yellow dress. She had a blue bow in her hair. For a moment, Daniel was transfixed more by her outfit than her eyelids. Yellow was his favorite color.

He took her down into the stacks. He showed her where they kept the oversized folios. He explained what a folio was. He pointed out where the light switches for the individual aisles were located. He encouraged her to flip some of the switches. He mentioned that they were now deep below Bryant Park. Finally, he indicated the location of some of the very sensitive smoke detectors.

Sasha seemed uninterested in the books and the smoke detectors. It wasn't clear to Daniel if she followed his definition of a folio. She seemed unimpressed by the idea of being beneath a park. And she had a hard time flipping the light switches with her tiny, thin fingers.

He led Sasha to the table. He asked her if she wanted to sit down. He drew her attention to the books piled in front of them, and the pictures of flowers they displayed. "Look at that," he said, picking up one of the books. He showed her the title: *The Flora and Fauna of Colorado.* He asked her if she wanted to see some pictures of the kinds of plants and animals that lived in the state she would be visiting soon. Sasha nodded uneasily. She seemed particularly uncomfortable at the end of the aisle, in the half-light.

Daniel began to leaf through the book. He told Sasha that if she closed her eyes every now and then, she could imagine herself inhabiting the pictures: perched on the tip of a flower, perhaps, or spinning in the sky. He said that this was a very enjoyable thing to do, daydreaming like this, if she had never done it before. She didn't seem to believe him, however. Her eyelids would shut only tentatively, but then they would flip open again, revealing her gigantic eyeballs. Daniel continued to turn the pages.

They went through one book, then another. Sasha was barely blinking at all now. She looked like an owl, perched next to him. Daniel had begun to perspire profusely. He realized that Sasha would never fall asleep, that he would never be able just to gaze down at her eyelids, or press his cheeks against her face. So he could no longer see himself as a beautiful flower with which a butterfly would be thrilled to come into contact. He couldn't see himself as beautiful at all. He had brought a girl down here with the intention of touching her eyelids, of feeling her eyelashes flicker against his face, but she didn't want to be touched. She probably didn't want to be in the stacks in the first place. And suddenly he no longer felt insulated and hidden by all the books that surrounded them: by the shadows and the low ceiling. Instead, he felt as if he were suffocating. He wondered if perhaps he might pass out.

He rose from his chair. "I have to . . ." He tugged at the collar of his shirt. "Excuse me, I must . . ." And he rushed through the stacks and over to the elevator. Back on the first floor of the library, he hurried across the reference room, toward the main staircase.

When she saw him coming, Mrs. Higgenbottom rose to her feet. "Where is the girl?" she cried out after him. "Where are you going?"

Daniel didn't answer. He sped out of the library. He rushed over to the subway station. He rode out to Astoria, to the stop closest to their apartment building. But he didn't go into their building. Instead, he went into the corner store across the street.

He walked through the center aisle, filled with bags of potato chips and beef jerky, up to the counter. His mother watched him approach.

"What are you doing here, Daniel?" she asked him. She was wearing a light blue vest with a nametag and a blue visor. "Is everything okay?"

Daniel leaned against the counter, out of breath. He wiped the sweat from his brow. He sniffled, his mouth filling with mucus. He wondered if he had caught a cold from Sasha.

"It's not enough to pursue approximations—parts for wholes. That doesn't work."

His mother looked at him with a pained expression. "I don't follow you."

"Trying to look for substitutes . . ." He glanced around the store.

She followed his eyes, as if they would point her toward an explanation of who he was. "Please, Daniel." She held her hands out toward him. "Please, tell me what it is that consumes you so. I want to know. Even if it's awful. Just tell me, please."

He laid his hand flat on the counter. "It is the slightest of things."

"If that's the case," she said, shaking her head, "then why are you so . . . why are you so withdrawn? I don't understand."

"Because it is the slightest of things."

131

Her eyebrows wrinkled. "Maybe you just need to get out more. You never go out."

"I'm out now." For a moment, he wanted to reach out and touch the bill of her visor. He wanted to put his cheek against the side of the cash register. "I am entering a new life cycle. I have to leave my cocoon. Do you understand what I'm trying to tell you?"

He could put it no other way. Otherwise he would crush his loves.

She stared at him with her mouth ajar. He was dressed so oddly, in a purple shirt and green pants, and his skin—which she rarely saw in the sunlight—was pale and chalky, like wax paper. "No, I don't understand what you're trying to tell me."

Several people had lined up behind him, waiting to purchase lottery tickets and bags of pretzels and chocolate bars. Daniel stepped aside so that his mother could ring them up. Then he stepped back in front of the counter. "I have to go away. I can't stay here anymore. There is no room left for me. I have to go." He noticed a package of thin, spearmint gum on a display stand just to his left and picked it up and placed it next to the register. His mother rang in the amount. He paid her with exact change.

She watched him open his package of gum, remove a single piece, unwrap it from the foil, and place it on his tongue. He didn't chew it right away. Instead he stood still, his mouth open slightly but his eyes shut as he rocked on his feet. Then he turned and began to make his way down the aisle.

"Where are you going?" she called after him meekly.

But he said nothing. He just stepped through the doorway. She watched him disappear into the city. She doubted that she would ever see him again. The truth was, she had been waiting for this day. Ever since he had flung himself off the gazebo when he was just a little boy, she had always known this day would come.

AFTER THREE DAYS HAD PASSED and Daniel had not returned to work, Mrs. Higgenbottom called the maintenance staff and asked them to send someone over. When one of the custodial workers finally swung by, she instructed him to force open Daniel's top desk drawer. He said he didn't understand. "That!" She pointed at the drawer. "That needs to be opened." He fiddled with the lock for several minutes, first with a paperclip, then finally with his pocketknife. When the lock finally sprung, the drawer flew back. Daniel's pictures began to pour out onto the floor. Some of them were also kicked up into the air, so that for a moment this small portion of the reference area was filled with images of butterflies, freed from their narrow confines, left to scatter into the wider world.

The Detroit Frankfurt School Discussion Group

AFTER HIS DIVORCE WAS FINALIZED, Colin made a list of all the activities he wanted to try during those days of the week, Thursdays through Saturdays, when he didn't have his kids. The idea was to keep himself busy. That way, he wouldn't mope around his house too much. But he also wanted to try to find a girlfriend, and he wasn't entirely sure how to go about doing this. Colin's list had six items on it.

1. *Join a yoga class.*

Meg said it would be a great way to meet women. And they'd all be fit, too. Meg was Colin's sister.

2. *Take golf lessons.*

3. *Enroll in a Thai cooking class.*

4. *Learn Russian.*

5. *Give Internet dating a whirl.*

6. *Volunteer for the Ann Arbor Meals on Wheels.*

One by one, Colin ruled out participation in all of these activities. Or they were ruled out for him. Yoga was dismissed by his friend, Ted. "Middle-aged guys who try yoga," he spoke with mysterious authority on the subject, "regret it. For starters, you won't be able to do any of the poses because, like every guy our age, you never stretch." *Our age* meant thirty-five, and Ted was right; while he dragged himself to the Y two to three times a week to spin his legs on an elliptical machine, Colin never stretched. "Secondly," Ted continued, "it's a well-known fact that yoga makes you fart. I would recommend, as a new single guy, avoiding any activities that make you fart in public." This argument was irrefutable. Yoga was out.

Golf was abandoned fairly quickly, mostly because Colin was pretty terrible at it, and having to face what a failure he was at golf made him reflect on other things he had failed at—most recently, his marriage—and that depressed him. Plus, it was expensive—not just the lessons, but the greens fees; the balls; getting a new putter, since the one in his bag seemed to have rusted somehow; getting a new bag—and it took forever to play a round. Flailing around in the rough one day, Colin asked himself how exactly he expected to meet a member of the opposite sex with a golf club in his hand. The only scenario he could envision was one in which he hit some poor woman in the head with one of his errant shots. He had a better chance, in other words, of entering litigation by playing golf than a relationship. Thus ended his dabbling in the sport.

There were no Thai cooking classes offered anywhere in or around Ann Arbor, so it wasn't Colin's fault that this activity quickly fell off his list. Washtenaw Community College did have courses devoted to German cooking, and one designed for single men, in the description of which Colin read the following line. *We will begin by learning how to boil water.* For some reason, that sentence depressed the hell out of him, not because Colin didn't know how to boil water—he did—but because he could now, as a divorced man, be reasonably placed within a demographic of men who actually did not know how to boil water. It was almost as if he were moving down, rather than up, the evolutionary ladder, and occasionally Colin would picture himself enrolled and standing around a stovetop in a classroom outfitted for cooking lessons at the community college. "All right," the instructor would say, "can everyone see the bubbles forming there, on the surface of the water? Right there. See that? Take note: that water is boiling!" And Colin would be left thinking, *My God, what has become of my life?*

Learning Russian was also something Meg had suggested because, ever since he had been a teenager, Colin had talked about studying the language. Nonetheless, this was a particularly insane idea; Colin was busy enough to begin with, working and parenting. Besides, if he was going to learn any foreign language, it really should have been German, since Colin was ostensibly an expert on the Frankfurt School of Criticism and Social Theory, and all the original members of this group had written in German. Colin was an adjunct lecturer in the English Department at the University of Michigan, and he regularly taught a course on the history of critical theory that began with the Frankfurt School. Learning German might have proven to be academically useful, but it also would have felt like an extension of his work life. Besides, Colin reasoned with himself, he had always loved writers like Tolstoy and Chekhov. Maybe trying to learn Russian was crazy, but weren't you supposed to do some crazy stuff after a divorce? Wasn't that a part of the rebuilding process? So he took Meg's advice and signed up for the Introduction to Russian Language course offered in the Slavic Department, just across central campus from where he normally taught.

The first day of class, as he took a seat in the front row and opened his brand-new notebook, on which he had magisterially written **Russian** on the front cover, Colin admitted to himself that his extreme excitement over his impending linguistic adventure really had very little to do with Chekhov or Tolstoy. Rather than great male Russian writers, Colin was really thinking more about great female Russian tennis players. It was undeniably true that, when he daydreamed about meeting a beautiful woman in Ann Arbor, say, standing in line at the Starbucks on State Street, or walking through Nickels Arcade, he tended to imagine encountering a Russian beauty—if not Anna Kournikova exactly, perhaps it was fair to say Anna Kournikova inexactly. It was this fantasy, more than anything intellectual, that had landed Colin in this Russian language course, and now, as he sat there in the front row, he felt an undeniable thrill at the fact that he had acted on such a whim.

The problem, however, Colin discovered in class that same day, was that Russian was a really hard language to learn. First of all, the letters were all fucked up. He had known about the whole Cyrillic thing, but knowing that and then trying to make sense—however preliminarily—of the squiggles and jabs that constituted the language itself was really too much to bear. And Colin found his instructor, a woman who wasn't beautiful at all but rather overweight and severe, to be too blunt and direct for his tastes. "You will fail at this," she said to him the first time she called on him and asked him to choose a Russian name. "Boris, you will fail. You are too old to learn Russian. And you are lazy; I can tell. This is a terrible idea for you."

Of course, she was right on all fronts. Colin dropped the class the next day.

INTERNET DATING WAS MORE DISASTROUS than anything else Colin undertook. To begin, he found the information that he was asked to provide in order to fill out his profile page to be daunting and, in many fundamental ways, unknown and unknowable. Did he believe in God, for example? Well, *kind of*, but on the one hand, he didn't want to date someone who *really* believed in God, and on the other hand, he wasn't very excited by the idea of going out with someone who was an outspoken atheist. Nothing that accurately reflected his wishy-washiness on the subject of religion, God, morality, and so on was provided as an option on the list of responses. Moving on, he came to a series of questions that asked him to identify his interests and hobbies. Well, he didn't really have any. There were things he thought he *might* be interested in, but his life as a divorcé seemed to be eliminating these possibilities quite systematically. Plus, Colin wasn't sure he liked people with hobbies. They seemed, in all honesty, quite unbearable. So he left the category blank.

The second-to-last step prior to making his online profile complete involved uploading a photo of himself. But Colin didn't have any decent photos of himself, at least nothing that was up-to-date. Why did he have no photos of himself? Because he wasn't in a relationship. What single person with two young kids had photos taken that would have been suitable to upload on an Internet dating site? Wasn't the search for a partner—on the goddamn Internet, no less—an open admission that one *had no life*, and therefore no photos detailing the absence of said life? And while he wouldn't so much as consider reading a profile of someone else that didn't have a picture attached, Colin felt outraged that *he* was expected to provide a photo of himself. Surely his circumstances precluded such an obligation, and surely, somehow, some absolutely gorgeous, perhaps new émigré from Saint Petersburg, would stumble upon his self-description, with its lack of a photograph and its blank spaces next to all of the personal categories, and nonetheless, somehow, find him irresistible. At least, this is what Colin told himself when he finally paid the membership fee and his profile, or lack thereof, became visible.

Horrifically, however, even though he appeared more or less as a ghost on the dating website, Colin was immediately approached by women, only not the kind of women he had ever imagined meeting. A grandmother in Toledo, for example, repeatedly offered to bake him a cake. A woman with the username *Rightplacethistime* offered preemptively to explain that her felony record was due to a remarkable string of bad luck, although she didn't use the word *remarkable*. A nineteen-year-old said she'd meet him at the casino in Battle Creek for "dinner" (her quotation marks), but she'd need two hundred dollars up-front.

Finally, one afternoon, all in an effort to improve his online dating profile, Colin set a trap for his eight-year-old son, Mark. As he often did, Mark reported being bored right around four thirty in the afternoon. Usually when he complained like this, Mark could expect his father to tell him, somewhat sternly, although without looking away from his laptop, that under no circumstances should he ever be bored, that the world was filled with things to do, that boredom was an admission that one wasn't sufficiently engaged with the world, that everything wrong with the world could be traced back to the ease with which the young reported being bored, because people who remained bored long enough ended up becoming susceptible to the lurid temptations posed by groups like ISIS, not to mention really bad pop music, and so on.

Instead of launching into one of these tirades, however, Colin nearly pirouetted into the hallway. *You're bored? Hey, I know what we could do that would be fun! You could take photos of me! Close-ups! Doesn't that sound like fun!* And with that, Colin ditched his laptop and handed over his iPhone to Mark, which only further aroused his son's suspicions. Since dropping his father's last iPhone in the toilet a month before, Mark had not been permitted to handle this new, sleeker model. Now he was being asked to take pictures while his father leaned like an idiot against the bookcase in the living room of their house, his head cocked to the side, eyes slightly crossed, with a forced smile on full display. It made no sense. Nonetheless, Mark snapped away.

After the kids had gone to bed that same night, Colin uploaded one of the photos Mark had taken of him onto his online dating profile. Then he formulated some answers to those haunting, banal questions he had previously sidestepped. Yes, he decided, for the sake of this enterprise, yes, he did believe in God. And while he had never windsurfed or rock climbed, he put them down as hobbies because he thought they made him sound daring and fun. Next, he knocked two years off his age and claimed one tattoo on his body where there were none. He also took a cue from the profiles he had read and insisted in his self-description that he was a really "laid-back guy" who loved "just hanging out with friends and taking it easy," when, in fact, nearly all of his friends lived far away and nearly all of his "hanging out" time took place with his kids, both of whom he did mention in his self-description, but neither of whom—if asked—would have characterized their father as easygoing, what with his coffee-induced finger-tapping and his endless puttering around their house, picking up dirty clothes and sweeping dust out from behind their furniture, all while he whispered to himself: little phrases and asides and even sometimes exclamations that his children sometimes asked him to repeat. "Speak up, Dad! We can't hear you." And Colin, sheepishly, would shake his head. "I was just talking to myself," he'd say. "Sorry."

About a week later, Colin exchanged a series of messages with a divorced woman from Plymouth who—like him—enjoyed "hanging out" and "taking it easy." In all of her profile pictures, she came across as really attractive, with very long black hair; smooth, unblemished skin; and a pretty, demure smile. They ended up talking on the phone. She told him her name was Candy, and Colin asked her if she wanted to have dinner that Friday. She said she did, so when Friday rolled around, Colin headed out to Plymouth to pick her up.

The GPS directions to Candy's place were complicated. Technically, she lived outside Plymouth, in what turned out to be a ranch-style home on a dirt road. When Colin pulled up to the home, he was struck by how unkempt the yard was: the tall grass nearly covering the large foreclosure sign that sat just a few yards from the mailbox.

"They're kicking me out, the fuckers," she said, once she let him in. Actually, Candy had a much fuller figure than Colin had anticipated, and he realized now in hindsight that all of the pictures she had posted of herself on the dating site were headshots. Just *how* full a figure she had was hard to tell; Candy was wearing a white sundress that fell in rippled folds from her waist, making her lower body resemble a Greek column. Still, her face was just as appealing as it had appeared online, and she had glitter eye shadow on, which Colin found thrilling: not the eye shadow itself so much as the fact that he was going on a date with a woman who was wearing such makeup. Colin was pretty sure glitter eye shadow had been invented during the decade in which he was married.

Candy led him into the kitchen. There was a staggering number of appliances on the counter: a blender, microwave, food processor, toaster oven, waffle iron, sandwich press, and some machines Colin couldn't even identify. All lined up as if in a showroom. And yet, it looked as if no one had ever actually used any of them, or even done any cooking in the kitchen. There were no crumbs on the counter, no stains on the floor from spilt milk and juice, as in his house, and no smell of grease or burnt toast. Moreover, Colin knew that—like him—Candy had an eight-year-old son. They had shared observations on the subject of parenting in their messages. Surely she had to prepare meals for him, and yet there was no evidence that she did.

"Do you want a drink?" she asked him.

Colin shrugged. "Okay."

Candy opened a cabinet beneath the kitchen counter, in which a single bottle of vodka sat. "Sorry, I don't have anything to mix it with."

"That's okay."

She withdrew two water glasses from one of the cabinets above the counter and filled each of them with vodka.

"That's a lot of vodka for me," Colin said. "I mean, I'm driving us—"

"I thought we were going to party?"

"Well—"

"Do you want some ice? To water it down?"

"Sure."

"I don't like ice." She set his glass beneath the ice maker and pushed it against the plastic lever. As the ice cubes fell, vodka splashed onto the floor. "See how the ice wastes the vodka?" she observed.

Colin thought of a few responses he might make on this front, but instead he just nodded. They clinked glasses and Candy led him into the living room—a vast space, with white carpet and white walls. A white leather sofa faced an enormous flat-screen TV. Off to the side was a treadmill, around which plastic toys were sprinkled: a yellow dump truck, a pile of Legos, and several Star Wars action figures. Except for a glass coffee table, there was nothing else in the room: no books, no photos, no magazines, no clutter whatsoever.

Candy took a long sip of her vodka and then set the glass down on the table. "My ex-husband," she began, "he told me I could buy whatever I wanted for the house once we closed on it. He gave me a credit card. I don't even know what the limit on it was. I just bought and bought. The next thing I know, he's lost his job and we have all these collection agencies calling. Then he decides he wants to start fucking this whore he went to high school with, so I tell him to get the hell out. So he moves out—this is last summer—and for a while he comes back on the weekends to mow the lawn and take Taylor to his baseball games. But then, one weekend, he doesn't come by. Then another weekend, he doesn't show. And then another. We've already signed the divorce papers by this point. I supposedly got a great deal—credit card debt wiped out, the house and car in my name, alimony, child support, and on and on. But the first alimony check he sends me bounces, and he never ends up paying any child support! He just disappears, the fucker. I can't make the mortgage payment or the car payment. I don't know how to operate a riding mower, so I can't cut the grass, and I'm not going to pay someone to cut the grass. I started living off my credit card back in February and by May—what's that, like two months ago now? Anyway, I maxed out my card before Memorial Day. I tried to get another one, but no place would approve my application, because once you're down, you know, they just want to fucking bury you. So I had to declare bankruptcy. Now, we're just waiting for the bank to take the house. Then we're going to move in with my mom. She's over in Romulus. My mom is, like, the last white person to live in Romulus." She took a gulp of her drink. "They're all Jews, you know," she offered matter-of-factly. "The fuckers at the bank. Every one of them is a Jew. Even the ones without the obvious last names, once you talk to them, you just know they're Jews."

Colin hadn't been entirely shocked by the dismal story of financial ruin, but the Weimar-era anti-Semitism did catch him a little off-guard, along with the casual racism, and he didn't know quite what to say. Instead, he sipped from his enormous glass of vodka, all while Candy's cell phone buzzed again and again from the counter in the kitchen.

"You can take that call, if you want," he said finally.

"Oh, you don't want me to take that call. That's Tony; he would be very unhappy to know I'm hanging out with you. *Very* unhappy."

Colin looked at her with some confusion. "Tony is your ex-husband?"

"No, my boyfriend." She caught herself and waved her hands at him. "Ex-boyfriend."

Colin exhaled slowly as he took in this new information. Maybe he should steer clear of asking any more questions about Tony. Since religion, race, economics, and—one could safely assume—politics were also topics best left unexplored, he wondered what the hell they were going to talk about over dinner.

"So Tony's a drug dealer," Candy said. She drank some more. "He works out of Toledo. He was supposed to be my fling after my divorce. You know, you're supposed to have a fling when your marriage ends, right?"

"That's right." Colin had never admitted this to himself in so many words, but he had implied as much when had written *Give Internet dating a whirl* on his activities list earlier that year.

"But, you know," Candy continued, "he just won't go away. He's a cool guy—fun to party with. But he has a temper. Like, a psycho temper, you know? You aren't like that, are you? I can tell you aren't."

"No," Colin confessed. "I mean, I lose my cool, but probably not like Tony."

"Oh, you have no fucking idea." She chuckled. "I've seen him, like, throw a guy out of a car. That's not cool, you know? Not when you're going fifty through downtown Toledo and there's blow all over the dashboard. That's not a good time to push your best friend out of your car. Am I right?"

With a telling nod, Colin agreed that such behavior was really inappropriate, what with the blow, the friendship, and the speeding.

"But our boys really dig each other . . ." Candy seemed, for a moment, lost in thought. Her cell phone buzzed some more. Suddenly she redirected her gaze at him. "Can I be, like, totally straight with you, Chris?"

"Actually, it's Colin—"

"I don't really want to have dinner. I mean, we could, if you *really* want, but then we got to drive into Ann Arbor and all that crap. I kind of want to get high. Like, the only person I've been high with lately is Tony and he's a fucking psychopath. I would so love to get high without Tony, you know?"

Candy's voice sounded flat and uninflected, as if she were describing how to use a TV remote control, but now she took her foot, shorn of its sandal, and rubbed her toe against Colin's shin.

"You mean, smoke pot?" he asked.

"What are you, in high school? Come on! I mean, let's get *high*. Taylor's at my mom's. I got nowhere to be tomorrow. The only thing is, I don't have the cash to buy any shit because of the fucking Jew bankers and this fucking foreclosure crap. So I was thinking, instead of dinner, we could go to Novi. I know someone there we could buy from. We can't buy any shit in Ann Arbor or Ypsi because Tony knows *everyone* in Ann Arbor and Ypsi. But he doesn't know this dude I partied with last weekend in Novi, I'm pretty sure. So I was thinking, we could buy some shit there and afterward, we can come back here and once we're high, you can fuck me if you want. You know, that's the least I can do, if you're buying the shit. I promise you can fuck me, if we get high first."

Colin elected at that moment to take a pass on the getting of the shit and the subsequent fucking and explained instead that he was sorry but he had been doing a lot of thinking over the last few minutes and he had decided that he really wasn't ready—on the heels of his divorce—to be dating after all. Candy let him know very clearly, as he headed for the front door, that he was coming across as incredibly lame—not nearly as laid-back and chill as he had sounded over the phone. A couple of minutes later, Colin was driving home in his car, rattling along on the dirt road that led from Candy's foreclosed home over to M-14, thinking to himself as he drove, *I have reached some kind of end, here in Plymouth. I have fallen to some kind of limit.*

This happened in July, after which Colin took a break from Internet dating, and a break from tackling the post-divorce activities on his list. At least, he never bothered to volunteer for the Ann Arbor Meals on Wheels.

SUMMER TURNED TO FALL, and Colin found himself once more teaching his History of Critical Theory class, along with two sections of English composition, all to undergraduates who mostly hid their enthusiasm for these subjects, if they had any, with staggering completeness. Fall then turned to winter, and then the spring came, and Colin approached and finally passed the one-year anniversary of his divorce. His kids seemed finally to have adjusted to living in two separate homes, but he felt lonelier than ever, and out of ideas as to how to improve his personal life.

Lacking better options, Colin decided—reasonably, or so it seemed—to become an alcoholic. Not a raging alcoholic, or someone who drank *every* night, or drank vodka out of a water glass. Rather, Colin would just get drunk on two or three drinks—he had always been a lightweight—those nights when he didn't have his kids. This seemed very manageable. He even thought he could be a fairly harmless alcoholic. For example, since he always walked to work, Colin didn't have to worry about getting a DUI, or running over some college kid who had a lot of promise and was up late, practicing the viola or studying for her MCATs and very decidedly *not* deserving to get run over by some alcoholic in training. As Colin hatched this new plan, its simplicity grew on

him. Three nights a week, he would teach, get drunk, then stag-
ger home and fall asleep. And maybe, while stumbling home one
night, *he* would be the one to step off a curb and get walloped
by a car—not an SUV, or something that might end his days, but
a Honda Civic or one of those new Kias—perhaps one driven
by an attractive woman of Russian descent who would hop out
of her car, rush over to him, and—maybe simply out of pity for
running him over, which Colin would be fine with—offer to take
him out for dinner. Maybe something positive, in other words,
might emerge from not trying so hard to meet someone, or learn
some new skill other than how to get drunk by himself. The
whole concept was counterintuitive, but that appealed to Colin.
Everyone in his life, from his parents to his ex-wife, had always
commented on how tightly wound up he was; well, they wouldn't
say this if he were smashed half the time.

Since he passed right by the Old Town Tavern on Liberty
Street each night on his way home from campus, Colin decided that he'd work on becoming an alcoholic there. Old Town
was popular among older, townie types who drank at the bar,
and graduate students who usually occupied the booths that
ran along the far wall. As an adjunct—which meant, more than
anything, *not* being a tenure-track professor—Colin usually took
one of the small tables off to the side: not close enough to the
townies to become mired in one of their conversations about
where they liked to park downtown, or buy cheap patio furniture, but not so close to the graduate students as to give them the
creeps. The graduate students at Michigan tended to avoid the
adjuncts because they didn't want to end up in their precarious
professional situation. So Colin would give them their space, as
if acknowledging that he possessed some kind of communica-
ble disease, like chlamydia or herpes or any of the things surely
waiting for him out there in the terrifying world he had glimpsed
through the portal of Internet dating.

Although he was better at drinking than playing golf, Colin
discovered that he really wasn't that good at getting drunk. Beer
made him feel bloated, and when he consumed hard liquor, he
seemed to skip the drunken stage and go right to the I'm-falling-

asleep-in-public stage. Hemmed in on one side by older men and women sitting at the bar on stools, people who quite likely *were* alcoholics, Colin was distressed to see just how much they drank, and just how high their bar tabs were. So he gave up on his dream of someday having cirrhosis. But Colin continued to stop at Old Town once or twice a month to have a single drink and put off, by at least half an hour or so, the crushing silence that constituted his home life when the kids were at their mom's.

THAT'S WHERE HE WAS on an otherwise thoroughly mundane Thursday night in early April, when—after having only drunk about half of his Two-Hearted Ale—Colin decided to call it a night and asked for the check. It was barely 6 p.m. He left his money on the table, slipped on his blue backpack filled with ungraded student papers, and stepped outside, onto Liberty Street. It was a beautiful spring night—the sky uncharacteristically clear, the temperature cool but not cold. He took a right to head home when, at the corner of Liberty and First, a light-brown Buick Skylark screeched to a halt in front of him. The undercarriage of the car, along with the hubcaps and the frame of the doors, were all rusted out, and the muffler was suspended just a few inches off the street by a web of thin wires.

A very young woman sat behind the steering wheel, her elbow poking out of the open window. She looked up at him. She couldn't have been much more than twenty years old.

"Hey," she said.

"Excuse me?"

"Hey."

Colin squinted at her in confusion. "Hello," he replied.

"You want to party?" she asked him.

"Excuse me?"

With her mouth open, the girl took her pierced tongue and laid it on her lip before lifting it up and rubbing it against the top row of her teeth. She had fair skin and very bright dyed-red hair. A string of tattooed stars ran down her neck, beginning just below her earlobe and disappearing beneath the collar of her white

147

tank top. A metallic object of some sort also protruded from her right eyebrow, about the size of a toothpick.

"A party. You want to go to a party?"

"Do I want to go to a party?" For a moment, Colin was reminded of the Russian class he had taken for one hour, the way in which they had duly repeated phrases that none of them could understand. Then he thought of Candy in her foreclosed home out in Plymouth and her idea of a party. Is that what this girl meant?

"We want to party with you, Colin." This voice came from in back. Colin crammed his head down and saw a young, attractive African-American girl in the backseat, with high cheekbones and her hair set in a bun atop her head. She, too, might have been around twenty, although Colin really had no idea. College age, he would have said to be safe, although neither one of these girls seemed to be in college. The girl in the back of the car was also in a tank top, her cleavage pouring out before him.

"How do you two know my name?"

The back door wheezed open. "Because we want to party with you. You're Colin! Come on. Get in."

Colin thought of identity theft. They had managed to steal all of his personal information and now they were coming to get him so that they could bludgeon him to death and then bury his body in a hole somewhere in southeastern Michigan. But if they had already stolen his identity, why would they need to kill him?

"We have a friend who works on critical theory just like you," the girl behind the wheel added. "He knows you, but you don't know him. You two will get along great. He's all about the Frankfurt School. Come on! You can meet him, and party with us. It'll be awesome."

Colin peered at her over the top of his rectangular glasses. She wasn't making sense. No one in Ann Arbor wanted to party with Colin. No one in the Upper Midwest wanted to party with Colin. Colin did not himself want to party with Colin. But it was a little thrilling, talking to these young women. They were so sexy and alluring, with their piercings and their skimpy clothing.

And they had just plopped down into his world, as if someone had spliced some show from MTV into an infomercial about closet storage containers. And this all pointed to another problem, another factor influencing the present situation. Colin was horny. He had been horny for more than a year now. He had not had sex in . . . a very long time. Not that these girls were offering him sex, exactly, unless *party* could be taken as a euphemism for sex. Not that it would have been appropriate for him on any level to engage in sexual activities with either one, or both, of these girls. He knew that. But he was horny; he couldn't help but want to talk to them.

And then he caught himself and shook his head. He was being an idiot. "I'm sorry," he said, "but I have to get home."

"Why?" the girl behind the steering wheel asked him. "What's waiting for you at home?"

He shrugged. Whole-grain pasta and frozen broccoli, to be consumed while watching *SportsCenter* and throwing out junk mail. Since discovering six months before that his cholesterol was terrifyingly high, Colin had gone on Lipitor and begun eating only food that he did not enjoy eating. That was what was waiting for him at home. But he said nothing.

"We so want to party with you," the girl in the back said once more. She had slid over to the open door, and Colin could see her fingers, softly stroking her neck.

Colin stood there on the corner. He looked around, waiting for a familiar face to pull him back into the Ann Arbor he was accustomed to traversing as he marched from home to work and then back from work to home. But there was, curiously, no one around at that moment. Just him standing there, and these two girls in the car. He could see, below him, the purple bra of the one in front, barely covered as it was by the white tank top. They knew his name. That was really weird. But they had explained that; they knew someone who worked on critical theory. Who in the world could that be? Maybe someone who had read his one publication? "*Absalom, Absalom!* In the Age of Mechanical Reproduction" (*Theoretical Inquiry Quarterly*, volume 71, number

2, 2012). Regardless of how sketchy this whole scene seemed, if these two young women had friends who were academics, what did he really have to worry about? Besides, how inappropriate of him to dismiss them with such suspicion, just because their car was a piece of shit and they were young and their breasts were spilling out of their clothes. He was being judgmental.

"Come on, Colin." The one in back said his name sleepily, as if the two of them were lounging together—in a hammock or on a beach or next to a pool.

This is crazy, this is crazy, he whispered to himself. Crazy that this was happening. Crazy that he was no longer thinking about his walk home. Crazy that he had never bothered to put something like this on his post-divorce list of activities. *My God,* he muttered to himself. It was here to stay, this tic he had developed since his divorce. Muttering to himself. *My God, I am a really lonely person, aren't I? I am seriously lonely.*

And then he just stopped thinking and stopped muttering. Without any more hesitation, Colin stepped into the car.

AS SOON AS HE SHUT THE DOOR, the Buick peeled away from the curb. They raced down First.

"Where's the party?" Colin asked the girl next to him in the backseat. She had already scooted far from him so that she was leaning against the passenger door on her side of the Buick. Now she bent down, picked up a gray sweatshirt from the floor, and put it on.

In the silence, as they appeared to near warp speed, Colin fumbled with his seat belt. "I can't . . ." The belt had somehow been shorn of the metal piece that fit into the seat attachment next to his thigh. "There's something missing—"

"Would you please shut the fuck up," the girl in the front said. She eyed him in the interior rearview mirror, as if he were some annoying child, just as they took a sharp left onto William Street.

Colin let the belt go as he flopped toward the middle of the seat. Well, this little scenario wasn't unfolding quite as he had been led to believe. Or at least the collective desire of the girls in the car to "party" with him seemed to have cooled rather quickly. Colin noticed now the not-so-gentle bouncing of the car's carriage on its axles. The shock absorbers were clearly shot.

They took a quick right onto South Main, at which point the girl driving whipped out her flip phone and called a number. "Yeah," she said, "we got him. No, we're almost there." She tossed the phone onto the seat next to her just as they took a left onto Hoover and then a quick right into the alley that led behind the Hoover Street Auto Repair.

When they pulled into the tiny parking lot, the girl shifted the car into park but didn't kill the engine. A moment later, a tall, lanky black man walked out from behind the auto shop. He was wearing baggy jeans and a black T-shirt, and in his hand—which was nestled up against his chest—he held a green hardcover book. He looked considerably older than the two girls in the car, even older than Colin himself, although how much older was hard to gauge. *This* was the friend who, like him, worked on critical theory? Or were they running some kind of scam? As the man neared the Buick, Colin began to think that he looked a little familiar. Perhaps he had been following him around town for some time, planning this abduction.

Without mulling any more over the strange predicament he had now found himself in, Colin grabbed his backpack and flung open his passenger door with the intention of running straight out of the parking lot, back onto Main Street, up to Pauline, and then home to his safe, small, two-bedroom rental house on Hutchins Street. But before he could slip out of the car, the girl in the back grabbed his arm. He managed to squirm away from her, but she had slowed down his escape. By the time he rose to his feet, the black man was standing right in front of him, about ten feet from the car.

"Well," the man said, looking at the girl behind the steering wheel, "I told you he'd be wearing Dockers or some such thing. I didn't think he'd *actually* be wearing Dockers. That is a white

man's pair of pants, Colin Spanler, PhD." And now he was looking right at Colin, who was nearly panting with fear. "Come on
now," he said. "Take it easy."

"I've got kids," Colin stammered. "I'm a divorced dad. I've
got kids. Please let me go. There's been a misunderstanding."

"No misunderstanding here. I got kids too! Calm the fuck
down, Colin. Tina, tell him to calm the fuck down."

Tina was apparently the name of the girl driving. "Calm
the fuck down, Colin," she said, with hardly any inflection at
all. Looking back over his shoulder, Colin noticed that she had
slipped on a plaid shirt. So the skimpy clothing, that had just
been for show.

"That sounded a little bitchy, didn't it?"

"Fuck you, Ty. I'm tired; I've been working all day. This was
your stupid-ass idea anyway; you calm him down."

"I have majority custody," Colin was stammering. "My kids
need me—"

"Kids need their parents, Colin," Ty interrupted him.

"*Parent,*" the girl sitting in the back added. "He said he's divorced."

"But his kids see their mom, Missy. He said *majority custody.*
He didn't say *sole custody.* You want to start a revolution, you got
to *listen* first. So my point, which *was* meant to calm him down,
Tina, is that we are aware as a group of the need that Colin's
kids have for *both* parents, just as we are aware of the needs that
all children have, wherever they fucking live, for a solid support
system. For schools with toilet paper, and maybe a few books in
the library—books that aren't so damaged you can't read them
any more. And streets you can cross without getting shot at. So
we are all on the same page. No one has any reason to be concerned. Let's just all get in the car and we can be on our way."

Colin had stepped back, and now he was leaning against the
side of the Buick, just next to the opened passenger door. Let's
just all get in the car! What the hell was he talking about? There
was no way Colin was getting back in that car.

Ty loomed there, just a few feet from him. He was quite

tall—at least six four. Colin was closer to five ten. He felt the man looking him over, studying him. "Hey!" He was trying to get Colin to look him in the eye, but Colin hesitated. "Look at me, C." And Colin did, slowly. "This is not some fucked-up shit. I assure you of that. There is nothing for you to be afraid of here. We were just hoping to maybe pick up some insights from you about critical theory, and we thought—no, Tina's right, *I* thought—that giving you a lift to the meeting was the best way of picking your brain. Please, don't be scared. It's all good." And he gestured toward the backseat.

Now that they had made eye contact, Colin felt for some reason that he shouldn't look away, that to do so would be to admit some kind of weakness, even though he felt incredibly weak: cornered against the car, with those two girls in it. So he continued to stare at this guy, who was making no sense at all, but who was also not sounding entirely crazy, either.

"What the hell are you talking about?" Colin asked him. "Are you guys trying to take me to a lecture? Is that what they meant earlier when they said *party*? A lecture? Because no one is speaking about critical theory tonight at Michigan. I would have heard—"

"There are places other than the University of Michigan where people care about critical theory and the Frankfurt School, Colin."

"I'm not saying there aren't—"

"Let me start over. All this obfuscating, it's my fault. You hear that, Tina?" Ty twisted at his waist and looked over at the front of the car. Colin didn't turn to see Tina's reaction. "I'm giving you props here, girl, because you're right; this was a fucked-up way to approach this whole matter." He put his hands on his hips and looked back at him. "Colin, My name is Ty Bartell and I've started something we are calling the Detroit Frankfurt School Discussion Group. Our third meeting is tonight, at the abandoned Roosevelt Warehouse, over on Fourteenth and Marantette in Detroit. You know the place? No? All right, well, anyway, we'd like you to come along. That is, we are inviting you to speak at our meeting. And I'm sorry, but there's no honorarium."

Colin mumbled and stuttered for a moment, nothing that anyone could understand. This guy was running a Frankfurt School discussion group? That's why these girls had lured him into their car? To talk about the Frankfurt School? Twice a week, on Tuesdays and Thursdays at ten in the morning, Colin tried to get Michigan undergraduates who had willingly signed up for his course on critical theory to discuss the Frankfurt School, and the results were decidedly mixed. Sometimes a conversation broke out. Much of the time, his questions were greeted with silence. And now he was supposed to believe that there were people, non-students, non-academics, who were driving around southeastern Michigan, combing the streets, looking for Frankfurt School specialists to pick up and take to meetings?

He shook his head. "I really need to go home, man." Colin was appalled by his own, blatant attempt to mimic the way Ty spoke, ending a sentence with *man* for the first time in his life. As if such a transparent move would suddenly spring him free.

"Come on, Colin." Ty straightened his arms at his side, as if he were a little cold. He had long, very thin arms: wiry, with nicks and scars up and down them. These were not the kind of arms Colin saw routinely on his walks through Ann Arbor. "Be real, C. Get out of your ivory tower for a night. Come help out some people who are trying to understand some readings that are pretty fucking hard to understand—especially for folks who didn't finish high school, much less college. These are people who want to make sense of their city, and the future of that city. Come with us to the D. This is the chance to do some *real* teaching. Doesn't that interest you? Man, don't worry; you'll come back in one piece. You got nothing to be afraid of."

Colin hadn't grown up in Michigan. He was from Connecticut. He had come to the university with his ex-wife when both of them had been accepted by doctoral programs: Colin in English, Nicole in psychology. Almost immediately after beginning his graduate studies, Colin became interested in the Frankfurt

School, that group of German intellectuals who, leading up to and following World War II, had reimagined Marxist theory in order to critique the failures of modern capitalism, and who had also proposed some strategies by which workers and intellectuals might escape the oppression posed by all-encompassing commodity production. What these thinkers developed, to varying degrees of coordination with one another, became known as Frankfurt School Critical Theory: an account of the problems posed by unfettered, state-organized capitalism. Beginning in the graduate seminars in which he enrolled, Colin wrote about Walter Benjamin, who had explored the relation between aesthetics and literature and technology, and Theodor Adorno, who had dissected the culture industry of twentieth-century Europe. For his preliminary exam and prospectus, Colin tried out Frankfurt-School-inspired readings of *Moby-Dick* and *Middlemarch*; he proposed the existence of proto-critical-theory ideas in the novels of Thomas Hardy and Charles Dickens. In the dissertation that followed, Colin tried to make unlikely connections between Frankfurt School members and their contemporaries, as in his article on Benjamin and William Faulkner. Once he had finished his dissertation, in part aided by the fact that Nicole had been offered a tenure-track position by the Psychology Department, Colin was hired as a lecturer at Michigan.

Now, three years into his lectureship, Colin continued to write about, and teach, critical theory as it had evolved after the flourishing of the Frankfurt School, but he had never once thought of anything Benjamin or Adorno had written as being related to Detroit, or any city he might visit in twenty-first-century America. How could he really refuse an invitation to hear people discuss Frankfurt School ideas with the conditions of a specific urban environment in mind—one just forty-odd miles from his house? Even if it would be clearly insane to get back into this car. Even if he did have majority custody of two small children. Even if it was entirely possible that these people weren't intending to take him to a Frankfurt School discussion group at all. He still wasn't sure how he could pass up the chance to hear critical theory discussed by non-academics in Detroit.

"Have you ever even been to the D?" Tina asked, interrupting his train of thought.

"Just to see the Tigers a couple of times," Colin mumbled.

"Going to a Tigers game, that isn't going to Detroit . . ."

She seemed prepared to explain why, but Missy interrupted, her voice dripping with sarcasm. "You should see the D on a nice spring night, Colin. They say the poverty is really beautiful, as the sun goes down."

"Don't mock Colin's white, bourgeois pretensions, Missy," Ty said. "That's not the way to disabuse a man of his white, bourgeois pretensions." Ty looked Colin up and down, tapping his fingers together as he did so. He had enormous hands with very fine, thin fingers, and his eyes were slightly milky and opaque. "I got to tell you, C, we really want to understand these dudes: Horkheimer, Adorno, Marcuse, Habermas. We've started with Max Horkheimer. At least, that's the only one we've read so far. All his essays that are in this book." Ty held out the book that, up to now, he had clutched to his chest.

Colin turned his head to the side so he could read the spine. *Critical Theory* was visible on its binding, as well as the call number from the graduate library at the University of Michigan. This guy had read Horkheimer's *Critical Theory*? Colin remembered checking out this very book as a graduate student. He still taught one of the essays in his course on the Frankfurt School: "Traditional and Critical Theory." *Critical Theory* was early Horkheimer—the phase during which his thinking was the most idealistic, before the 1940s, when he and Adorno wrote the *Dialectic of Enlightenment*, in which they both pretty much gave up on the idea that the worker could fundamentally improve his or her life. It was the takeover of all German industrial capabilities on the part of the Nazis that made Horkheimer and Adorno so fatalistic. They watched as a political ideology and a manufacturing capability were sutured together, and it made them think that not just the worker but the political subject, the autonomous human being who just wanted a life of small, manageable pleasures, didn't have a chance.

"This fucking book," Ty went on, "this book has changed my life. It's given me a purpose, you know what I'm saying? Even if I don't understand all of it, this book has given me a reason to get up in the morning. It's some fucking wonderful shit. And you of all people, you have to get where I'm coming from, teaching this stuff on a daily basis."

"How do you know what I teach? How do you even know I'm a teacher?"

"I asked you for a copy of your History of Critical Theory syllabus first day of class last semester. In the basement of Angell Hall. Remember?"

Colin nodded his head slowly. He did remember. When Ty had approached him and requested a syllabus, Colin had handed him one, assuming that he worked somehow for the university, even though he wasn't wearing an ID badge. More precisely, Colin had assumed that Ty was in building services.

"I liked the one essay by Horkheimer you teach so much, I went ahead and picked up this book so I could read more of his stuff. And I got to say, he's just the guy we needed to launch our group. He's asking the central question we're trying to answer."

"What is the central . . ." Colin was lagging behind in their conversation, distracted as he was by the unlikely web of connections that seemed to be unfolding between them.

"How would the Frankfurt School rebuild Detroit? That's what we're trying to figure out. Because we want to take advantage of the moment. The system of capital production is paused, you know what I'm saying? In Detroit, it's paused. But it isn't going to be paused for much longer. So before it starts up again, I was hoping to begin a conversation about what we as Detroiters want as a community—how we might be able to recreate a sense of the individual in the postindustrial landscape of the D. Horkheimer is very clear. The two are linked. You can't have the individual without the community, and vice versa. But to have the community and the individual mutually enrich one another, you have to rein in the capitalistic machine, and that's what we're trying to figure out how to do. First conceptually, by reading up on the Frankfurt School, but next organizationally. On the ground. How can capitalism be more responsive to the needs of impoverished communities than it has been in the past, particularly with the dismantling of labor unions? What can we reasonably ask of those companies now moving into the city in terms of giving back to the community? How can people in Detroit help rebuild the city's infrastructure? All those questions we need to have answers to. We got so much to do, man. And it's going to be hard work, too. So what do you say? Want to give us a hand?"

Ty gestured toward the open door of the Buick, and Colin Spanler, who had dropped Russian after one class because the teacher had called him lazy, who had given up becoming an alcoholic because liquor made him tired, and who had easily re-vamped his entire diet to lower his cholesterol because he didn't really care what he ate, the staid and steady and—by his own reckoning—somewhat boring and profoundly depressed Colin Spanler, looked at the torn, stained backseat of the Buick Skylark and decided that he would get back into this awful car, even if doing so had to be the stupidest thing he had ever done in his life. He would do it not because he trusted any of these people. He would do it not because he entirely believed in the existence of the Detroit Frankfurt School Discussion Group. He would do it because hearing Ty Bartell—this wiry, tall black man—reference Max Horkheimer, and witnessing Missy and Tina taunting his unquestionably white, bourgeois pretensions, made Colin realize that at some point he had simply stopped thinking about the world around him. He had thought a lot about what he hoped to extract from this world—a girlfriend, for example—but not about his connection to any sort of community. And that realization troubled him, even more than getting back into this car. Plus, and this was undeniably true but also a ridiculous reason to drive off with these people, he really didn't want to go home to an empty house. He was willing to choose these complete strangers over spending another night alone, in front of the TV.

"Just don't kill me," Colin said as he let his backpack slide off his shoulder and stepped once more into the Buick Skylark.

"Shoot, the only thing that might kill you, C," Ty said, his loud voice fading away for a moment while he walked around the car to let himself into the front passenger seat, "is this girl's fucking driving."

As if on cue, Tina hit the gas, and they were off.

THEY TURNED BACK ONTO MAIN STREET and drove through downtown Ann Arbor, passing within a block of Old Town Tavern. As they inched through the traffic, Ty sat with his back to his door, looking at Colin, the long fingers of his right hand tapping the glove compartment.

"I got so many questions for you, man," he said. "Horkheimer is kind of a trip for me because it's like, one minute, I get him real tight, and then the next minute, he loses me." With his left hand, he opened the University of Michigan's library copy of *Critical Theory*. "Do you mind if I ask you a few questions?"

"Not at all."

Ty began to flip through the book. "Okay, so tonight we're just talking about the essay you teach in your class, 'Traditional and Critical Theory.' That's his shit from . . . when did that piece first get published?"

"1937."

"See?" Ty winked at Tina. "The boy knows his shit. So early on in the essay"—he peered intently at the book while he scanned the pages—"Horkheimer talks about resisting the Kantian ego. Here it is. Yeah, he's going on about some issue he's got with *the ego of transcendental subjectivity*. What the fuck is that?"

They had made it across Huron Street, shedding some cars in front of them as they did so. Colin bit nervously at his nails. "Right, so if you're adapting Kantian philosophy to sociology, you might be tempted to think that society as a whole represents some kind of collective unconscious. A transcendental power, in Kantian terms. But Horkheimer rejects that, which is important for other Frankfurt School thinkers, because it helps them to establish their desire to be less dreamy and idealistic in their approaches to social issues."

"Right, okay." Ty nodded. "That helps me. And part of being less dreamy, I suppose, means rethinking what it means to be a person in the first place. Because we might *think* we are engaging, you know, with society and what have you, only when we choose to be, but actually society is up in our shit from the minute we open our eyes in the morning. Am I feeling that right?"

"Yes, you are." In spite of his language, Ty's account of Horkheimer's reevaluation of the bourgeois subject was pretty much spot-on—as keen as anything Colin's undergraduates produced in class. As they merged onto M-14, Ty dug a crinkled sheet of yellow paper out from the back pocket of his jeans. "I got to explain that Kantian bit to the group, I think. My plan is, I'll say a few words about the essay in general, and then kind of hand things over to you."

"What exactly do you want me to say?"

"Well, imagine Horkheimer was living in Detroit right now and elected mayor. All right, what would he do? You know what I'm saying? What the fuck would he do?"

"Like with Livernois Avenue," Missy added.

"Exactly! How the fuck would Max Horkheimer clean up Livernois Avenue? That's what we'd like to know. If you could help us figure that out . . . well, that'd be one kick-ass meeting of the Detroit Frankfurt School Discussion Group."

The Buick Skylark rattled loudly on the highway as Tina snaked her way through what remained of rush-hour traffic. "That's, uh"—Colin chose his words carefully—"that kind of analysis is not where I typically go when I'm teaching 'Traditional and Critical Theory'—"

"Well, you're smart," Ty interrupted him. "You can figure it out."

With the lack of shock absorbers, and all the swerving they were doing, Colin felt a little carsick. He was still thinking about Ty's account of Horkheimer's work. Had he really come up with that entirely on his own? "Are you taking any courses at Michigan?" he asked him.

"Courses?" Ty cocked his head. "I don't even have a high school diploma! I don't have any money! How am I going to take courses?"

"Well, how do you check out books from the library then, if you aren't a registered student?"

"I don't check them out. I just walk out with them. Those mousy little white girls they got working at the counters there, you think they're going to ask a black man for his ID? I take the books, but I return them, after I've made photocopies for the rest of the group over in Dearborn. My sister works for Ford there."

"What does she do?"

"She cleans, but they've got photocopier machines all over the place."

There was a pause in their conversation. Colin's body swayed as Tina swerved to avoid a pothole in the middle of the highway.

"There was some dark shit in that essay," Missy observed.

"I told you, girl!" Ty slapped the dashboard. "You think you're an individual just because you have a name. Then you read Horkheimer, and you learn that what you think makes you special is just what the market has told you makes you special. And it's told you that just to get you to buy a bunch of shit you don't need—work some job that turns you into a robot. Hell, he's dark, Horkheimer. Isn't that right, Colin? Hopeful at the same time, but dark."

"Yeah, that's true."

"I mean, if we're reading him wrong, tell us so. Don't pull any punches."

"Otherwise, what's the point of us driving your ass to Detroit?" Tina added. They had crept up on the bumper of a semi in front of them, and now Tina swung out from behind the truck and slammed on the gas. They rocketed ahead, the engine of the Buick straining loudly, the noise filling the car.

"No, you're not reading him wrong," Colin said. "Certainly

not 'Traditional and Critical Theory.' The question becomes, later in his career, do his views change? That's all."

No one said anything, and Colin wondered if they were waiting for him to answer his own question. "But remember, I'm not a Horkheimer expert," he added. "I just teach that one essay of his—"

"You don't have to be modest, C." Ty had produced a cigarette from somewhere on his body and, now cracking open the window, lit it. "Tina's right. We're bringing you along to teach us, not to make us feel good."

Colin didn't say anything. Ty shifted in his seat. "So what'd you mean, C, just then, when you said your analysis of Horkheimer doesn't usually go in the direction of, you know, Detroit? Real world stuff. What'd you mean by that? I ask because I got a theory—"

"You got a theory for everything," Tina interrupted him.

Colin couldn't see the speedometer, but they had to be going at least ninety miles an hour. They had already made it onto I-96 East, the trees and shrubs on the side of the highway just a green blur.

"Well, I got a theory for this most definitely. It goes like this." Ty ashed his cigarette out the window. "Capitalism has been designed so as to discredit the views of people like Horkheimer. It's like a conspiracy. And the people who were raised during late-stage American capitalism, prior to the Great Recession. . . . Well, no offense, Colin Spanler, PhD, but clearly your generation is just not equipped to talk in revolutionary terms. Especially, again no offense, white suburban kids—people who have benefited from the consolidation of capital in the hands of a comparatively few—you guys aren't the ones best suited to explore the full ramifications of the Frankfurt School message."

"Well, remember, in my course, I'm doing a survey of the Frankfurt School and its impact on subsequent critical theories—"

"That's a dodge. Excuse me, C, but that's a total dodge. You could be making a difference in that basement classroom of yours. You could be giving tools to the next generation of young Americans to try to take back their economic system. They aren't going to have the opportunities you did—not even the white suburban kids. They're all pretty much fucked, it seems to me."

Traffic was congested up ahead but—rather than slow down—Tina swung onto the shoulder and drove around a string of cars that were backed up behind a fender-bender.

Colin tried to give Ty's comments some thought, but it was hard to focus on their conversation. Like everyone else in the car, he didn't have a seat belt on, and Colin wondered for a moment what would happen if they all died in a car accident. What theories would be concocted back in Ann Arbor to explain his presence in this automobile?

"I don't disagree with what you're saying," he said after a little bit. "I mean, in my classes, it's easier for me to talk about the Frankfurt School in relation to literary texts, so that's what I do. Plus, at a school like Michigan, we have these kids whose parents are paying tens of thousands of dollars to send them to college, and I'm not sure how many of us would be comfortable critiquing an economic system that their families have profited from." He caught himself. "But in my defense, I *do* teach in a literature department."

"But that's what I don't get, C." Ty squirmed some more in his seat. "Even if you were teaching economics, you wouldn't be talking about Detroit. You academics have learned all this stuff *from* books, right? You've taken this shit *out of* books, but what you all end up doing is just putting it right back into books. Why is that? Why make books just talk to other books? Why not take this shit and try to use it to change the world, or at least change Detroit? It's the goddamn *University of Michigan* we are talking about here. Detroit is in Michigan, last I checked."

Colin looked out the window. Really, he didn't have an answer to Ty's question, except to say that it had never occurred to him to think in such terms, and that would have been such an embarrassing admission he preferred to say nothing at all. They cruised along in the Buick, past Livonia and into Dearborn. A minute or so after it became clear that Colin wasn't intending to speak, Tina turned on the radio. A hip-hop song came on that everyone except Colin knew. Their heads bobbed with the beat. Colin felt hopelessly, irretrievably, old and uncool. When the song ended, and the station went to a loud commercial, Tina clicked off the radio. "Why'd you get divorced, Colin?" she asked him.

Missy seemed to have been mulling over the same question, because she jumped in quickly. "Were you banging your students?"

"No," Colin said.

"Do you have a temper?" Tina peered at him in the rearview mirror.

"No."

"Are you an alcoholic?" Missy again, only this time nodding her head slowly at him.

"No, I tried to become one, but it didn't take." No one said anything for a moment, and Colin added, "My wife, my ex-wife, she's a psychologist. She fell in love with a colleague of hers. They were working together a lot, on a longitudinal study, and I guess all the time they spent together . . ." But he couldn't go on.

"Why do you have majority custody?" Tina asked. "Your wife don't want to be with her kids?"

"Is she on drugs now?" Missy chimed in.

"No, she's just in the lab a lot. She runs these experiments that use human subjects, and they take a lot of time. Her schedule isn't really conducive to getting the kids from school. So I have them four nights a week."

"Man, that must leave you with no life," Tina observed.

"No life? You must be the horniest motherfucker in Michigan!" Ty cried out. "No wonder you got into this car."

"You should not get into cars like this one, Colin Spanler, PhD," Tina added, shaking her head. "Some people, they would fuck you up. Take you God knows where. Some place even worse than Detroit, wherever that might be."

"Flint," Missy added.

"That's right. They'd take you to Flint. Kidnap your ass. Drug you and harvest your organs."

"They wouldn't drug him," Missy countered. "That might fuck up his organs. They'd just kill him, then cut out what they wanted."

"Oh, and killing him isn't going to do anything to his organs?"

"You put fucking drugs *in* his system, you don't know what you're fucking with! You might mess up his kidneys, or his liver. You don't know."

"I'm just saying, people do that shit. They kidnap other folks, handle their insides like they're in the produce section of a supermarket."

"And I'm just saying we're not talking about kidnapping! We're talking about cutting this guy up. Who's going to pay a ransom for Colin Spanler, PhD?"

"Ladies," Ty interrupted them, "I have a feeling C would like us to change the subject."

"That would be great," Colin said.

"But I'm making a point," Missy explained. "About no one paying a ransom for Colin. I'm saying his place in the political economy is culturally privileged but economically marginal." She turned and looked right at him. "I mean, they can't be paying you that much to teach those classes, can they?"

"Well . . ." Colin cleared his voice.

"You don't got the . . . what's it called, Ty?"

"*The tenure.*"

"You don't got *the tenure*, right?"

Missy stared at him. Occasionally, Colin could hear the muffler beneath the car, scraping against the highway. "No, I don't have the tenure," he admitted. Actually, Colin received child support payments from Nicole, but he wasn't about to reveal that piece of information.

"Looks like we got ourselves another person who is being put to use to enhance the world of capital, rather than benefit from it."

"That's right, girl," Ty said.

They sped along. Colin was aware that everyone in the car was waiting for him to issue some kind of response to this characterization, but he felt that he could neither defend the institution that employed him nor agree with Missy's assessment. Did he feel taken advantage of somewhat, teaching as much as he had to teach, being subject to yearly contracts and the most meager of salary increases? Of course he did. But he didn't want to admit that he felt these things to this group. Why? Was it because he didn't want to feel as if they had too much in common?

Missy was studying him. "You're all receded up in your head, C," she said. "Like you're afraid to breathe. We got to get you breathing, man. Interacting with the world."

"Yeah," Tina added. "Missy's right. You're too withdrawn. It's like your brain's an empty room, and you're standing in the corner."

"Oh no," Missy countered. "He's got thoughts up there, racing around. He just doesn't let on what he's thinking. That's the worst kind of man. You know why?"

"Cause one day," Tina jumped in, "they just snap."

"That's right, girl." Missy clicked her tongue. "They fucking snap. That's why"—she pointed her finger at Colin for emphasis—"if you're a man, you want to be the kind of man who puts it out there. What you're feeling. What you're thinking. As bad as it is, you just got to put it out there. Women respect that. But they don't like sneaky, quiet shit. That's creepy."

"Yeah, Missy's right. You kind of got a creepy vibe, C. You're kind of a creeper."

Ty slapped the dashboard again, laughing loudly. "Listen to these two, C! Man, they are taking your shit *apart!*"

Colin was mesmerized by what they were saying. Did he really give off a creepy vibe? It was certainly true that he sometimes became self-conscious when he tried to articulate what he was thinking about a given subject and found that he couldn't—that the right words eluded him or, more unnervingly, that his mind had just gone blank. At those moments, Colin could feel himself receding from whomever he was with, a feeling he hated because it made him worry that he came across as boring. That was bad enough, but creepy? The possibility had never occurred to him.

"Can I give you some advice," Missy continued, "on the dating front?"

"How do you know he doesn't have a girlfriend?" Ty asked.

"Please."

"Boy with a girlfriend," Tina offered, "does *not* get in a car with two girls like us. Not if he likes that girlfriend one bit."

"And Colin would like a girlfriend, you know that," Missy added.

"That we have established," Ty said. "Since he is the horniest motherfucker in Michigan. But the dating advice, Missy. Come on, girl; don't leave us hanging."

Missy shifted in her seat. "All right, C, so you're kind of funny. Like, when you talk, in your soft little white guy way, with your head bobbing up and down, you sound like you're a turtle, talking to another turtle, trying to get her to poke her head out of her shell. *Come on little turtle. It's okay. Look at me! Look at my head, out of my shell.* Women don't like men who talk like that. You got to put it *out there*, you know what I'm saying? Like I said before, you're all up inside yourself. You got to get more out in front."

"That's so right," Missy agreed wholeheartedly.

"And that backpack . . ." Tina added, her head shaking as she steered the Buick.

"Yeah, what is with the fucking backpack, Grandpa?" Missy asked. "Why don't you have one of them book bags?"

"Since I walk to work," Colin explained, "it's better for me to distribute weight evenly across my back, instead of just over one—"

"Jesus, see what I mean?" Missy interrupted him. "You sound like a creeper, Colin. Next time you're with a girl, make sure you don't talk about your backpack. Even if she asks you about your backpack, you don't discuss it. Try to put your shit more out there, but not that shit. Next thing we know, you're going to be telling us what you had for breakfast. Put real shit out there, you know what I'm saying?"

Colin shrugged. They thought he was so boring that he was creepy as a result. Well, that was nice to hear from complete strangers. Granted, they were young, but that didn't necessarily mean their judgment was faulty. It could mean instead that they were just more willing to speak bluntly. Nicole had never called him boring per se, but she had cheated on him. And she had moved on without any apparent regrets. She never cried: during the separation, when they signed the settlement, when they made their court appearance. The whole time, she never betrayed the slightest hint of regret.

"My boy C might not be emoting that much," Ty observed. "But he got in the goddamn car with you two, and then he got in the car again with me! You aren't going to give him any props for that? You think the average white man in Ann Arbor his age—how old are you, C?"

"Thirty-five."

"You think the average white, thirty-five-year-old *dude* from Ann Arbor gets in this car and drives with us to Detroit? The boy has layers, girls, I'm telling you. Layers like a cake."

"A vanilla cake," Missy added.

"And Dockers for frosting," Tina deadpanned. She was herself Caucasian, but she wasn't white like Colin was white. She was working class—urban. Tina clearly identified a hell of a lot more closely with Ty and Missy than she did with him.

How had stepping into this car somehow turned him into a leper? Or at least a leper by virtue of his extraordinary squareness? Colin doubted that he had ever, in his entire life, felt so ridiculously, so glaringly, privileged and suburban and sheltered and lily, lily white. He hated feeling this way. He hated feeling so exposed by these three, so laughed at, so easily—and accurately—categorized. He wanted desperately *not* to be the person they thought he was, and he wondered how in the world he might achieve this end. What would it take for Colin Spanler, PhD, to be more interesting than the average white guy who lived in

Ann Arbor? Because he wanted to be more interesting than the average white guy who lived in Ann Arbor. Ty was right; he had stepped into this car twice in the course of about ten minutes in part because that was exactly what he wanted.

THEY WERE NO LONGER ON THE HIGHWAY. They had taken an exit ramp, and now they were in Detroit, on Rosa Parks Boulevard. Colin looked around, first at an abandoned building, about eight stories high, its windows all broken, its ground floor boarded up, and next, half a block down, a pristine auto parts shop with a pharmacy across the street. If you took a picture just of the shop and the pharmacy, he realized, the intersection might pass for any street corner in urban America, but if you widened the lens to capture the abandoned buildings and empty lots on either side—the deserted sidewalks, the garbage piled at the corner of the alley up the street—then you'd suspect you were looking at one of those cities that had fallen on hard times. A relic of the era of industrial manufacturing in America. Maybe Toledo. Maybe Buffalo. Maybe Cleveland. Maybe Detroit.

Colin continued to stare out his window. He spied several people waiting at a bus stop, and just beyond them, a city block that had been more or less razed. Just a single, narrow brick building remained, with a liquor store on the ground floor advertising lotto tickets. What struck him most about Detroit was all the empty space: how few people were out and about, how much room existed for more buildings, more cars on the street, more life. There was emptiness everywhere, perhaps especially in the hollowed-out, abandoned buildings that seemed to occupy space in a qualified way.

He felt Ty's eyes on him and turned away from the window to meet his gaze. "Not all Detroit is the same," the founder of the Detroit Frankfurt School Discussion Group said to him. "You can't paint it in one brushstroke. All around Wayne State, that area's popping. There are folks with money here—black folks as well as white."

"Yeah, but this here," Missy said, "this is shitty right here. And when Detroit wants to do shitty, Detroit can *really* do shitty."

Colin continued to take in his surroundings, but now he wasn't so much looking *at* the neighborhood as he was looking *through* its empty lots and gutted buildings, thinking as he did so that in a funny way, he felt—on the inside at least—much more like Detroit than he did Ann Arbor. Largely razed, sorely in need of reinvestment, but with space to grow, as well. Maybe the similarities stopped there. *I'm so timid*, he muttered to himself. *Detroit isn't timid, but I'm so timid*. What kind of person, after all, sat in a car with complete strangers and said virtually nothing while they took him apart, down to the backpack nestled between his feet? What kind of person ended up in this situation in the first place? Perhaps it wasn't so much that he had layers, as Ty had generously claimed, but that he was just pliable and blank—all too easily talked into anything, all too easily led astray.

They took a right onto Marantette Street. "That's it up there." Ty pointed at an enormous brick building, two stories high, that stretched across an entire city block. A chain-link fence, with looped barbed wire at the top, circled a wide patch of weeds and dirt around the building. Tina pulled over to the curb, and they all stepped out of the car.

"You got those folding chairs in the trunk?" Ty asked Tina. "And the flashlights?"

"Yeah," she said, circling toward the back of the car.

"We're going up to the second floor, right?" Missy asked.

"That's right," Ty said.

"Because I'm not dealing with no rats, Ty. I told you. I'm all good with the Frankfurt School, don't get me wrong, but I don't do rats."

"None of us do rats, girl. What the fuck are you talking about?"

Colin was staring at Missy in horror. She nodded her head at him. "You can hear them, down on the ground floor—nibbling away at the books."

170

"I hate to break it to you, girl," Tina shouted playfully while the trunk wheezed open, "but you can hear them on the second floor too."

Colin was confused. "What do you mean? Why are rats eating books?"

"The warehouse was a book depository before the fire," Missy explained, while Ty and Tina lifted several folding chairs and flashlights out of the trunk. "There are books everywhere in there, but they're all ruined. Ty wants us to think about what that means in a metaphoric sense. That's why we meet here."

"In a metaphoric sense?" Colin wanted her to say more.

"Where do books end up?" Missy struck a languid pose and slowly waved her hands in front of her, clearly imitating Ty. "They end up rotting, turning to ash. Books are just things. You got to take the ideas that are in books and move them out into the world to make them matter. That's the central message of the Frankfurt School. Am I feeling you, Ty?"

The trunk of the Buick slammed loudly. Colin jumped. Ty stepped out into the middle of the empty street. "Where is everybody?" he asked no one in particular, ignoring Missy's question.

"Devon said they were going to park on Dalzelle, meet us inside."

"Upstairs?" Missy inquired.

"Yes, M, upstairs. Damn." Tina snickered as she handed Colin a flashlight and a folding chair. "The rest of them probably already went up."

"Let's go then." Ty began to walk.

"Are we . . ." Colin felt his left eyelid twitching—some kind of newly emerging nervous tic—while his right hand, the one holding the folding chair next to his body, drummed his thigh with his fingers. It was like he had been guzzling coffee for the last little bit, only he hadn't had any caffeine since lunch. They headed toward a portion of the fence that had been bent back on itself, like the folded-down corner of a page. "Is it a good idea to go into a condemned building?"

And his three companions burst into laughter. "That's a good one, C," Ty said half to himself. "That's a real good one."

They stepped through the weeds and into the warehouse, passing through a window frame after Ty carefully removed the board that sat in its cavity. Now they were in a damp concrete stairwell. Ty turned on his flashlight, and the rest of them followed suit. They took the stairs up to the second floor. Stepping out of the stairwell, Colin saw a sea of ruined books, spread across the floor like sand: textbooks with their covers missing, paperbacks that had curled like enormous seashells, books that had fused and morphed with other books. They had to step over and around the piles, but even as they did so, their shoes came down on printed pages. In the dark, with the beams of their flashlights revealing more ruined books in the distance, Colin inhaled the tart smell of rotten pulp.

"Be careful," Ty called out. It's easy to twist an ankle."

The four of them slowly made their way toward a dim set of flickering lights in the middle of the room. Not until he was nearly upon them could Colin see that the rest of the Detroit Frankfurt School Discussion Group had arranged an assortment of candles and some kind of lantern, around which they had also cleared a semicircle and set up their folding chairs. There were about a dozen of them standing there in the cavernous space, their flashlights held loosely in their hands. Standing on the periphery, Colin watched as Ty greeted everyone individually, exchanging hand slaps and bear hugs with some of the men, shaking hands almost deferentially with some of the women. As far as he could tell in the half-light, most of the members of the Detroit Frankfurt School Discussion Group were black, and most of them looked to be in their twenties and thirties, wearing dark jeans and T-shirts, a few with jackets either on or tied around their waists. Still, a few of the women were clearly much older. One lady, in dark slacks and a purple blouse, could have been a grandmother, and Colin wondered how in the world Ty had induced her to join his group.

"I don't know if all of these candles are a good idea, folks,"

Ty said in a loud voice, just as the members began to drift over to their folding chairs. "You know, open flames, when we are surrounded by paper."

"Yeah, we would hate to have a fire here, in a building that was abandoned because of a fire," one of the other men observed.

Everyone got a laugh out of that, Colin included. He had already followed Missy and Tina's lead and had squeezed his folding chair into the ring that had been formed. This meant kicking aside books and wiggling the legs of his chair in and around clumps of pages that wouldn't budge from the floor. By the time Colin was seated, Ty had strolled over to the candles and was standing just in front of them, so that their flickering wicks cast a shadow of him across the semicircle, out into the darkness that loomed behind them.

"So how you all doing?" he asked, his voice low and measured. There were murmurs in response. "Before we get started, I thought we'd go around the circle and introduce ourselves to our guest, Colin Spanler, PhD, from the University of Michigan."

Ty shone his flashlight at Colin, who instinctively shielded his eyes from the glare. In the near darkness, people began to call out their names. Colin caught just a few; he was too distracted by too many things to be able to listen carefully. He thought of rats chewing the pages of the books around them. He wondered what the chances were that they might all get arrested for trespassing. If he ended up in a Detroit jail, how would he explain that to Nicole and the kids? To the English Department? Who in the world would ever believe that he had come to this warehouse to discuss the Frankfurt School of Criticism and Social Theory?

"So I'd like to say just a few words about our reading for tonight." While Ty pulled out his crinkled sheet of yellow paper, the rest of the members of the group began to withdraw their photocopies of Horkheimer's "Traditional and Critical Theory" from their coat pockets and purses. The sound of these pages being neatly unfolded and smoothed echoed in the room. "I checked this with Colin on the way over; no need to worry about that *ego of the transcendental subjectivity* stuff at the beginning of the essay. Instead, let's focus on the heart of what Horkheimer is saying. Let me try to paraphrase his shit here." Ty fumbled some with his notes, and Colin wondered if he wasn't perhaps a little bit nervous. "All right, so according to Horkheimer, eventually free markets—which are never really that free to begin with—but in any case, they end up getting replaced by more controlled markets. These are markets in which the government is really exercising its influence. So what happens, and we all know this, is that the people in control of the government, and the people in charge of industry, all the folks who manage the production of goods, and the laws that govern this production, they all end up amassing far greater wealth than the people who actually *make* the goods. We're talking about the one percent here, you know what I'm saying? So commodity production, which is just a fancy way of describing how all the stuff we buy gets made, this production inevitably creates a situation in which the individual working, for example, on the factory line, the guy who initially thought a job was going to bring him independence, purchasing power, a nice life, and so on, eventually that guy—"

"Or woman," Missy interrupted him.

"Yes, thank you, Missy. Or woman. Eventually, he or she ends up with less independence, less purchasing power, and a pretty crappy life. Now, we all know this, right? But why does it happen?"

He stood there, his shadow swaying, and let his question sink in. Like an experienced teacher, Ty seemed comfortable in the silence. "Well, Horkheimer says it happens because industrial production is actually *designed* to eat up the freedom of the working person. Freedom or happiness, it turns out in the end, is just a mirage—just another feature of commodity production. You tell a person if he or she works hard, they can buy a new TV, that they'll love that TV, that it will make them so happy, owning it. So they work hard just like you told them to, and they get that new TV, and you know what? Maybe they're happy for a while, but then you tell them they have to buy something else, and on and on it goes. You're telling them to go out and purchase shit so that you get the money back that you're paying them in the first place. The worker, he or she is stuck in the system, laboring away. It's all rigged, see? And Horkheimer saw this way back in the 1930s. Isn't that amazing?"

Several people shifted in their seats. Colin felt the coldness of the warehouse settling now on his shoulders and arms. Ty spoke slowly and deliberately, but with intensity, too. There was something slightly mesmerizing about his performance.

"In capitalism," he went on, "the worker thinks he or she has freedom because he or she can sell and buy goods, but that is *all* they can do—run after material interests that are actually being dictated to them. The market serves the market; it doesn't care about people. And it leads toward a completely automated, totally managed social environment. So what I'm saying is, even if some jobs come back to the D, that's not enough. We can't think that a renewed economy in our city is necessarily going to make us happier. Sure, they might turn some of the street-lights back on. They might fix some of the potholes. But it's not enough for us to be satisfied with that. We need to ask for more. We need to change what defines our city. And I know what you're thinking right now. You're thinking, *Ty is full of shit. How are we going to change what defines Detroit, the group of us, sitting in this abandoned warehouse?* But here's the thing I want you to realize. It takes less than you think to change a city. Let me give you an example. Less than fifteen percent of the Detroit popu-lation voted in the last mayoral election. That means, to become mayor of Detroit, you need fifty-one percent of fifteen percent of seven hundred thousand people. Well, I did the math. That's fifty-three thousand people. That's how many votes you need to become mayor of Detroit. Fifty-three thousand."

A member of the Detroit Frankfurt School Discussion Group coughed a few times, but otherwise it was quiet, save for the settling of the building in which they sat, the occasional rustling of pages out in the darkness, and the dripping of water from pipes that still, somehow, had a little liquid left in them.

"How many people did you say live in Detroit?" one of the men asked.

"Seven hundred thousand."

"How can a motherfucking city of seven hundred thousand people only have two decent grocery stores?"

"I was thinking the same thing," a woman on the other side of the gathering chimed in.

"Well, maybe we can get an answer to this question from our reading," Ty said. "What do you all think Max Horkheimer would say on the subject of how a city of seven hundred thousand people can have only two decent supermarkets?"

There was silence among them.

"I think, maybe with that, I should let our friend Colin take the reins here, since he is an expert on the Frankfurt School. He's going to talk to us about the concrete things Horkheimer says we can do to make our city work for us—to make it breathe again. Come on up here, C."

Colin rose slowly to his feet. When he reached the candles, Ty shook his hand, pulled him in close, and patted him on the back. Colin could smell the sting of the man's perspiration. He watched Ty walk over and sit down in his empty chair. Now that he was standing there alone, in front of the group, Colin became aware of his own shallow breathing, the sound of his heart pounding in its cavity, the eyes settling on him, the flashlights pointed at his feet.

"I want to thank you all for having me here," he began. Since he had been more or less abducted, he thought that was a pretty gracious way to get started. "I haven't had the chance, ever, to hear the ideas of the Frankfurt School considered in a context like this. In an abandoned building, in a city that needs to be rebuilt. And I also want to thank Ty for doing such a great job summarizing the main points of Horkheimer's essay 'Traditional and Critical Theory.'"

Colin kicked at a pulpy mass of a book stuck to the concrete floor in front of him. Beyond their semicircle, coal blackness fell. Not being able to see anyone's face actually made it easier for him to gather his wits. "I was saying to Ty, Missy, and Tina earlier tonight that I don't normally discuss Horkheimer's ideas with any contemporary urban context in mind, so if I sound as if I'm grasping for words a little . . . well, I probably am." He tried to recall the essay now with its applicability to Detroit specifically in mind. "Horkheimer says pretty clearly that for capitalism to benefit an entire society, it has to be reconceptualized. As Ty explained, we are taught by capitalism to think that our material desires are really our own, when, on the contrary, they are largely scripted for us. Does that make sense?"

There were murmurs of affirmation around him. Colin clenched and unclenched his hands, thinking as hard as he could. "So what we have to accept," he continued, speaking slowly as he tried to piece together his ideas, "is that our concept of the individual is a largely false one. The paradox is that when we think more communally, we are actually thinking in ways that better serve our personal interests. So in terms of Detroit . . ."

But now he was stumped. Colin didn't know how to situate Horkheimer's ideas in the middle of this city; he wasn't sure how to situate himself in the middle of this city—wasn't even sure, at this precise moment, if he was actually *in* the middle of this city. It was a sprawling place, Detroit, if not by virtue of its dwindling population, then simply by its vast acreage. So he was left with one option—the only move he knew how to make as a teacher in this situation. "Let me ask you," he said, preparing to throw Ty's question back at the group, "how might we, in the spirit of Horkheimer, think more communally, with Detroit in mind?"

There weren't even murmurs among the members of the Detroit Frankfurt School Discussion Group. Just silence. Colin stood there, his legs warmed by the mass of candles behind him. He heard someone's folding chair creak. Then, a male voice came out of the darkness—raspy and deep.

"I've been out of work now for two years," he said. "And I want a job. I want a living wage. I don't begrudge a man or a woman who has more than I do; I really don't. But I do miss the sense of being part of a larger whole. Whatever companies move in here now, they are going to want to pay us peanuts to work for them, right? Otherwise, what's their incentive for coming here? I just don't want to see all the money they make taken out of the city. I'd like the mayor and such . . . the city council . . . I'd like to see them ask these companies, no, *demand* that these companies invest in Detroit. Give them tax incentives, that's fine, but also make them help fix up this place too, you know what I'm saying?"

Several people shouted out "Yes!"

"No more new buildings," a woman announced. "You want to set up a business here and pay us minimum wage? Fine. You're right, Devon; we've got no leverage in that regard. But my God—fix up a building or two! We got the most beautiful buildings in this country here in Detroit, but so many of them have fallen on hard times. It's mighty tough to have a sense of community with all of these smashed windows."

"That is so true," Missy observed.

"People don't talk about it anymore," one of the older women interjected, "I guess it's a tired subject, but I'm telling you, drugs are *still* ravaging this city. Just ravaging it. That's one thing you got to admit, Ty. Horkheimer didn't know diddlysquat about crack cocaine."

Before Ty had a chance to respond, a young woman, her jacket unzipped to reveal a Taco Bell uniform beneath it, piped up. "If there is no money to be made," she said, "the market isn't going to be there, right? Isn't that what this man Horkheimer says? So no wonder we've only got two decent supermarkets! Our city is so poor now, you won't make any money trying to sell us fresh green beans. We're just trying to afford the basics. So with all of these abandoned lots, why can't we turn more of them into community gardens—start growing fruits and vegetables ourselves?"

"That's what they're doing over in Rouge Park."

"Yeah, well, I don't live in Rouge Park. They aren't doing anything like that in my neighborhood."

"Like Ty says, we got to vote," observed someone else. "We can get all the money we can from these companies, but if we got corrupt government officials running things, we're fucked."

"As long as we have an emergency manager running the city, it doesn't matter who we elect," a woman observed. "They won't have any power anyway."

For a moment no one spoke. Then the elderly woman in the purple blouse, seated just a few feet from Colin, cleared her throat. "These young people on the sidewalk, or on the bus, they'll walk right into you because they're staring at their phones and listening to their music. How are we going to build a community with everyone on their gosh darn phones all the time? It's a problem."

"The ultimate example of capitalism," Ty observed from his folding chair. "Not just telling you what you have to buy, but teaching you to experience the world through what it sells you. So that you block out the real for the fake."

In hearing this, Colin thought of how much he was himself tethered to his iPhone, and wondered when he had last checked his email account. It must have been while drinking half his beer at Old Town earlier that night. What was that, two hours ago? And yet it seemed like forever.

"I'm so sick of white people on TV, talking about how much they love animals." The woman's voice came from the far side of the semicircle. She spoke slowly, lingering over each word. "There are people getting their water turned off, children hungry, wearing clothes that don't fit, and every time I watch a show, the same commercial comes on with that white girl crying because there are dogs being mistreated all over the place. Not that I condone abusing dogs, but we have brothers and sisters in some serious need, and we don't talk about them. We talk about animals instead."

And so it went, comments and anecdotes, declarations and reflections, about Detroit and the experience of living in Detroit. Colin stood there in the middle of the group, listening, his hands dug deep into his pants pockets, until Ty finally stood up and walked over to him.

"Thank you, Colin," he said, "for coming down here tonight. Not that we gave you much of a choice."

"Thank you for having me," he said. And then they clapped for him. The Detroit Frankfurt School Discussion Group applauded Colin Spanler, PhD. He stepped away from the candles, walked over, and sat down in his folding chair.

As he did so, Tina leaned over and tapped him on his knee with her flashlight. "That was pretty good," she said, "the way you got everyone involved. Ty, he'll just start talking and never stop, but you didn't do that. That was cool."

They blew out the candles and folded up their chairs. Someone in the group asked if they were all going drinking, and the collective response was overwhelmingly favorable. Ty, by this point, had rejoined Colin, Tina, and Missy. "I suppose I need to get you back to Ann Arbor, huh, C?" he asked Colin.

"Yeah," Colin said. "I'm teaching tomorrow morning."

"Tina, can I borrow your car?"

She handed Ty her keys. "You better put gas in it. Take this, too." She handed him her folding chair, as did Missy. "See you, Colin," she added.

"Yeah, see you," Missy said.

"Bye," Colin said.

While the rest of the group headed out the far end of the building, toward Dalzelle Street,

Ty and Colin made their way back around and over the same mounds of books they had already navigated, down the same stairwell, and out the same window frame through which they had first entered the warehouse. Ty reaffixed the board that had covered the window frame prior to their arrival. Then they crossed the street and put the chairs and flashlights in the trunk. A minute later, Ty gunned the Buick and they were on their way.

FROM THE FRONT PASSENGER SEAT, Colin looked down the deserted streets of Detroit, at the gutted buildings and dilapidated, American-made cars. Then, as they moved farther out of the city, he took in the boarded-up homes and empty lots, the scattered clusters of young men in their hoodies and baggy jeans. Ty, so voluble and animated ever since Colin had met him, was quieter now.

"I'd really like to attend your next meeting," Colin said. "Volitionally."

Ty veered onto the entrance ramp for I-96 West. After they had merged onto the empty highway and he still hadn't said anything, Colin looked over and noticed that he was smiling. "What is it?"

"Oh, man . . ." Ty shook his head.

"What?"

"I'm not a fool, C. You probably think I am, but I'm not. I know that Horkheimer was a little naïve early on in his writings."

"Did you read some of his later work?"

"No, but I looked at the Wikipedia entry on his ass. The fact is, Horkheimer doesn't have that many concrete things to say about how to make Detroit a thriving city again. His only solution would seem to be a communist workers' revolution, but everyone in Detroit knows that isn't going to happen. And most Detroiters wouldn't want it to happen. We invented the goddamn Cadillac, after all. So when you got up there in front of the group and didn't have much to say, you more or less confirmed my hunch."

"Thanks for using me as your guinea pig."

"Well, a man has to be resourceful in my situation." He laughed a little. "Ah, hell, C, the Detroit Frankfurt School Discussion Group isn't about the Frankfurt School. I'm not interested in *teaching* Max Horkheimer. I'm interested in *using* the idea of Max Horkheimer. If those folks you met tonight, if they encounter someone in something they read describing economic conditions that they can relate to, even if there aren't any clear, viable solutions offered for how to improve those conditions, it still resonates with them. Especially when it's challenging material. An essay like 'Traditional and Critical Theory' tells them they aren't crazy for thinking the way they are—that they might actually be really smart. Reading the writings of the Frankfurt School, I don't care how much goes over their heads—my head—because just trying to understand the ideas gives us *power*. And that's all I want to do. I want to empower people." He had rolled down his window and the air, whipping into the car, made Colin shiver. "Do me a favor, little man. Check that glove compartment for tobacco, would you?"

Colin opened the compartment. Receipts, crumpled bits of paper, empty packages of sunflower seeds, two lighters, and a bottle of hair detangler spray spilled into his hands.

"Right there." Ty pointed at a folded pouch of tobacco wedged in the back of the compartment. "Yeah, see if there's any rolling paper in that bag."

There was paper, along with plenty of tobacco. Colin passed the bag to Ty, who set it on his lap. Using his knees to steer, he rolled himself a cigarette.

"I think it's great, what you're doing with this group," Colin said.

"I'll tell you something, C." It was almost as if Ty hadn't heard him. He stared out the windshield, his eyes not quite set on the road in front of them. He seemed lost in thought. "The greed of some people, the people who control markets . . ." His profile was lit only intermittently by the passing headlights on the other side of the highway. "It can be a supermarket. It can be a stock market. It can be a city plaza. But the greed nowadays . . . it's got more than a tinge of desperation to it."

Colin was only half listening. He was lost in his own thoughts. He and Ty had read the same book by Max Horkheimer, the *exact same book*, and yet its impact on each of them had been so different.

"I sold a means of escape on those streets back there." Ty gestured over his shoulder and out the back of the car, toward the city now cloaked in darkness. The slow cadence of his voice brought Colin's musings to a halt. "I'm not going to term the merchandise by its usual name. I'll just call it a means of escape, the possession of which, in its freebase form, carries with it harsher penalties under the law than in its powder form. And I'll add that even though more white people use the powder form than black folks use the freebase form, the rate of incarceration for the latter is much higher. Five grams of this means of escape in its freebase form means a felony. You want to get charged with a felony with powder, you're going to need five hundred grams. I'm just saying. . . . But I sold the freebase form. Back in the day, like a good capitalist, I sold that shit to anyone who wanted to buy it, regardless of age. Right in front of the Bradley Playground. Kids, girls, mothers. I think about the mothers the most. I helped turn some of them into whores, pushing that poison on them. Then I saved myself. I didn't have a moral awakening; I just got bored. And I was scared. Want to know something? You can be scared and bored at the same time. I should have been killed more than once, but bullets missed me. I should have been picked up by the cops when others were, but I slipped away. You think my story is something special? Shit, it isn't special. I just fell out of that world when my crew got busted up: two guys sent to prison, a third shot eight times and left in a dumpster over on Fenkell. I had to move out of my place, watch my back for a long time.

"I still watch my back. But I got a job through a cousin—working as a groundskeeper at Wayne State. At night, in the real early morning, after we'd clear the walks of snow, we'd go up to the top floor of the library—place as quiet as a cemetery—and look at pornography on one of the computer terminals. Hell, I even got tired of that. That's when I started reading. Back then, I wanted to know all about Karl Marx. I had heard he was a badass, a real revolutionary. So I read his stuff—at least I tried to. Then I read some about him. That's how I heard about the Frankfurt School. The Wayne State Library, they have a shitty selection of Frankfurt School texts, I must say. So I ended up spending my free time on your campus."

They sped along, passing from Wayne County into Washtenaw. Ty continued talking. "The books I read now," he said, "sure they're unusual fare for a black man from Mack Ave., but once you've sold drugs in the D, then you've already begun to critique the capitalist system. You have already started to think about how things fit together." He whistled softly. "Back in the day, I was the opposite of an urban planner, man. I was an urban destroyer. The human byproduct of a dysfunctional market economy. I was the end result of what Horkheimer feared self-consuming capitalism could produce, only I wasn't some abstract sociological concept. I was skin and flesh. I was an angel of death."

"Well, you're not"—Colin's voice was scratchy from the cloud of nicotine in which he sat—"you're not an angel of death anymore."

"I hope not. We each have different challenges, it seems to me. Yours is complacency tempting you just to let the world do its thing. Mine is hopelessness tempting me to take the world apart."

He flipped on the radio. The station they had been listening to earlier in the evening had been replaced by static, but rather than fumble with the tuner, Ty just turned it off. They drove in silence, merging onto M-14, and finally closing in on Ann Arbor. Ty never asked Colin where he wanted to be dropped off. Instead, he just drove right up to the front of Angell Hall, where the English Department was housed, and pulled over. The building was dark—central campus empty, save for some kids skateboarding over by the loading docks behind the Natural Science Building. From State Street, Colin could hear their boards scraping against the concrete.

Ty shifted the Buick into park and leisurely rolled himself another cigarette. "There's an avalanche of the new coming to Detroit, C," he said, shaking his head slowly as the smoke rose up and trailed out of the open window. "I think we're kind of lucky in one sense, those of us in the D. We know there's an avalanche coming. But it's coming here, too. To Ann Arbor. You can hear it rumbling. We'll get it first, the poor people, but then other people, other cities, other towns, they'll get it too."

He smoked his cigarette. When he was done, he flicked the butt out the window and turned toward Colin. "Maybe you could check out the books for me for our readings, so I don't have to sneak them out of the library?"

"I could do that."

Sitting in this car, while Ty was smoking his cigarette, Colin had been thinking about his life since his divorce. He had been forcing things. He wasn't cut out for hobbies or activities. He wasn't a golfer. He wasn't suited for Internet dating either, at least not at the moment. Small steps first. He needed to be more engaged with the world, like he lectured to his son. So he'd join the Detroit Frankfurt School Discussion Group. Everything else he'd think about down the road.

He opened the door. "Thanks for taking me into Detroit, Ty."

Ty extended his right hand and, very slowly, took Colin's and clenched it hard so that their thumbs linked together tightly. "You're all right, C." He let his hand go as Colin stepped out of the car. "Hey, this was a good night for you. An important evening in the life of Colin Spanler, PhD. Know how I know?"

Standing on the sidewalk, Colin shook his head.

Ty pointed over his own shoulder. "You almost forgot your backpack."

Sonnet 126

{}
{}

THEOBALD KRISTELLER SETTLED INTO HIS CHAIR in the early printed texts room of the British Library. He preferred the reading desks closest to the circulation counter, because he liked being right next to the bank of terminals one used to find and order books. He also appreciated the relative bustle in this part of the enormous room. The rest of the early printed texts reading area was deathly quiet and nearly void of distractions, save when one of the younger, gung-ho librarians stumbled upon someone not using one of the book cradles properly, or writing notes in pen. Theo had himself once been upbraided for letting a first edition of Robert Persons's *De Persecutione Anglicana* slip into his lap. "But it's Persons!" he had exclaimed incredulously. "No one cares about Robert Persons!"

This transgression had occurred in 1990, when the BL was located in the British Museum and Theo had just arrived in London, having escaped—thanks to his mom leaving him more than a bit of money in her will—the awful prospect of spending his entire career as an English professor at Excellence University in the American Upper Midwest. He could still recall, after being caught with Persons in his lap, how he had been ushered into the circulation office smack dab in the middle of the two reading rooms at the BL and reprimanded by one of the senior librarians, a withered man encased in worn tweed, the stench of pipe tobacco—Chartwell blend, Theo discovered soon thereafter—pouring from his mouth. "In the British Library, patrons handle the books properly, or they don't handle them at all," the man had said, his voice dripping with disdain, his line of vision fixed above Theo's head, as if he were too appalled to make eye contact. Theo had apologized profusely and left the library immediately, too embarrassed to return to his seat. Two hours later, he emerged from Harrods, having purchased his own Harris Tweed blazer and his first of many pipes, all from salesmen who had looked down their noses at him. "I will never be accepted in this city," he had thought as he walked down Brompton Road, the black taxis passing him on what would seem for years to be the wrong side of the street. "And I will never, ever leave."

Skip ahead twenty years and Theo spent between three and four days a week at the British Library, depending on his teaching schedule at Roehampton, which was hardly laborious. He taught an introductory course on Renaissance literature, a class on research methodology, and—less frequently—a graduate seminar on paleography. More than proper research or proper teaching, though, Theo valued scholarly distractions. Since his teenage years, he had always had a romantic appreciation for the figure of the reader. He liked the look of intensity in his eyes: the tapping of fingers and toes while the rest of the body remained motionless, even languid. This combination of resignation and fierceness was what had drawn him first to the academic subject of early modern, Catholic martyrs and then to the Anglican Church as a devout parishioner.

It was the second Tuesday of October, 2010. Theo had come to the British Library that day to look at a 1606 edition of Robert Southwell's *A Poem Declaring the Real Presence of Christ in the Blessed Sacrament of the Altar.* The poem—just a single quarto page—had been printed in Flanders. After its publication, some poor sop had smuggled the work into England, risking his life in the process. Southwell was an English Catholic, martyred in 1595. Possessing one of his poems would have attracted the interest of authorities, and easily brought a charge of treason.

Southwell was also, without question, Theo's favorite martyr. When he was hung, having been arrested for celebrating a mass at Uxenden Hall, near Harrow-on-the-Hill in Middlesex, the Jesuit had not died right away, because the knot that secured the rope had loosened when he fell through the scaffold. According to eyewitnesses, the hangman had been forced to pull down sharply on Southwell's legs in order to finish him off. But Southwell was still breathing even when the rope was cut, and was said by some to have been mouthing last rites for himself just before he finally expired on the baseboard of the cart that had wheeled him to Tyburn in the first place. Whenever Theo pictured all of this, Southwell's suffering, the savageness of the execution, the press of the crowd around the spectacle, he always came away ever more convinced that this martyr's death was the most scintillating scene from the whole English Reformation.

While the years of his expatriation had flown by, encompassing several moves from one flat to another, a brief marriage to the inimitable Fiona Tartleton, and his seasonal retreats to Italy each August, Theo's interest in Renaissance English Catholics had never really wavered, even if his progress on the book he had been intending all these years, *Torture and Torment: The Question of Catholicism in Tudor and Stuart England*, was nowhere near to being drafted, much less completed. Perhaps the examples of devotion and self-sacrifice that these subjects set forward were just too mesmerizing for Theo to comment on in prose. But their piety wasn't even what he liked best about martyrs like Southwell. What really floored Theo wasn't their commitment to God so much as their appreciation of culture. That was the real reason behind their willingness to offer up their lives on behalf of stained-glass windows and rosary beads. They believed that

God inhered in these things, but they also knew that if such objects were destroyed, what remained in their wake would lose all beauty, luster, and vitality. Theo's sympathy for just such a worldview, not to mention his fondness for blazers and vests, made his drift toward the Tory side of the political spectrum inevitable and now—in this, his fifty-fourth year as an animate being—irreversible.

When the light on his desk blinked, indicating that the book he had requested was now available at the circulation counter, Theo set down that day's copy of *The Daily Telegraph* and ambled over to the queue. In less than a minute, he was summoned to the counter by the nearly imperceptible nod of one of the clerks, a young man whom Theo didn't recognize, with a thick head of curly black hair and a neck speckled with moles. Not until he had lived in London for more than a decade had Theo begun to pick up on all the subtle twitches and smirks of the English—that nervous, melancholy race. But once he could read the mysterious, subtle mannerisms of these pale-faced, painfully demure types, Theo began to notice how many people—on the Tube, in the public parks, and in the grocery stores—weren't pale faced at all, not to mention demure. They were, rather, Indians and Pakistanis, Black Africans and Black Caribbeans. Theo didn't feel nearly as confident intuiting their manners and sensibilities, although he often inferred muted rage and disdain when they returned his stares with their own. Then, in the wake of 9/11, the papers devoted so much attention to the radical mullahs preaching in and around London that Theo stopped taking public transportation, a choice validated when those horrible bombs went off in the summer of 2005. Not even the Tories had a credible immigration policy: just chatter about quotas, which struck Theo as crass. None of the people either standing for office or babbling about politics on television seemed to have any idea how to maintain the integrity of British culture, which exasperated Theo. British culture was the reason he had stayed in London all these years. Or at least high British culture. Its existence justified, to no small degree, his entire life.

"Name, please?" the boy asked.

"Kristeller." Theo said his last name so softly he had to repeat it again. All these years and he was still a mumbler, still trying to hide his flat Midwestern accent.

The young man nodded. He was halfway between readably British and unreadably other. He had the appropriate mannerisms, but that dark hair and mustardy complexion meant that either his mother or father was from somewhere probably Mediterranean. The boy retreated to one of the book carts behind him, before returning with not one, but rather two books in his hands. He withdrew the call slips and placed them on the counter. "Sir?" The boy squirmed with discomfort. "May I just say how I much I have learned from your work on Italian Humanism."

"Oh, no, no!" Theo waved his hands. "You've learned nothing from me. That's a different Kristeller: Paul Oskar. I'm Theo. No middle name. The chap you have in mind, he died in 1999."

For his entire career, Theo had been regularly mistaken for the famed historian of Renaissance Humanism with whom he shared a last name and nothing else. This other Kristeller had authored ten books and dozens of articles and had taught at Columbia for thirty years. Fiona, his ex-wife, witnessing yet another one of these mix-ups, had once burst out, "For goodness sakes, why not at least claim him as a cousin? It couldn't hurt."

The boy, now undergoing the full, British response to embarrassment—head twitch, nervous biting of the lip, et cetera—managed a hurried, "So sorry, sir," but Theo quickly brushed it off. "No worries at all," he replied.

His cheeks still flushed, the boy cleared his throat. "I noticed, sir, that there was another copy of the book you requested, so I took the liberty of bringing that one up as well."

He must have been a brand-new clerk; this kind of unprompted helpfulness would be thoroughly beaten out of him in another week or two. But of course, he had also thought that he was helping the foremost historian of Renaissance Humanism, not a fifty-something lecturer with two article publications to his name (one technically just a note).

"The same . . ."

"Sorry?"

He cleared his own throat, not that it had been obstructed. What a pair of human awkwardness the two of them were. "I said, is it the same edition, 1606?"

"Yes."

"And this copy is not in the database?"

"No, I saw it when I was retrieving your item. We're understaffed today, so I was helping out in the stacks. It was right next to the volume you requested. Its card must have been misplaced at some point in the old British Library. Probably was misshelved, too. Then, when they moved the books from Russell Square over here to Saint Pancras, someone no doubt corrected the shelf position but forgot to update the electronic database. It's not that uncommon. I've made a note to let data processing know so they can update the computer file."

Theo's eyebrows had already perked up. If this book had been unaccounted for until now, that meant no one had seen the copy for quite a few years.

"Yes, by all means, I would like very much to take a look at it. Thanks for bringing it up."

The clerk nodded, and Theo lifted the books off the counter and returned to his desk. Upon sitting down, he placed his original request of Southwell's *A Poem Declaring the Real Presence of Christ* off to the side and instead opened this other, more mysterious copy. The musty smell of the decaying rag paper wafted up to his nostrils. Oh, these pages had not been perused in a long, long time. Theo scanned for marginalia. He noted light annotation: clearly an early seventeenth-century secretary hand, although one with characteristics that made him pause. God, he did love old books: the feel of their paper, the fixture of their print. He turned to the back to see if the same annotator was inclined—as were many in the period—to take notes on the final leaf. Well, no markings per se, but this was interesting. Someone had apparently folded a loose leaf and then glued it between the back page and the binding.

Theo traced the rectangular shape of the protrusion with his index finger. Then he flipped the book over. Yes, the binding was early seventeenth century, contemporaneous with the poem; he should have noticed that right off the bat. So someone, in a rush to have the book bound, had neglected to remove this added leaf, which pressed now between the binding and the book. Or someone had deliberately bound the book with this leaf lodged within it. Someone with a secret, which anyone in possession of a poem by Southwell in England in the early 1600s was likely to have. And then, centuries had passed, and no one had noticed this protuberance until now? That seemed hard to fathom, although Southwell's work had been quickly relegated—after his martyrdom—to the margins of the English literary tradition. No one had fussed over the poem for centuries, why would anyone have noticed a bump beneath the back leaf of a single copy?

Theo glanced around. No library monitor in sight, and no one seated near him, which was a real stroke of luck. He could make a request for this irregularity to be examined, and the preservationists would get back to him in a few weeks. If they took the leaf out themselves, he would hardly be the first to see it. He was thinking like a Philistine, really. The temptation was outrageous. Then again, if Fiona were here, presented with the same set of circumstances, what would she have done?

He took a quick inventory of his possessions: two mechanical pencils and his legal pad. But there was also a nondescript metal paper clip affixed to the first page of the pad. Theo removed the paper clip and unfolded it. Once more, he surveyed his immediate vicinity. He would have to do this swiftly and quietly, and he could kiss his reader's pass goodbye if he were caught.

With the end of the paper clip, he cut into the crisp paper, around the rectangular bulge, then rotated the book and carefully folded out the leaf in question. It was glued to the binding as he had suspected. Lest its provenance be questioned, Theo went to great pains to unfold the sheet without separating it from the vellum.

He knew what he had uncovered less than a minute later, as the blood rushed to his head and his hand started to shake. He read the lines once, then once again, all while his heart pounded in his chest. Finally, after he was done panting with wonder, he picked up his pencil and copied the last two lines of the scribbled text he had discovered onto his legal pad. He could barely read his own writing. Done with his copying, he hopped to his feet and returned the books to the circulation counter. The same boy as before called him forward—another bit of good fortune. How curious . . . the cards were really falling his way, after not lining up for him for years and years—decades, in fact.

"Could you put these items on hold for me, please?" he asked the young clerk. "I'll be back tomorrow."

"Of course."

Theo's next request was highly unorthodox, and he ventured it with some trepidation, leaning over the counter slightly, the chain of his pocket watch swinging out as he did so. "And perhaps . . . well, if you could put off letting your mates in data processing know about this other quarto just for a day or so, until I have another look, I'd be enormously grateful."

He gave a hopeful smile. The boy paused. He had to know the impropriety of such an arrangement. But he had also committed that *faux pas* with Theo's identity. So there was some guilt there, made all the more prominent by the boy's wobbly status as a Brit. Being an immigrant, the boy had probably tried his hardest for years and years to be as British as possible. Overcompensation. That meant he would either certainly help Theo, or certainly not.

"For one day, sir?"

"A day, yes. Really just this afternoon. I wish to consult another expert on the matter. Once she confirms my hunch, which should be before lunch tomorrow, you might be a part of a rather significant little story—all the more significant if we keep things quiet today."

The boy's bushy eyebrows furrowed. He was thinking hard—too hard. Theo's heart sank. But then the boy suddenly

193

nodded. "Very well. No problem, sir."

Theo thanked him curtly. If he appeared too grateful, his own questionable status as a scholar would be even more glaring, and the gig would be up. He sauntered through security and rushed out of the library proper, nearly running back to his flat—just off of Euston Road on Endsleigh Street. He did have a call to make, to an expert, no less . . . in Renaissance British literature. All of that was true. But Theo didn't need Fiona Tartleton's expert opinion. He just wanted to share his bit of good fortune with her.

Once settled in his flat, with his slippers on and his pipe lit, Theo poured himself a large glass of Bowmore. Perfectly respectable Scotch, although not like the Macallan he used to keep around. Being forced to economize in the arena of alcohol . . . that was a sad state of affairs. Amazing that he had plowed through his inheritance the way he had, but living in London, and spending time in Italy every summer, wasn't cheap. He picked up the phone and dialed Fiona's number. Her phone rang and rang. She must have been out in the garden. He sipped from his drink. Really, he would have let her number ring all afternoon if need be. Finally she answered.

"Fiona, how are you?"

"Theo! What a pleasant surprise."

There was an uncomfortable pause, then some kind of rustling.

"Fiona?"

"Yes?"

"Was that you?"

"No, that was the line, darling. We have a bad connection. I've been tending to my peonies. Please hold on for a moment; let me wash my hands."

He listened to the phone clank against the counter, then heard the water running, like a pleasant stream in the distance. Fiona had beautiful English hands—the fingers long, slender, and pale—and Theo pictured them now, beneath the tap, the soapsuds gathering on the delicate knuckles. Her kitchen was probably fantastic as well, although he had no way of know-ing for sure. He did know that she lived in a restored, seven-teenth-century manor outside of Oxford with her second husband, Ian Teddleton, famed historian and cultural critic. Tartleton and Teddleton, what a pair.

"How are you, Theo? It's so nice to hear your voice."

"I'm fine. I'm actually calling on business. I wanted to ask you what you know about Sonnet 126?"

"Shakespeare?"

"Uh huh."

"You've phoned to ask me about Shakespeare's Sonnet 126?"

"That's right."

"Have you reached the point in your premature dotage, Theo, when it strikes you as acceptable to call and ask me for help in preparing your lesson plans?"

"Indeed, I'm past that point, but I could never use anything you gave me in class. You're too clever; my students would see right through it."

"Oh, you flatter me." Fiona was a sucker for obsequious praise, always had been. "Well, let's see, Sonnet 126. Of course, it's the only twelve-line poem in the sequence, the last poem be-fore the turn to the Dark Lady. It begins, let me see . . . 'O thou, my lovely Boy, who in thy power / Dost hold Time's fickle glass, his sickle, hour . . .'" She did have a score of verse committed to memory, like so many Brits. Theo loved that. "Yes," she went on, "I quite like it. Underappreciated, I should say, as far as the Sonnets go. 'Yet fear her, O thou minion of her pleasure.' I quite like that line: the diminution of the addressee in the face of na-ture's power. That's an ingenious way to circle back to the topic of procreation, don't you think? Without being too obvious."

"I do, yes." Although in truth, Theo wasn't following her entirely.

"Why do you ask about the poem?"

"No reason. Well, that's not true. I just thought you'd want to be the first to be set straight. It turns out the poem isn't twelve lines, it's fourteen."

"Darling, it's twelve. You've been confused by the 1609 Quarto printing, which places brackets at the end, implying missing lines. The printer was ignorant, see? He didn't know that *sonnet*, while typically referring to a fourteen-line poem, could also be used in the Italian sense: *sonnetto*, or little song, in which the number of lines is irrelevant."

"No. Fiona, I have found a manuscript version of the poem. It's fourteen lines long."

There was a slight pause. "Theo, my goodness."

"And it's in Shakespeare's hand." It was the one thing she wouldn't dare question. As someone who could sense where the field of literary studies might turn next, and as a result which authors deserved renewed attention, Fiona was unmatched, but as a paleographer, she was worthless. Theo, however, although incapable of either anticipating coming trends or producing scholarship that might attest to such trends, was nonetheless an excellent paleographer. And, as was true for any scholar of handwriting who specialized in early modern British, he had first cut his teeth on Hand D from the *Sir Thomas More* play. Shakespeare's hand. He knew the Bard's handwriting as well as his own.

Fiona was silent.

"There's more." Theo was just beginning to process fully what had transpired in the British Library. Perhaps that was the real reason he had wanted to phone Fiona: telling her what he had found would make the discovery real. Although it was much too late to save their marriage, Theo still wanted to impress her.

"I'm waiting, Theo."

"The missing lines confirm homosexual entanglement, I'm guessing with Henry Wriothesley, but that's as much because of the Cobbe portrait as anything in the verse itself."

"Theo, Theo, there are plenty of homoerotic suggestions in—"

"This is more, shall I say, pointed." Theo finished his drink with a gulp.

Fiona sighed. "This is all terribly interesting, Theo, but my Yorkies are begging for a walk and I really must run along. Please ring again sometime. Lovely to hear—"

"Shakespeare was Catholic, Fiona. I have irrefutable evidence."

He was hoping for a hushed silence, but instead there was the crackle of the line, combined with the unmistakable sound of her tongue clicking with disapproval. "My goodness, Theo. You simply must get out more, and not to the library. You need to find a pub to call your own, I'm afraid. You are the only adult male in England who needs to drink more, not less."

That cheered him a little, her advice. Teddleton, her husband, was brilliant and famous, but also a lush.

"Have a nice walk, then, Fiona. Great to hear your voice."

"Likewise."

He hung up and poured himself another Scotch. Perhaps he wasn't quite as abstemious with liquor as Fiona thought. But he knew her well, even after all these years, and he was convinced she would ring him back sooner as opposed to later. He sat back down in his chair and cracked open his *Complete Stories of Evelyn Waugh*. Not more than ten minutes later, the phone rang.

"Theo?"

"Fiona, what a pleasure."

"I was thinking here. . . . Well, I don't want you to do something rash with the press on this one. You know how they seize upon anything Shakespeare related and run with it. And you do not, I repeat *you do not*, want to be branded as one of those authorship loons. Perhaps, as a favor, I could swing down tomorrow and take a look at whatever it is you've stumbled upon. A second pair of eyes is usually a good idea with this sort of thing. But before I make the trip, do give me the context: the textual context."

"I'm sorry, I can't." He was too nervous to provide her with any paper trail whatsoever. What if she ended up scooping him? Not intentionally, but what if he became hopelessly stalled with his discovery—began wrestling with minor details, collating this and that—and she ended up publishing the material herself? No, Theo had to hold his cards very close to his chest.

"Well, then, at least read me the lines. The two that you've found. Give me the end of 126 or I won't be able to sleep tonight. *I shall die.*"

She was mocking him with her reference to another poem attributed to Shakespeare five years before. In the intervening years, the case for its attribution had been systematically picked apart by a whole legion of scholars. Well, "Shall I Die?" was hardly Sonnet 126; Theo had the damn poem in Shakespeare's hand. For once he would have the last laugh.

"Please, Theo." She sounded quite desperate, at least by her incredibly high standards of cool. He exhaled slowly. He had thought it would feel good, the whole shoe-on-the-other-foot sensation. And it did, but it wasn't quite as transformative an experience as he had hoped. He was still a failed scholar, and Fiona remained her indomitable self, just momentarily in the dark.

When he had first met her in 1994, Theo had been ahead of Fiona in terms of a first-book project. Fiona's monograph idea, pedestrian in comparison to *Torture and Torment*, was a little study of Queen Elizabeth's private chapels. Upon Fiona finishing her book, and securing a publishing contract, she and Theo decided to celebrate with a holiday in Italy. There, on the heels of an utterly fantastic meal on Lake Como (Theo, at the time, still flush with funds), the two of them decided, impulsively, to marry. When they returned to England, and to reliable gossip that Queen Mary, University of London would very likely be hiring in their field in the coming fall, Fiona declared her intention of writing another book over the course of the next five months so as to improve her chances of landing the position. Theo hardly paid her pronouncement any attention, but sure enough, Fiona did manage to complete a book on the Leicester Circle and Philip Sidney's *Arcadia*, really not bad work at all. Before the winter lifted that following year, the job at Queen Mary was hers. Still, all remained just fine between them. Theo was now officially moving slowly on *Torture and Torment*, but it was a big book, and big books—they both agreed—took time.

Then, in that same calendar year, Fiona finished *another* book—on Francis Bacon and court intrigue. This one had sent her deep into archives all across England, places where the most prominent and esteemed early modern scholars spent their time. And now, just as it became clear to Theo that his wife was on her way toward the primum mobile of the academic universe, whereas he was just a disheveled, wandering star, word trickled back that Fiona was engaged in some improprieties with an academic far more successful than was he.

The news of Teddleton's seduction of his wife, combined with the avalanche of praise and awards heaped on Fiona's book on Bacon, all made Theo panic and do something quite ridiculous. He abandoned *Torture and Torment* to write a monograph on Giambattista della Porta, an Italian scientist who had penned a book called *Natural Magick* in the 1550s. *Natural Magick* was a quasi-scientific treatise filled with absurd assumptions about the material world. Theo had imagined that a study of this book would serve as a kind of counterpoint to Fiona's stately meditation on the birth of empiricism. He would win her back by countering her Bacon, her Teddleton, with a man who believed that frogs came into being when the sun's rays mixed with mud. A small victory for the crackpots. Instead, Theo's desperation made Fiona lose the last bit of respect for him. So when an offer from Jesus came down—Jesus College, Oxford, that is, where Teddleton, coincidentally, was chair of the hiring committee—Fiona accepted it immediately. A short time later, she served Theo with divorce papers.

Their divorce actually proceeded with little acrimony. At the time, what pained Theo more than his marriage crumbling was the status of his own academic career. Della Porta wasn't quite the crackpot Theo had assumed; in the field of optics, for example, some of his theories ended up being accredited by subsequent experimenters, which Theo would have learned in a more timely manner if he had bothered to consult secondary materials on della Porta early on, instead of focusing exclusively on primary materials for months and months, as he always did. Feeling betrayed by the unanticipated legitimacy of his subject, Theo cast the scientist aside and returned once more to *Torture and Torment*. This return, though, was less the recommencement of a stalled journey than a sinking ship itself, turning around once more to strike the rock that had crippled it in the first place. Theo continued to poke around in archives, looking at books written by or about Catholics—most of which he had already examined—but he didn't even attempt to turn any of his notes into academic prose. By that point, *Torture and Torment* referred in his mind less to those who had suffered for their religious beliefs than to Theo's own, unrealizable treatment of such figures.

"The missing lines, love. From the poem?"

"Sorry." No need to check his scribblings for the couplet in question; he had memorized these two lines without any effort whatsoever. "'Yet still I wait, one Will to thou will's slight, / Whilst behind our dark love pricks nothing's right.'"

The pun on *Will*, not to mention the juxtaposition of the anus (*behind*) with the period's slang for vagina (*nothing*) made it patently clear that Theo hadn't made up the lines himself. They were far too clever for his talents, and far too bawdy for his taste. There was, he was quite certain, no more direct reference to sodomy in any of the other sonnets, nothing that so precisely *pricked* a "dark love" in the butt. Perhaps the closest one got to such tomfoolery was in Sonnet 20, where "nature" was said to have "pricked" the speaker's male friend, but that was a female figure fiddling with a male, however indecorously. The end of Sonnet 126 was clearly man on man. Indeed, that last bit was probably punning on the homonym *right/rite*, thereby juxtaposing the sexual relations between the men with sanctioned marriage relations. Of course, the two lines spilled over with insinuation and meaning, like everything that dripped from Shakespeare's quill.

"And you believe it is Wriothesley being referenced there?"

"It's less the pairing that interests me than the context in which I discovered the sonnet."

"The context that you refuse to provide for me?"

"Yes, at least for the time being."

"Perhaps I will be able to convince you otherwise tomorrow morning?"

"Yes, perhaps. But for now, I must run along. I'm, uh, going to take your advice and meander over to a pub."

"Oh, Theo." He was a terrible liar and pictured her shaking her head at him. "Theo, Theo, Theo. I think I preferred your brief dabbling in early modern quack science to this devout, Tory phase of yours. It has really taken a toll, I'm afraid."

"Please . . ."

He wanted her to stop there, but she didn't. "I had always assumed—when you started going to church—that eventually you'd come out of the closet. But you really aren't gay. Even though you read Evelyn Waugh. You actually believe in the whole Christian God business, don't you? Choirs of angels and blest kingdoms and virgin births. That's probably hardest for me to swallow, you gobbling up all that malarkey."

"That's a little intolerant, don't you think?"

"I'm just being honest."

What people got away with saying these days by virtue of claiming honesty appalled Theo. How he longed for a time when men and women kept their daggered words to themselves, even if it meant the occasional public execution.

"Give my best to Ian, Fiona."

"See you tomorrow morning, Theo."

"See you tomorrow."

THEO AWOKE EARLY THE FOLLOWING MORNING, made himself a strong cup of tea, along with a piece of toast, and hustled off to Mass. He was one of a handful of parishioners in attendance. Among the others was a woman who had to be in her eighties, accompanied by an oxygen tank. During the celebration of the Eucharist, the click of her breathing machine became oddly synchronized with the priest's pauses, so that it sounded as if God were being asked to work his miracle of transubstantiation to the beat of a metronome. With each click, Theo would lurch in his pew, but he was alone among the congregation in acting perturbed. Even the priest seemed entirely unfazed by the interruptions. Everyone was so passive these days, so accommodating, which didn't mean—in Theo's estimation—that people cared more for other people, or were more empathetic. It just meant that they cared less about everything than they once had.

When the doors to the British Library opened, Theo was among the very first readers to queue up. He dutifully removed his belt and placed it, along with his two mechanical pencils and legal pad, on the conveyor belt that ran beneath the X-ray machine. Then he stepped through the metal detector, just as it emitted a rather hideous buzz. The burly guard with the wan, freckled skin, red hair, and bushy sideburns stepped over to him and asked him to spread his arms.

With a gasp, Theo realized that he had neglected to deposit his Swiss Army knife keychain in one of the small lockers in the lobby. What an unprecedented oversight on his part, although—in his defense—he had never had anything like Sonnet 126 to distract him before.

He pulled the tiny pocketknife from his pants pocket, only to have the guard swipe it from his hand.

"What have we here?"

"Yes, so sorry about that. I neglected—"

"You can't bring this into the library!"

Theo could hear the shuffling of impatient feet behind him. "Of course I didn't intend . . ."

The guard had strode away from him. Now he folded out the miniature blade from one of the knife's three small compartments and peered at it as if it were a very small Rosetta Stone. The seconds felt like hours. Finally he closed up the instrument. Theo prepared to bask in what would surely be a mortified reaction when this guard handed over the knife and realized how rudely he had treated him. It was, after all, Theobald Kristeller here, someone security had observed entering and leaving the library thousands of times. But as he returned the Swiss Army knife to Theo's open palm, pointing back toward the lobby with his other hand as he did so, the guard betrayed no hint of familiarity.

"Hurry along now," he said, waving him off. "You're slowing down my line."

Theo assembled his belongings and stepped once more through the detector, which buzzed again. He made his way to the lobby, past the now serpentine expanse of scholars, each of whom manifested supreme annoyance with him in one way or another: a sigh here, an upraised lip there, and so on. He locked away his keychain and then queued up once more. This time, he made it through the detector without causing any problems. And the same burly guard, who watched as he reaffixed his belt for the second time that morning, said nothing at all.

For his workspace that day, Theo uncharacteristically chose a desk in the far corner of the enormous room. At the circulation counter, he asked for the two copies of Southwell's *Real Presence* he had placed on reserve the day before. The boy wasn't there; Theo's items were retrieved by one of the miserably crabby older clerks—bespectacled, with a crooked moustache. Theo carried the books like a Communion chalice toward his desk. After placing them squarely in front of his chair, he sat down.

He began by rereading the sonnet. Like the venerable Samuel Johnson, Theobald Kristeller found himself irritated by the Bard's incessant wordplay. "Who hast by waning grown, and therein show'st," line three of Sonnet 126, was surely playing around with the homonym *grown/groan*. Had Shakespeare been similarly disposed to such shenanigans in conversation? Must have driven his friends batty. With the poem now fresh in his mind, Theo peered at the lines themselves, looking for the telltale, paleographic features of Shakespeare's rather shabby secretary hand: the bold, slightly loopy *s* in "glass" (line two), and the "show'st" of line three, although where the Bard's handwriting most clearly distinguished itself was probably in line four: "Thy lover's withering, as thy sweet self grow'st." Whether or not anyone else had ever written as well as him was perhaps debatable (Donne was certainly as smart, and Cervantes's prose style was admirable, although Theo's appreciation was limited to the English translation), but no one had—strictly speaking—*written* like the Bard in early modern England. Those *s*'s were Shakespeare's alone. Really not such a complicated paleographic case to prove, this one. Theo leaned back in his chair contentedly.

Then, for some reason, he thought of the security guard again. On the prowl for knives, the man should have been checking for paper clips. He had failed to recognize him, after all these years. . . . Well, quite soon he would know Theobald Kristeller all too well. Theo would have his revenge on him.

He had rocked back in his chair imagining this man's comeuppance, but now the wooden legs rested firmly on the floor. Would he really have revenge? The guard would certainly never admit as much. How could the discovery of Sonnet 126 really make up for all the time Theo had frittered away in the British Library?

With an unpleasant, nearly audible *hiss*, Theo felt the balloon of his rising expectations begin to deflate. What exactly was he supposed to *do* with this discovery of his? Hold a press conference? Then what? Well, he'd find himself mired in the high-stakes world of literary scholarship. The reading room would be an absolute zoo. Once they discovered he had butchered one of the books, they'd snatch away his pass, probably get a search warrant to check his flat for pilfered items. And it wasn't as if All Souls College would come calling: not for someone his age, with his résumé. No, regardless of what he did now, regardless of what he might have found, Theobald Kristeller wasn't going to get another chance at an academic career. He had had his career, or more accurately, had missed his opportunity to have one. Not even Sonnet 126 could change that.

As he thought about his situation more, from this new, more earthly perspective, Theo realized the sheer magnitude of what he faced. Sonnet 126 did present opportunities for him, of course, but it also promised certain humiliations. For starters, he would never be able to pull off successfully some public unveiling of the poem. He would stutter and bumble; he would sweat and shake. Theobald Kristeller had always been a little shy, but he was more so now than ever, having failed to achieve the scholarly station he had once dreamt of, and having chosen to settle in London, where—even if he had grown up in one of the neighboring enclaves, like Amersham, rather than Missouri—he would have always been viewed as an interloper.

He slumped in his chair. Wouldn't being a sudden *cause célèbre* just throw into greater relief how little he had accomplished as a scholar? Not to mention, it wasn't as if he'd ever be able to follow up on something like the discovery of Sonnet 126. He would be a one-hit wonder, but his life would still be flipped upside down as a result. Much to his surprise, Theo found himself resisting the scenario he had first imagined the day before—getting the last laugh, or however he had put it to himself. Perhaps he actually *liked* his little life more than he had assumed, save for the fact that he was lonely at night and felt like a loser during the day. Perhaps notoriety, what Fiona had always hungered for, really didn't hold much appeal for him, after all.

So what *did* he want, if not the fame of having discovered the end of Sonnet 126? Theo stared out across the library, adrift in the emptiness of thought. What a fool he had been to organize his life so that, when he wasn't alone in his flat, he could be found either in a church or a library, places where interaction with others was more or less forbidden, unless one was being harassed for a penknife the size of a postage stamp. Far too much opportunity to mull over things. Yet again, he recalled the hostile gaze of the security guard, and next he thought—for some reason—of the elderly woman from mass that morning, the one with the clicking oxygen tank. He had wanted to scoff at her for being a nuisance, but like her, he was tethered thinly to life. Everyone was just one small accident, just one trivial misstep, from annihilation. And he was in his fifties now—certainly not getting younger.

Theo folded his hands on his desk. Ian Teddleton. What an

ass. In these quiet enclaves, in naves and reading rooms, Theo had been stewing over that injustice all these years. *That* was his real problem. Being cheated upon, being *left*, had been so hard for him to accept. Not right at the time, but over the years that followed. All that blather in the media about adulterers being gnawed at by their guilty consciences, all the trumpeting of the merits of fidelity and monogamy, all of that crap was just intended to give solace to people like Theo. People who had been left behind. The truth was, adulterers were the ones who gained by virtue of their behavior. They remade themselves. They took charge of their lives. And, in the process, they had fun. Whereas the people who were dumped, they felt sorry for themselves. They withdrew from others, grew lonely, drank too much, watched too much TV. Their moral superiority garnered them nothing.

He rose to his feet, picked up the two copies of Southwell's poem, and returned to the circulation counter. The boy from the day before had apparently just begun his shift. Theo waved along several patrons until he was able to approach him and set the books down on the counter.

"The scholar Fiona Tartleton shall be calling up these items in a little bit," Theo announced stiffly. "Please permit her access to them. She'll need a moment or two with your head preservationist, as well."

The boy nodded. If Fiona Tartleton's name had impressed him, and Theo assumed it must have, he had kept it to himself.

"There is some interesting material here, which your industry helped uncover." Theo placed his hand gently on the volumes. "You shall make a fine librarian."

"Thank you, sir."

He rapped the counter authoritatively with his knuckle and headed for the exit. After passing through security with utter anonymity, and retrieving his keychain from the locker in which he had deposited it, Theo decided to wait for Fiona in the foyer. He had calculated that she wouldn't be on the first train down from Oxford—she'd begin the day fussing around with her dogs or what have you—but she would be on one soon thereafter. And sure enough, in no time at all, he made her out, barreling across the concourse outside, a Burberry comet headed right toward him. Her raven-black hair. Plus, she had cuckolded him. Yes, of course, she was his Dark Lady.

She stepped through the glass doors and rushed over to him. "Theo!"

"Fiona." He embraced her awkwardly. She tapped his back once with her flat hand. "Tea?" he asked her.

"No, thank you."

She was all business. He stepped over to the side, away from the stream of readers flowing toward the library doors.

"The find has been confirmed," he said matter-of-factly.

"Has it? By you alone, I suppose?"

He nodded. Fiona inhaled deeply, then adjusted the pearl brooch in her hair that didn't need adjusting. "Theo, if we are to embark on this adventure, we must proceed in a highly systematic manner, which is to say, we'll have to follow my playbook more than yours. To begin, we shall need to conduct a thorough chemical evaluation of the rag paper and ink to establish period authenticity, which means touching base with the head preservationist—"

"I've left word that you'll need to see him."

"*We*, you mean. I'm not doing that grunt work on my own."

From the moment he had phoned her, Fiona had just assumed that Theo was offering to partner with her in announcing the discovery of Sonnet 126. Even when he had claimed otherwise, she had ignored him, no doubt confident that he would recoil when faced with the prospects of confronting the media—not to mention other scholars—all on his own. He had told himself blithely that he had reached out to Fiona simply to gloat, but that was ridiculous. Deep down, he had known right away that he would need her guidance. And that was yet another problem with regard to Sonnet 126. Like everything from that blasted literary period, it anchored him to his ex-wife.

"I want you to claim the discovery, Fiona. On your own."

Her small head, so birdlike and angular, rolled back on its neck. "What are you talking about?"

"You can have Sonnet 126."

"Have it? But this could change your life, Theo!"

"In more ways than one. For example, I'm afraid I wasn't as orthodox in my handling of the book in question as I might have been. I used the end of a paper clip to liberate the poem from the back binding—"

"The means used to achieve your discovery do not mitigate the discovery. But desecrating a rare book! Good God."

Perhaps, if presented with the same set of circumstances, Fiona Tartleton wouldn't have behaved in a similar fashion.

"It was an impulsive—"

"You'll be a marked man in libraries from now on, in more ways than one."

"Precisely. And I don't want to be marked."

"You don't want to be famous? After all the setbacks you've endured?"

Clearly she was thinking of their divorce as much as scholarly accomplishments, or lack thereof. "I don't think I do want to be famous, in fact. Funny, isn't it? I think I quite like my little life, although it does need some rather serious alterations."

Fiona shook her head. He could see her slowly wrapping her brain around the tremendous opportunity being presented to her. The ambition colored her face like a drug. "To give this to me, Theo, after . . ."

"Your infidelity to me . . ."

". . . It's incredibly generous. Unusually so. I'm not sure if I can fathom entirely—"

"I've let the young boy at circulation know that you'll be requesting the items reserved under my name. Do make sure he is appropriately lauded, as he found the book in the first place."

"Slow down, Theo. Please. I'm dizzy. What is going on here?"

Theo breathed deeply through his nostrils. He did feel a little lightheaded himself. "I think, Fiona, that this uncovering of mine, this little book of wonders I've stumbled upon, I think it might open up other possibilities for me. Or bring to a close a very long . . . a very long chapter in my life."

"Well of course it will, Theo! That's why I came down from Oxford. To help you manage this opportunity. It's a grand thing."

"Yes, it is, but not in the way *you* think it is, Fiona. At least not to me. You see, I think I want more than books for my life. I think I want more than rag paper and ink. What you said about me finding a pub to call my own. . . . Well, you were onto something—figuratively, if not literally. I want to bloom, Fiona. Like one of the flowers in your garden. I'm not too old to come alive. But not here—neither in this library, nor in the learned world it represents. So I'm going to leave you here, with Sonnet 126, catch a taxi, and go over to the Tate Modern. Even though I hate modern art, I'm going to go over there, meander around, and look for a woman whose appreciation of sculptures made of toilet paper rolls and canvases with cow dung smeared on them is as strained as mine. And, God willing, perhaps I will approach such a woman and ask her if she might want to have tea. I'm done with the business of old books, Fiona. I *want* to be done with it. Enough torture and torment."

How remarkable. A tear had welled up in the corner of Fiona's right eye. What sounded like rebirth to his ears must have rang like suicide to hers. Further confirmation that he was doing the right thing. Theo withdrew a handkerchief from his back pocket and blew his nose. "He just turned his back and left it all, too, you know?" he added.

"Who's that?"

"Shakespeare. The biggest mystery in all of literature. How could he have just retired to Stratford? Just left London and the theater behind? But, see, it was *because* he had given so much of himself away. That was why he could just stop. He wasn't after eternity, not when he glimpsed the arc of his own life coming to an end. He just wanted, before he died, to enjoy his time on this distracted globe. If literature should teach us anything, surely it should teach us that literature is not the only thing that matters in life."

He clasped her hand, a more genuine gesture of intimacy than that ridiculous hug he had attempted a few minutes before, and then made a move to doff his Ascot cap. But Theo wasn't wearing an Ascot. He hadn't worn a hat in years and years—since he and Fiona had first been married. What, were the muscles in his body taking him back in time so that *he* could be the first to leave the other behind? With a smile and an out-of-the-ordinary hop in his step, Theobald Kristeller bid adieu to Fiona Tartleton, then unceremoniously dumped his pencils and legal pad in the trashcan just inside the front doors. Outside, it was drizzling and a touch cold. He headed over to Euston Road and began to walk up the street, his hand extended above his head, waving for a taxi as he marched past bookshops and Indian restaurants. All he had needed to change his life, it turned out, were two lines of poetry. Granted, lines written by Shakespeare, but still—just a couplet did the trick. At long last, Theo was off to pastures new.

Faucets

MALCOLM RADRICK, A THIRD GRADER at Edison Elementary in Middletown, always went to the bathroom right at the beginning of recess. He preferred being in there when his classmates were outside because it was quieter then and more private. Although he was only nine years old, Malcolm was particular about a few things: going to the bathroom, obviously, but also not mixing up his foods when he ate and keeping his shirts and pants sorted in the left- and right-hand drawers, respectively, of his dresser. That way, in the morning, it was easy for him to reach in, pull out an item of clothing with each hand, and be dressed and ready to go just like that.

Archibald Masterson, six-term Middletown mayor, who—in addition to being an architect—also fancied himself as something of an urban planner, had designed Edison Elementary School in 1955, right on the heels of the Brown versus Board of Education Supreme Court decision. Archibald felt that central bathrooms at Edison might provide too much of an opportunity down the road for future black students at the school to plot some kind of violent, mob activity. His plans dictated that a bathroom be located in the corner of each classroom. Like many

211

of his fellow Middletown residents in the late 1950s, Archibald's imagination tended to run wild on issues of race. Still, the anticipated deluge of black students never arrived in Middletown, and even now, fifty years later, the town remained overwhelmingly white.

The dingy state of the bathroom in his classroom at school usually encouraged Malcolm to get his business done as quickly as possible. After flushing the toilet and washing his hands, he would normally sprint straight outside to join his classmates on the playground. That day, however, he altered his routine ever so slightly, for rather than turning off the faucet after he was done washing his hands, he left the water running.

Over the course of the next several weeks, Malcolm would be asked again and again to explain this decision on his part. Principal Peters would ask him. So would Dr. Shannon, the child psychologist he would eventually see. And his parents, more than once. Why, they all wanted to know, had he made this curious choice?

Unfortunately, Malcolm was incapable of giving a satisfactory answer. He came up with responses, but none of them ever rang true either to him or—he suspected, based on how they reacted—to the adults who heard them. The truth was, Malcolm had no idea why he had decided abruptly not to turn off the faucet. At the very end of that first day, when Mrs. Henry lined up Malcolm and his classmates to march them outside to their parents' idling SUVs, she let everyone know that someone had left the water on in the bathroom before recess. Wasn't everyone aware, she asked incredulously, that wasting water hurt nature? But even as Malcolm nodded and intoned with the rest of his classmates, "Yes, Mrs. Henry," he realized that from now on, he was *always* going to leave the water running, regardless of whether or not he hurt nature in the process. As of that day, leaving faucets on was just something that Malcolm Radrick knew that he needed to do, even though he had no idea why.

Faucets

MALCOLM'S PARENTS, JIM AND LIZA RADRICK, had been married for twelve years. They were a *mixed couple*: local lingo for a husband and wife who weren't both from Middletown. Liza had grown up two towns over, in Naderville. Folks in Middletown called the place Nadir. *Nothing middling about Nadir*, the joke went. Jim had ended up spending some time there in his mid-twenties, however, building homes for Frank Lufkin's construction company. He met Liza while she was waiting tables at the Greasy Spoon, a popular Naderville diner.

If Jim hadn't ventured into Naderville for work, he and Liza probably wouldn't have ever met. Liza certainly wouldn't have run into Jim in Middletown; if you weren't from that enclave, you tended not to visit. For starters, it was confusing, just driving into the place. This was deliberate. During his tenure as mayor, Archibald Masterson had redesigned the city to keep the outside world at bay. Rather than a patchwork of different neighborhoods, Middletown was comprised of nine distinct districts, or *loops*, as they were known. Each loop was contained within two broad boulevards, each of which formed a concentric circle around the center of town. There were nine such loops. The business route that branched off the interstate actually circled Middletown. A motorist therefore couldn't simply drive *into* town; he or she had to choose an exit. But the exit signs themselves didn't make this choice an easy one. They were numbered, although not sequentially, and not so as to correspond with the well-known loop numbers.

Malcolm and his parents lived in a two-story, redbrick, three-bedroom home in the decidedly middle-class third loop, just a few blocks from Edison Elementary. Three years earlier, Jim had left Lufkin Construction and became a self-employed carpenter and wood craftsman. Liza was employed as a bookkeeper in a carpet wholesaler over in the sixth. Her job paid very little—she barely worked thirty hours a week—but her schedule enabled her to pick up Malcolm from school. They'd come home, Malcolm would have a small snack, and then they'd do something together: play a board game or drive to Old Town (the first loop) and walk through the pedestrian mall. Between five and six, Jim would arrive home, and Malcolm would rush out to the driveway and help him unload the back of his truck. Then they'd have dinner, after which Jim and Malcolm usually headed upstairs for showers while Liza did the dishes. Around eight thirty, they would put Malcolm to bed, and usually by ten, Liza and Jim were asleep themselves.

That night, both Jim and Liza were tired, so it wasn't very long after Malcolm was asleep that Liza put on her nightgown and went into the bathroom. Much to her surprise, she discovered that the faucet in the sink was running.

"Honey?" She stepped back through their narrow hallway. Jim was in bed, reading *Sports Illustrated*. "Did you leave the faucet running in the bathroom?"

"Nope," Jim said from behind his magazine.

"Well, that's strange." Liza proceeded to brush her teeth, apply her facial cleanser, and rub her cocoa butter smoothing lotion on her arms and legs. Before joining her husband in bed, she checked to make sure the faucet was turned off. Then, in a matter of minutes, she was fast asleep.

THE NEXT DAY, A TUESDAY, Malcolm once more left the water running in the bathroom in his classroom. Again, when they lined up at the end of the day, Mrs. Henry reminded the class to conserve resources. The following day, after finding the water running during recess, she called Malcolm over to her desk during independent reading time.

"What's going on?" she asked the boy in a soft, hushed tone. "Why won't you turn off the faucet after you use the bathroom?"

Malcolm shrugged.

"Are you forgetting to turn it off?"

He thought that maybe by answering in the affirmative she'd drop the subject, so he nodded.

"Well, what can we do to help you remember? Is this something we should meet with your parents to discuss?"

That was really the last thing in the world Malcolm wanted to do. He shook his head.

"Okay, then I'm going to ask that you stop using the restroom right before recess, and I'm also going to ask that you try extra hard to remember to turn off the faucet. We'll see how you do tomorrow and take it from there."

Malcolm nodded in agreement. The next, day, however, didn't go very well. First, when he tried to go to the bathroom earlier in the day than he normally did, Malcolm found that he couldn't. Then, about ten minutes before the bell rang for recess, Lucy Hinkler projectile vomited onto her desk. Some of this vomit ended up in Adam Wiltner's backpack. Adam Wiltner was very particular about his stuff—much more so than Malcolm or, indeed, anyone else in the class—and when he discovered his backpack sprayed with puke, he began to cry and shake.

In the midst of this chaos, Malcolm suddenly had to pee very badly. He knew not to pester Mrs. Henry during a crisis, so rather than ask permission, he simply walked over to the restroom. Before going in, however, he swore to himself that he wouldn't leave the water running. One thing led to another, however, and after just a few seconds Malcolm realized he had to do a lot more than pee. In the meantime, the bell rang, signaling recess. Mrs. Henry waved her children out onto the playground and found Mr. Evans, the school custodian, in the hallway. He said he'd take care of the mess—Malcolm heard this from the restroom—so Mrs. Henry rushed off to the front office with both Lucy and Adam in tow.

It only took Mr. Evans a couple of minutes to wipe up and disinfect the desk and the floor around Lucy's chair. He was half-way to the front office when Malcolm finished going to the bathroom. After he flushed the toilet, he considered not washing his hands at all. That way he wouldn't have anything to do with the sink. But for his entire childhood, Malcolm's parents had always drummed into his head the importance of combating germs at every opportunity, so he just couldn't bring himself *not* to wash his hands; and once the faucet was running, Malcolm couldn't bring himself to turn it off.

After dropping off Lucy and Adam at the principal's office, where Mary Jo Martin, the school administrator, could arrange their pickups, Mrs. Henry headed back to her classroom. On the way past the faculty lounge, however, she was reminded of the birthday party for Mrs. Greenwald. So she dropped in for a piece of cake.

When the bell rang to announce the end of lunch, Mrs. Henry walked over to the cafeteria to fetch her students. Unbeknownst to her, the sink in her classroom bathroom had been partially clogged for years and years. This hadn't mattered when the faucet was turned on and then off after a few seconds, or after a few minutes—as had been the case all three times Malcolm had previously left it on. But when the water just ran and ran, as it did that day, eventually the drain clogged completely.

The minute she stepped into her classroom and saw the water pooling on the floor, Mrs. Henry realized what had happened. Without thinking, she rushed to turn off the faucet. Her feet slipped beneath her, though, and she came down hard on her side. When she hit the floor, she let out a terrifying scream.

The ambulance didn't pull up at Edison for another twenty minutes. It took an additional ten before the paramedics managed to lift the somewhat plump Mrs. Henry onto a gurney. Principal Peters, who had been meeting with a group of parents, caught up to the gurney just as they were about to lift it into the ambulance. When Mrs. Henry saw him, she reached out and grabbed him by the arm. "Dan!" she said. "One of my kids, Malcolm Radrick, won't turn off the damn faucet in the bathroom. It's like he's trying to flood the school. You got to help me out on this one. Please!"

THE NEXT MORNING, BEFORE SCHOOL STARTED, Malcolm and his parents met with Principal Peters in his office.

"As I explained over the phone to your parents," the principal said to Malcolm, after a few pleasantries had been exchanged between the adults and the Radrick family had sat down in the row of chairs in front of his desk, "we cannot have students disobeying their teachers, particularly if their behavior is going to make school dangerous for others. Mrs. Henry has a contusion now on her hip from her fall. Do you know what a contusion is, Malcolm?" Malcolm shook his head. "Well, it's a very serious kind of bruise: very painful. So I'd like to ask you a question, Malcolm, regarding the faucet in your classroom bathroom. What I'd like to know is why, suddenly, you have decided *not* to turn it off?"

Malcolm sat very still, hoping that an answer to this question would spring to mind. Nothing sprang, though. Everyone was waiting for him to explain himself. He cleared his throat. "I like the way the water looks," he said softly. "The way it coils toward the drain. I like the sound the water makes. It's pretty loud, if you think about it."

He could tell, by the way Principal Peters and his parents sat still, staring at him, that they weren't very satisfied by his answer.

"Are you, in any way, trying to damage the school? Flood it, perhaps, so we have to cancel classes?"

Malcolm shook his head.

The principal tapped his desk. "Well, until you're absolutely sure you won't leave the faucet running, I'm going to ask that, if you need to use the restroom, you let your teacher know. She'll page us via the intercom, and Mrs. Martin will come down to get you. Then you'll use the bathroom here in the front office. Okay?"

Malcolm tried to nod but it was hard, moving his head. His lip was quivering. He didn't want to have to leave his classroom every time he needed to use the restroom. That would be embarrassing. He wondered if there was a different faucet somewhere else in the building that they might keep on for him. Maybe one in the basement? But he didn't dare ask.

"All right, then." Principal Peters clapped his hands. "Now I'm going to request that you take a seat on the bench outside my office. I just want to talk to your parents for a moment."

Malcolm nodded and left the room.

"We're so sorry about all this, Dan," Jim said, sighing. He had been ahead of Dan in high school and hadn't really known him growing up, but he had played baseball with his older brother, Brad, and he was incredibly embarrassed to be sitting there, talking about his son and faucets.

Principal Peters rolled back from his desk in his chair and crossed his legs. "Look, if it makes you feel any better, there has been a rash of this kind of behavior all across town. The kids get ideas, you know? From TV and stuff."

Liza took note of this comment because Malcolm, in fact, had very little exposure to TV. They had one, of course, in the living room, but except when Jim watched sporting events on the weekends, it remained off.

"For example," Principal Peters continued, "a couple of months ago, a child at Abe Lincoln over in the fourth loop was opening windows, over and over again. In the middle of the winter! And another kid at Jefferson, he started emptying the napkin dispensers in the cafeteria. This was last fall. He'd take all the napkins out and pile them on a chair. Crazy, huh?"

Jim and Liza shook their heads.

Principal Peters ran his fingers through his thinning brown hair. "Malcolm's going to have to whip this thing, and he might need a little help. There's a child psychiatrist named Mary Shannon who has a great reputation, working with kids who are struggling, you know, with mental . . . things. I know the napkin kid, for example, has been seeing her—"

"I'm not sure that Malcolm needs to see a psychiatrist," Liza interjected. "He has always done very well in school—"

"Liza, please," Jim whispered.

Dan Peters cleared his throat. He reminded himself that Liza was from Naderville. People from outside the loops didn't always see things the same way as Middletowners. "You're right, Liza. Malcolm *is* a fine student. But I think we can all agree"— and now the principal turned to Jim in the hopes he'd at least understand what he was getting at—"that your son might have some kind of—and, again, I'm not a doctor—but some kind of . . . obsessive-compulsive thing with regards to faucets. Dr. Shannon might be able to help."

He slid his card across the desk, on the back of which he had written Dr. Shannon's number. Jim picked up the card and handed it to Liza, who put it in her purse.

"We'll give her a call," Jim said. He was relieved that a solution to their problem had so quickly appeared. In the coming weeks, Jim had a lot of work that needed to get done. Moreover, he didn't want people talking about them. He just wanted a simple, quiet life—the kind that Middletown was known for offering.

Liza said nothing. The three of them stood up and shook hands. In the midst of their conversation, the bell had rung, and Malcolm had been shepherded to class. The Radricks made their way out to the parking lot, where—knowing they'd have to rush off to work—they had driven separately and parked next to one another.

"We aren't putting our kid on drugs because he's been forgetting lately to turn off the faucet," Liza said to her husband.

"No one said anything about drugs." Jim leaned against the tailgate of his truck.

"That's what Dan was implying."

Jim sighed. "You got to admit though, Liza, this is a strange one—what we've got on our hands here. Don't you think we should explore our options? Get this fixed so that we can move on?"

"We aren't putting our kid on drugs," Liza said once more. She hated to hear her husband describe their son as if he were a problem that needed to be fixed, like a cabinet with a faulty hinge. So without another word, she stepped into her car and drove off to work.

THAT SAME AFTERNOON, prior to picking up Malcolm from school, Liza swung by the house to change into some sweatpants and jogging shoes. Then she drove Malcolm over to

219

the Middletown Oval, or the M-Oval, as it was known in town, so that the two of them could take a walk together. Among his many innovations as mayor, Archibald Masterson had eliminated all sidewalks in town, and passed city ordinances prohibiting people from walking in the streets. His concern had been for the safety of Middletown's youth; he wanted to protect them not simply from being run over, but also from being abducted by people who might somehow infiltrate the loop system from the outside and then find themselves free to prey upon the innocent children of Middletown.

After parking and filling up a water bottle, Liza and Malcolm began to walk in adjoining lanes on the oval.

"So how was school today?" she asked Malcolm.

"Good," he said.

"Who did you play with at recess?"

"Mostly Charlie and Andrew."

"What'd you do?"

"We did kickball, then tetherball. Andrew really likes tetherball."

Liza reminded herself to swing her arms as she walked. It was supposed to help raise your heart rate.

"How did things go, in the bathroom?"

"Mom . . ."

"We did meet with the principal this morning. I think I can ask."

"It went fine."

"I'm glad."

Of course, Liza wanted to ask her son what he thought might have caused the whole thing with faucets to take hold of him, but she didn't want to press too hard. "Would you like to have Charlie and Andrew over this weekend for a play date?"

Malcolm nodded.

"Remind me to call their moms. You all can build a fort in the living room."

"With *all* the pillows and comforters from the bedrooms?"

He looked up at her, his blond hair slightly spiked, his cheeks rosy, his new, adult teeth jutting over his lip. "Every one," she said.

THAT SAME NIGHT, Liza felt that their home life had returned somewhat to normal. When Jim arrived home, Malcolm helped him unload the truck, stacking the two-by-fours in the garage and carrying his dad's tool belt down to his workshop in the basement. Jim had some drawings to go over that night, but after Malcolm finished his shower, he lingered until Liza came upstairs and offered to put their son to bed. While Liza started the bedtime process, her husband said he was going to lie down for a minute or two. He dozed off. When he woke up, Liza was in bed, reading a magazine next to him, and Malcolm was fast asleep. Liza suggested he put off his work until the next morning, but Jim said he'd rather just get it done, so he said goodnight and headed down to the basement. A minute later, she heard footsteps as he rushed upstairs.

"He turned the . . ." Jim stood in the doorway to their room, fuming: his cheeks flushed red, his eyes wide. "He left the faucet running in the basement!"

"Jim, please. He's sleeping. Don't alarm him—"

"Don't alarm him! Liza, there's water all over the floor!"

He turned and marched into Malcolm's room. Liza leapt out of bed. She had never seen her husband so livid before. From the doorway to their boy's room, she watched as he pulled down the sheets in Malcolm's bed and lifted the boy off the mattress by his shoulders.

"You've got to stop this, son!" he said, holding him so that their faces nearly touched. The boy's sleepy head rolled from one side to the other. "Malcolm! You have to stop this!"

Malcolm's eyes opened. "Dad?"

"You cannot let the faucets run! That sink in the basement has a slow drain. When did you turn that faucet on?"

"Jim, please!" Liza stood in the doorway. Where was all this anger on his part coming from? Simply a running faucet?

"I . . ." Malcolm's lip quivered, just as it had in Principal

221

Peters's office.

"When did you turn on the faucet? When you took my tool belt downstairs?"

Malcolm nodded, his eyes filling with tears.

"Jim, calm down!" Liza rushed to the bed. She took her son in her arms, resting his head against her chest. Jim stepped back from both of them.

"This is not acceptable," he said. "Do you understand, son? This is unacceptable."

Malcolm was crying.

"You have to stop this!" Jim said. "You have to."

"I can't," Malcolm said, sniffling. "I, I can't stop."

"You have to stop!" Jim shouted at him. "You have to stop!"

"We'll help you, honey," Liza said, stroking his head. "We'll help you."

Jim stared at Liza from the hallway until her gaze finally met his. "Make the call," he said. "Tomorrow morning. It's our house, Liza. Make the call."

And then he went down to the basement to mop the floor.

THE FOLLOWING MORNING, Liza phoned Dr. Shannon, who had a cancellation that afternoon at four. When school ended, Liza picked up Malcolm and drove straight to the doctor's office. Jim met them there.

Before seeing Malcolm, Dr. Shannon asked if she could chat with the two of them for a few minutes. She asked them a number of questions about their son. Had there been any recent disruptions in his home life? Any problems at school? Any problems with friends? Any complaints on his part of not feeling well? Of not being happy? Again and again Liza and Jim said no, and again and again Dr. Shannon nodded knowingly. Finally, she called Malcolm in and asked his parents to take a seat in the waiting room.

"So," Dr. Shannon began once they were alone, "I think we both know why you're here. Let's talk about faucets."

When his mom told him in the car that he was going to see a

doctor and that it was the kind of doctor you talked to, Malcolm knew what they were going to be talking about, so he had been thinking over the last several minutes about what he might say to try to satisfy her curiosity. "I don't like the idea of water just sitting in the pipes," he said. "I think it should be let out. That's why I haven't been turning off the faucet at school or at home."

"Why do you think that water should be let out?"

He shrugged.

"What if water poured into your room? Would you like that?"

He didn't understand the question, since there was no faucet in his room. Clearly she wasn't following him. He didn't want the water to pour anywhere except out of faucets. When he left a faucet on, he never imagined where the water was going to end up, although lately he had been thinking what a shame it was that drains didn't work better.

Dr. Shannon asked at least a dozen or more questions. Then she took Malcolm out to the waiting room and called in his parents. Before they had reentered the consulting room, she paused in the doorway. "I forgot to ask earlier, has Malcolm by chance had strep throat recently?"

Jim turned to Liza. "In the fall," she said. "There was a case in his classroom, and he caught it. But we took him to the doctor right away."

"I ask because I'm slightly concerned," she said, shutting the door behind her, "that Malcolm's recent OCD tendencies with regards to faucets might indicate something more troubling. Have either one of you heard of PANDAS? Not the animal, but the condition?"

They both shook their heads no.

"Well, the full name is pediatric autoimmune neuropsychiatric disorder associated with streptococcal. What happens is a child gets strep throat, and then suddenly his or her behavior changes dramatically."

"That's it." Jim nodded furiously.

"If it remains untreated," Dr. Shannon continued, "PAN-

DAS can have serious consequences. That is, children with it can become very agitated, even violent."

Jim was tapping his feet on the floor. Liza was reminded of a racehorse at a starting gate. She just wanted to calm him down, to get him thinking more slowly and deliberately. "Malcolm had strep right before Halloween," she said, looking back and forth between her husband and Dr. Shannon. "That was months ago."

"This could be late-onset PANDAS." Dr. Shannon touched the tips of her fingers together. "I'm not saying it is; I'm saying it could be. In light of this possibility, though, I would recommend an aggressive treatment plan. That is, in conjunction with therapy, I'd like to prescribe a small, daily dose of something like Prozac."

"Prozac!" Liza's head recoiled. "For a nine-year-old boy! He's not depressed!"

"Prozac has been proven to treat OCD in children quite well, and can be safely prescribed to kids as young as six. Plus, if he's on the PANDAS spectrum, Prozac would help mollify his mood fluctuations."

Jim's head was bobbing up and down. "I don't think we can wait and see if he gets better just from talking to you. Not that I'm saying that won't help him as well, but he nearly broke his teacher's hip . . ."

"Jim!" Liza wanted him to stop talking so that they could discuss this at home. Just the two of them. She couldn't stand how rushed he sounded, and desperate.

"Is everything all right, Liza?" Dr. Shannon asked her.

Liza nodded, trying to compose herself. She wondered, if she engaged in a conversation with Dr. Shannon, would that make Jim slow down? "What are the possible side effects? Of the . . ." But she couldn't say the name of the medication.

"Loss of appetite and sleeplessness are the two big ones with Prozac," Dr. Shannon explained. "Sweating, as well."

"I'd like to see him get back to normal as soon as possible," Jim added.

"I think Dr. Shannon picked up on that," Liza said wryly.

And then she couldn't help it; she began to cry. It was hearing this woman, this stranger, describe her son in such alien terms that upset her. He had a thing with faucets. That was it. It was about faucets.

Jim leaned over and patted her on the shoulder. Liza put her head in her hands. She was sobbing now.

Dr. Shannon reached over and tapped her knee. "There, there," she said. "It's going to be okay."

After Liza had calmed down, Dr. Shannon wrote out a prescription for Prozac and handed it to Jim. "I'd start him Monday morning," she added, standing up to shake their hands. "Before school."

THAT NIGHT, THE THREE OF THEM ATE DINNER in awkward silence. Shortly after putting Malcolm to bed, Liza tried to fall asleep, but she couldn't; she was too agitated and irritable. When she flipped on the light, she was surprised to find Jim lying there with his eyes open.

"I don't like where we live," she said bluntly. She hadn't planned on saying such a thing. She wasn't even aware that she was thinking along these lines. The sentence just exploded from her mouth.

"Not everyone can live in the fifth loop, Liza."

"I'm not talking about the fifth loop. I'm talking about Middletown."

"What's wrong with Middletown?"

Sometimes, in the winter, their parkas and coats would accumulate on the closet floor and, in search of a missing glove or a scarf, Liza would plunge her hands into the arms and hollows of their outerwear, grasping for the familiar feel of whatever garment had disappeared. She felt as if she were doing this now, only she was looking for something, the contours of which she could not visualize.

"Don't you think this place is perhaps a little *too* structured? With all these loops, and the rules against walking in the street, and—"

"You want to get run over? That's your idea of freedom?"

"I just wonder . . . the way everything is so controlled . . . I wonder if that's why Malcolm started leaving the faucets running. Maybe he senses all of this structure around him and wants, instinctively, to resist it. And who knows, maybe that's a good thing."

"You think it's a good thing when he takes out his teacher? You think it's a good thing that he could have flooded our basement?"

"I'm just saying . . . I don't think I want to live here anymore." She didn't know if she really felt this. More than anything, she wanted to hear Jim's response.

"All my clients are here, Liza; all my references. I don't know what to tell you."

"They'd still be your references and clients if we lived in another town."

"I'm not so sure that's true." He paused. "No offense, but I'm not interested in raising our son in Naderville."

She turned over on her side, away from him. "What's wrong with Naderville?"

"Nothing. Well, you know, all the neighborhoods, all the people . . . everything is just all mixed together. It's not organized like Middletown, that's all."

"What do you mean by that phrase *mixed together*?"

Jim sighed. "I don't know, Liza—"

"Because maybe that's what we need. Maybe we all need to be a little more mixed together."

Neither one of them moved. Jim's breathing was heavy beside her, like some kind of animal. "If Middletown is such an awful place," he said, his voice straining to remain subdued, "why do the homes sell so quickly? Why is the crime rate so low? People want what we have, Liza. We're lucky. We're just going through a tough time as parents, that's all."

Liza listened to him breathe.

"Kids just go through phases," Jim added. "We've got it pretty good, all things considered. Sometimes, you know, counting your blessings isn't a bad thing."

MONDAY MORNING, Jim stuck around for breakfast. He never had breakfast at home; usually he was gone by seven. Liza knew why he was lingering. Before Malcolm had finished his waffle, Jim placed a tiny, baby-blue pill next to his orange juice.

"Hey, buddy," he said, leaning over his plate. "This is what Dr. Shannon prescribed for you. It's a vitamin that will help you remember not to leave any faucets running." Dr. Shannon had told them that was how they could refer to the medicine if it made them more comfortable. "Go ahead and wash it down with a swig of orange juice."

Malcolm set his fork down by his plate. "I don't want to take a vitamin."

"Dr. Shannon wants you to."

"But I don't want to."

"I'm not asking what you want to do. I'm telling you that you need to take this . . . vitamin. It's for your health."

"If you don't like it," Liza interjected, "then you won't have to take it again. We're just asking you to try it."

Jim shot her a glance, then turned back toward his son. "What do you say, buddy? Don't you want to make your parents proud? And your teacher? And your principal? And Dr. Shannon? Don't you want all of these people to be proud of you?"

Actually, Malcolm thought that he would prefer to leave faucets running than to have everyone be proud of him. If they were all proud of him, wouldn't they observe him that much more, smiling and giving him the thumbs-up all of the time? Malcolm didn't like the idea of adults watching him more than they already were, and he thought that older people looked ridiculous when they gave the thumbs-up. Then again, if he took the pill and ended up leaving a faucet running here and there, maybe they would blame the pill for not working rather than him for not being able to control himself. With that in mind, he put the pill on his tongue and took a gulp of his juice.

MALCOLM BEGAN TO FEEL DIFFERENTLY right when he stepped out of the car in front of Edison Elementary. It was like he heard a tiny buzz in the back of his head. He thought about this buzz most of the morning, while he did his math worksheet and copied the information about grasshoppers from the chalkboard into his science folder. He decided that the buzz he felt was more or less the same as running water. He still pictured the faucet running in the bathroom back behind his desk, only now it felt very far away from where he was: so far away that it never occurred to him to try to go and turn on the faucet.

Later, when they were doing their math, Malcolm realized that he hadn't been thinking about faucets at all. For a moment he pictured water pouring into the sink in the bathroom. The image didn't make him feel one way or the other. He just pictured the faucet running. Then he went back to his work.

"I DON'T LIKE MY VITAMIN, MOM," Malcolm said to Liza Wednesday afternoon of that week. He was sitting at the kitchen counter, his unfinished math homework laid out in front of him.

"Why not, honey?"

"I don't know. It makes me feel funny, like there's something buzzing in my head. And, at night, I can't sleep."

This was true. On Monday night, he had been up until ten. The night before, it had been closer to ten thirty.

"You told me I wouldn't have to take it if I didn't like it, and I don't like it."

Liza was still upset about the medication, but it was true, there hadn't been any incidents, either at school or home, since he had been on it. And Jim had been much calmer around the house as well, much easier to be around.

"Yes, I did say that you could stop taking your vitamin if you didn't like it," she said, "but can you stick with it until you see Dr. Shannon again tomorrow afternoon?"

Malcolm shrugged. When he was done with his homework,

he surprised Liza by asking if he could go outside. While third-loop children were prohibited from keeping permanent play structures outside, they weren't forbidden from playing outside, although most tended not to.

It was overcast and chilly, but the snow from the previous weekend had melted. Liza took him out into the garage. They found an old four-square ball. She inflated it and then watched Malcolm bounce it in the driveway. A few minutes later, she went inside to get dinner ready. Jim arrived home right at six, and they had a pleasant dinner together. Afterward, while she did the dishes, Jim sat at the counter with Malcolm and folded paper airplanes. Then they went up to bed.

That same night, a little past ten, the Radrick doorbell rang. Jim and Liza were already in bed, and Malcolm had just fallen asleep. Jim threw on his bathrobe and went downstairs. It was their next-door neighbor, Max. Jim opened the door.

"How you doing?"

"Fine. Sorry to get you out of bed. Hey, a funny thing here: Muffins, our cat, got out, so I was poking around the side of my house looking for her just now when I noticed that our spigot was on. Yours too; the one on our side of your house. I turned them both off, but I just wanted to let you know."

"Thanks, Max." Jim tapped his foot. His hands strummed his thighs.

"Strange, huh?"

"I'll say."

Upstairs, he told Liza what had happened. They didn't wake up Malcolm. They were worried, if they did, that he wouldn't go back to sleep.

AFTER DISCUSSING THE SPIGOTS WITH MALCOLM over breakfast, Liza and Jim called Dr. Shannon to tell her what had happened. "We might want to increase his dosage," Dr. Shannon said. "What he's taking now wears off by the early afternoon. If we increase his dosage, he'll feel the effects right through the day."

"If the effects of the pill wear off in the early afternoon, why can't he fall asleep at night?" Liza asked. She was on the phone in their bedroom while Jim was on the one down in the living room.

"That's a side effect. That's different. You can always give him a couple of milligrams of melatonin at bedtime; it's a natural supplement that will help him fall asleep."

"All these pills . . ."

"Think of them as a resource," Dr. Shannon suggested. "A managed resource. We can talk about it more this afternoon if you want. I'd be happy to explain the medication to Malcolm."

Liza told Dr. Shannon she would appreciate that, so right after school, she drove Malcolm over to the psychiatrist's office. First she listened to Dr. Shannon as she explained the merits of increasing Malcolm's dosage. Then Dr. Shannon called Malcolm into her consultation room and instructed Liza to wait outside.

"How are you feeling, Malcolm?" she asked him, after he had sat down in the chair facing her.

Malcolm shrugged.

"Are you wondering about the vitamin we're having you take?"

He nodded.

"Let me explain it to you." She reached into the bottom drawer of her desk and used both of her hands to lift out an enormous book. "This is a book that psychiatrists like me use to determine how to diagnose and treat our patients. It's called the *Diagnostic and Statistical Manual,* but us doctors refer to it as the DSM. Do you know what *diagnose* means? It means figure out what is bothering someone. We use the DSM to figure out such things, and to prescribe medication, or vitamins, if you will. Like the one you're taking. Do you think your vitamin is helping you?"

Malcolm bit at his lip, lifting his left shoulder ever so slightly as he did so.

"Well, from what I hear, it seems to be helping you. But your parents and I think maybe you should take two vitamins each day instead of one, just to help you that much more. How does that sound?"

Malcolm tried to remain very still. He didn't want Dr. Shannon to interpret any movement on his part as signaling that he was fine with taking an extra vitamin. He didn't understand how this book knew that the buzzing from the vitamin he took in the morning went away in the afternoon. He didn't like the idea that this book was helping Dr. Shannon read him. He wanted to destroy the book. If only it wasn't so big, maybe he could have slipped it under his shirt when Dr. Shannon stepped into the hallway to get his mom. But they would notice if he tried to take it. And then, if they caught him trying to steal the book, maybe they would make him take even more vitamins and the buzzing would never ever stop. All because of a book.

"Do you have any questions for me, Malcolm?" Dr. Shannon asked him.

Malcolm shook his head.

THE ADDITIONAL PILL NEEDED TO BE TAKEN after lunch each day. The school nurse handed out such medication from what had once been a storage room in the basement. Students, almost all boys, lined up right when the bell rang. The first day Malcolm joined the line, he noticed Adam Wiltner standing in front of him. He had always wondered why Adam was late to class after lunch; now he knew.

With this second pill, Malcolm found that the effects of his vitamin changed. He no longer thought about faucets running, even in the distance. Instead, a lot of the time, he found himself thinking about what he was thinking. This was a little weird, though, since what he was thinking about was usually the fact that he was thinking about what he was thinking. He was also surprised to find how absorbing it could be, thinking about thinking. At recess, he had always wondered why kids like Adam sat on one of the benches and just watched the other kids play.

But now that he was so caught up in his own thoughts, Malcolm didn't feel like playing, either. He was content to sit there, with the other boys who took vitamins after lunch, and say nothing.

A WEEK PASSED, AND THEN ANOTHER. There were no more faucet incidents, either at Edison Elementary or in the Radrick home. Malcolm now took his vitamin in the morning without being reminded. In the afternoon, while his mom prepared dinner, he would sit at the counter and look through her, or so Liza felt. At night, he would chew two peppermint-flavored melatonin tablets and go to sleep.

One weekday morning, just a few weeks into their new routine, Liza felt very down. She recognized that Malcolm wasn't just *behaving* differently; he seemed changed to her. Outside, the ground was blanketed with light snow. It was late March. Just as her son was wiggling into his boots, her cell phone rang. Jim didn't usually call right after he left in the morning, so Liza assumed something was wrong.

"No, everything's fine," he said. "I just got off the phone with Ed Talston." Ed was an electrician with whom Jim sometimes worked. "His son, Paul," Jim went on, "got into trouble at Edison a few days ago. You know what for?" Liza listened intently. "He's been taking the pebbles out of the beds in front and placing them in his locker. So they're taking him to see Dr. Shannon the day after tomorrow. She must be making a killing, by the way, Dr. Shannon."

Liza cupped her hand over the phone so Malcolm wouldn't hear the sting in her voice. "Why are you telling me this?" she asked him sharply.

"What do you mean? I thought it'd make you feel better, knowing we aren't the only ones, at least not in our loop."

"Well, it doesn't make me feel any better."

"All right, then. Geez. I'm sorry. Everything okay over there? You sound crabby."

"I'll talk to you later, Jim." She hung up on him, then noticed

Malcolm standing in the hallway, staring at her.

"Are you upset, Mom?" he asked.

"No, of course not, honey," she replied. "I'm fine."

He opened the door that led into their driveway, where Liza's car sat. She grabbed her coat from the closet to follow him. So this was her life now. Out of the corner of her eye, Liza spied the plastic bottle filled with Prozac pills on the edge of the counter in the kitchen. How many would she need to take to feel some effect? Two, three? She palmed two of the baby-blue pills, then reaffixed the cap. What a strange world I have found myself in, she thought as she stepped outside. What a strange, strange world.

Easy Writer

Of bodies changed to other forms I tell . . .

Ovid, *Metamorphoses*

CHARITY JACKSON WALKED THROUGH the fifth floor of Hypnos Applications amid rapturous, although soft, applause. Alex had encouraged his team to show its appreciation and excitement at seeing Professor Jackson, but also to be mindful that she might be nervous. It wouldn't serve their research ends any, agitating her before their most significant harvesting to date.

In fact, Charity wasn't particularly nervous; she was hungry, having skimped on dinner for reasons that didn't make any sense—as if the people at Hypnos were going to analyze her eating habits. Now she wondered if her brain waves, her storytelling, would be adversely affected by this change in routine.

Alex and his assistant—a young, very kinetic woman named Kim—ushered her through the pristine, bustling lab space of the Hypnos Applications Storytelling Team. When the three of them stepped into the glass-partitioned room and Kim shut the door behind them, nearly all of the background noise disappeared. Charity, at long last, came face-to-face with what she considered to be Alex's creation, even though—of course—many others had also been involved in its design and fabrication.

In size and shape, Easy Writer appeared almost identical to an old-school MRI machine, save for the coils of different-colored wiring that mushroomed out of its top hatch, cascading down the near side of its hull and then snaking across the room before disappearing into the floor and then—presumably—connecting to the bank of computers on the other side of the glass partition, where a row of programmers sat, their brows furrowed. How much money had gone into the R&D for this project? Many, many millions, to be sure.

"*This* is going to replace books?" Charity asked Alex, gesturing toward the enormous machine. "Isn't it a little bulky?"

"Yes, as a prototype. For harvesting, we need our human storyteller to be in a relatively immobilized, resting state. That way, his or her brain can be scanned continuously for a full night's worth of REM sleep. But that won't be necessary for implantation. We hope to have a working model that inserts narrative—that is, synchronizes neural firings—by the end of the year. We're talking the size of a motorcycle helmet."

Alex gestured toward a small cluster of three folding chairs. When Charity sat down, she placed her tote bag, in which she had packed some toiletries and pajamas, next to her feet.

"Please tell me you're a little tired." Alex seemed nervous himself.

"I am. I went for a walk late this afternoon, as you suggested." Having mentioned exercising, Charity looked down at the round swell of her stomach beneath her considerable breasts. She was spilling over the edges of her plastic chair, but so was Alex. "I'll be able to sleep. I'm not worried about that."

Alex grinned with relief as his black-rimmed glasses slipped down the bridge of his nose. He was lacquered over with a film of perspiration that made his nearly pink skin shimmer under the fluorescent lights. Beginning in high school, when she had first found herself surrounded by white guys, Charity had always been amused by the profuse, rather desperate manner in which they sweat, especially the ones who were overweight.

"And you've got your story to tell?"

"Yes. It's more of a vignette, actually—really dreamlike, which I assume is good."

"That is good. The shorter it is, and the more ethereal, the easier it makes neural insertion."

"I've been meaning to ask about revision." Charity shifted in her chair, the seat of which pinched her bottom. "Let's say I begin my story, but then I decide to add an element, or subtract something . . ."

Both Alex and Kim were looking at her with an attentiveness that verged on the parental. "Easy Writer should be able to assemble the storyline as it is rethought and reimagined," Alex explained, "because the narrative pieces, and their corresponding regions of neural stimulation, won't be synched until *after* you've cycled out of REM sleep. The story isn't finished, per se, until you wake up in the morning and we roll you out of the scanner."

"But don't worry about trying to imagine a completed story," Kim added. Like Alex, she was dressed business casual—on the scale of such things, slightly more glamorous than your typical academic, but only slightly. "What matters most to Easy Writer is the emotional content. That's what it uses to target neural stimulation. So the more personal your narrative is, the better, since— without strong affective cues—we can't do implantation."

"Although hopefully," Alex jumped in, "with our newest software modifications, we have a larger margin of error than before. But remember, Charity, as I told you in your office: implantation is not for you to worry about. You're here to generate content for us."

He made it sound like she was just fodder for this machine— like branches for a woodchipper, or vegetables for a food processor. Once more, she questioned her decision to participate in this enterprise.

"If you'd like to prepare for bed, I can show you to the ladies room down the hallway." Kim stood and gestured toward the glass door through which they had entered a moment ago. Alex helped her up, and Charity followed Kim out of the room and back through the lab.

Once she was in the restroom, Charity took off her black slacks and beige blouse, folded them neatly, and placed them in her tote bag. She had deliberately worn one of her sports bras in order to feel a little more covered up, as she was going to be sleeping surrounded by Hypnos employees. After slipping on her favorite pair of silk pajamas, she brushed her teeth. When she stepped back into the lab, Kim was waiting with a pair of slippers in her hand. Charity thanked her and put them on.

As she passed several workstations, Charity noticed as the programmers and scientists stepped back from their computer screens to nod deferentially and smile at her. They were mostly white and Asian men who were dressed in jeans, T-shirts, and retro Converses. Charity knew they were a mix of computer specialists and neuroscientists, because Kim had told her as much during the lengthy information session she had conducted with her over the phone the week before. Back in the glass room, Alex had been joined by two technicians—these men in white lab coats—who were in charge of the on-hand programming of Easy Writer. One of them was carefully adjusting a series of dials on the side of the machine while the other punched in numbers on a keypad, all while Alex looked on attentively. Without breaking his gaze, he motioned over to Kim, who held out her hand to lead Charity over to Easy Writer. All this doting on her . . . well, it wasn't a typical Sunday night, to say the least.

Several thin blankets had been spread on the narrow, padded table that extended, like a tongue, out of Easy Writer's gleaming, white hollow sphere. Charity eased herself onto the table, worried it might wobble beneath her. Then she scooted herself up and—with Alex's help—swung her thick legs around. With her head now resting on a small, foam pillow, one of the technicians walked over and attached electrodes to either side of her temple.

While Alex stood there with his arms crossed over his considerable pouch, smiling down at her, Charity suddenly remembered a question she had been meaning to ask. "What about layering my story? You know, I'm a Classicist. The piece I have in mind is allusive; it plays around with the myth of Proserpine and her mom, Ceres. Are you familiar with Ovid's version?"

Alex and Kim—who had joined him next to Easy Writer—shook their heads.

"Pluto kidnaps Proserpine and takes her to Hell. Ceres tries to save her, but she can't rescue her daughter if she breaks her fast, which Proserpine does when she eats seven pomegranate seeds among the orchard trees of Hell." The two of them stared down at her blankly. "When you partake in the offerings of Hell," Charity added, "you become irreconcilably linked to the place. Hell isn't other people for Ovid, as Sartre would have it. Hell is the loss of self-control."

Alex's mouth wrinkled as he seemed to chew on Charity's words. "Easy Writer can code the references," he explained, "but your reader's brain won't go to Ovid unless he or she has read him before. Instead, that content will be replaced with material that matters to your reader the same way Ovid matters to you."

But Charity wasn't listening. She felt a need to talk, to lay out her creative vision. "I'm going to switch the mother and daughter's roles, so it's the mother who's kidnapped and the daughter who goes looking for her. Otherwise I'm pretty much following the myth. Oh, and I want to make a fairly obvious allusion at the end to Daphne's story."

Alex nodded. He seemed, if not slightly annoyed by her attention to source details, then at least not very interested. "Just don't hold back," he said. "Remember, I'm going to be your reader at this stage of development, and my subconscious is going to seize on allusions and symbols and enigmatic characters to make your story mine. If you give me a seamless narrative, or one in which every possible ambiguity or symbol is explained . . . well, that's not how the brain tells itself stories in sleep, so that's not the way we think about narrative here. Trying to make everything perfectly clear, that's what causes writer's block, right?"

Charity didn't say anything. She felt a chill and asked for another blanket, which Kim quickly produced.

Several minutes passed while the technicians fussed about, one of them even wiping down the hull of the machine with what looked like a damp cloth. While these final preparations took place, Alex occasionally stepped out of the room, only to rush back in a moment later. Whenever he vanished, Kim would scoot over slightly, taking his place next to Charity. It was as if they didn't want her to feel alone.

"The table is going to shudder and hum a little," one of the technicians said after several minutes. "Nothing to worry about." And sure enough, the table vibrated for a moment before settling into a more subdued, but constant, buzz. Like a massage chair in an airport.

"We're going to insert you now," Kim said.

Easy Writer rumbled, and then Charity began to move slowly into its yawning chasm, its donut-like hole of open circuitry and softly blinking lights.

Alex stepped back into view just before Charity disappeared completely into the machine. "Sweet dreams," he said, giving her ankle a squeeze before she was completely enclosed in Easy Writer. "Now go write us one hell of a short story."

CHARITY JACKSON HAD A TUMULTUOUS UPBRING-ING—one that formed the basis for the celebrated short story collection she published at twenty-five. The youngest of three kids, she was also among the last generation to grow up in the Cabrini–Green Projects on the Near North Side of Chicago. Her family was a microcosm of the projects—both its tragedies and triumphs, its most egregious caricatures and its most astounding singularities. She and her two brothers were the products of a single mom and three different dads, each of whom managed to go nowhere but still disappear completely from view. Their mother worked behind the counter at a convenience store right on Clybourn. Each night, when her shift ended, she would bring home dinner from the store, and one of Charity's earliest memories was eating dinner at their tiny kitchen table—SpaghettiOs and saltines—and her mom falling asleep, her head slumping forward while the three of them sat there, chewing and slurping quietly to the sound of her snores, trying not to wake her up.

One January night, Charity's mother didn't come home. She stumbled into their unit the next morning smelling of the streets— her overcoat torn, her hair disheveled. Charity would always believe it started then. Her mother was addicted to crack cocaine by Valentine's Day, a ghost of herself by Saint Patrick's, a whore by the Fourth of July, and dead by Halloween. A week after the funeral, her only daughter turned thirteen.

Charity's oldest brother, Jayden, was dealing crack by the age of seventeen, and was shot twice by the age of twenty. In and out of juvenile hall and then jail, at twenty-one he was convicted of first-degree murder and went away to prison. Four years passed before Charity had the opportunity to visit him out at Stateville. In the visiting room, when he lumbered in, she barely recognized her brother. Jayden had put on considerable weight, and added ridges of muscles above his collarbones, but that wasn't it. There was, rather, some glint in his eye now lost—the way he looked through her—that signified he was no longer the same person as before. In her absence, a metamorphosis had occurred. *Omnia mutantur.* Right then, albeit unbeknownst to her, out of a dark patch of fertile soil in her brain, her book *Cabrini Dreams* began to sprout.

Charity's other brother, Michael, two years younger than Jayden, took the lesson of his mother and brother to heart and stayed away from drugs and out of trouble. Because he was dyslexic, school was a challenge for him, but Michael—lean, angular, and nimble, and named after Michael Jordan, no less—excelled at basketball. Even by Chicago standards he was a fantastic point guard, and had just signed a letter of intent to go to DePaul when he was gunned down in front of their building—mistaken for a gangbanger who had a similar build.

Charity was fourteen at the time of Michael's death, living—

as she had since her mother's passing—across the hallway from their old place in the one-bedroom unit of an elderly woman by the name of Ms. Lynette. How Charity and her brothers ended up in the care of Ms. Lynette rather than social services forever remained a mystery. Fortunately for Charity, the old woman—an attentive, gentle, even doting figure—became her second mother.

After Michael's death, Ms. Lynette resolved that Charity would not be matriculating at the local public high school. "Too many bad apples," she observed. Besides, Charity had already begun to display an interest in reading and books, and she was still turned in, as she had been ever since her mother had died. Ms. Lynette felt strongly that Charity needed to be in a quiet, strict environment where learning was taken seriously. A Baptist, she nonetheless thought the Catholics had schooling figured out. So she enrolled Charity at Holy Trinity, where the young woman's most unlikely gift soon manifested itself.

Charity Jackson's gift, it turned out, was Latin, to which she was introduced her first semester at Holy Trinity. She loved everything about the language. She loved the block units that constituted a Latin sentence. She loved that the words themselves would fit together to form such sentences, changing their endings like otherworldly pieces of a fluid jigsaw puzzle. Just a few months into her first year at Holy Trinity, Charity started to meet early each morning with her Latin teacher, Father Thomas, in order to memorize declensions and vocabulary. Over the ensuing years, Charity read Cicero. She read Catullus, Seneca, and Horace. Finally, with much anticipation, she read Virgil. And while she loved these writers, none moved her as much as the final poet whose work she took up in the fall of her senior year: Ovid.

"If this wasn't in Latin," Father Thomas announced with his customary tone of quiet affability, waving his tattered, bright red Loeb edition of the first eight books of the *Metamorphoses* over his head before handing it to his star pupil to borrow, "I'm not sure it'd make it past the Papal censors." And it was true; there was so much violence in Ovid, so much horror—girls being plucked from their families, and men doing such awful things to them—that Charity felt at once shocked and engrossed. Regardless of how long ago he had written, Ovid was describing human nature in conditions she had herself witnessed. Somehow, he knew a thing or two about Cabrini–Green.

The winter of her senior year in high school, at Father Thomas's insistence, Charity applied to all of the fanciest colleges in the country. Who would have ever guessed? Latin could be her ticket out of the projects; a dead language might save her life. Despite having cast her net wide, she still kept her hopes firmly bound within the Windy City, longing to be admitted to DePaul or, in her best-case scenario, the University of Chicago. When her acceptance letters began to pour in, however, Father Thomas pointed out the previously unthinkable: Charity didn't *have* to remain in Chicago. Ms. Lynette, her only other tie to the city, concurred. Shortly thereafter, Charity accepted a scholarship to attend Stanford University.

Just a few months after she left for the West Coast, authorities closed the last Cabrini–Green building. Ms. Lynette was transferred to another public housing unit, this one on the South Side. She died before Charity completed her first year at Stanford. In the wake of her death, and having been assigned several short story collections to read in one of her humanities courses, Charity now had some sense of an artistic form in which she could document the losses and experiences that had shaped her life. By the beginning of her sophomore year, she had four stories drafted. She submitted them as a portfolio so that she might be considered for one of the selective, creative writing courses offered to Stanford sophomores. Upon reading her file, the director of the undergraduate program gave her a call in her dorm room. "Don't do a class," he said to her. "Your fellow students, they wouldn't be able to help you with this material. Just keep working on your own, and give me the collection when you think it's done."

She was nineteen. She was twenty. She loved everything

about Stanford—her classes, her classmates, the weather. She was twenty-one and finished a draft of *Cabrini Dreams*, but she still wasn't ready to show it to anyone. She was twenty-two and—at graduation—received the Latin Prize. She applied, and was admitted, to the Stanford Doctoral Program in Classics. She was twenty-three, had rewritten *Cabrini Dreams* from beginning to end but still couldn't imagine actually approaching the creative writing professor who had responded so enthusiastically to her work. And then one afternoon, just out of nowhere, the man called her once again in her dorm room to see how her stories were coming along. The next day, at his insistence, she gave him a copy of her manuscript. He called her two days later. "My agent is coming to see you," he said. "I gave her your book to read. She wants to represent you. You have written something that will last, Charity. I think you're an amazing talent."

Charity signed with the agent a week later, and the woman sold her book a month after that. In November, the budding writer turned twenty-four. Charity spent some of the fall doing final revisions on her book, but mostly she stayed focused on her academic work. She learned how to do archival research, how to read Carolingian minuscule, how to handle and decipher vellum codices. She wanted to write a dissertation on Ovid, but her thesis advisor recommended Cicero instead. "He's more political," he explained. "You'll be more marketable with a dissertation on Cicero. After you get a job, write about Ovid." Charity did as he recommended. As an academic, she always followed advice.

Charity turned twenty-five the day *Cabrini Dreams* came out. It promptly exploded on the literary scene. A front page, effusive review in the *New York Times Book Review*. More praise on NPR and in *USA Today*, the *Washington Post,* and the *New York Review of Books*. Even the *Wall Street Journal* had positive things to say. *Cabrini Dreams* made every top-ten fiction list for the year. It won the PEN/Hemingway Award and was short-listed for both the Pulitzer Prize and the National Book Award. Charity was called the American Zadie Smith. She was called the next Toni Morrison. Once more, her agent flew out from New York to see her in

Palo Alto. Offers were coming in, substantial offers, for Charity's next work of fiction.

"You can drop out of graduate school tomorrow," Charity's agent told her. "I can get you a deal that will support you comfortably while you write your next book. It needs to be a novel, though. That's what writers do. They write a collection of stories, or a novel in stories. Then they write a novel proper."

But Charity didn't want to drop out of graduate school. Had anyone else from her building in Cabrini–Green, had anyone from her generation there, ever gotten a PhD from Stanford? Besides, she had an idea for a book; why couldn't she do both? Her agent asked her what she had in mind, and Charity explained that she wanted to write a historical novel set in ancient Rome, detailing the relationship between Catullus and Clodia Metelli. It would be too easy for her to write once more about her family, about what she had seen growing up in Cabrini–Green. She needed to branch out as an artist, to push herself. "Instead of branching out," her agent countered, "why not think about going deeper into a subtext of one of the stories you've already written?" She didn't have to spell it out; she wanted Charity to tackle her mom's drug abuse more directly than she had in *Cabrini Dreams*, where the effects of her mother's addiction on Charity and her brothers had received more attention than the addiction itself. But Charity didn't want to do that. Neither did she want to start a novel with the added pressure of being under contract. Instead, she just wanted to see where her writing took her.

Her agent reacted to this proposed course of action with the bodily contortions one might otherwise associate with acute pancreatitis. Charity, however, would not be swayed, even though a part of her knew, even then, that she was hedging her bets on being able to finish another work of fiction. She was already feeling her writer's block coming on.

She was twenty-six. Her dissertation was almost done, but her novel about Catullus was stuck in mud. Charity decided to scrap what she had and focus on something entirely different. Again, her agent suggested she do something autobiographical, but now Charity wanted to write about Augustine's debauchery during his Manichaean phase. The working title of the novel was *Augustine's Concubines*.

She was twenty-seven years old, a PhD from Stanford in hand, a Classicist but also a young black woman who had—not so long before—been short-listed for the Pulitzer Prize and the National Book Award. The Stanford Classics Department offered her a tenure-track position as an assistant professor, and Charity began to work on her own translation of Ovid's *Metamorphoses*.

She was twenty-eight. *Augustine's Concubines* was going nowhere. Charity went back to her notes on Catullus. She went back to her notes on Augustine. She tried to combine the two. She tried, for a time, to write in Latin. Nothing worked. She was twenty-nine.

She was thirty. Her translation of the *Metamorphoses* came out and won the PEN Translation Prize and the MLA Translation Prize. She was thirty-one. She won an I Tatti Fellowship. She was thirty-two. She won an NEH. She was thirty-three and received tenure at Stanford. She was thirty-four and garnered the Rome Prize. A revised version of her dissertation, *On Ciceronianism: The Rhetoric of Roman Polity*, was published by Harvard University Press. It won the International Classicist Award. It won the Vatican Prize. It won the Karl Deutsch Award from the International Political Science Association, which made Charity Jackson the first Classicist ever to be so honored. She was thirty-five. She won a Guggenheim. Once more, her agent checked in with her. "Forget what I said," she told Charity. "Forget about writing a novel. Just be a short story writer. Do another collection."

So Charity tried to write a sequence of stories that wasn't set in either the late Roman Republic or Late Antiquity, but rather, back in the Chicago of her youth. Still, she couldn't seem to weave any of her sentences together. They sprouted on her computer screen like weeds, but they refused to commingle. She was thirty-six. She won a MacArthur. She was thirty-seven. She tried to write a freestanding story, just a ten-page piece about a little girl who gets turned around and goes into the wrong stairwell at a public housing complex, which any girl who grew up in a public housing complex knew you absolutely could not do, but she found herself incapable of writing so much as a few lines.

She was thirty-eight. Since leaving Chicago, Charity had avoided the convenience-store food on which she had been raised until her mother died. For nearly two decades, she had eaten kale salads, veggie wraps, and sushi, and yet her body had remained substantial and hefty. Now, to encourage her efforts at writing nonacademic prose, Charity began to stock her cupboards with cookies and candy, and fill her cereal bowls with chips and Cheetos. She began to buy two-liter bottles of Coke. She could snack and drink soda, she told herself, as long as she was trying to write creatively.

She was thirty-nine. Doing archival work in a monastery in Germany, she found an extant copy of Lucretius's *De rerum natura*, one with significant deviations from both the *Codex Oblongus* and the *Codex Quadratus*. Re-examining the well-known emendations of folio twenty-two recto of the *Oblongus*, Charity was able to establish that this alteration was based on the manuscript she had discovered, which meant the *Oblongus* wasn't the oldest Lucretian codex after all. Kind of a big deal. So she retranslated Lucretius, adding a critical introduction. Once more, she won all the major translation prizes.

She was forty. She found herself avoiding the small kitchen table where she had always tried to write fiction. Instead, she often came to, as if awakening from a dream, standing in her small pantry while her hands shoveled junk food into her mouth. She couldn't remember ever feeling so absolutely, insatiably hungry before, and diagnosed her compulsive eating as a symptom of her writer's block.

She was forty-one. The calls from her literary agent were infrequent now, and Charity never picked them up. More academic accolades came her way. She didn't need to be a short story writer; she was a tremendously accomplished woman of color—one of the best Latinists in the entire country, the entire world. Pictures of her—behind podia, in front of chalkboards—were ubiquitous in all of the promotional literature produced by Stanford. Still, Charity was haunted by the fact that she was so blocked as a fiction writer. She felt like a failure. She was forty-two. She was voted into the American Academy of Arts and Sciences. She was forty-three. She received a phone call in her office informing her that her brother, Jayden, had been killed in prison. So she was the last one left. Everyone else, everyone who had been seated at the kitchen table of her childhood, was gone.

Perhaps this was what caused the flood of story ideas to engulf her. Day after day. Haunting stories, all Ovidian in nature, darker than any that had made their way into *Cabrini Dreams* but similar in terms of their Chicago settings. The city she had fled and then avoided now seemed to overtake her imagination, her subconscious, entirely. But still, she couldn't so much as draft a single sentence.

She was forty-four. No longer hovering on the border, Charity Jackson had crossed into the land of chronic obesity. Her joints ached when she walked. She acquired a wheeze that sometimes made it difficult for her to catch her breath when she lectured. While receiving her annual physical exam, her doctor expressed shock that she had yet to develop diabetes. At parties, without the insulation of Latin, she would sit shyly in the corner, unless there was a word game to play—Boggle, Scrabble, Scribbage—in which case her self-consciousness quickly evaporated. Charity loved word games.

She was forty-five. She tried once more to write stories, but now she was so blocked, she couldn't even conjure titles. She couldn't even choose a font. She felt as if a corner of her, one of her organs, one of her limbs, had darkened and died. She held a named chair now as the Head of the Stanford Classics Department. She received the Medal of Freedom at the White House. Her regular class on Latin poetry was so oversubscribed, most students who squeezed into the seminar room weren't even registered. Some weren't even students. They stood against the walls, their notebooks held just beneath their chins, and wrote down everything Charity said, much of which was in Latin because she would forget, reading Ovid aloud, reading Virgil—in medias res, as it were—to switch back into English.

Outside of the classroom, outside of the lecture hall, Charity Jackson saw herself as a loser. She would mutter self-abuse as she tried to walk without waddling. *Pinguis es. Immo pinguissima. Turpis vero*, she would whisper. *You're fat. Really fat. Disgusting, actually.* But still, her binge eating continued. At night, when she read her favorite passages from Ovid, she would begin to weep. She had let her family, she had let all traces of Cabrini–Green, vanish. Her childhood. What she had escaped. Sometimes, Charity thought of what it might feel like to step off an overpass, into the flow of Northern California highway traffic. To be like Philomela, to be like Procne—turned into a bird so as to escape the horror that chased her, the feeling that most of what had been inside of her, all those stories she had wanted to tell, had instead withered on their vines, her fingers too clumsy and swollen to pluck and grind them into wine.

She was forty-six. Her agent retired. Charity would look at the spine of *Cabrini Dreams*, never daring to lift the thin volume and open it, and say to herself, *Vitam meam recedere vidi. I have seen my life slip away.*

And then, an old acquaintance, the neuroscience PhD who had lived across the hallway from Charity her first year in graduate school, the amiable and forever-sweaty Alex Reeves, called her out of the blue and asked if he could pay her a visit.

He came out to Palo Alto to see her during her office hours the following Wednesday afternoon. "What I have to ask you," he explained, after a brief exchange of pleasantries, "is exciting but also complicated and personal and maybe a bit strange."

Charity folded her hands on her desk and regarded Alex with a mixture of interest and caution. People from her past, many of whom she didn't remember at all, regularly sought her out to ask if she could help their daughter or son, their niece or nephew, get into Stanford. But Alex had yet to mention any family, and his chubby left hand—like hers—had no wedding ring on it. Presumably he didn't have kids himself.

"I'm listening," she said noncommittally.

He shifted nervously in his chair, not unlike her students often did, although with far less agility. His hair had thinned considerably over the years, and if he had been chunky in their youth, Alex was now—also like Charity—seriously overweight, with a rotund, firm midsection and baggy pants, the seams of which seemed to meet around his kneecaps.

He exhaled slowly through his mouth. "Charity," he began, "I've spent the last decade, since 2028, working in a subfield of neuroscience known as neural symbiosis. Basically, we know how to trigger brain cells, we know what specific parts of the brain are stimulated by emotions and narrative, and we're getting better and better at moving into these regions, at the neural level, and inserting data. We're already confident in our capacity to safely record such data; we've been successful on that front now for more than a year. As you can probably imagine, the implications of our research are immense, and we have different teams looking at different possibilities—psychotherapeutic treatments, pedagogical initiatives, and so on. Our team is looking at storytelling."

Charity's head tilted.

"Let me start over." Alex folded his hands in his lap, perhaps in an attempt to imitate Charity's pose, but this clearly didn't suit him, and a moment later his legs were crossed while his hands tapped the arms of his chair. "Most people don't have time to read anymore," he remarked. "Not pleasure read, at least. Not stories. I certainly don't have the time to read. Or more to the point, I don't make the time. Do you . . . are there stories you still want to tell, Charity?"

She straightened her posture. "Why do you ask?"

"Well, there was *Cabrini Dreams* . . . I mean, right after we first met, you published that book, and it really spoke to me. I thought it was magnificent. But that was a while ago now. See, I ask because"—he re-crossed his legs—"we're looking for someone—"

"Who's *we?*"

"Our startup. Hypnos Applications. We're looking for someone who is a proven storyteller, but also someone who hasn't
published anything in a while."

"You mean someone with writer's block?"

He smiled a little painfully. "Kind of. Our idea is to bring
writer's block together with reader's block. We want to give people stories to absorb in their sleep—real stories that their brains
can then reimagine as their own. We've built a machine, Charity.
An amazing machine that can read, record, and insert narrative
at the neural level. It's called Easy Writer." He leaned toward her.
"May I admit something to you?" She nodded by briefly shutting
her eyes. "As a reader, as much as I love *Cabrini Dreams*, to this
day, when I try to inhabit its stories, as a white guy who grew up
in San Diego, who's never owned a parka, not to mention . . . you
know, I didn't grow up like you did. So let's just pose the honest
question. How much of what you rendered on the page do I
really *see* when I read your collection?"

Charity weighed his query. "If I do my job right," she responded slowly, "as a writer, you should see the world I've conjured."

"But will I *feel* your story, if it comes from a place completely
alien to my own? Wouldn't I feel it more if the building blocks
of your narrative were transformed into the building blocks with
which I would assemble your story if I had experienced it as my
own in the first place? Wouldn't that be even more powerful?"

"But doesn't that already happen? Isn't that an inherent part
of reading fiction, of reading poetry?"

"Is it? Or is it maybe the case that fewer and fewer people
read stories now because fewer and fewer people feel like they
can take that imaginative leap? Technology enables us to experience so much so intimately, but with fiction, we're still stuck
with an ancient delivery system. Maybe even a misguided one.
If I had been raised by an abusive father named Arnold, and
the central character of one of your stories was named Arnold,
wouldn't that impact my processing of your story? What we're

doing at Hypnos, Charity, is taking the next, long overdue step in the sharing of narrative. Because books will be done very soon. In a certain sense, they're already done."

Charity glanced around her office, which was lined with books. Old books, nearly all of which were in Latin.

"So you're talking about replacing prose narrative with what, a video game? Film?"

"No. Easy Writer isn't visually based, or game-oriented. Easy Writer is predicated on the idea that, to be truly moved, your own emotional landscape and experiences need to be tapped directly. So if you are haunted in your nightmares by clowns, but I am haunted in my nightmares by penguins, your story about clowns is more powerfully felt by my brain if those clowns become penguins."

She wondered for a moment, with some amusement, just what the hell he was getting at. "I'm sorry, Alex, but I don't see how this works at the level of narrative. How is what you're describing even storytelling?"

He rose slowly to his feet, wiggled his chair out from against the wall, and stood behind it, his fingers resting on its top rail, his stomach pressing through its slats. "We have the technology, Charity, to read your story as it emerges in your brain, record that emergence, and then implant it in the brain of a reader, who will then absorb your story not through the page, but rather from within his or her own psyche. The key for harvesting is REM sleep. Ideally, you'll begin your storytelling at bedtime, in a conscious state, and then fall asleep. Easy Writer will read your story both as you deliberately render it and as it is subsequently shaped by your subconscious. It records the story, see, but not as a narrative would be set down in a book. Instead, it's rendered as a sequence of neural firings. Then Easy Writer inserts that sequence into the brain of a sleeping subject. So we're not even asking people to make the time to read a short story. We're just asking them to take a nap."

Charity glanced out her window, at the students milling about. None of them, she couldn't help but notice, held any books.

251

"If you agree to participate," Alex continued, "we'll harvest a story from your brain and insert it into mine. That is, I'd like to be your first symbiotic reader, with Easy Writer's help."

She didn't know if this made her feel better about the proposal or worse. As she mulled all of this over, Charity rearranged the legal pads strewn in front of her. Yes, she still used legal pads to take notes; she had to special order them online. "You're talking about the death of writing, Alex. It's one thing to have the material book disappear, but you're talking about narrative itself being changed."

"It's already changed, Charity." Alex circled around his chair and stepped over to the front of her desk. Was his prior bout of fidgetiness just an act? He seemed every bit the salesman now, trying to close a deal. "Easy Writer isn't going to kill storytelling. Storytelling has already killed storytelling. But Easy Writer is going to bring it back to life. *You*, Charity Jackson, *you* are going to bring it back to life. If you choose to, you can create the stuff that dreams are made of. You can be the first writer to tell a story from inside the brain of someone else."

She looked down at her own hands, her palms so coarse, so dry. Of course, she had to say no. But then she hesitated. She thought, as she so often did when forced to make a decision, of Father Thomas's advice about going away for college—advice that changed her life for good. Was this a similar opportunity to leave a colder place for a warmer clime? And what was going to happen to the stories in her brain anyway, now that she no longer seemed remotely capable of writing them down? Would they otherwise be destined for oblivion?

Alex leaned across her desk. Beads of perspiration welled in his pores. "Wouldn't you like to write fiction again, Charity? Write without having to stare at a computer screen? You are the person we have designed Easy Writer for. You are brilliant. You still have stories to tell, but you're blocked. Let us help you. Try Easy Writer."

Charity leaned back in her chair, away from Alex. The ergonomic frame creaked beneath her weight. What if she failed, even with a keyboard taken out of the equation, to produce a story? What if her ideas were themselves no longer any good? But then again, what if it worked? What if Easy Writer enabled her, once more, to feel like a writer? And what did she have to lose if she failed, except that she'd know once and for all that she was done as a storyteller? She nodded slowly.

Alex clapped his hands. "Thank you, Charity. You won't regret this. My assistant, Kim, will be in touch regarding logistics." He turned to leave, then caught himself. "God, I almost forgot, maybe the most important question."

"What's that?"

"Tell me you sleep on your back?"

For the first time in their meeting, for the first time in a long while, Charity grinned with satisfaction. "As a matter of fact, I do."

Pomegranate, or Proserpine Redux
[Charity's story, as told to Easy Writer]

Ceres lies awake in bed, staring at the stains on the ceiling. She can sense that her mom isn't home, and that it is very late. It feels as if she has been resting like this for a long time, but she has no way of knowing, since there is no clock in the room.

She shifts onto her shoulder and looks over at the futon, on which both her brothers are deep in sleep. As quietly as she can, she rolls out of bed. She doesn't need to put on clothes; in the winter, they sleep in their clothes, to stay warm. She tiptoes out of the bedroom and steps into the tiny living room, which is separated from the kitchen area by a narrow counter.

Her mom isn't on the couch. Ceres checks the clock on the microwave; it's three thirty in the morning. What if something terrible has happened? It doesn't seem right just to lie in bed and wait for her mom to return, but Ceres doesn't want to alarm her brothers, either. She decides to go look for her mom by herself, in the streets of Chicago.

She steps into her rubber boots on the mat inside the door, because if you leave your shoes in the hallway, they will go walking fast. She puts on the parka that her eldest brother wore until it no longer fit him, at which point it became her other brother's parka. Now it's hers, although the fit is tight, on account of her body type. Where there had once been a hood, there remain only snaps to attach one. So she grabs her black knit hat, checks to make sure she isn't wearing any red or blue, and opens the door.

The hallway is dark. She walks through it and opens the door to the stairwell, which smells of marijuana. There are voices talking and laughing a few floors down. During the day, if the teenagers want to smoke pot, they'll go down into the part of the stairwell that leads to the boiler room in the basement. But that's during the day. At night, everything changes. The teenagers have the run of the stairwells then. That's one of the reasons why Ceres and her brother aren't supposed to go out at night.

She begins to descend the stairs. She goes down one floor, then another. The laughter and smoke is coming from a group of boys on the second floor. When they hear her footsteps, they grow quiet. "Where you going, fat girl?" one of the boys asks her when she reaches them. Well, that isn't very nice, but Ceres has heard worse. Twelve years old and she's heard all sorts of things. "You want to get high?" another jumps in. "Want to suck my dick?" asks a third. The taunting is bad enough, but do all the kids in her building have to be taller and thinner than she is? Ceres keeps her head down and tries to squeeze by them, which is hard, on account of her being big-boned. For whatever reason, maybe just because they're high in a good way rather than a bad way, they let her by. She steps into the foyer, always empty, because of the surveillance camera, and makes her way into the courtyard.

The courtyard has changed hands twice in the last week. The gang that's controlling it now is the one whose members wear blue, not red. There are four members of the blue gang, standing together right in the center of the courtyard with their backs to each other, keeping watch. The rules in the courtyard are straightforward. If you're young and a girl and you mind your own business you can cross it, unless you're wearing the wrong colors. Then you have to go around the complex on the outside, which takes time. Plus, it's dark in spots on the perimeter and if someone grabs you and you scream there's a good chance no one will hear you. So really the best thing to do if you're a girl is just to check your clothing before you leave home and go through the courtyard.

Ceres walks quickly. The four guys say nothing to her; they just watch her move. In less than a minute, she's on Clybourn. She starts to walk toward the convenience store where her mom works. The store is open twenty-four hours, but Ceres's mom doesn't get scheduled to work the night shift much because she has kids. Ceres glances through the window just to make sure her mom isn't behind the register, then passes through the group of men standing on the sidewalk in front of the store. They're drinking from bottles and cans wrapped in brown paper bags. One of them calls out to her. "Isn't it past your bedtime, girl?" he asks. Ceres ignores him.

She walks one more block, then another, before feeling as if she has gone too far. She spins around and begins to retrace her steps. Halfway up the block, Ceres notices a small alleyway on her left. She turns down it, skirting around puddles and passing in front of reeking dumpsters. The alley angles downward, running deeper and deeper into the bowels of Chicago.

The moon disappears behind a thick bank of storm clouds. Ceres quickens her pace. The alley suddenly veers sharply to the left and she notices a withered old woman—hunched against a crumbling brick wall, her chin buried in her neck, her body bundled in rags. The woman sits atop a pile of crushed liquor boxes. Ceres approaches her. Slowly the woman lifts her head.

"What is it, child?"

The old lady has no eyes, just empty sockets, the skin inside of them worn and wrinkled, but for some reason, Ceres is in no way unsettled by her appearance.

"I'm looking for my mom," she says. "Have you seen her?"

The woman nods slowly. "I have, yes. A man led her down this alley not that long ago. She had a very sad look about her, your mother. She looked very tired and sad."

Ceres believes what the woman has said, even though she has no eyes. She hurries past the old lady, following the alleyway. As she walks, she begins to notice—beneath her feet—what looks like blood, running in thin rivulets along the cracks in the asphalt.

She walks faster and faster and finally reaches the end of the alleyway, which is sealed off by a high, concrete wall. On her right, a rusted metal door is open slightly, beneath which the blood trickles out in a steady stream. Ceres hunches over this stream to get a better look, noticing as she does that the red liquid is not as thick as blood should be, and that it carries on its surface a thin layer of very tiny, red seeds. She steps over the stream, and pushes against the heavy door. It wheezes open.

She steps into what appears to be some kind of electrical room. The wall on her left is hidden behind a row of metal panels—some with dials, others padlocked shut. The panels hum and vibrate. On the floor Ceres sees crushed red fruits. Apples? No. She looks closer and realizes they're pomegranates, although how she is able to identify them is a mystery to her, since she is certain she has never seen such a fruit before. At the end of the room, a black door is cracked open, behind which—over the hum of the transformers or generators or whatever they are on her left—Ceres can hear what sounds like an animal, lapping.

She steps over the crushed pomegranates, over the scattered pools of red-seeded juice. Her hand shaking, she pushes open the door.

The space is no bigger than a broom closet—dimly lit from above by a single light bulb that hangs from a cord. Ceres's mother is propped against the wall that faces the door. She is barefoot. Ceres cannot recall ever looking—really looking—at the soles of her mother's feet, with their dead, flaking skin. Her dress is hiked up above her waist, and Ceres can see her mother's underwear—frayed and worn. A large man in baggy jeans and a hoodie squats next to her, a pile of squashed pomegranates at his feet. He is so focused on her mother, he doesn't even turn around to acknowledge Ceres. With one hand, he crushes a pomegranate in front of her mother's mouth, slurping up the juice as it dribbles off his hand.

Ceres looks at her mother. For a second, their eyes lock. "Do not taste the fruit," Ceres says to her without speaking. "Come home with me instead. I can rub your feet on the couch until you fall asleep." And her mother is listening. She looks back at her, saying with her eyes, "So my little girl wants to take care of her mom. What a kind child you are." But then her mother seems to look through her. Ceres fights for her attention, but she can't seem to regain it. The man has the fruit right at her lips. He's forcing her to taste it, but there is nothing Ceres can do to stop him. And now her mother's silent voice changes tone. "You don't understand how hard my life is," she says to Ceres. She sounds bitter, angry even. "I need to try this fruit, just once. I need to see what it tastes like."

The man begins to thrust the pomegranate into her mother's mouth, pushing so that the juice stains her cheeks and chin. As he presses against her face with one hand, with the other behind her head, he begins to slide Ceres's mother onto the concrete floor, like she's a baby he's putting to sleep. And now her mother's eyes look up, the pomegranate juice having filled her mouth, and now they roll back in their sockets in bliss, while the man—now on top of her—starts to slide her underwear down her leg.

Ceres turns away. She rushes out of the electrical closet, slipping and sliding on the pomegranate juice. Back in the alley, she begins to run. Her eyes are filled with tears, and she is so unsteady on her feet, she worries that she might crash into a dumpster, or the alley wall. She runs past the pile of liquor boxes—now shifting in the wind—where the woman with the empty eye sockets had been sitting. She turns onto Clybourn. As she approaches the men who linger in front of the convenience store, one of them holds out his arms, saying, "Come here, you little round thing. You need a hug." But Ceres runs around him. And the gang members in the courtyard back at Cabrini–Green, they also try to get her attention, calling out to her as she dashes by, "Slow down, boo. Come here." And the teenagers in the stairwell, now high in a not-so-good way, try to block her path, but Ceres barrels through them.

She re-enters their unit, quickly locking the door behind her. Soon she hears voices and feet scuffling. She looks through their peephole. Some of the men she just eluded are now gathering in the hallway. They call out to her to let them in. "I want to feed you," one of them says. "I want to cradle your head in my hands," another one cries out, "and slide you onto the floor." Ceres backs away from the door. She sees a book on the kitchen counter—its cover fire-engine red. Where did this come from? She grabs it and goes into the bedroom. In the dark, she can hear her brothers sleeping. She reaches beneath her bed, scoops up her flashlight, and shines it on the book.

When Ceres opens the front cover, she discovers that what she's holding isn't an ordinary book. Actually, it's a portal. Looking into it, she can see an entire world: ruins and arbors, rivers and streams, temples with inscriptions in a language she doesn't recognize.

Now she understands the choice in front of her. She can either enter this world or she can remain here, with her brothers, in their unit. But she has to choose, and once she chooses, she can never change her mind. Where one world opens, the other closes up. The noise in the hallway grows louder. They are trying to break down the door to get to her. Ceres is so frightened, she can't be sure if she is thinking clearly. She tells herself she will be safe in this other world, like a girl in a tree. Heart pounding, she whispers goodbye to her brothers, then lets herself fall—head first—into her book.

The Pro Shop

[Alex's version of Charity's story, following implantation by Easy Writer]

Hal can't seem to fall asleep. He stares at the rosette molding that lines his bedroom ceiling, recently refinished by a carpenter hired by his stepmother, Adele, who then produced a bill that his father found—at dinner the other evening—to be a little steep. "How are we ever going to sell this dump," Adele had countered, "if we don't fix it up? You know, technically, we live in La Jolla, but we can barely see the ocean. Practically speaking, we might as well be in Mission Valley."

Hal stumbles out of bed, shaking his head at the thought of how clearly he can hear Adele's voice, with its distinct, nasally twang. He's still dressed in his tennis clothes. Strange, he usually naps pretty easily after one of his lessons, but today he just couldn't sleep. Laurel and Hardy, their pugs, are wheezing away on their orthopedic dog bed. Hal is stretching his arms just as his stepmom's voice comes in over the intercom.

"Hal?"

He walks over and presses the small button next to the speaker. "Yeah?"

"Your father's probably forgotten that we have a fundraiser tonight for the symphony at the Hotel Del Coronado. Go tell him he needs to be ready by five."

Hal glances at the digital clock on his bookshelf. It's three thirty in the afternoon. "Can't you just text him?"

"I have texted him and he hasn't answered. I assume he's on the court. I mean, he's always on the court, isn't he?"

Hal ignores her question. "Did you try calling the pro shop?"

"Yes. No one answered. Jesus, Hal, the club is three blocks away! Maybe the extra cardio would do you some good."

She was referring to his jiggle, which wasn't very nice. "All right." Hal picks up his racquet, then remembers he isn't actually going to play tennis and puts it back down. He laces up his sneakers, which he keeps in his room with all of his other shoes, since the last time he left his tennis shoes in the downstairs hallway, his stepbrothers filled them with dog shit.

Hal knows Todd and Teddy are around because he can see their truck in the driveway, with their surfboards in back. His own personal rule is to stay in his room with the door locked when they're at home. That's why he moved Laurel and Hardy in with him. If he's got the pugs, his laptop, and his mini-fridge stocked with food, he doesn't need to leave his room, unless it's time for a tennis lesson. They hate him, his stepbrothers. You'd assume they'd just ignore him, as they're three and five years older respectively, but they want to torture him—why, Hal has no idea. Maybe because, since declaring bankruptcy, their own father lives in a duplex in Chula Vista? But it isn't like they have any problem mooching off his dad.

He checks to make sure his shirt isn't tucked in, unlocks, and then opens his door. From down below comes the booming laughter of Todd and Teddy as they exchange insults. Hopefully they're in the rec room—hard to tell with the way the vaulted ceilings throw the noise around. Hal begins to head down the wide, spiral staircase of their seven-bedroom, Spanish Revival home. Funny *that Adele hates the place so much in that she picked it out after the wedding.*

Todd and Teddy were actually headed out of the main hallway, but hearing their younger, chubby stepbrother has caused them to reverse course. They meet him at the base of the staircase, stinking of marijuana.

"Hey, douchebag."

"Hey, you fat fuckwad."

"Your tennis coach called. He asked you to stop sucking."

Hal steps around them without saying anything and keeps on walking. For whatever reason, maybe just because they're high in a good rather than a bad way, they let him by.

Outside, he takes Camino del Sol over to Avenida De La Playa. Once more, Hal checks to make sure his shirt is untucked. Otherwise, if the cool kids from Country Day are out, they'll give him crap. Of course, no one sets out to look like a dweeb, but La Jolla Beach and Tennis Club rules stipulate that players dressed in tennis attire keep their collar shirts tucked into their shorts. Hal's instinct is to follow all stated rules, but sometimes unstated rules matter just as much, if not more.

Sure enough, the cool kids are out in force, lingering in front of the kayak shop, in their blue baggy swimming trunks, no shirts. They all have those braided necklaces, whatever they're called. Does every one of them have to be thinner and taller than he is? He walks with his head down, and for once, the boys are too busy—hawking loogies at each other—to bother him.

He opens the side gate with a wave of his member card against the scanner. Now that Hal is on club property, he carefully tucks his shirt into his shorts, noticing when he's done that the groundsmen have been watching him. At their feet, nestled against bags of fertilizer, are cans of beer carefully wrapped in brown paper bags. One of the older guys, at the moment holding a hedge trimmer, releases his hand from the trigger. *"Where's your racquet?"* he asks in a friendly, heavily accented tone. Hal just shakes his head.

He walks past the main entrance of the club, then past the bocce court, so he can check the tennis facility in one long swoop, heading home as he does so. He doesn't see his dad anywhere. He approaches the central courts, where there is covered seating on the far side of court one, and permanent bleachers set up behind courts one and two. Looks like a ladies round robin is about to get underway, led by the silky-smooth head pro Dan Dennens (former qualifier for the ATP Challenger Series), who is dressed in his white USTA tennis cap, white Izod shirt, and white tennis shorts, and holds his Roger Federer–endorsed Pro Staff Six tennis racquet loosely at his side.

Hal passes by the swimming pool and approaches the club restaurant and guest rooms, all of which face the beach on the far side of the club. Now he has the feeling he's gone too far, so he doubles around, exiting the pool area through the arched passageway on the left. The light shifts abruptly, and Hal looks up. Storm clouds above. When's the last time it rained in La Jolla?

He's cutting through the courtyard of the club when he comes upon an elderly lady in a white tennis dress, sitting on one of the wrought iron benches, zipping up her racquet cover. Hal approaches her. She looks up at him, her eyes hidden behind a pair of oversized sunglasses.

"Yes?"

"Have you seen my father?" He doesn't know the woman's name—he doesn't even recall ever seeing her before—but everyone at the club knows his dad. For a moment his eyes are drawn to the wrinkled folds of skin that hang from her thighs. Even though most of the time he is intensely aware of the perfection of other people's bodies, particularly when he is on the grounds of the La Jolla Beach and Tennis Club, aka the Bitch and Tits Club, for whatever reason, Hal is in no way unsettled by the lady's withered form.

"Your father?" she replies. "Your father . . ." She seems to be gathering her thoughts. "Yes, he passed by here not that long ago with Ms. Katie, the assistant pro. I thought he only took lessons with Dan Dennens?"

Hal shrugs and is about to thank her when she adds, "Check the pro shop. Your father, you know . . ." she pauses again and Hal stands there in suspended animation. "Your father is not a happy man. You know that, don't you? He's a very sad man."

This is news to Hal, but he believes what the old lady has said, even though he can't see her eyes. He moves along. The pro shop sits just behind the seating area off court one. Someone must have spilled a hopper, as there are tennis balls scattered all along the side of the shop. Hal steps over and around the balls, worried about turning an ankle. The wide, rusted side door—out of which Dan Dennens regularly wheels his ball machine—is ajar. Hal pushes it open a little more and steps into the pro shop.

There are tennis balls everywhere—rolling on the floor and piled against the walls and racquet displays on his left. Softly, just above the sound made by an oscillating fan set on the counter, Hal hears the voice of a woman. She sounds maybe like she's practicing her backhand, grunting with each swing, but the sound is coming from the tiny room in which Dan Dennens strings racquets. Hal walks over to the black door—open a crack—and presses against it lightly with his shaking hand.

Ms. Katie is flat on her back on the floor, her white tennis skirt pushed up past her waist. Atop her, his bare ass rising and then falling with a kind of savageness, a kind of hatred, against her crotch, is Hal's father. Hal can't remember when he last saw his father's butt—the cheeks hollow and pale, with long black hairs matted against them. He stands there for a moment, debating whether or not he should slip away, when he remembers that he has been sent there to tell his father to come home and that he wants his father home because when he isn't home, Hal doesn't feel comfortable outside of his bedroom. Also, he knows that his father shouldn't be here, in the pro shop, on top of Ms. Katie. Maybe, it occurs to him, his father is sad precisely because he is spending too much time here. So Hal stands there, pleading silently with his father to come home with him, but he is too abashed to say anything.

He looks at Ms. Katie, lying on the floor, her eyes shut tight, head and shoulders rocking, her mouth emitting a volley of tennis-like exclamations, and watches as his father—holding himself up with one hand, his slender trunk extending as he does so, lats tightening, his butt's jackhammering slowing down— picks up a tennis ball and presses it against Ms. Katie's mouth. Alarmed by this, Hal steps back. The heel of his sneaker hits the door.

His father turns and looks at him over his shoulder. For a moment, their eyes meet. "Come home with me," Hal says without speaking. "Please. I promise I'll practice harder, so we can do better in the father-son tournament next year. Just come home now. Please." And his father for a moment seems to hear him. "I know it's been hard," he says silently, "since your mom died and I remarried. And I know I play a lot of tennis these days, but I'm still your dad. That won't ever change. I just . . . I need this, to relax. I'm under a lot of pressure. You don't know what it's like."

He turns back around and begins to stab and thrust again. Ms. Katie's head slowly lifts off the floor, a tennis ball lodged between her lips. Hal neither wants her to see him, nor can stir himself to move. Once more his father's head swivels, his eyes now wide with rage, in the throes of some feeling, some attachment, that is actually much bigger than what they share—something more precious, more elemental. "Get the fuck out of here!" he screams.

Hal stumbles backwards through the doorway, his foot landing squarely on a tennis ball. He falls to his knees, rises, then scampers out of the pro shop. Outside, the storm clouds have thickened, but no rain has yet to fall. Hal runs through the courtyard, past the empty bench where the elderly lady had been sitting. His nose fills with snot, and he focuses on breathing through his mouth, worried that otherwise he might start to cry. He runs through the grounds of the La Jolla Beach and Tennis Club, passing the groundsmen, who are still trimming the shrubs. The same older guy as before calls out to him, but Hal keeps on running. Back on Avenida De La Playa, the cool, shirtless kids from Country Day taunt him, saying, "Hal! Where you going?" Saying, "Hal, come hang with us and eat your feelings." He runs down Camino del Sol, re-entering their home. His stepbrothers still haven't left. They're lingering in the entryway; perhaps the weather is too ominous for surfing. "You look like you need a puff on your inhaler, jackhole," one of them says. "Where you going, bro?" the other one asks. "I feel like hitting you in the arm. Come here." Now they seem high in a not-so-good way. Hal hurries past them.

He steps back into his bedroom, quickly locking the door behind him. Loud footsteps echo from the staircase. Oh, great, Teddy and Todd are coming upstairs. Hal snatches his laptop off his desk, grabs his noise-cancelling headphones, and climbs back into bed. Laurel and Hardy are still sleeping. He opens his web browser and does a search for the human brain. On the heels of what has just transpired, he wants to understand how people make the choices they do.

He finds an interactive site on which he can click on different parts of the brain and then read a list of the primary cognitive functions associated with that part. His heart pounding, Hal looks over the rudimentary data in front of him, none of which provides him with the information he really covets. As he tries to think about how the human brain thinks, his own brain surveys his situation. "You will never lose your jiggle," it informs him. "You will never be good at tennis." Hal accepts these predictions, noticing as he does that he is not just looking at a computer screen—that the brain displayed in front of him is opening up, its coiled tissues retracting, inviting him in. Now he understands the choice in front of him, between the world of bodies and the world of cognition. The racket in the hallway grows louder as his stepbrothers bang on the door. Hal is so scared, he's not sure if he's thinking clearly anymore. He tells himself he'll be left alone if he gives up the world of bodies for the world of the brain— that he'll be mercifully ignored by others. His heart pounding, he says goodbye to the pugs and, like a snake that has shed its skin, plunges into his laptop.

FOLLOWING HER NIGHT SPENT IN THE BELLY of Easy Writer, Charity puttered around her condominium the next day, making bad snack choices and coming up with a list of books for her graduate research assistant to fetch from the library. She kept herself busy, but she was distracted the entire time, thinking about the story Easy Writer had extracted from her brain. Was it the most revealing, the most exposed, she had ever made herself? Or was the story too compressed, too otherworldly, to work? She couldn't recall if her subconscious had returned to the story in her REM sleep, and of course she had no idea what her story looked like as read by Easy Writer, not to mention as reconfigured in Alex's brain. She didn't even know if Alex had gone through the implantation yet, or—if he had—if it had been successful. When would they let her know? She realized they hadn't even discussed a timetable.

She slept poorly that night. The next day, she taught her classes—giving what was, in her mind at least, a very poor lecture on Book Four of the *Aeneid*. The day after that, exhausted from tossing and turning unsuccessfully in bed, she held her office hours. Perhaps partly owing to the fact that she and Alex had met in her office, Charity found herself distracted as she listened to her students and watched them fidget nervously in front of her. She kept thinking again and again about her choice to give Easy Writer one of her stories. After she published *Cabrini Dreams*, on her book tour, when white men approached her at readings to tell her how much her stories meant to them, Charity had never felt like their appreciation of her work in any way resembled an attempt to appropriate her material. But now she wondered, in giving Alex her story, what he had taken from her in the process.

The next morning, after yet another night of fitful sleep, Charity decided she had had enough. Rather than call, she got in her car and had it drive her all the way over to Hypnos Applications in Sunnyvale. When she buzzed from the entrance, Kim came down to let her in. In the elevator going up to the fifth floor, Kim exclaimed about how excited Alex would be to see her, how thrilled everyone was about her involvement with Hypnos, and so on. Stepping out of the elevator, she showed Charity to Alex's corner office—also enclosed in glass, like the room in which Easy Writer still sat.

Alex circled around his desk and greeted Charity enthusiastically before pointing to two chairs, around which some potted plants had been arranged. Once Kim had left them alone, the two of them sat down.

"I was going to phone you later today," he said. "We've had a lot of post-implantation diagnostics to process, but it looks like the experiment worked brilliantly. Your story certainly felt like my own story when I experienced it. I mean, it blew me away."

For a moment, Charity forgot the purpose behind her visit and instead just coveted feedback. "Did it feel"—she leaned toward him, trying to find the right word—"Ovidian?"

"I don't know, since I've never read Ovid. The only real literary classic I tried to tackle on my own was *Infinite Jest* years ago, because of the tennis stuff. When I was young, my dad really wanted me to be good at tennis. Anyway, I didn't even make it a quarter of the way through that book, but that's where my version of your story went. Which is just to say, there were lots of tennis balls, and it was set at the club where I played as a kid."

Charity looked at him, dumbfounded. "Tennis?"

"Did you ever play, growing up? No, I don't suppose—"

"No, I did not play tennis as a child, Alex." She rose to her feet. "I'm afraid I made a mistake. I should have asked at the outset if I could . . . if there would be any way to take my story back. Or, I don't know, scrub it from your brain. I've had misgivings. I've been worried about my material being appropriated by your machine—about my identity being erased. And then to hear you talk about tennis . . ."

Alex looked at her, crestfallen. "I, uh," he struggled for words. "I don't know, short of a frontal lobotomy, how we'd extract your story from my brain. It's a part of me now. An important part. My version of your story, it wasn't *about* tennis. It was a story that tried to explain why my father abruptly sent me off to boarding school right before I started seventh grade. My dad, he chose his life at that time, including my awful stepmom and my stepbrothers, over me. Or at least that's how I felt when I was shoved on a plane and flown across the country to

Eaglebrook. My dad never explained his choice. So your story, whatever it was to you, in my head it was a story about my father abandoning me, and me being saved—I guess you could say—by my interest in neuroscience. That's what I should have said just now."

Charity didn't know how to respond. She stood there, thinking about her mom—what it was like to lose her, first to drugs, then to death itself.

"I'm not saying my version of your story would matter as a work of fiction to anyone other than me, but to me, it was a revelation." Alex shook his head slowly, as if his eyes were seeing it once more—her story, now his, taking shape again in his brain. "There were such mysteries in my home back then, like I guess there are in every home. Why, when my mom died, did my father marry the woman he did? Why did he ship me off, when I thought we were pretty close? When I was really the only link he had to my mom?"

Charity knew none of this about Alex's childhood. Out of sympathy, she felt compelled for a moment to reach over and squeeze his hand, but she held back. Would that be a betrayal of her story, of the experience she had tried to relate, to show sympathy for his brain's rewriting of her experience as his own? Charity had wanted to communicate a story about losing her mother, and Alex had clearly absorbed that story, although in very different terms. But still, there was no question; he had absorbed it.

"I've never had a way of thinking through this stuff before." Alex was staring down at his stomach, which swelled out over his belt and crotch. "Even in therapy. Nothing has ever done for me what your story did. My father was so self-destructive. I always suspected that, but now I feel like I know it for certain, and that makes me feel better—like it wasn't my fault he made the choices he did. Thank you, Charity. Thank you so much. I mean, when I finished *Cabrini Dreams*, I remember saying to myself, *That was a great book*. But this experience wasn't about absorbing a narrative; it was about me, only more about me because it came from somewhere else, if that makes any sense."

He exhaled, shaking his head, then slowly rose to his feet and clasped her hands. "We'll be in touch," he said. "If you want to work with us again. We'd like your permission to have your story implanted in some more test subjects. Then, maybe in a year or so, when we're ready to go out with the Easy Writer product—maybe then we could retain you under contract as one of our writers? It could be very lucrative for you, I suspect, if that interests you."

"It doesn't."

He opened his office door. "Does that mean you're ruling out the possibility of maybe, down the road, doing some more work for us?"

She still felt as if Easy Writer had co-opted her experience growing up as an African-American girl in Cabrini–Green. But now Charity felt other things, as well. Her story, however Easy Writer had translated it, had moved Alex. After many, many years, she had produced a narrative that mattered to another human being—mattered more, maybe, than anything else she had ever produced. But it mattered because Easy Writer had effaced any need for empathy on the part of her reader. The machine had literally whitewashed her story. Was this the promise that technology held? How would difference—not just personal singularities, but historical difference, the writings of Ovid versus the writings of David Foster Wallace or Zadie Smith or, yes, Charity Jackson—how would such difference be maintained when scientists and programmers could so easily fuse them all together? "I just don't know, Alex," was all she could muster.

They began to move slowly toward the elevator bank, each of them breathing a little shallowly. From what Charity could judge, they were the two heaviest people at Hypnos. How would a thin person's subconscious have processed her story, she wondered? Or someone with a stable family? Does everyone experience some traumatic moment of abandonment in childhood, even a kid growing up in La Jolla? Did Easy Writer only neutralize the particularities of her life, or was that an oversimplification? Did it also make her life more resonantly mythic, as Ovid would have it?

They waited in silence for the elevator doors to open. When they did, Charity stepped inside the carriage. Alex stood still. He didn't speak until she had turned around and was facing him.

"Be a part of what we're building," he said to her. "Going forward, being a self, being a storyteller, is going to be all about dispersal. Letting ourselves go. Into other people, other experiences. You should be proud. You're going to change lives, if you choose to." The doors began to shut. Alex moved with them as he spoke. "You can change lives from the inside out, Charity. Call me if you—"

He disappeared from view. Charity pressed the button for the ground floor and felt the elevator shudder slightly before beginning its descent. She wasn't mad at Alex so much as she was disappointed. Boys, regardless of their age, were so easily mesmerized by their newest toy, their newest gadget. The way he had spoken of pride just now made her think of hubris: Ovid's Jove with all of his plots, all of his arrogant stumbles. What if Alex was right about selves and storytellers being dispersed into other people, other frames of reference? She had always wanted her stories to be out there, commemorating her experiences, testifying to what she had seen and felt. Was this now just a hopelessly old-fashioned wish?

Charity saw herself reflected in the gleaming doors of the elevator. She straightened her posture. When she got home, she'd need to throw out all the junk food in her pantry. She also had to start walking again in the late afternoons. What if she tried just to write down the story she had given to Easy Writer? Reclaim it via pen and paper. But were pen and paper any match for that machine? As the elevator dropped, past one floor and then another, Charity Jackson could feel herself falling—faster and faster, into the future.

Acknowledgments

It was a joy to work again with Michelle Toth and Andrew Goldstein at SixOneSeven Books, as well as Eliyanna Kaiser. My thanks to Michelle in particular for her editorial work on these stories. Whitney Scharer did an amazing job designing the cover. I'm also grateful to Sharon Dynak and her staff at the Ucross Foundation, where I was in residence when I began this collection in 2012. Several of these stories were drafted while I was a fellow at the University of Michigan's Institute for the Humanities; my thanks to Daniel Herwitz and Sidonie Smith for their support of my work during that time.

Editors at a number of journals vastly improved many of these stories before first ushering them into print. My thanks to Michael Byers for his edits on "The Librarian," and Jonathan Freedman for his insights on "Sonnet 126." Both of these pieces appeared in the *Michigan Quarterly Review* (Summer 2010, Fall 2013). I am also indebted to Janell Watson at the *Minnesota Review* for her work on "The Novelist and the Short Story Writer" (Issue 82 [2014]); to Kathleen Canavan at the *Notre Dame Review*, where "The Program in Profound Thought" first appeared (Summer 2014); to Robert James Russell and Kelly Nhan, who brought out "Faucets" in *Midwestern Gothic* (Winter 2015); to Harilaos Stecopoulos, Lynne Nugent, and the rest of the staff at *The Iowa Review*, where "Endymion" was published (Fall 2015); and finally, to Ladette Randolph and her staff at *Ploughshares Solos*, where "The Detroit Frankfurt School Discussion Group" came out in 2016.

"Endymion" is a retelling of the myth of the same name, and is also in conversation with John Lyly's play *Endymion* (1588). In "Easy Writer," I had some help from my friend Leonard Nalencz, an extraordinary Latinist. The various early modern texts and authors referred to in "Sonnet 126" all exist in the archive, as do the critical writings mentioned in "The Detroit Frankfurt School Discussion Group," although the characters and events in both of these stories are—as in all the others—entirely fictive.

Friends such as Michael Byers, Peter Ho Davies, John Davis, Nicholas Delbanco, John Ducker, Tarfia Faizullah, Jonathan Freedman, Linda Gregerson, Danny Hack, A. Van Jordan, Laura Kasischke, Kevin Kopelson, Megan Levad, Eileen Pollack, Kirstin Valdez Quade, Claire Vaye Watkins, Maya West, and Helen Zell make the labor of writing more bearable, and its rewards more keenly felt. My beloved agent Miriam Altshuler has managed somehow always to be not just supportive but ebullient, and her colleague Reiko Davis was also incredibly helpful and generous throughout this process. Most importantly, my kids—William and Cecelia—sat next to me on the couch, or at the dining room table, as I worked on this book, and I thank them for their patience and love.

This book is dedicated to my mom, Libby Trevor—a great lover of books, and the most resilient person I have ever known.

About the Author

Douglas Trevor is the author of the short story collection *The Thin Tear in the Fabric of Space* (winner of the 2005 Iowa Short Fiction Award and a finalist for the 2006 Hemingway Foundation/PEN Award for First Fiction), and the novel *Girls I Know* (winner of the 2013 Balcones Fiction Prize). His short stories have appeared in dozens of publications, including (most recently) *Ploughshares Solos*, *The Iowa Review*, and *New Letters*. A professor of English literature and creative writing, he is the current Director of the Helen Zell Writers' Program at the University of Michigan.